P9-DDB-150

A FIERCELY INDEPENDENT WOMAN,
A PROUD AND STUBBORN MAN—
BOUND BY PASSION,
TORN APART BY INJUSTICE

# *The*
# BELOVED WOMAN

# The
# BELOVED
# WOMAN

## DEBORAH SMITH

BANTAM BOOKS
NEW YORK · TORONTO · LONDON · SYDNEY · AUCKLAND

BELOVED WOMAN

A BANTAM BOOK / APRIL 1991

ISBN 0-553-28759-1

PUBLISHED SIMULTANEOUSLY IN THE UNITED STATES AND CANADA

Bantam Books are published by Bantam Books, a division of Bantam Doubleday Dell
Publishing Group, Inc. Its trademark, consisting of the words "Bantam Books" and the
portrayal of a rooster, is Registered in U.S. Patent and Trademark Office and in other
countries. Marca Registrada. Bantam Books, 666 Fifth Avenue, New York, New York
10103.

PRINTED IN THE UNITED STATES OF AMERICA

OPM        0 9 8 7 6 5 4 3 2 1

Many thanks to BETTY SHARP SMITH, Cherokee teacher, lecturer, and author, for translating and proofreading the Cherokee language used in this book.

Many thanks also to the eastern tribe of the Cherokee Nation, who provided invaluable help through their publications and their museum at Cherokee, North Carolina.

Last but not least, thanks to Carolyn Nichols and Nita Taublib, who guided this book from the start.

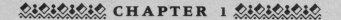 **CHAPTER 1**

*Your soul has come into the very center of my soul,
never to turn away. I take your soul.*

—CHEROKEE LOVE CHARM

North Georgia, Cherokee Nation, 1838

THE DAY was too pretty, too painfully serene in its fresh spring promise, with the late-blooming dogwoods lacing the woods in white and the sweet smell of wild honeysuckle wisping through the air. A man could hurt from thinking about it, hurt so badly that he cried.

"She wasn't more than half grown, God. You turnin' your back on all the Cherokees now, even the children?" Justis Gallatin asked out loud.

He inhaled raggedly, gagged on the scent of honeysuckle and death, then took his shirt off so fast, several of the wooden buttons tore from it. He knelt beside the small, naked form and wrapped it quickly but gently, arranging the long swath of coal-black hair over the shirt.

Cradling Sallie Blue Song's body in his arms, Justis walked out of the woods, past the burnt hulls of barns, past orchards standing untended, fields empty, fences broken—the utter destruction of what had once been one of the best farms, white or Indian, in this part of the Nation.

He entered a sandy yard canopied by grand old oak trees and watched his partner drop a saddle blanket across one of the four bodies stretched out there. Sam Kirkland glanced up at Justis and saw what he was carrying.

Sam gave a low moan of distress, walked to a blackened timber at the jumbled ruins of the Blue Song house, and leaned over it, retching. He began a chant in Hebrew as Justis laid Sallie by her father. Sam kept his religion a secret from the people over in town, but now he let the odd, melodic words of it ring out. Justis had no idea what the words meant, but he found them soothing.

He covered Sallie's head with the sleeve of his shirt. "That's the best I can do for her right now, old friend," he whispered to her father's corpse. He sat down beside Jesse Blue Song and gazed sadly at the bronzed face capped by inky black hair. Jesse had kept his hair cropped short because he wanted everyone to know that he was as civilized as any white man. Intelligence and kindness had given him a dignity that few people, of any color, possessed.

"You outdid 'em, friend," Justis told him hoarsely. "And the sons of bitches couldn't stand it."

He gently tugged a folded packet of paper from the pocket of the Cherokee's bloodstained shirt. Opening it, Justis squinted at the delicate, beautiful handwriting. Shock poured through him.

*Dear Papa and Mama, I dreamed about home again. After more than six years away—forever, it seems to me—I still see the beloved mountains so clearly, and all of your dear faces. I can stand this dreadful loneliness no longer.*

Justis read on, shaking his head in frustration when he came to long passages written in Cherokee, frowning when he couldn't make sense of the parts written in formal English. Jesse's eldest daughter had more education than anybody he knew.

He waved the letter in the air. "Sam, come read this and tell me what this gal's trying to say. She doesn't use many words less than a foot long."

Sam took the letter and read it anxiously. The breath soughed out of him. "She's had some sort of falling out with her guardian in Philadelphia, she's homesick, she's given the rest of her bank account to a maidservant who's needy, and she's worried over newspaper rumors about the Cherokees being forced to give up their land."

Sam handed him the letter. "In short, my friend, she's broke and she's coming home. Judging by the date of this letter, she'll arrive any day now."

Justis stared grimly at his business partner. He'd never met the eldest Blue Song daughter—she'd already been sent up north to get an education when he arrived in Cherokee country six years before. Shaking his head, he cursed softly. "The army's fixin' to kick her tribe clear across the Mississippi. She hasn't got a home anymore."

Justis looked around at the Blue Song place and swallowed harshly. He owned it now.

"What are you going to do?" Sam asked.

Justis slowly lowered his gaze to Jesse Blue Song's body. Jesse had led him to a fortune in gold and treated him like a son. There was only one way to pay him back.

Justis closed the dark, unseeing eyes. "I'll keep her with me and take care of her no matter what," he promised softly. "I swear it."


KATHERINE BLUE SONG sat properly with her head up and shoulders back, but she thought her spine would snap if the carriage bounced over one more rut in the trail. Either that or she'd crack her head on the coach's low ceiling. The trail was worse than she remembered, just a pair of wagon tracks in the hard Georgia clay.

It was such a typical Georgia road that she began laughing. She loved the terrible road, every inch of it. She loved the unbroken blue-green hills on either side, and the smoky mist that filled the valleys in the afternoons, and the little creeks that leapt through the ravines. They belonged to Cherokees, had belonged to them for generations, and she was going home.

*Home.* She gazed happily out the carriage's window. It would be only an hour or two more.

Katherine heard the hogs approaching before she smelled them. The sound was amazing, like a grunting, snuffling army. They topped a grassy rise, hundreds of them, and fanned out across the wagon trail. She grasped the window ledge and looked out in amazement while with a bellow of dismay her driver tugged his horses to a stop. The coach rocked as the hogs swarmed around it and under it.

Katherine peered down and hogs peered up. What in the world could anybody need with this sea of pork, she wondered. She knew there were many more people living in the Nation now, but this herd would feed thousands.

"These barnyard bungholers wanta rest a spell!" a loud male voice called out. Katherine arched a raven-black brow at the coarse language and watched as several scruffy drovers ambled over the rise. One of them led a pack mule; the others swung tall, stout poles, prodding the hogs as they went.

"Clear the road!" Katherine's driver yelled.

"Get offen that coach and try to make me, you ugly mule arse!" came the reply, along with a loud chorus of guffaws.

The driver snapped his whip. "I got me a lady here! Hold your tongues!"

"A lady!"

Katherine watched as the drovers jerked their floppy felt hats off and trudged toward her. Their quick change of attitude looked sincere. But when they pushed their grizzled, sweaty faces into the windows on one side of the coach, shock filled their eyes and politeness fled.

"A Injun!"

"In a fancy dress!"

"Cain't be! I never saw a squaw dressed thisaway!"

"A good-lookin' savage, ain't she?"

Katherine drew herself up so tightly, the fear churning in her stomach had no place to go. People in Philadelphia might disapprove of her or call her names, but they did it behind her back. She wasn't used to this kind of blatant scrutiny with its insulting undertone.

"Good afternoon, gentlemen," she said evenly.

"She speaks real good English," one of the drovers said in awe.

"Some of 'em do. She must be one of them missionary-taught squaws."

Katherine folded her hands on her lap and clenched the fingers tightly. "I'm on my way home, sirs. My family has a farm near the town your people call Gold Ridge. My father is the chief in this district. Would you allow my driver to proceed?"

They gaped at her. "I've heard about Cherokees like this 'un," one drover told the others solemnly, and Katherine suddenly realized he wasn't trying to insult her. He was just stating the facts as he saw them. "Mostly they're mixed-bloods. Some're almost as civilized as white folks." He studied her face. "But damn, this 'un is a full-blood."

Gritting her teeth, Katherine picked up a small silver-gray umbrella that matched her skirt and rapped on the coach's ceiling. "Go ahead, Mr. Bingham, please." She met the drovers' curious stares and said coolly, "I'm afraid I don't have any more time to chat."

Mr. Bingham called down weakly, "Miss Blue Song, you oughten to be so quick with these boys."

Katherine heard the fear in his voice and knew with sinking dread that the driver—hired up in Nashville for his respectability, not his toughness—would be of no help.

"Come on out," one of the drovers ordered, his gaze darting over the snug black bodice of her dress. "Let us have a look at you. We ain't never seen a squaw like you before, that's all."

"No, thank you. I'm not an exhibit for the entertainment of rude men."

"Get out," another said curtly.

"Miss Blue Song, they just want to take a gander at you," Mr. Bingham squeaked.

Katherine eyed the drovers for a second, considered her options, then nodded. But before she left the coach she opened a bulky black satchel by her feet and reached into a box of surgical implements.

The drovers moved back a little, forming a semicircle to keep the hogs away, then pulled the coach's door open. Katherine stood, fluffed her skirt, and stepped to the hard-packed ground. She concealed a razor-sharp scalpel in her right hand.

"Lord, what a beauty," one man breathed.

"Kinda skinny and tall. A little long in the tooth too," another complained.

"Nah. How old be ya, sister?"

Katherine quivered with rage. "Twenty."

"Not too old to keep a man plenty warm at night."

"Is this the way you always talk in front of ladies?" she asked.

A stream of tobacco juice barely missed the toe of her shoe. "Ain't no such thing as an Injun lady."

A man stepped closer to her. "My wife shore would like this dress. Why don't you shuck it off?"

"Don't touch me."

He grinned and grabbed a handful of the skirt. The man was near enough that Katherine barely had to move. She simply lifted her hand and made a quick, skillful movement across his arm.

"She cut me!" he yelped. Hogs squealed at the smell of blood. The drovers stared at their injured companion in openmouthed surprise, then at her. Katherine slashed again as another man reached for her. He stumbled back, his forehead bleeding profusely. "She's trying to scalp me!"

"Now, really, you men calm down," Mr. Bingham begged. "She's no savage."

"Get that damned knife outer her hand!"

Katherine swung again, and a drover grabbed her wrist. He squeezed painfully. "Let go of that cuttin' piece."

Panic grew inside Katherine's chest. "My father will have you in jail before sundown!"

"Squaw, you're plumb crazy." He wrenched her arm a little and still she refused to drop the knife. "If we weren't gents, we'd strip that dress off you and haul you into the woods for an hour or two."

"You would regret that." She lashed a sharp-toed shoe into her captor's knee, and he howled.

"That done it! Grab her, boys!"

Mr. Bingham gasped and began flailing the drovers with his whip. One man grabbed her around the waist and another sank his fingers into her throat. Katherine jerked her fighting hand free and swung the scalpel wildly, hearing curses when it connected.

In the midst of struggling she suddenly heard something else—a deep, resonant thud, the sound of wood hitting a skull. A drover slumped to the ground, then another, and she realized that someone new had waded into the bunch, swinging one of the drovers' own wooden staffs.

The men let go of her and backed away, shielding their heads and squalling oaths. Katherine stumbled on a wagon rut and grabbed the coach door for balance. Dust rose off the trail in a thick cloud. The hogs scattered in every direction.

The devil was loose in the middle of hell, and she could only watch in amazement.

The newcomer was lean and tall, but he had the shoulders of a prime bull and the strength to match. His big-knuckled hand brushed a shapeless, wide-brimmed hat off his head. Dust swirled around shaggy hair the dark, rich color of chestnut. Under a thick mustache, his mouth curved into a lethal smile.

Now, apparently, he was ready to do serious battle with the drovers. She stared at the newcomer as he punched one drover in the head and swung about gracefully to kick another between the legs. Katherine covered her nose to keep from choking on dust and excitement. Her rescuer, if that was who the devil was, began uttering inventive and filthy curses in a deep, drawling voice.

When only one drover was left standing, he jerked a pearl-handled pistol from his belt and leveled it at the drover's forehead. "Get your asses and your hogs outta my sight," he warned in a deadly tone. "And if you're takin' 'em to Gold Ridge, keep your goddamned selves out of my sight there too. You hear anybody say 'Justis Gallatin,' you tuck tail and run, or you're dead. Understand?"

"Yeah."

"Yes, *sir*," Justis Gallatin corrected the drover.

"Yes, sir."

Katherine wiped perspiration from her forehead and tried to catch her breath. She barely noticed as the drovers staggered off without looking back, taking their hogs with them. She was too busy studying Justis Gallatin.

He stood with his booted feet braced apart, a rangy chestnut wolf guarding his territory, his eyes never leaving the drovers, his arm bent lazily so that the pistol pointed upward, ready to be leveled again if need be. His dark trousers were rusty with dust, and his loose white workshirt had turned a pinkish color.

He wore a wide belt with a gold buckle, and tucked

into it was another pearl-handled pistol, plus two large knives sheathed in leather scabbards. His shirt was unbuttoned halfway down his chest, revealing a thickly haired expanse and a gold nugget hanging from a leather string.

A gold miner, she thought suddenly. Her father had said they were all over the place now. And most were mean-tempered thieves, not to be trusted.

This one might be no better. She stared at his drooping mustache. No gentleman wore hair on his face. She couldn't recall when she'd seen such a hearty growth of hair on a man's upper lip, and it was as intriguing as it was shocking.

She must be overstimulated from fear, she decided, because she had a sudden mental image of him tickling his mustache across her naked breasts. Swaying, she nearly fell backward into the coach.

Sometimes she saw things in her mind, and then they came true.

Katherine shook her head ruefully and began to sweep the dust from her skirt. She still held her scalpel and glanced at it, distractedly noting that blood had run onto her fingers. At least it wasn't her blood. She smiled.

"Smiling. Lord, she's smiling. If I live to be old and toothless, I'll never see the likes of this again."

The rich, teasing drawl made her look up warily. Justis Gallatin headed toward her, grabbing his hat from the ground and tucking his pistol back into his belt as he walked, his gaze never wavering from a head-to-foot study of her.

Katherine froze, her body on alert in strange ways she didn't have time to analyze. He was a big man, tall and powerful, with corded arms that looked as if they could squeeze a bear to death, and legs that glided along in an easy cadence.

He walked like an Indian, she thought. Silent, graceful. A woman wouldn't hear him slip into her room, but once he was there, she wouldn't want him to leave.

"Thank you for your assistance," she said formally, and waited for him to stop a polite distance away.

He didn't. He strolled right up to her, coming to a halt so close that she felt threatened by the potently masculine smells of sweat and dust and leather. Then he licked one forefinger and brushed the tip of her nose with it. The finger came away covered in damp red dirt.

"You okay under that war paint?" he asked gruffly.

She stared up into a youthful face already tending toward rugged squint lines and creases, thick, wickedly arched eyebrows, eyes the color of new green leaves, and that infernal mustache.

"I'm unhurt, thank you, sir. Thank you very much."

Mr. Bingham hung over the side of his seat atop the coach, watching them. "I'm sure sorry about all of this mess, Miss Blue Song."

She forced her gaze up to the driver's. "Are those drovers typical of the men roaming the woods in Cherokee country now?"

"Yes'm."

"My father will send the Lighthorse patrol after them."

"Nope," Justis Gallatin interjected.

She swiveled her gaze to the man, who was now watching her with a different kind of intensity that made her feel increasingly uncomfortable. His eyes drooped a little at the corners, giving him a sleepy, satiated expression when he smiled. But he wasn't smiling now—he seemed far from it—and his hooded scrutiny was guarded, perhaps even angry.

"What do you mean, sir?"

"There's no more Cherokee courts. The state of Georgia took over the law a few years ago. I figured your folks wrote you about it."

"I read about it in the Philadelphia paper. But my

father said it wasn't so." She frowned. "My name's Katherine—Miss Blue Song. Do you know my family?"

He hesitated, his wide, generous mouth tightening under the mustache. Then he said, "Your pa sent me to meet
you on the road. I've been waiting for you the past
week." The green eyes were shuttered now, half closed.
"He's working a new field and couldn't come himself, but
he was a little worried that you'd run into trouble—just
like you did."

She tilted her head and looked at him curiously.
"You're employed by my father?"

"No. Friend of his."

"Your name is Mr. Gallatin, is that right?"

"Justis Gallatin."

She inched back in wary consideration. "My father
wouldn't send a stranger. This isn't like him."

"Lots of things have changed since you went north."
Abruptly he took the scalpel from her hand. "Never seen
anything like it," he said again. "Swiping at those boys
like a cat with one mean claw. Damned good." He pulled
her hand to him, jerked the long tail of his shirt from his
trousers, and wiped her bloody fingers.

Katherine was angered by his familiarity, surprised by
the gentleness in his big, lethal hands, and flushed from
the thought that her fingers were being cleaned by material that had recently been tucked against his thighs—
and more.

"You obviously share the drovers' opinion of me," she
said in a crisp but genteel tone. It had taken years of
practice at the Presbyterian Academy for Young Ladies to
acquire that soft, ice-cold voice.

He stopped ministering to her fingers and looked up in
surprise. "Huh?"

"You wouldn't be so forward with a white woman,"
she said, pulling her hand away.

He frowned, sincerely puzzled. "Yes, I would."

"Well, that's honest."

Amused despite herself, Katherine pivoted gracefully and climbed back into the coach. Dust puffed around her as she sat. Her heart still thudded painfully from the encounter with the drovers, and she wasn't in any mood for Mr. Gallatin's unsettling brand of chivalry.

"You may ride along behind the coach if you like," she told him. "And when we arrive at my home, you'll be welcome to stay for supper."

She tried to ignore the anger rising in his face and nodded toward the huge gray horse that waited beside the road. Its gear gleamed with care, and there was gold plating on the bridle. "Close the coach door and go to your mount, sir," she ordered as calmly as she could.

"I'm not some hired jerktail you can steer any way you like. I told you, I'm a friend of your pa's."

She raised her chin and stared stubbornly at a speck of peeling paint on the coach's inner wall. "My father doesn't have many white friends, and he never mentioned you in his letters."

"Be that as it may. Don't take on airs. You're in no position to be choosy."

"I appreciate your help, Mr. Gallatin, but your manners leave a lot to be desired."

"Yes'm, I know, but you'd better get used to 'em." With that unsettling remark he turned and whistled for his horse.

Katherine watched in consternation as he tied the horse to the back of the coach. Then he climbed in and sat down, pressing himself close to her in the narrow seat, his shoulder and thigh firmly welded to hers. The intimate contact made her feel like covering her torso with both arms, as if he had just undressed her. He flicked the door shut with a quick movement of one long arm.

"Move on, Mr. Bing-ham," he called loudly. "And make it fast."

The coach lurched forward just as Katherine, quietly

furious, rose to move to the seat facing him. She tottered and he latched one hand into the back of her skirt. Through skirt, petticoat, and drawers she felt his fingers brush the cleft of her hips. She'd never been touched by any man there, much less a white, mustached gold miner.

She twisted around, wrung the skirt from his grip, and saw from the gleam in his eye that he knew exactly what he'd done. She sat down hard on the opposite bench, and dust poofed up like some kind of boudoir powder she'd used too liberally. He grinned.

"Give me my scalpel, sir," she said. He had tucked it behind his ear.

"I don't attack women, Katie. I coax 'em. Rest easy."

"It's *Miss Blue Song.*"

He looked down, saw her satchel, and dropped the knife into it. "Who's the sawbones?"

"I am."

The disbelieving look he gave her was no more than she expected. "A lady doctor?"

"Not certified in any way, of course. But then, there are quite a few men practicing medicine who have no claim to formal training at all."

"There's no such thing as a lady doctor. Nobody'd teach you."

Katherine smiled grimly. She'd have to put up with this blunt rascal only until she reached home. "If you're an Indian, people don't expect you to act like a lady. They aren't shocked when you do eccentric things."

"But what doctor had the gumption to risk his reputation by trainin' you?"

"My guardian in Philadelphia, Dr. Henry Ledbetter. A friend of my father's. Dr. Ledbetter is a progressive. He let me assist him—with female patients only, of course."

"Oh. You're a midwife, then."

"No, I'm a doctor. I don't see why not."

He thought for a second. "Well, I reckon I don't see why not neither."

To her surprise, Katherine found sincere admiration in his eyes. Then he gave her a solemn, lopsided squint. "But you got enough trouble just bein' an Injun. Don't tell people you're a Yankee free thinker too."

She took several slow breaths, a technique that always served her well, then gave him a hard look. "Sir, get out of my coach and ride behind it."

He shrugged his answer and picked up the slender leather-bound book he'd wedged into a corner when he sat down. Though he tried to be nonchalant, from the way he frowned at the title she doubted he could figure it out. Not many people in these regions could read or write.

"*Romeo and Juliet,*" she offered with a polite smile.

"Shakespeare, huh?" He nodded smugly, a gleam of triumph in his eye. "I saw it acted once, down in Savannah. A boy played Juliet. Romeo couldn't marry him, so he killed himself. Seemed unreasonable to me." He tossed the book down. "Waste of time."

"How nice. You saw a play once. With a little more culture you'd reach the level of a barbarian."

His eyes snapped. "You didn't care about my lack of culture when I was savin' you from those hog-kissers."

Remorse mingled with undeniable gratitude. "Mr. Gallatin, you're entirely right. I apologize for offending you. You saved my honor, and possibly my life. And you risked your own safety to do it."

He frowned, studying her raptly, then said in a slow, thoughtful tone, "I guess I've rescued myself a real lady. The kind that makes a man want to fight dragons for her."

A shiver ran down her spine. Had she discovered some remarkable brand of backwoods cavalier, a white man and gold miner who fancied himself a crusading knight? He leaned forward, spit on his fingertips, and began cleaning her face. She drew back so quickly, her head thumped the coach's wall.

"Sir!"

"Easy, gal, easy. Katie Blue Song, full of vinegar."

He pulled a handkerchief from his trouser pocket, took her chin in one hand, and went on about his cleaning while she sat in transfixed silence.

"You and those drovers," he murmured, shaking his head. "I never saw a woman defend herself with so much courage before. Not a squeak, not a tear, just laid into 'em. Weren't you scared at all?"

"Certainly." The heel of his hand brushed her cheek; his fingertips outlined every bone in her face, or so it felt. Katherine had never cast her gaze down before any man before, but now she did it to keep from studying him with the same fascination he directed toward her.

"I'll be damned," he said in his low, breath-stealing way. "I knew that Jesse and Mary had three pretty daughters, 'cause I saw 'em each time they came home from the mission school up in Tennessee. But I never figured the fourth one was the prize."

In her mind's eye Katherine saw the slow, easy journey of a man's hand along the length of her bare stomach, and then lower. She knew exactly whose hand it was. *No.* There was no way that could come true.

She twisted her face away from Justis Gallatin's touch. "If you're really a friend of my father's, why are you trying to trifle with me?"

"When you've got a lot of gold, you don't *trifle* with women," he told her solemnly. "You lure 'em into wicked, wicked sin, just like the dime novels say."

"You have no manners or education, but you do have a lot of gold. So you think gold gives you the right to do as you please."

He sat back, propped one foot on the opposite knee, and smiled calmly. "Done some mining. Done all right at it. Now I'm trying to get respectable. Or at least learn to *act* respectable."

"You've mined Cherokee land—stolen from it—just like all the other white men."

He looked out the window, and his jaw worked a little. She could almost see the tension rising in him, and it made the coach feel much too small for the two of them.

"Your pa's one of the best friends I ever had . . . have," he said finally, still staring out the window. "I've mined his land, but I've put half of the profits aside for whenever he wants to claim 'em."

Shock sliced her breath in two. Her father had never been interested in large-scale mining, and especially not with a white man as partner. He and her mother had scooped gold out of the creeks occasionally—Cherokees had traded gold among themselves for centuries—but they had kept the locations secret. They knew that showing them to white men would only cause trouble.

"My father would never willingly help a white man find Cherokee gold," she told Justis Gallatin.

"Times have changed, I keep tellin' you. Your father changed." He gestured impatiently. "Look, gal, it wasn't no big deal, all right? I set up a dredge on a little bitty creek in the middle of the woods. Closed the operation down when the vein ran out three years ago. 'Cept for some piles of dirt, you can't hardly tell anybody was there. Now I got me a big mine in the hills east of town."

"Not far from a little spring surrounded by laurel?"

He looked at her cautiously. "Yeah."

"My parents were the only people who knew about that spot! They led you there. Admit it."

He swore under his breath. "All right. But half the profits from that mine was . . . are theirs too. Waitin' to be claimed."

Katherine tried not to raise her voice, but she felt angry and confused. "Why haven't they claimed them already?"

"Too risky. It's illegal for Cherokee and white to have a business deal."

"*What?* Are you saying that everything I've read is true? The Georgia courts are trying to force us out?"

He gazed steadily at her, his expression tight and hard. "Times have changed a lot since you went off to Philadelphia, gal."

She clenched her hands into fists. "Mr. Gallatin, if you say that to me one more time—"

"Hullo," Mr. Bingham called. He pulled the horses up. "Miss Blue Song, is this the road toward your homeplace?"

Katherine grasped the edge of the coach window and looked out. Everything else was forgotten as she gazed lovingly at the wagon trail that disappeared into shadowy forest. "It is, sir, it is. Turn onto it, Mr. Bingham!"

Justis Gallatin called out, "Whoa, Bing-ham! Straight on, to Gold Ridge."

Katherine looked at him in exasperation. "I have no business to conduct among a passel of log cabins filled with gold miners."

"Your pa said for you to meet him there."

"But my mother and sisters are at home."

"I was told to make sure you went into town and waited for Jesse there. Don't cause me any trouble. You're goin' to town."

He spoke with an authority that stunned her. Gone was the teasing rogue, and in his place was a man who gave commands easily and expected them to be obeyed.

Katherine straightened, feeling angry but also worried. "What's the truth? Tell me. Please."

Shaking his head in consternation, he leaned forward and took her hands. "I'm sorry for snappin' at you. Your pa just wants to surprise you, that's all." Now the voice was friendly again, the eyes reassuring. "Don't make me ruin it by telling you."

She exhaled slowly but couldn't relax as long as his

thumbs moved in slow circles across her palms. "I'll have to have a talk with my father about his choice of messengers. You're not very good at presenting surprises. And stop tickling me."

"I like to make a Cherokee gal blush. It takes more work, but when it happens, a man knows he's really done something right."

Katherine realized that her face was burning. She pulled her hands away and rapped on the coach wall. "Onward, Mr. Bingham. To Gold Ridge, where a secret awaits."

Justis Gallatin lounged back in his seat and nodded with satisfaction. It puzzled her that for just a moment he looked so sad.

## CHAPTER 2

JUSTIS asked enough polite questions to get her loosened up and talking without his help. She was still unnerved from the business with the drovers, and seemed grateful for any diversion. So he got her to tell him about railroad trains, something hardly anyone outside a big city had seen.

Her talking left him free to curse his situation silently. What was he going to do with her? And how could he tell her that she had no family, no home, and no money other than what few dollars she might be carrying in the little satin purse anchored to the waist of her dress?

She was part of a doomed tribe, and he couldn't change that. In this part of Georgia, as in the states bordering it, the new settlers had long ago given up talk about sharing the land with Indians. Get the darkskinned devils out and take the country God meant for white folks to own, they said.

Most of the tribe still hung on to the old ways, spurning the missionary schools, avoiding the whites whenever possible, keeping to the riverside villages and little farms tucked deep in the hills. Justis couldn't help but admire their stubborn pride and independence. Katherine Blue Song's feisty nature didn't really surprise him. She was one of the Principle People, and ages earlier the Great Spirit had told the whole world to kowtow to her tribe.

Their lives were part of the land, and the ancient place-names had been born in the lilting songs of wind and water—Etowah, Chestatee, Chattooga, Hiwassee. Justis could only maul the names with a stiff tongue.

But at least he respected them. Most people thereabouts were disgusted with the Indians for hanging on so hard, especially those who had adopted white ways, built prosperous businesses, and traded their war cries for fancy arguments supported by white laws.

You mean them Injuns wrote up a constitution that calls their hunting grounds a nation? You sayin' that they started a newspaper—a *newspaper* with that bastard scribble they use for writing? And they had the gall to send chiefs to Washington City to tell the President of these United States that his treaties weren't no good? Lord have mercy, what kind of uppity notions will they get next?

Justis watched Katherine Blue Song and felt a dull ache in his chest. Even if she were white she'd never fit in anywhere. She had too much education for a woman, not to mention that odd idea about being a doctor. Hell, if he had his way, she could doctor everybody from here to the Mississippi, but few folks in Gold Ridge would agree.

It would've been better if Jesse and Mary had sent her to the mission school in Tennessee like their other daughters. The missionaries wouldn't have let her get dangerous ideas, and they sure wouldn't have turned her into someone so refined that every woman in Gold Ridge would feel jealous.

Justis forced himself to stop looking at her. He stared

out the window and thought, Refined and beautiful, and it'd be easy to stir up the fire behind those black eyes.

What else did he want from her? Too much, he admitted. Friendship and trust. Good Lord, what he was thinking added up to a helluva lot more than a woman like Katie Blue Song would ever give to a slap-hazard renegade like him. He had grown up in a world that demanded he fight for his survival; she had been raised like some kind of royalty.

How would she feel when she learned that he owned the Blue Song place? And where could he send her so that she'd be safe from men like those damned drovers? And if he didn't send her away, how long would it be before he got her into his bed?

Not long, if he could help it. He admitted that too.

He'd never forget his first glimpse of her—backed against this carriage, glaring at the world; her thick onyx hair, which she wore braided around the top of her head, catching the sunlight like some sort of dark crown; her generously curved chest thrust out in defiance; and that skillful, slender hand moving with deadly accuracy. An enemy would do well to protect his throat around her.

"Mr. Gallatin?"

Justis looked back at her. She had her head tilted to one side, and her deepset eyes examined him from beneath a luxurious ruffle of lashes. He caught his breath.

"Yeah?"

"You were rubbing your neck and frowning. Are you too hot?"

He laughed softly. He was way too hot, and if he told her why, she'd get the scalpel out again.

"I'm fine, thanks." He caught the edge of her skirt and idly fingered the shiny gray satin. "Lady like you belongs back in Philadelphia." Where he wouldn't be tempted by her.

"No, I've come home for good."

When he saw the happy anticipation in her face, he

almost choked. "Frontier's going to be mighty boring after a big city."

She smiled and shook her head, then nodded toward the window. "This land's in my blood. When I was little, my mother fed me a spoonful of soil mixed into some corn mush. She said the land was part of me now, and I'd never stop loving it."

He grimaced. "What kind of husband are you gonna find around here? Some buckskinned feller with a log shanty back in the woods? Nah, you wouldn't be satisfied."

She raised her chin and said calmly, "That's no problem, Mr. Gallatin. I don't intend to marry."

More odd notions. She had a ripe, dusky pink mouth that ought never to be wasted on such talk. "You'll marry," he told her with confidence.

"I won't. I swear it. I'll be owned by no one but myself."

He tugged playfully at her skirt. "I bet some pearly-faced dandy up in Philadelphia broke your heart and busted your pride. Told you he wouldn't marry an Injun gal." Justis paused. "He allowed that he might fancy you as a mistress, though. Hmmm?"

The quick flare in her eyes told him that he was probably right. "I'm certain that you could write sonnets about romance, Mr. Gallatin, but I'd prefer not to hear your opinions. I assume you're not married."

"Not yet. Been plannin' on it for some time, though."

"Oh?" she said quickly. "Are you betrothed to one of the local she-bears?"

He laughed again. "I'm an important man hereabouts. Got ambitions to be more important, and I need the right kind of wife to make me look respectable. I might even go up to New York and hunt for one in high society."

"Trap one," she corrected him dryly.

He grinned, fascinated by her. Behind that sweet smile was a sharp tongue. He'd wager that six years in Philadelphia hadn't tamed the free spirit of a Cherokee upbring-ing.

"Your mama told me how you ran buck-wild when you were little," he said cheerfully. "Said you got into more trouble than a Cherokee elf. I disremember the de-tails, but there was a story about a big powwow, some sort of festival. Seems little Katie had a girl-size blowgun for hunting rabbits, but she went huntin' trouble instead. Slipped into the woods and snuck up on an old chief and his wife who were enjoyin' a particular sort of entertain-ment at the moment . . ."

"My mother told you that?"

"Gospel truth." He solemnly held up a hand. "She said you made that old chief nervous for the rest of the festi-val."

Her mouth crooked up at one corner. "I'll have to speak to my mother about her tall tales."

"She was . . . she's a fine woman, your mother."

"Yes." Nodding, Katherine smiled pensively. "I've missed her so much. I wanted to come home a long time ago, but she and Papa wouldn't let me."

Justis knew why—they'd have gone crazy worrying about her safety. Jesse and Mary had feared for their other three daughters as well, and that was why the girls had all been enrolled up at the mission school in Tennes-see. If they hadn't come home to visit, they'd still be alive.

Justis cleared his throat and pointed out the window. "Look. We're on the edge of town."

She clasped the window ledge and gazed out intently. "The creek's nothing but a ditch between mounds of dirt! Somebody cut down all the trees! There are stumps ev-erywhere! And all those shanties—how many people live in Gold Ridge now?"

"About five thousand," he said carefully, watching her reaction.

Stunned, she was silent for several minutes, studying

the ugly overflow of a booming gold town. Pigs and chickens roamed among the shanties, searching for food through piles of garbage. Men sat on canvas stools, using tree stumps for tables as they played cards or drank from umber-colored bottles.

A few women and children squatted around campfires, waving away flies in the warm April sun. Between two lopsided tents a pair of men punched at each other drunkenly until one fell backward and brought his home down in a heap around him.

Finally Katherine turned away, her face drawn with worry. "Is it all like this?"

"Nah, there's a real nice square with a new brick courthouse. Got some decent homes, couple of churches, some respectable hotels. That's where we're going—to a hotel just off the square."

She unpinned a pearl brooch from her bodice and took the handkerchief that it had held. Dusting herself delicately, her eyes clouded with thought, she murmured, "What do all these new people think of their Cherokee hosts?"

Justis was saved from answering that question when a man trotted his fat bay horse alongside the coach. Slouched over the saddle, his white coat flopping in rhythm with the brim of his white hat, he tried to steer his mount, smile, and stick his face as close to the coach window as possible.

"Welcome to Gold Ridge, mister," he said to Justis. "You need land? I got land bought directly from those lucky souls who won it in the lottery. Forty-acre gold lots, hundred-and-sixty-acre farm lots, some with improvements the Injuns made on 'em. Good prices— Well, I'll be damned!"

He stared at Katherine, then looked back at Justis. "You taking this squaw to one of the cathouses? Which one?"

By the time Katherine's sharp gasp hit the air, Justis

was already leaning out the window, and a second later he'd jabbed the barrel of his pistol into the man's fleshy throat. With a squeak of alarm the man reined his horse around and galloped back toward the shanties. Justis swore softly as he settled back in his seat and put the gun away. He finally looked at Katherine and saw the horror in her expression.

"These people really believe that they can have Cherokee land and anything else they want," she said with soft torment. "They're convinced of it."

Justis sighed. She looked so stricken, he reached over and cupped her face in both hands. Her skin felt fantastically smooth to his callused fingers, and desperation gave her eyes a wide, limpid appeal that sank into him like a knife. She might be tough, but she was scared too.

"Everything's gonna be just fine, Katie," he said soothingly. Then, telling himself that he needed to distract her from further questions, he kissed her lightly on the mouth. She tasted like sweet cologne and dusty sweat, a unique combination that he found wildly provocative.

"Oh, dear," she said, trembling.

His mouth brushed hers again. "You stick with me, Katie, and I'll fight any man who looks crossways at you."

"Why are you like this?" Her breath came in soft, ragged puffs. "Are you as wicked as you act, or as sweet as you sound?"

"Both."

Because she made a murmur of amusement, he ran his tongue over her lips before he sat back. He held her shoulders and nodded solemnly. "Now you got clean lips."

*Jesse, I promised to take care of her, but I didn't count on this.*

She blinked a couple of times and shivered. Her eyes filled with tears of shame as she shoved his hands away.

"I'm sorry for letting you do that. I feel very confused right now."

"It was just a friendly kiss."

"And the Alamo was just a skirmish."

"Hullo, down there," Mr. Bingham yelled. "Where to in town?"

Justis stuck his head out the window. "The Gallatin-Kirkland Hotel. It's on the edge of the square."

"The *Gallatin-Kirkland Hotel*?" she repeated. With her handkerchief she dabbed quickly at her eyes, then brushed the material over her mouth, shooting him a reproachful look as she did.

"Me and my business partner own it," Justis explained. "Sam Kirkland. He and his wife live there."

"What *else* do you own in the Cherokee Nation?"

"Besides the mine I already told you about, a store, a stable, and a saloon." Plus two hundred acres of the prettiest land in this part of the state. Blue Song land.

She arched a black brow. "Is there anything left for anyone else to own?"

"Plenty." He pointed. "Take a look-see. Yo, Bing-ham! Take us around the courthouse once!"

The coach rolled into a neatly kept square, at the center of which stood a majestic two-story brick building with a pair of white colonnades framing the entrance. Saddle horses and mules hitched to heavy wagons stood lazily in the shade of a massive oak tree by the courthouse steps.

"The bricks were made by a local man," Justis told her proudly. "There's flecks of gold in 'em. And after it rains hard, you can go out in the street and pan nearly a pennyweight. There are fortunes just waitin' to be found here."

"Too much to resist," she murmured.

The buildings around the square were a variety of styles, everything from an old log cabin to clapboard stores with canvas awnings and nicely painted houses complete with rocking chairs on the porches. Even though the sun had barely reached noon, raucous piano music filtered out the open doors of the Buzzard's Roost Dance Hall and several similar establishments nearby. A half-dozen drunks lay in the alleyway between the rather grand Gallatin-Kirkland Saloon and the ramshackle Golden Lady Billiards Emporium. They were piled up like sleeping puppies. Flies circled them in the shadows.

Men hunkered around dice games on the porches and in the street. A mud-covered gent in overalls danced a jig with a woman wearing an overstuffed carmine-red dress, the perfect color to match her hair. They had no musical accompaniment, at least not any that matched the rhythm of their feet. They did, however, have a nanny goat and her nursing kid for an audience.

A wide variety of people traveled the street—miners carrying pans, picks, and shovels; businessmen in snug cutaway coats and top hats; barefoot farmers wearing coarse homespun; women in gingham and women in silk. They had one thing in common—except for a black slave or two, they were all white and seemed very much at home.

"Why didn't anybody write me about this?" Katherine asked in desperation.

Justis shrugged elaborately. "It was hard for them to put into words, I reckon. And they didn't want you to get worried and come home."

"Can you send someone for my father right away?"

"You bet."

He'd tell her the truth as soon as they got inside the hotel, he told himself. He wasn't very good with words and even worse with hysterical women. Thinking about her reaction made him feel sick.

Mr. Bingham finished his circuit and headed off the square toward a handsome white building set not far from where thick forest closed in on a trail leading out of town. Double galleries ran across the top and bottom levels, flowers formed a colorful border out front, and a small garden flourished beyond the limbs of a stately beech tree near one side of the building. A sign hung from the edge of the bottom gallery, with "Gallatin-Kirkland Hotel, Est. 1835" scrolled in large gilt letters.

Dread pooled in Justis's stomach as he stepped from the coach. Bingham jumped down and went to remove Katherine's trunks at the rear. Justis followed him there.

"You been paid in full?"

"Yes, sir. Miss Blue Song took care of it in Nashville a few days ago. Look, I don't feel right, going off and leaving her with strangers . . ."

"Here." Justis planted a ten-dollar gold piece in Bingham's hand. "Get going soon as you unload. I'll take care of her from now on."

When the driver looked at the coin his eyes bugged. "Yes, sir."

Justis heard a sound and strode to the coach door too late to do more than watch Katherine shut the door behind herself. She looked around anxiously while she set a black bonnet over her hair.

"Don't wear that thing," he told her. "Makes it hard to see you."

She peered at him from under the bonnet, her face like the center of a darkly exotic flower. "I just want to be ready when my father gets here."

"You think he's gonna know by magic the second you set foot on the ground in Gold Ridge?"

"Perhaps." She removed the bonnet and gave him a mild look of exasperation.

"Mr. Justis! Is this the Injun?"

A robust black boy, barefoot and shirtless but dressed in good trousers, ran up and grabbed Justis's hand, then gazed at Katherine in awe.

"This is Miss Blue Song." Justis shifted awkwardly. Introductions were one of many social graces he hadn't mastered yet. He gestured from Katherine to the boy. "Meet Noah."

She could have ignored the boy, nodded silently to him, or reproached Justis for introducing her to a house servant. Any of the three would have been acceptable. Instead, she smiled gently and said, "How do you do, Noah?"

Justis watched her with a troubled heart. She was a real lady, he thought, and after that kiss he knew he'd do whatever it took to keep her.

Noah ducked his head in a vague sort of bow. "You be an orphan like me, huh?"

Justis hurried him to the stallion pawing impatiently at the back of the coach and shoved the reins in his hands, along with a nickel. "You take Watchman over to the stables, you hear? And don't get trampled."

"Okay!"

After the boy left, leading the huge gray horse behind him, Justis sighed in relief. Katherine turned her attention from Bingham's work with her baggage. "What did he mean by 'orphan'?"

"Some fool game of his. I don't know."

"You own him?" The disapproval was obvious in her voice.

"Yeah. But I didn't buy him. Him and his sister were bartered for goods at the store. They were both sickly and bruised up. Wasn't any other way I could get 'em away from their master."

"I'm an abolitionist, Mr. Gallatin. I just want you to know that. A free-thinking abolitionist."

Lord, why didn't she just strip naked and do a dance in the road? he thought. That couldn't make her any more controversial than she was already. He pulled a long Spanish cigar out of the band of his hat and jabbed it between his teeth.

"I'm not really opinioned on the subject, Katie, but I don't own slaves. When Noah and his sister are older, I plan to sign their manumission papers and send 'em up north to school. Good enough?"

She looked remorseful. "Yes. I apologize." He nodded, satisfied. When she was wrong, she admitted it. Not many women did that. But after a moment she added, "Please don't call me by a pet name. It's crude. A gentleman would call me 'Miss Blue Song.' "

Justis felt embarrassment creeping up his cheeks. One minute a smiling angel, the next a high-falutin' queen. "I'm not a gentleman, *Katie.*"

She clamped her lips tightly together and turned away. "Just put those trunks on the veranda, please, Mr. Bingham. I won't be here long."

The sound of footsteps on a wooden floor heralded the appearance of Sam's wife, her cheeks rosy from housework. She wiped her hands on a white apron as she pulled it from her calico dress. Rebecca Kirkland radiated the same wholesome sweetness as a pot of honey. She was made up of wheat-blond hair and buxom womanhood, with kind hazel eyes. When people wanted good chicken soup and tenderhearted treatment, they went to Rebecca. Justis had never looked at a female with brotherly affection before he met her.

"Welcome home, Miss Blue Song," she said kindly, and held out both hands. "I'm Rebecca Kirkland. My husband and I are partners with Mr. Gallatin." She shot an anxious look toward Justis, and he shook his head.

After a startled moment Katherine went up the steps and clasped Rebecca's hands. "I'm sorry to intrude on you. I really don't understand why Mr. Gallatin brought me here."

"Jesse's supposed to meet her," Justis called. This had to stop. It gnawed at his insides more with each second. As soon as Bingham pulled away, he'd tell her.

*White trash murdered your family. Your pa was full of bullets and the rest—well, they died in other ways.*

"Why don't you fix Miss Blue Song some tea?" Justis

suggested loudly. He bit his cigar in two and had to grab
the front end before it fell to the ground.


NOAH AND HIS SISTER, Lilac, were hiding beyond the
arched doorway to the parlor, and they kept peeking at
her. Katherine smiled at them, but they looked sorrowful
in return. Rebecca Kirkland's hands shook each time she
raised her teacup. Justis Gallatin had quickly downed
two glasses of whiskey from a cupboard in the corner.
Now he lounged by the marble fireplace, scowling.

Something was wrong, very wrong, and fear grew inside Katherine until she could barely sit still.

"You know my family well?" she asked Rebecca.

"Oh, yes." Her smile was too wide, her voice too gay.
"They trade at the store."

"And the people from the Talachee village? Do they
trade with you also?"

"They moved on a month ago," Justis said. "Went to
the Indian territory out west."

Katherine looked at him in bewilderment. "They deserted the settlement? They'd been there for generations."

He cleared his throat, stared at the carpeted floor, and
said finally, "Settlers claimed their land. That's the way it
is now. Since the lottery. Man shows up with a deed,
Indians got to move. The treaty said so."

"No chief of any importance signed that treaty. And
it's still being fought in Washington City."

He slammed a hand on the mantel. "Dammit, this isn't
Washington City! It's over, you hear? There's nothing you
or I can do to change it."

The blood stopped in Katherine's veins. She and Justis
Gallatin shared a long, intense gaze, and regret slowly
softened his features. "I'm sorry," he said wearily.

Her hands felt so icy, she curved them around the
teacup for warmth. Gazing down into the amber liquid,
she tried to think. She was not ordinarily given to ner-

vous moods, but right now a bleak sense of doom was crawling through her stomach. "I want to go home," she said softly. "Right now. I have missed my family for six years."

Rebecca made a strange noise. Katherine looked at her quickly, searching for answers. Delicate footsteps tapped on the porch, and Rebecca left the room hurriedly when someone knocked at the door.

Katherine stood and faced Justis. "Please take me home."

He struggled for a second, then shook his head. "I can't."

"Surely you understand my impatience to see my loved ones."

"Nope. I've got no loved ones. Never have had any."

"Oh, you're being deliberately argumentative! Why not simply—"

"Justis, my dear, you've finally found her. I'm so glad."

Katherine pivoted to find a petite young woman breezing into the parlor, voluminous pink skirts flouncing around her, her cheeks flushed just as pink, her eyes as hard as blue sapphires. A pile of beautiful red-gold hair was arranged in ringlets around her head, and her features were striking despite the thick pattern of freckles that covered most of her face.

She went to Justis, took his hands, and looked up at him sweetly. "You were terribly kind to do it."

"Amarintha, wait," Rebecca called frantically, following her.

"This is the poor thing," Amarintha cooed, turning to Katherine. "You brave dear."

Katherine's mouth dropped open as the visitor threw both arms around her and hugged delicately, brushing a cool cheek against hers. When the woman stepped back her gaze swept over Katherine with intense appraisal.

The pink mouth tightened. "And such a fine example of what civilization can do. It's so very tragic."

Suddenly Justis inserted an arm between them. "Amarintha, let's you and me step outside for a minute."

Katherine had had enough. "Stop it." Her fists clenched, she backed away from the group, away from Rebecca's strained expression, the newcomer's rather melodramatic one, and the fierceness in Justis Gallatin's eyes as he started toward her.

"Someone tell me the truth," she ordered.

"You mean she doesn't *know*?" Amarintha asked. "No one's told her that her whole family's dead?"

Justis swung about and glared. "Dammit, you did that to be spiteful!"

Katherine sagged against a chair, grasping its back. In a second Justis reached her. He latched on to her arms and held tightly, looking down at her in anguish.

"This isn't how I wanted to break it," he said hoarsely. "But I reckon it's as good a way as any."

She stared up at him and frowned in concentration. Whole family dead. No, of course not. "Where are they, really?" she asked.

His fingers dug into her arms. "They were killed four days ago. All of 'em. We don't know who did it. The farm was robbed and most everything was burned."

The words glanced off her, making sense but not penetrating her shield of disbelief. "But you don't understand," she murmured, and raised her hands to grip his dusty shirt. "My family tries very hard to fit in. Papa enlisted when Andrew Jackson asked Cherokees to help him fight the Creek Indians. He's a veteran. My mother's mother was a medicine woman and my mother was a Beloved Woman in the Blue clan. When the first missionaries came here, she convinced the people at the Talachee settlement to trust them. Don't you see? No one would want to hurt my family."

"Katie gal," he whispered, shaking her a little. "They're dead. Believe me."

She pulled away from him and walked out of the parlor, out of the hotel, and across the side yard, where she stopped by the beech tree and wondered how she'd gotten there. Coming up the dusty trail past the hotel was a team of oxen pulling a large wagon filled with barrels. The two teamsters on the wagon seat gaped at her and pointed, then yelled something, she didn't care what. She turned and stumbled blindly.

"Easy, gal, easy," Justis's drawling voice said close to her ear, and his thickly muscled arm latched around her waist. She wasn't certain whether she was walking or being carried, but she ended up behind the hotel in the midst of a flower garden.

Her knees buckled but she didn't fall. Instead, she was lowered to a sitting position among the flowers, and Justis sat beside her, holding her to his chest and stroking her shoulder.

"There was no shaman to speak formulas over the bodies," she whispered. "And no preacher to pray for them."

"Sam said the right things," he assured her. "And we buried 'em proper." His arms tightened around her. "Go ahead and cry. I'm so sorry, Katie."

After a minute passed and she only sat silent and stiff in his embrace, he drew back to look at her. Katherine gazed past him to the sunlight streaming into the hearts of the flowers, carrying power to them, to the earth, to everything that was strong and eternal.

"They're buried on the land?" she asked.

"On the ridge beyond the house."

"Then they'll always be part of it, and it's part of me. And I'll always have the land. I've dreamed it."

He didn't say anything for a moment. Then, "You'll never want for anything, Katie. Before I buried your pa, I

promised him that I'd look after you. And I want to—it's
not just a duty."

What was he saying? Look after her? Why was it his
concern? She was no child, and she didn't need any help
from a white man.

She stared at him dry-cyed. "Take me home."

JUSTIS KNEW SHE wasn't heartless, and he was relatively certain that she had a sound mind, but her reaction to her family's death was the most puzzling thing
he'd ever seen. She acted no more hysterical now than
she had two hours before, in the garden.

She sat on the wagon seat beside him, her bonnet in
her lap, her expression blank. He knew Indians could be
stone-faced when they wanted, but this was different.
The Blue Song farm was nearly three hours from town—
a long trip in a mule-drawn wagon over a rutted trail—
but she'd been still as a statue the whole way.

They turned onto the trail to the farm, but even that
seemed to have no effect on her. The trail wound between steep hills covered in hardwood trees. As it neared
the farm, clumps of purple irises and yellow jonquils
dotted every sunny spot along the sides.

Suddenly she laid a hand on his arm. "Stop, I want
some flowers," she said in a low, calm voice, and he felt
as though a woodthrush had just murmured in his ear.
"My mother planted these when I was little. My goodness, spring must have come late this year. I'm surprised
that they're still in bloom."

She climbed down before he could help her and spent
the next ten minutes filling her arms with yellow and
purple blossoms. Justis watched her in silent worry.

She hardly knew what was happening, he thought.

Back in the wagon again, she nuzzled her face against
the flowers, then smiled. "Just as I've remembered them.
It will be good to be home again."

"You're gonna be all right," he said gently. "You're just a little confused in the head right now."

"No." She gazed up the trail. It disappeared over a rise, and beyond were the first fields. "It's all burned and broken, I know. The springhouse is the only thing that still stands."

"How do you know that?"

"I see things in my mind sometimes, and they're usually true."

He inhaled sharply. "You see anything else about the place, or what happened?"

"No."

"Good." This was not a line of conversation he wanted to pursue. When she offered no more words, he was relieved. The mules crested the hill and he pulled them to a stop.

This part of the land was too hilly for farming. Jesse and his field hands had cleared it for grazing, so it dipped and rose under a green carpet of grass, dotted by an occasional cluster of shade trees in the valleys.

Dread grew inside Justis as the fields passed behind them and the forest closed in again. After a short distance it opened on the main clearing. A row of burned cabins bordered the road.

"Papa freed his farmhands when he joined the church," Katherine said casually, as if the cabins weren't heaps of charred pine logs. "The families stayed on and worked for shares, though."

Justis noticed that her hands were digging into the flowers as she talked, crushing them. He patted her knee. "Your pa sent the hands away last year. North. He couldn't protect 'em from kidnappers."

She wasn't listening. Leaning forward, her body rigid, she gazed at the rubble of the main house and outbuildings. Her feet hit the ground before he stopped the wagon. Cursing under his breath, Justis followed her as she walked through the grounds, the flowers falling from her arms unheeded, scattering in a breeze that suddenly whipped over the ridge.

He trailed her silently, waiting for her to do something, say something, to fall on the ground and sob like he expected a woman to do. She held her handsome gray skirt up and walked through the debris the raiders had spread in their hurry to find everything of value.

Justis winced as she stopped here and there to pick up small items—a button, a broken ivory comb, the stem from a pipe—all of which she tucked into her purse. She halted under the oaks in the front yard, and he prayed that she wouldn't notice the bloodstains beneath her feet.

She didn't seem to see anything around her, though. Her head was up, her eyes alert as if she were listening to voices he couldn't hear, or talking silently to one of the Cherokee spirits. "Where are they buried?" she asked.

"Over yonder, overlookin' the valley."

The Blue Song land was beautiful, but the valley made it magnificent. Jesse had grown corn taller than a man's head in those rich bottomlands. A meandering stream crossed the valley's farthest edge, and hazy blue mountains rimmed the distant horizon.

Justis had made certain that all five graves faced that heavenly view.

He stood back and watched Katherine walk from one mound of red dirt to the next, her hands hanging motionless by her sides. What kind of grieving thoughts churned behind her mysterious eyes, he wondered. She took a bit of dirt from each grave and dropped it in her purse.

"It'd do you good to cry," he hinted.

She stared blankly at the graves. "I'm hollow inside. There's nothing there to make tears."

She walked toward the yard again, moving with short, unsteady steps. He sighed with relief. She was in shock, that was all. He'd never seen such a bad case of it before, but he knew it would pass eventually.

She veered toward the small log structure a little way

from the house. "I shall live here until the house is re-built," she announced. After stumbling, she regained her composure and opened the door. Justis went over and stopped behind her, his mouth open in dismay. She was worse off than he'd figured.

She stood in the doorway and surveyed the dark, cool interior, where the farm's butter and eggs had been stored. A stone well stood at the center, unharmed.

"I'll sleep in the springhouse on a cot," she said.

Sorrow and determination boiled up inside Justis. He took her by the arm, slammed the door, and swung her to face him. Be merciful, he told himself. Make the cut clean and quick.

"You're not gonna live here, Katie. It's not your home anymore."

"I was born here," she explained patiently. "My mother was born here. Her father was a half-breed fur trapper. He settled on this land in 1797. The date's carved on an old walnut tree over there." She pointed. "See? The tree with the bench under it . . ."

"The land's been given away!" Justis yelled. He shook her hard, trying to break through her heart-wrenching blindness.

Finally agony and panic showed in her eyes. Her voice rose. "I can buy it back!"

"No, you don't even have the right to do that! If you had all the money in the world you couldn't buy it, or even lease it. The law says so!"

"It's mine. My family's here." She shook her head as she talked, breathing heavily, her hands clenched. "Who stole it and killed them?"

"Nobody *stole* it," he said between gritted teeth. "I don't have an answer about the other. Gangs roam all over these hills, doing whatever they want to the Cherokees, and the state lets 'em. Come on, let's get out of here. I'm not armed well enough to protect you if a gang was to wander up."

She looked as if she might bolt into the woods, and Justis suddenly wondered how he would ever get her back to town. He pulled her to him gently and wrapped his arms around her. She trembled and balled her fists against the center of his chest.

"It's because of this," she said in fierce anguish, raising the gold nugget that hung there. "This poison is responsible for bringing every worthless white soul in the country here to murder innocent people." She slung the nugget aside and dug her hands into his shirt. *Who stole this land?*

"Let's go back to town," he said. He'd have to take her back by force if she didn't cooperate. "I'll tell you once we get there. Only when we get there. If you want to know who owns the land, you have to come with me."

The horror was taking its toll now, and she swayed against him. Finally she hung her head and said hoarsely, *"Swear it."*

"I swear."

Released by that vow, she fainted in his arms.

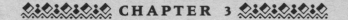 

## CHAPTER 3

KATHERINE woke with bright sunshine stinging her eyes. A hazy sense of despair and half-formed thoughts swam in her mind. It was easier to gaze around the room than to remember why she felt so hopeless.

Starched white curtains swayed stiffly at an open window. The walls were papered rather than painted. The rich floral print made her dizzy, and she looked away. The room contained a tall dresser and a marble-topped washstand complete with a bowl, a pitcher, and colorful cotton towels. Rugs dotted the wooden floor.

She lifted her covers and squinted at them groggily. Clean sheets and a pretty patchwork quilt. No bedbugs. The Gallatin-Kirkland Hotel provided lodgings that were far superior to most on the frontier.

*They're dead. Papa, Mama, Anna, Elizabeth, even little Sallie.*

Katherine let the covers fall, and her hands dropped limply on top of them. Memories nearly smothered her— her mother's walnut-brown eyes, warm with affection;

her father's way of laughing; her sisters' merry pranks. The sound of footsteps made her jump. Feeling too weary to move, she managed to push herself into a sitting position against the ornately carved headboard.

Her door opened and Justis Gallatin stepped into the room carrying a breakfast tray. Startled to find her staring at him, he halted. His sudden appearance jolted her senses. Like yesterday, he was dressed in a white shirt and dark trousers, but this morning he had tucked the trousers into knee-high boots.

His skin was so weathered that had it been a little darker, he would have passed for part Cherokee, except that no Cherokee had ever had such wavy chestnut hair. His mustache made him look like the handsome villain in a play. The gold nugget gleamed on the light background of his shirt.

Grief and anger fought within her, equally matched. She felt yesterday's anguish settling into her bones with fresh, sharp agony. It would have to work its way to the surface before she knew who she was again. Katherine wanted to hate every white settler in north Georgia.

"How do you feel?" Justis asked gently as he walked to a bedside table.

Could she hate this dangerous man who'd befriended her?

"Leave me alone. I don't need your help. You're trash, just a thieving settler no matter how kindly you act. Men such as you aren't fit to set foot on Cherokee land. Not so many years ago we would have burned you alive and laughed while you begged for mercy."

He stood beside the bed, looking miserable. "Katie, I know you hold it against me. Against every white man. If I thought it'd do a damned bit of good, I'd . . . All right, I will."

He set the tray down and went to her trunks and valises stacked neatly beside an armoire. Searching among them he found her doctor's satchel and took the scalpel from it. He came back to her and laid it on the covers by her hand.

Then he pulled his shirt off and sat on the edge of the bed with his broad, muscular back so close, she could see every hair, every freckle, the smallest workings of the flesh. "Go ahead," he said gruffly. "There are plenty of scars there already. I don't mind another one."

She stared at his back in horror. "I see them," she whispered.

"I've been in a lot of fights." He waited for her to do or say something else. He never looked over his shoulder to see whether she'd picked up the knife.

In the space of those few seconds she felt herself lose something deep and irretrievable from her soul. She began to cry silently because she knew she'd given it to the stranger who sat with his back bared to her, waiting stoically for her to hurt him.

She choked on a sob and flung the scalpel to the floor. "I don't hate you. Dear God, what are you trying to do to me?"

His shoulders slumped. "I wish I knew, myself. I'm not prone to acting crazy." Slowly he put his shirt back on. "Thank you, Katie."

Trembling violently, she pressed her hands to her forehead and tried to remember the evening before. As soon as he'd brought her back to the hotel he'd insisted that she drink some tea. Her recall ended with the soothing sound of his drawling voice. *Shut those sad eyes and rest, gal.* And it had been so easy to do that, especially when he slipped his arms under her and carried her here.

Katherine leaned her head back, shut her eyes, and said dully. "You put something in the tea to make me sleep so that I wouldn't question you anymore about my family or the farm."

"You needed the rest first."

She groaned at the headache that began pounding in her forehead. "Last night . . . I woke up once . . ." Her gaze darted to the rocking chair in one corner. "You were there. Why?"

"Shhh." He turned to face her, the weight of his big frame indenting the mattress so much that she rolled toward him, her hip nestling tightly against his. If he noticed the contact, he wisely said nothing. Instead, he lifted a strand of her hair. "I bet this almost reaches the floor when you stand up," he murmured, rubbing the satiny black tresses between his fingertips and thumb. "And it's so black that it's got no shadows."

His frowning gaze traveled up her body, and Katherine finally realized that the quilt lay bunched at her waist and above that she was barely covered by a thin, sleeveless undershirt. Never be fooled by this man, she told herself. His sympathies were of the most selfish sort.

"I didn't undress you," he said immediately. "Rebecca did."

He might as well have, she thought, the way his green eyes studied her. She pulled the covers over her breasts.

"I'll get out and give you some privacy in a minute." Unfazed, he poured tea into a heavy ceramic cup, dribbled honey into it from a small pitcher, and handed the cup to her. "But I'm not budgin' until you finish the whole cup." He met her eyes. "It's not drugged."

She drank the tea quickly.

"You wanted some answers yesterday," he said when she finished. He took the cup and thumped it on the tray angrily. "I won't put you off any longer. I just wanted to wait until you were a little stronger, that's all."

She shut her eyes. "Who took the Blue Song land?"

"Easy, now. I want you to know how it was from the start."

"It won't make it any better."

The regret in his eyes changed to grim determination. "Right after you went off to Philadelphia the state held a lottery for the Cherokee lands."

"I know that. It was illegal."

"Maybe then, but not now. People went to Milledge-ville and drew their lots, most of 'em without knowin' anything about the Indians, havin' never seen the land they were drawin' for."

He frowned. "So a dirt-poor, hardworking man won a lot, and he got the deed, and he spent his last dollar to hurry up here and start a new life. But when he got here he saw that his land had your family livin' on it, and they'd built it into the finest farm he'd ever seen. He felt bad about showing 'em the deed. But if he hadn't claimed the farm, some other white man would have stolen it from them."

When she didn't comment, he looked disappointed. "But this hardworking man had a conscience, and he couldn't kick a family off their farm, even though the state gave him the right to do it. So he made a deal with 'em, and it turned out real well."

"For the white man," she interjected, rubbing her forehead. "Hurry. I feel strange."

"Your family showed him where to find gold, and in return he left their farm alone—even made sure that no-body else bothered them. That white man was willing to live and let live, and he did the best he could under the circumstances, wouldn't you say?"

She felt sleepy again, and her lips moved slowly. "Sounds like a saint. Too good to be . . . true."

"He's sure not a saint, but he's not a bad feller either. And he got real involved in your family's problems, and the problems of the tribe, and he made a lot of enemies among his own people because he took the Injun side of things. How can you fault that man?"

Katherine sank down into the comfort of her feather pillow. "I miss my family," she whispered raggedly. "And I want . . . to go back to sleep. Tell me the rest . . . later."

Something was wrong, she realized hazily. This wasn't

how she'd felt a minute before. The reason managed to seep through her thoughts.

"You lied," she said, frowning. "The tea . . . was drugged again."

He moved closer to her. His thigh pressed lightly against her side. As he leaned over her, she gazed into his eyes and found them shadowed with regret.

"I lied, sure enough," he whispered. "I wanted to make things as easy for you as I could—and for myself. Katie, I'm that man who won the Blue Song land in the lottery."

She moaned bitterly, then turned her face to one side. "Get out."

He smoothed the backs of his fingers up and down her cheek. "Katie, try to understand."

"You tricked me . . . all along. You own the land. You think you . . . own me too."

"No, I'm your friend." He grasped her hand, holding it gently. "You're a fine, beautiful lady, and I can't let you go off alone in the world. There're too many men who think Injun gals are theirs for the taking, and when they see one as special as you, they'll do anything to have her."

She began to cry again, to her shame, but coherent thought had nearly deserted her and she was half asleep. "You're no better than them. You want to make me *a-tsi-na-Ha-i.* A captive. A slave."

His hand tightened on hers. He bent close to her, his mustache brushing her ear, and said gruffly, "I reckon that's partly true. I'll do anything to have you." He kissed her cheek. "Now rest, Katie. I'll leave you alone till you say different."

JUSTIS PACED THE aisle of the Gallatin-Kirkland General Store, a cigar clenched between his teeth. Rebecca and Sam stood behind the counter, safely out of his way.

"One more day," he said angrily. "If she doesn't eat by tomorrow, I'll force the damned food down her."

"Justis, she's lost her whole family," Rebecca said. "Let her grieve."

"It's been a week! What has she swallowed—a little soup, a few glasses of milk. That's all! I've done what I said. I've left her alone, I've not set a foot in her room or spoken a word to her!"

He stopped pacing to punch his fist into a smoked ham hanging from a low beam on the ceiling. "She never comes out!"

"I can't blame her." Rebecca slapped a ledger shut and shook a finger at him. "She feels cornered. You ought to give her a fair share of gold and send her back to Philadelphia, where she can start a life among people who'll offer her a better chance at happiness."

"Who's she got there? Nobody! She even admitted to you that she couldn't go live with that doctor again, not after his nephew caused such a scandal in the family."

"Justis Gallatin, if you *ever* let her know that I told you that story, I'll have Cookie put a purgative in your biscuits!"

"Becky!" Sam exclaimed reproachfully, fighting a smile.

Justis tossed his cigar into the unlit iron stove at the center of the store, then rammed both hands through his hair in frustration. Thinking about Katherine's experiences with that young dandy in Philadelphia made him itch to fight.

"Blue-blooded bastard," he muttered. "He courted her, did all his fancy stuff—read poetry to her, all that high-falutin' nonsense—and after she decided that he was a fine gentleman, he tried to kidnap her! And then told everybody she was the one at fault! He just wanted an exotic doxy!"

"Isn't that what you want?" Sam asked bluntly.

The air seemed to freeze. Justis faced his friend and saw reproach in his eyes. Rebecca wore a look of horror.

Guilt was all that kept Justis from anger. "I don't know what I want," he said finally, defeated. "Except I never met a woman like her before, and I'm not gonna let her get away."

His goal in life was to lord it over the kind of people who had turned up their noses at him for being born the son of dirt-poor Irish immigrants. Courting an Injun, whether for wife or mistress, was not exactly a smart thing to do if he wanted to rise in society, but Katie Blue Song's appeal overwhelmed her liabilities. And frankly, he wanted her so much, he didn't care about the consequences.

"Let her go," Rebecca urged, shaking her head. "She deserves a husband, white or red, but a husband. I know you can sweet-talk her into some kind of arrangement. I've seen how women humble themselves just to get in your good graces."

"If you think I can sweet-talk that Injun princess, then you haven't listened to her boss me."

"No, but I've sat in her room many an hour over the past week, and I've answered a hundred questions about you—are you an honest man, did you really keep her family out of trouble—and I tell you this much, she's drawn to you despite herself, like a rabbit to a trap. I tried to warn her, without being obvious, about the trap's success."

"I've never claimed to be a lonely man."

"I told her about Qualla and Big Pumpkin."

He thought for a moment. "She sees that I respect Cherokee women, then."

Rebecca rolled her eyes. "She sees that you lived with those two widows and they both called you 'husband.'"

"They never took that serious, and neither did I. Just because three people share the same cabin—"

"The same bed," Rebecca corrected him drolly.

Justis sat down on a barrel of whiskey and rubbed his forehead wearily. "I reckon you even told her about the Cherokee name they gave me?"

"Yes. I blushed, but I told her."

Justis crossed his arms and contemplated a crack in the plank floor. He'd never learned to pronounce the name very well, but the English translation said it better anyway. The Stud.

"I hope she was impressed," he grumbled.

"She said that she wasn't surprised."

Justis thought there were hopeful signs in that answer. Before he could wonder about them, a half-dozen soldiers arrived outside the store's open double doors, stirring up dust and interest.

Over by the courthouse a group of men who were fancily dressed started toward the store. A few miners ambled out of a nearby saloon and gathered on the store's porch, gawking. Men halted their wagons in the middle of the street so they could stare at the blue-coated cavalry soldiers and their captain.

The soldiers hitched their mounts to a rail and followed their officer inside. Justis stood slowly, suspicion putting him on guard. He'd come to this wild part of Georgia to escape authority, or at least to have more control over how it treated him.

The officer tipped a snappy blue cap. "Good afternoon, gentlemen, ma'am. I'm Captain Taylor, and I bring you greetings from General Winfield Scott."

When Justis refused to respond other than by putting another cigar between his teeth, Sam came forward and made the introductions. Captain Taylor turned to his men. "Begin passing those handbills out."

By now a large crowd had swarmed into the store. The excited comments of those who could read provoked the nonreaders to anger, and some of the miners began threatening one another.

"I'll rip the eyes out of any man who starts a fight in

this store," Justis announced loudly, and that settled the crowd. Sam climbed on the counter and read General Scott's announcement aloud.

The army would build a temporary stockade two miles south of Gold Ridge, just as it was constructing stockades in other areas of the Cherokee Nation. The Gold Ridge station would be completed by the middle of May, in about three weeks. Every Cherokee within a fifty-mile radius would be brought to the stockade and held there for escort to the western lands.

There were whoops of joy from the crowd. "It's about time we had a rattlesnake roundup!" one man shouted.

"Hot durn! I promised my ma I'd kill an Injun before I came home again!" another said.

The captain held up his hands. "No violence," he called out. "General Scott will prosecute any white settler caught doing harm to an Indian. He wants them treated as kindly as possible."

Justis scowled at him. "He's a little damned late for that. Clear out of here. I've got no use for you federal loblollies."

"States' rights man, are you?" the captain asked.

"Just don't like the smell of the general's plan."

"Don't pay any attention to Mr. Gallatin, Captain," a man said. "He's an Indian sympathizer. He had two Cherokee wives and he's got a third shacked up over at his hotel."

Justis began to smile.

"Oh, no," someone whispered. "Get out of his way."

Justis started forward, but Sam grabbed his arm. "He's new in town, partner. Let him have one mistake." The man's friends were already hustling him out the door.

"Oh, I don't know," a majestic voice boomed. "Let Justis have at him."

The crowd parted to let a tall, regal figure stride down the aisle. Judge William Parnell, Amarintha's father, had snow-white hair, a slight paunch that only added to his imposing appearance, and dark eyes that one or two gossipers suggested came from an Indian relative somewhere in the illustrious Parnell family tree.

Judge Parnell had presided over Superior Court for the past four years, and his rulings were as stern as the black suits he wore. Justis studied him idly, seeing, as always, a smiling old lion who ate people alive.

"You getting into trouble, boy?" Parnell asked jovially.

"Every second of the day."

The judge was a grand politician, and after Sam introduced him to Captain Taylor he went through the crowd, finding new faces and shaking hands with the strangers. A respectful quiet had fallen as soon as he stepped into the store.

Only one other man in Gold Ridge could inspire that reaction. When Judge Parnell finished his campaigning and halted in front of Justis, studying him with smiling, soulless eyes, they both knew who the other man was.

"I'll have the hide and tallow of any rascal who mistreats our peaceful Cherokee brethren during this tragic, tragic time," the judge said in a solemn voice. He turned to the crowd. "It's our duty to treat these innocent children of nature with respect. They are doomed by the good and proper onrush of civilization, and though God has given us the right to bring light into their dark country, He does not intend for us to lose our own souls in the process."

Several *amens* and *here, heres* demonstrated the crowd's righteous support.

Justis silently cursed every pious thief who'd engineered the Cherokee treaty, and wondered how he was going to break this latest news to Katherine. *If* he ever got to talk to her again.



FOR TWO WEEKS Katherine alternated between periods of dull apathy and unnatural exhilaration. Either she sat by the hotel window for hours, gazing blankly at the activity on the town square, or she paced her room frantically, her mind fired by memories of her family and horrible imaginings about their deaths.

Justis was waiting in the outside world, him and his vow, *I'll do anything to have you*. She had twenty dollars left from her travel money, and until that ran out she wouldn't ask him for anything. Though Rebecca had tried to refuse, Katherine had given her six dollars for room and board over the past two weeks. Katherine sat by her window every night until dawn, clasping her remaining money and staring at the stars as if they hid answers.

"You can't go on like this," Rebecca exclaimed tearfully when she discovered Katherine asleep in a chair one morning. She guided her to the bed and stood beside it, arms akimbo. "Please talk to Justis. He won't take advantage of your situation."

Katherine lay on her back and stared at the ceiling. "But will he give me my land and a share of the Blue Song gold?"

"He can't give you the land. I'm sure he would if he thought the state would let you keep it. But no Cherokee can own land here anymore."

"My family is buried on that land."

"It doesn't matter to the state, Katherine."

"Then I'll find some way to support myself until I can change the state's mind. I'll find employment here."

Rebecca gently patted her shoulder. "Justis will give you all the money you need. Just be patient about the rest. He can't do anything to change it, but he wants to be good to you. He's bullheaded but not cruel."

"I'll never understand him."

"He grew up on the docks down on the coast, an orphan, fighting for every crumb he put in his mouth. His parents were Irish. Irish and Catholic, and they died in a

fire when Justis was little. Imagine, a little boy all alone,
dealing with prejudice and poverty. An outcast. So much
about his life has been brutal—even you came to him
under brutal circumstances. But there's honor, and courage, and a simple kind of idealism in him that tries to
right all that, even though his methods are sometimes
rough."

Katherine thought of the anti-Irish protest she'd seen
in Philadelphia the previous year. It had been sparked by
religious bigotry and a deep fear that the desperately
poor immigrants would take too many jobs from American workers.

"You've explained a great deal about him," she admitted softly. "I think he's more hot-blooded than you believe, but . . . he's reared himself very well, considering
what little life gave him to start with."

Rebecca smiled. "You see why he's got such sympathy
for other outcasts."

Katherine looked at her closely. "I heard you speaking
Hebrew to yourself. I've studied the language a little. I
recognize it." When Rebecca paled, she added quickly, "I
won't tell. But is it such a terrible worry?"

"We feared that the frontier was not the best place to
be . . . um, different from everyone else." She glanced
away, frowning. "Is that cowardly?"

Katherine sighed. "No, not in my experience." She got
up, went to the window, and inhaled the fresh, promising air of the spring morning. "But for me, at least, there's
no point in hiding from it any longer." She squared her
shoulders. "What day is it?"

"Sunday."

Katherine thought for a moment. "Does Justis ever go
to church, any church?"

"No. I think he's afraid a bolt of lightning might strike
him dead as soon as he stepped across the threshold."

"Tell him that if he wants to see me, he can escort me

to services this morning. I'll fight this battle on my own grounds."

Rebecca clapped merrily all the way out of the room.

JUSTIS WAITED ON the hotel veranda because it looked better than stomping back and forth at the base of the stairs inside. The last thing he wanted Katherine to see when she came down from her room was him pacing like a worried beau. The pretty red fox knew how to play her cards right, for damned sure.

He heard footsteps and quickly checked his appearance. He lived in a cabin at the mine, but he kept his fancy stuff here at the hotel, where it had a better chance of staying clean. Everything was spotless—the dark blue frock coat, the black vest and tan trousers, even the white linen shirt and cravat. The black dress shoes hurt like hell, but they were clean, too, and that was all that mattered.

"Good morning, Mr. Gallatin."

She stepped onto the porch and stopped, gazing at him in quiet amazement.

" 'Morning." He bowed slightly, a black top hat cradled in one hand. He felt awkward and figured she found him ridiculous in nice clothes.

But when he met her dark eyes he found them solemn and intense, more striking than ever in a face that was thinner than it had been two weeks earlier. Some folks said the Indians had wandered over from China a long time back, and when he looked at Katherine's tilted eyes he thought the idea might be true. But that nose— No China girl had a strong little nose like that, defiant and just a bit hawked in profile.

He felt as though he'd waited centuries to see her again. "You need to eat more," he said. "Beef up a little."

"Thank you." There was an amused tilt to one corner of her mouth. "How kind of you to put it so delicately."

She'd pulled her incredible mane of hair into a braided knot at the nape of her neck. The style accentuated the fine bone structure of her face and made him want to touch her smooth, burnished skin.

"It's good to see you out of your roost," he told her. Lord, she wore her simple black dress as if it were meant for a gala, and with her blue-black hair to top it off, the effect was more regal than somber. It made him think about unwrapping her and how lovely her cinnamon-colored skin must be underneath all that ugly cloth.

"You've used my share of the gold-mining profits very well," she murmured, her gaze flickering over his fashionable outfit. "You must be grateful to my parents for making you a rich man and then having the courtesy to die."

Her voice was throaty and low, a bedroom voice with an icy undercurrent. It sank straight to the pit of his stomach and made him ache. Crazy, he thought, to want her more even when she insulted him.

He held out an arm. "Step nimbly, gal. Do you mind walkin'? It's not far."

After a moment she reluctantly slipped her hand under his elbow. "Fine. Which church do you attend, Mr. Gallatin?"

"Methodist," he said firmly.

To his surprise, she laughed. Cutting wickedly shrewd eyes at him, she announced, "I just won a bet, Mr. Gallatin. Thank you. Rebecca said you'd pick the Baptist church because it's next door to your favorite gambling hall."

Justis stared at her in exasperation. Then, to retaliate, he asked, "What, no blinders, Katie?"

He stroked the side of her face with his fingers, brushed the tip of her nose, and even trailed his forefinger along the line of her stern, tempting mouth. "Don't you want to go get that ugly black bonnet and hide your face so nobody'll know an Injun is traipsing around town like she thinks she belongs?"

She raised her chin proudly. She knew he was manipulating her, but she could play that game as well. "No, let everyone see me with you. I think a savage and a heathen make a fine pair."

He nodded sardonically, but placed a possessive hand over the fingers she curled around his arm. They walked down the steps and into the sunshine side by side.

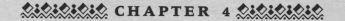 

## CHAPTER 4

THE CHURCH was just a big arbor built of poles and rough logs in a field down the road from the hotel. The backless benches were interspersed with tree stumps. Katherine decided that the people sitting on the stumps were lucky—the rough plank benches bristled with splinters.

She looked straight ahead and tried to ignore the stares as she and Justis entered the arbor. How many women were eyeing her with distaste not only for being an Indian but also for having this handsome, well-dressed rapscallion, undoubtedly the catch of the town, by her side?

He didn't wear his hat, which was just as well. It would have looked completely ridiculous on his shaggy chestnut hair, much like putting a fancy halter on a wild bull, she thought. Hair such as his made people wary, thinking that its unruliness implied rebellion and anger —which in Justis Gallatin's case was not far from the truth. She admitted that it intrigued her because of that.

A woman came over and tugged at her sleeve. Katherine gave her cautious attention. "I knowed your family," the woman said. "And they was fine folks. I was sorry to hear what happened."

More people came up to her and offered their sympathies. Some had done business with her parents and prized their friendship; some had been the recipients of Blue Song charity. Stunned, Katherine murmured her thanks. Tears blurred her eyes, and she held them back by sheer force of will. She would never cry in front of these people if she could help it.

"Come along," Justis said gently.

They sat down on a bench and were silent for several minutes. Katherine stared at the grassy earth beneath her feet, unable to talk without showing her grief. She still held Justis's arm, and the slow stroking of his fingertips on her hand was an act of compassion she couldn't bring herself to rebuke.

Finally she got herself under control and looked at him. "Thank you."

His green eyes were shrewd and thoughtful. "Reckon church was a good idea. You see that there are some folks who don't want to run the Cherokees off. You see that you've got friends."

"Good. Perhaps one of them will give me employment."

He frowned. "They're not gonna stir up trouble by encouraging a Cherokee to settle in town. You'd just get insulted, and then I'd have to beat the tarnation out of whoever insulted you. Besides, you don't need to work for money. I'll take care of you."

His leg was pressed tightly to hers; his hand clamped her fingers to his arm as if he demanded that she hold on to him throughout the service. She moved away and tugged her hand into her lap.

"I don't want you to take care of me. I want my land and whatever gold you owed my family."

"I'll give you anything that makes you happy." His

eyes glinted with determination. "Except your land—which I can't ever give—or enough money for you to traipse off into the world alone."

Gritting her teeth in frustration, Katherine opened the small Bible she'd brought with her. " 'The wicked borroweth and payeth not again: but the righteous sheweth mercy, and giveth.' "

He took the Bible from her and thumbed through it. " 'Two are better than one; because they have a good reward for their labor.' " He hesitated, deciphering the rest of the passage with difficulty. Finally he smiled. " 'If two lie together, then they have heat: but how can one be warm alone?' "

The slow tightening in her belly did not come entirely from anger. He rested his hand atop hers again and curled his fingers around hers, pressing them snugly into her palm.

Katherine was suddenly aware of him in a disturbing way that reminded her of the time he'd kissed her. She inhaled his scent and was oddly enchanted by the hint of shaving lather and aromatic cigar smoke. Such simple things, but so masculine that they made her feel very feminine by comparison.

His gaze held hers, challenging her to examine his features. His nose was charmingly crooked, his eyebrows thick and slightly arched at the centers, and the mustache a rakish addition that drew attention to the sensuality of his lower lip. His features were almost too strong—the kind that could express emotions with powerful effect.

She sighed and heard a quiver in her breath. What hope would there be for her if she let this man control her both body and soul? A white man. That alone would mean trouble.

"I like it when you look at me that way," he said, smiling thinly. "Like you either want to eat me up or bite me. I can't be sure which."

"Bite you, certainly."

She faced forward and focused her attention on the arrival of a tall, skinny preacher dressed entirely in black. He was a circuit rider, with mud still clinging to his boots and horsehair on his trousers. Katherine fidgeted, feeling Justis still looking at her, his fingers stroking the soft cup of her palm.

"That passage about 'two being better than one'?" she whispered. "It refers only to *friends,* not man and woman, and especially not a white man and Cherokee woman." She took her Bible and her hand back into her own lap.

Justis laughed softly and leaned so close that goose bumps ran up her neck. She was certain he was going to touch his lips to her ear. "That's what we are, Katie. Friends," he murmured. "The man and woman part makes it a helluva lot of fun. The white and Injun part is just something we'll have to deal with."

The preacher raised his hands for attention. "Welcome, sisters and brothers. Today, seein' as how I've got five couples to marry after the sermon, I'm goin' to preach about the glory of matrimony."

"Let's go," Justis whispered teasingly. "You got no interest in marryin', remember? You won't be owned by anybody but yourself, remember?"

"Let's stay for your sake. You ought to learn a little something about marriage, don't you think, before you try to capture a wife from the halls of *haute* society?"

"What kind of society?"

*"Haute.* It's a French word. It means 'high.' High society."

"You know French?"

She nodded. "And Latin, plus bits and pieces of a few other languages." She put her finger to her lips. People were frowning at them for talking.

"You know French," he said softly, more to himself than her. He plucked a blade of grass, stuck it between his teeth, and stared off into space, absorbed in thought.

\* \* \*

A WARM GUST of April air swept over the new graves, carrying the fragrances of pine, oak, dogwood, and honeysuckle toward the valley. The breeze lifted specks of red-tinted soil and dried the tiny spots where Katherine's tears had fallen. The already baked earth hinted that the coming summer would be dry and hot.

Justis leaned against a tree and watched Katherine place dogwood boughs on the graves, her face composed now, her manner as formal as her black dress. After church he'd changed back into his comfortable trousers and white work shirt—and his regular boots, too, which made him feel a hundred times more human—but she still wore the solemn outfit with its high neck and long sleeves.

She murmured Cherokee words over each grave, then added prayers in English. "I have to make certain that my family's spirits are residing peacefully in the Dark Land," she explained.

"You still cater to the old ways. Jesse and Mary did too. I've seen 'em throw food to the fire when they sat down to eat supper—asking the blessing of the fire spirit, they said."

Katherine glanced up at him and smiled wistfully. "A part of me will always believe the old teachings."

"I like 'em, especially the Cherokee idea of the hereafter," Justis assured her. "When you're alive you live in the Sun Land, and when you die you go off to a village in the Dark Land, where you get to carry on just as if you were still flesh and blood. Nobody makes you fettle with angels or harps or any of that."

"Do you know where the Dark Land is?"

He gave her a troubled look. "Toward the sunset."

"Yes. That's one reason so many of the people don't want to go west. They think of it as the Dark Land." She paused, her expression tragic. "In a way, it is."

Justis took a deep breath. He might as well give her the news now. "The army's settin' up a stockade south of town. To hold the Cherokees for removal. It'll be finished in a couple of weeks."

"I know." She hugged herself. "I overheard some of the hotel guests talking about it the other night as they passed my door."

"Don't worry about going to the stockade. I'm going to write the governor and ask him to give you an exemption. You'll be my responsibility."

"A white man's ward." She smiled coldly. Then her shoulders slumped and she looked at the graves again. "I'm finished. You may do the rest now."

Justis climbed onto Watchman and touched a blunt gold spur to the stallion's gray flank. Feeling sorry for her and not knowing how to say so, he tipped his wide-brimmed work hat in silent salute.

"Step back, gal, so you won't get trampled."

She walked down the slope a few feet and stood staring into the distance, her hands clenched together. While Watchman's hooves destroyed the mounds of her family's graves, she resolutely faced the ancient blue-green mountains. They had belonged to the Cherokees for centuries.

Justis finally reined the stallion to a halt. Katherine continued to gaze into the distance. After studying the rigid control in her posture and the quiver of restraint at the base of her throat, he knew she was very near to crying again. He'd never seen a woman so determined to be strong, and it filled him with both respect and tenderness.

He didn't want to examine those feelings too much because he'd never felt them so strongly before, and they worried him. It was hard to care this much about a woman who had good reason not to care back. He had never belonged to anyone heart and soul, and he wasn't certain that he wanted to now. But he knew without doubt that he wanted Katherine Blue Song to belong to *him* that way.

Justis sighed. He hoped that she'd come to feel something for him, even if it were only desire. He knew he could make her want him in bed.

"None of the grave-robbin' bastards around these parts will find your family now, Katie. You can count on it. If the greedy fools weren't so convinced that Cherokees bury gold with their dead—"

"Thank you," she said in a small, sad voice. "I know you had to make certain no one would find them. I understand."

He stepped down from Watchman, went to the small mare tethered to a sapling, and led her to Katherine. "Up you go, gal. It's not safe for us to stay here long. Too far from town."

She faced him, and grief and bitterness made her eyes glow like polished onyx. "Of what concern is my safety to you, sir? You've done your duty. Buried the dead. Rescued the orphan. I'll go west with my people, and you can put your conscience at ease."

"Goddammit," he said fiercely, hurt by her disdain. "You're determined to leave me. But I'm not gonna let you end up alone and like the rest of the Cherokee women around here. If you don't know what the gangs are doing to 'em, I'll tell you."

She swayed and raised a hand to her mouth. "Are you saying that my mother and sisters . . . even little Sallie . . ."

"*No.*" It was easy to lie, easy to tell any lie that would wipe away the horror in her eyes. Cursing his thoughtless tirade, he quickly wound the horses' reins around a tall shrub, then pulled Katherine into his arms. Her pride failed her, and she leaned against him.

"Forgive me, gal," he murmured. "No. That didn't happen to them."

"I don't believe you," she said sadly. "But I don't want to know the truth either."

He eased her head against his shoulder and felt her tears on his skin, though she made no sound. Finally she managed to say, "Not many people care. Why do you?"

He shut his eyes for a moment. Sitting there in church this morning, he'd made his decision—not that he'd been moved by some spiritual revelation. No, he'd simply admitted what he'd wanted all along, no matter how much trouble it caused.

"Come over here and sit down." He led her to a shady spot under a maple tree, and when they were seated he put his arm around her shoulders. "Why do I care?" he repeated. "I guess I've got selfish reasons, gal—Katie . . . Miss Blue Song." He cleared his throat. "You're a beautiful woman, a woman with education and culture. I want you for my wife."

She gasped softly, then gazed at him in absolute disbelief.

"I do mean it," he said grimly. "I really do."

"Do you think I'd ever marry a white man? Sitting in the midst of what white men have done to my family, how can you ask me to marry you?"

"Because I'm not your enemy, and you know it."

She pressed her temples as if trying to force calm thoughts into her mind. "This is amazing, sir. You think you can have whatever you ask for. And why do you ask? It doesn't make sense. You can have so many other women." She looked up sharply. "I knew Qualla and Big Pumpkin. They were friends of my mother's."

"And they were fine gals too. I cared about 'em. It wasn't easy for me to say good-bye when they decided to go west last month, but I knew that every day they stayed just put 'em in more danger."

"You've done without women since then, and now you're desperate?"

He made a sound of disgust. "If I was just lookin' for a pretty piece, I wouldn't have to marry to get it!"

"You should be perfectly happy using the girls at the houses of entertainment in Gold Ridge. Rebecca told me that you even considered buying one of the establishments, but Sam talked you out of it."

"I thought I could run it a lot more kindly than the old bitch who was in charge! If you'd seen the way those places treat their girls, you'd want to help too!"

She gazed at him askance. "You're a commendable humanitarian. Or so it appears on the surface."

"Look, Katie." He squeezed her shoulders and exhaled wearily. "I don't want to use those girls, all right? I don't want to pay for that particular kind of pleasure. I'd rather go without." He arched a brow. "Or get married."

"What about Amarintha Parnell? Or some other respectable girl in town?"

"Too much trouble. They got more webs than a spider. And Amarintha has a mean streak. Besides, what good would one of them do me? They don't know anything about the outside world. They don't speak French."

"Ah. It was my 'haute society' that convinced you."

"Dammit, you twist my intentions. Let's go back to the point. Will you be my wife?"

"What kind of benefit would you get out of marrying me?"

"If anybody could teach me manners, you could. That's what I'd get. In return, you'd get to stay in Gold Ridge. If you're betrothed to a white man, the governor might exempt you from the removal."

She laughed dully. "So you'll marry the Blue Song daughter out of duty. Well, sir, I won't marry just to have a roof over my head. Besides, you're addled for even thinking of marrying an Indian." Sarcasm tinged her voice. "You want to be an important man, you want to move in important circles. Marrying an Indian would make you scandalous in polite society."

"Not up north. That's where I'm heading eventually. Gonna put some Gallatin gold into New York investments."

"Blue Song gold," she corrected him. "Taken from Cherokee land."

"You'll never forget that," he said grimly. "So be it. Then look at things this way—if you want to have a say in how the gold's spent, marry me. We don't have to tie the knot until you get accustomed to the idea."

"How noble of you," she said dryly.

"Not the least bit. And I don't give a damn what polite society thinks of me. Never have. I just don't want to feel like a backwoods hick when I have to deal with nabobs. You can learn me everything I need to know."

"Teach you."

"See? It's already workin'."

"I'm not going to marry you."

"I figured you'd say that at first. You think on it, gal. You got nobody but me."

He stood, held out a hand, and watched her take it reluctantly. After he helped her to her feet he swept a predatory gaze around the woods. One hand came to rest on the pistol in his belt. "We best get back to town. I've killed my share of the trash roaming these woods. Like to avoid killing any on the day I proposed marriage to you."

"How very sentimental."

His mouth curled in annoyance. "I don't think you want sentiment, Katie. Neither do I. But I think we could be happy together."

Her eyes went dead. "I would never be happy with a man who uses my rightful inheritance to hold me in bondage."

"You marry me, the land and the gold will practically be yours. I think I'm doin' what your folks would want."

"And after you decide that you've soothed your conscience toward me and improved your social graces enough, you'll send me on my way."

"You'll probably worry me to death before that happens. Then you'll be a wealthy widow."

"I doubt the Georgia courts would let me keep a white man's estate."

Justis knew she was right. He also knew that there was no sense in talking to her anymore today about the subject of marriage. She looked exhausted and angry.

"Enough for now," he said as gently as he could. "I'll walk off a little ways. You say your farewells. Say 'em good—I don't want to bring you back here again. This part of the country will be even more dangerous when the army starts rounding up Cherokees."

Katherine watched him lead the horses away. Marry him? Teach him to be a gentleman and at the same time share a bed with him? Somehow, she didn't think he'd be a gentleman in bed if being one meant that he'd have to curb the virility that had earned him a Cherokee name such as The Stud. What frightened her, what made her clench a fist against her stomach, was that she wanted him because of it.

Slowly she turned and faced the valley. Sorrow welled up in her, pushing aside all other thoughts, making her feel half crazy with grief. This land held her family, it was part of her blood. It was all she had left.

She made a silent, sacred promise to herself. Nothing must ever take this land away from her. Even if she never saw it again, it would always be waiting.

Justis Gallatin would not keep it, or her.

THE SOUND OF silence was a warning to Amarintha After years of training herself to accept it, she knew without consciously paying attention that the judge's pen had stopped moving on the papers that lay atop his desk. The silence meant that he'd finished his work for the day. The squeak of his chair reverberated through the parlor as he reared back.

"Sweet baby, you're going to ruin your eyes staring out that window like a cat watching a bird. What is it, another good fight going on at the square?"

"No, Daddy, not this afternoon."

He chuckled. "Too bad." After a moment she heard him shift his chair again. His pen began scratching once more, putting wayward lives to rights, sentencing people to pay for their crimes, wielding more power than a knife or gun in a town where the law needed to be merciless to be respected. The judge was infinitely respected.

Amarintha renewed her concentration, and once again her fingers dug viciously into the piece of needlework that lay forgotten in her lap. Rage slipped through her veins like mercury, fueled by suffocating desperation.

She was going to lose her only chance to escape this hell if she didn't get Justis away from that pretty, red-skinned bitch.

"I'm just watching Justis Gallatin parade his squaw around the stores," she said casually. "How can he dote on her so? She doesn't look the least like a white woman. Her skin is coppery and her eyes are almost slanted, like a cat's. That hair of hers is blacker than sin—no white woman ever had hair that black. She draws stares everywhere she goes. You know that he took her to the Methodist meeting on Sunday, don't you?"

"The man has a right to squire her anywhere he pleases."

"But it's not proper. She acts as if she thinks she's going to stay here after the rest of her people are carried off. She couldn't, could she?"

"Not unless Mr. Gallatin can get an exemption for her from the governor."

"You ought to send a letter to the governor, just to make certain that he understands the situation."

The judge stopped writing again. A small muscle twitched in Amarintha's neck. "Now, sweet baby, why

are you so interested in whether or not Justis Gallatin
likes that lady?"

Amarintha swiveled on the settee and quickly smiled.
"I just like to stir up trouble, Daddy, you know that. It's
my favorite pastime."

His dark, suspicious eyes always seemed unnatural to
her because they contrasted so starkly with the white
hair and the fair complexion mottled by age marks. The
pouting look she gave him finally eased their shrewd
scrutiny.

He winked at her. "I'll write the governor about Mr.
Gallatin's lack of good judgment, and in two weeks,
when the stockade's finished, off his Indian lady will go."

She clapped in delight and blew him a kiss. "You chastise the lawless, Daddy, and I'll chastise the fearless."

Laughing with admiration, the judge drew a heavy
gold watch from his vest pocket and checked the time.
"I'm done with work for today," he said. "Pull the parlor
drapes, sweet baby."

Amarintha set her needlework aside and went to the
windows, taking the usual amount of time to close the
heavy damask coverings, subduing the usual brief swell
of nausea, then pivoting gracefully toward her father,
who had, as usual, begun to undo his trousers.

"Coming, Daddy," she said with a smile.

JUSTIS HAD A fine mahogany desk in his office at the
mine, and bookcases full of books he'd never read, and a
map of the United States on the whitewashed walls. His
desk was furnished with an astral lamp so rare and the
oil so costly that when it arrived from Boston, people had
come out to the mine just to see it.

The lamp cast its bright light on the paper, ink pot,
and pen that Justis shoved across the desk to Sam. It
wasn't that Justis couldn't write, but Sam could write

with the kind of beautiful penmanship that made important people take notice.

Sam, Charleston born and raised, was the perfect business partner for a man who had neither the delicacy nor the patience to be eloquent. He spent nearly a minute writing a date and salutation on the letter, then tapped his fingers on the thatch of light brown hair along his forehead and said solemnly, "Let's try again."

Justis twirled the tip of his hunting knife into a mangled block of wood that he held cupped in one hand. He had stared down the barrel of guns without flinching, but now a sheen of perspiration coated his forehead and his palms felt clammy.

After several seconds of listening to his abject silence, Sam said carefully, "Why don't you just outline the points you want to make and let me put them in final form? Then I'll read the letter back to you."

Justis ground his teeth together. Frustrated by his lack of expertise in a matter that meant so much, he stabbed his knife into the desktop. "It has to be perfect. I've gotta make sure Katherine gets to stay."

"I know, friend, I know. Tell me what you want to say."

"That Katherine Blue Song deserves to be left alone. That she's a fine lady and can do a lot of good here in Gold Ridge. Tell the governor that she knows how to doctor people and how she sewed up a cut on Noah's arm this week. Tell him that she graduated from the Presbyterian Academy for Young Ladies in Philadelphia. Tell him that she speaks French, for God's sake."

For several minutes Sam wrote methodically. Then he stopped to gaze solemnly at Justis. "Anything else?"

"Yeah. This oughta do it for sure. Tell him that I'm goin' to marry her. In church. With a preacher. The whole shebang."

Sam's fine-boned patrician features were schooled at hiding his reactions, but his mouth twitched with humor. "Has she agreed to even the first part of the she-bang?"

"No. But she will."

"Should I elaborate for the governor?" Sam cleared his throat. "As in adding something such as, 'Miss Blue Song is dear to my heart, the light of my life,' et cetera?"

"Hmmm. Sure. If that'll make it sound good." Justis glowered, then rose and paced the floor, aware that Sam was frowning at him.

"Do you think she feels anything for you?"

"Some gratitude for what I've done to help her. Some hate for what I won't do. As for anything else—" Justis gestured vaguely. "She needs me in the way any woman needs a man."

"The lady is not exactly smitten with you, then. I say that only to help you see the situation as it really is, without undue hope."

Justis thought of the carefully fathomless expression Katherine kept in her eyes so much of the time. "She's still grieving for her family. And she's not the kind that craves a husband. See, there's a lot of old-time Cherokee raisin' in her—she was taught to be in charge of things. Cherokee woman in the old days, well, she didn't take shit off any man. She owned the house and the children. She picked her own husband, and if she got tired of him, she'd just kick his butt out and marry another one."

Sam sighed. "You'd better accomplish something soon, partner, because if she doesn't marry you, she'll likely end up in the stockade with the other Cherokees, and then be sent west."

Justis stopped by a window and stared into the night. "I know," he said wearily. "Tell me what you wrote to the governor."

Sam read the letter back. It sounded just right, formal and not embarrassingly desperate. Justis returned to the desk, bent over Sam's elegantly drawn words, shook his hand several times to get the kinks out, then signed his name with as many curves and loops as he could manage.

He hadn't felt so worn out and worried since the back-busting days when he was a dock foreman down in Savannah. Now he had a good-sized fortune in gold and everything he could want. Except Katherine, and she might be the most difficult to gain.

"I need a drink," he said bluntly, and left the office with his work hat crushed in his hand.

THE QUICK CLATTER of childlike feet on the hotel stairs made Katherine look up from her afternoon reading. The feet ran down the hallway to her door, and a fist rapped hurriedly.

"Miss Katherine! Mr. Justis wants you over at the mine!" The high-pitched voice belonged to Lilac. "And bring your doctor's bag!"

Katherine flung the door open and looked down into wide brown eyes, pigtails, and a gap-toothed mouth. "Did anything happen to Mr. Justis?"

"No'm, one of the miners got his leg split wide open. Mr. Justis says to let you have a try at patchin' him."

Katherine realized that she had sighed with relief at hearing that Justis was unhurt. The fact that he had asked her to come doctor one of his workers amazed her. No other man would have trusted a woman with the job.

She grabbed her satchel and followed Lilac out of the hotel to a rickety cart hitched to a bay pony. "Can you drive this contraption?" Katherine asked the tiny Lilac as they climbed in.

"Like a li'l demon," Lilac said, grinned, and slapped the reins.

The Gallatin mine wasn't far from town, and Katherine would have sworn that they reached it in half a minute, considering the way the pony galloped and Lilac drove. Along the way they took a back street that ran through the middle of the brothel section. Katherine had never seen so many brightly clad women run for their lives before.

The Gallatin Mining Company was a small community unto itself, with cabins, sheds, barns, and a couple of saloons scattered around a square tunnel cut into the side of a hill. The thunderous, repetitive boom of a stamp mill sounded from a tall building near the mine entrance.

Justis came out of a shed as Lilac pulled her pony to a stop. Katherine clutched the sides of the cart to keep from sailing onto the pony's back. She caught a glimpse of Justis trotting toward her, his long, powerful legs swinging in an easy but purposeful rhythm.

"Any of your teeth shook loose?" he asked, lifting her out of the cart.

"Only a half dozen or so."

"Ever tend a busted leg?"

"On a woman, yes."

"Men got the same bones?"

"Undoubtedly."

"Good."

He led her toward the shed, where a crowd of men in canvas coveralls stood, watching her warily. Their consternation over the boss's choice of doctors was overcome by the boss's scowl, and they stepped back respectfully, doffing their hats.

"Why didn't you call a doctor from town?" Katherine asked Justis.

"Last time one of my men got a leg busted, the doc didn't fix it right. Man was crippled."

"I may not do any better."

"Couldn't do any worse."

"Why, thank you, sir, for the confidence."

A pathetic scream tore the air as they reached the shed's door. Justis blocked her way with an arm and looked down at her, frowning.

"This is a bad thing for a woman to see. Maybe I was wrong to ask you."

Katherine thought of all the gory, pitiful sights she'd seen while training with Dr. Ledbetter. She patted Justis's shoulder. "I doubt I'll faint."

Then she ducked under his arm and went inside the shed.

SHE WAS PLEASED with herself, exhausted but pleased, and more nearly happy than she'd been in several weeks. Katherine sat on a plushly upholstered sofa, her stocking feet tucked under her comfortably, the sleeves of her plain gray dress rolled up in very unladylike fashion.

The nicest thing about today's work had been seeing the respect in the men's eyes when she left their comrade sleeping, his leg expertly set. She admitted that Justis's proud smile had done more good for her feelings than anything else.

"Here," he said now, striding across the cabin that served as the mine's headquarters with two glasses perched easily in one of his big hands. Katherine looked at the amber liquid they contained. "Brandy," he told her.

She took a glass, recalling the few times she'd sipped alcohol, just sweet sherry. It had made her feel too warm. "I can't finish all of this."

"No hurry."

He sat down beside her and stretched his legs out, propping one booted foot over the other—looking deceptively lazy, she thought. His eyes were shaded by thick lashes that gave them a languid droop at the outer corners, as if he'd just come from bed.

He held his glass up. "A salute," he said softly, his cheerful green gaze holding her uncertain dark one. "To you, Doc. For the best doctoring I've ever seen."

Ridiculous claptrap. All flattery, she told herself. Then she smiled so widely her mouth hurt. He clinked his glass to hers, and, watching her carefully the whole time, put the glass to his mouth and swallowed the contents in one smooth movement.

Katherine sipped her brandy and liked the way it burned her throat. The rich scent and taste blended with the overtly masculine atmosphere of Justis's office. She glanced at the various guns hanging on wall pegs, the quality desk and lamp, the bookcases filled with the classics, and the heavy, colorful rugs on the plank floor. It was a place of contrasts, like the man himself, a roughly built place that nonetheless had a compelling sense of style.

*Bought with Blue Song gold.*

"I'll be going back to the hotel now," she said abruptly, and started to get up.

He caught the hand that held the brandy glass, then set his glass on the floor. With a graceful gesture he tilted her glass just enough to splash brandy on her fingers.

"That liquor favors the color of your skin," he murmured. "Makes me want to taste you."

She watched in dismay as he took the glass from her and drew her fingers to his mouth. "Please, let me go," she whispered. With a regretful shake of his head he kissed her wet fingers, his lips sipping at her skin. They produced a taut, sucking sensation that traveled inside her, tugging pleasantly at the pit of her stomach.

"I need to know something," he said. His mustache brushed her knuckles. It was the most provocative thing she'd ever imagined. His eyes were half shut but alert as he studied her. "I need to know that you want me as bad as I want you, at least in one way."

She jumped a little and murmured a soft sound of distress. "I'm tired, Mr. Gallatin, and the past few weeks have left me more than a little confused. Now is not the time—"

"We don't have much time left, gal." He slid closer, turned her palm toward his mouth, and nibbled it. "Do you like this, Katie? You look like you do. Did you know that you're touchin' your tongue to your lips right now?"

Katherine realized that she was. Shivering inside, she groaned at her weakness. "I've had my hand kissed before." But never like this, she admitted silently.

His jaw, covered in faint beard shadow, pressed against her fingertips as he delved his tongue into the center of her palm. "By that blue-blooded dandy in Philadelphia, huh? The one who broke your heart?"

"Yes."

"Yes, he broke your heart?"

"No. He kissed my hand."

"Did he do this?"

Before she knew what was happening he rose to one knee and leaned over her, then sank his fingers into the knot of hair at the base of her neck. She gasped as he gently pulled her head back.

"No. No more," she begged.

"Just a bit more, Katie."

He poured some of the brandy onto her neck. Before it could run into the tiny white ruffle around the collar of her dress, he bent down and trapped it with his mouth.

She cried out at the shock of his warm, mobile lips covering the pulse at her throat. It was an alarming sensation that made her heart race, yet at the same time drew away the strength to flee. She felt as if he had stricken her helpless, that perhaps the slow swirl of his tongue on her skin had seduced the part of her that controlled rational thought.

"It's like the brandy came alive," he said hoarsely, then drew his tongue up the front of her throat. "The brandy turned into the most beautiful woman I've ever seen."

Slowly he raised his head and met her eyes. She

blinked at him owlishly, afraid of her reactions and so overwhelmed that she couldn't speak. She heard herself make a small whimpering sound, half anguish and half desire, as he tipped the brandy glass over her lips.

His eyes gleamed with amusement. "Make a pucker," he ordered softly, and as she did he filled her lips with the remainder of the tingling liquor. He groaned with delight and covered her mouth with his, licking up the brandy, tugging at her lips gently.

It was an indecent kiss, like no kiss she'd ever seen described in a book or magazine, and it made her ache inside until she couldn't resist it any longer. She lifted her mouth for more, moving her lips against his, trying to taste him as he was tasting her.

"That's what I wanted," he said in a low, rumbling voice so full of emotion that it was nearly a growl. "Give me hope."

Tears burned the back of her eyes. "Not that. I didn't mean—"

"More," he said in a harsh whisper, and sank his mouth onto hers with a possessiveness that demanded response.

Katherine had not known that a kiss could be so many things at once—angry, gentle, unrelenting, tender. She'd never had more than chaste kisses before, and they had made her feel as if she were participating in a frozen tableau, two lovers pressing their mouths together in motionless passion for eternity.

There was nothing motionless about Justis's mouth. The pull and twist of it made her open her lips. When his tongue slipped inside she was so startled, she touched her own tongue against it. He taunted her, his tongue thrusting slowly, insinuating intimacies that made her feel weak.

She suddenly saw those intimacies in her mind, saw him lying between her thighs, his big, hard-packed body arching against their softness, and her feet curling contentedly over the backs of his legs.

"It can't be," she said out loud, and tried to push him away. "Not between the two of us."

"It can and it will."

His face was lined with passion and restraint. He sat back and pulled her to him, sliding one arm around her waist, gently trapping her. Her feet were still drawn up beneath her, and she suddenly felt his hand on her ankle.

His gaze held her immobile. "Just a bit more, Katie," he promised again. "Just a bit to keep you awake at night."

"You cannot seduce me. It's something that happens only to foolish women—"

"You're not foolish, and it's all right to be seduced by a man who'd never do you harm."

"I don't know that," she protested, shaking her head fiercely. "I don't know— Oh, Justis!"

His hand had glided up her leg to where the stocking ended, just above her knee. Now his fingertips caressed the naked skin in slow circles.

His eyes gleamed with pleasure and he lowered his head. "You'd burn me up," he whispered, his lips almost touching hers. "We'd burn each other."

"I'm afraid I agree," she admitted wretchedly.

"Good."

He slowly trailed his fingers upward, and the sheer material of her long-legged drawers was no protection against his touch. It seared through the cotton, making her shut her eyes and gasp at the fire rising between her thighs, making her breasts swell and grow tender.

She gripped his arm in warning, but her fingers dug in rhythmically rather than pushing him away. His hand slid toward the apex of her thighs. "You can't touch me there," she protested. "Even you wouldn't—" But he did, rubbing his fingers back and forth on the soft mound.

Her head drooped forward and she groaned in defeat. "Damn you."

"Remember this, Katie. Think about this. I can make you want me just by touchin' you through your clothes. Think what it'll feel like when my fingers are on your skin. Even now I can tell that you're ready for me."

She twisted away from him, covering her face. "You've proved that I'm a woman. Now please let me go before we make a terrible mistake."

"It's a start," he said softly, and slipped both arms around her in a stubborn embrace.

The sound of bootsteps on the cabin porch forced him to let go, reluctantly. She scooted away, and before the visitor was finished knocking she had jammed her feet into her tall black shoes.

"Hullo, it's Sam!" a voice called.

"Sam!" she said loudly. "I'm glad you're here!" She vaulted off the couch, grabbed her doctor's satchel, and ran for the door. When she threw it open, Sam looked down at her curiously.

"Is all well?" He gazed past her at Justis.

All was not well, and never would be, Katherine thought, if she let Justis's seduction blind her to reality. "I'm done here, Sam. Will you escort me back to the hotel?"

"Certainly, but—"

"I see your buggy. I'll wait there."

"But—"

"She's a mite shook up," Justis said calmly. "But she's gettin' her mind straight. She'll be marryin' me soon."

She pivoted and stared at him, speechless. Finally she managed to say, "You still don't understand the foolishness of what you're trying to do. I may not cry, but I never forget my grief. I may not live like a Cherokee, but I never forget my heritage." She trembled with emotion. "And as much as I am . . . as much as I am growing to *respect* you, I'd rather be carted off to the west than marry you."

His soft, stunned curses haunted her as she hurried out the door.

## CHAPTER 5

KATHERINE got out of bed while the May morning was still just a cool pink hint on the horizon. She dressed in a blue cotton work dress with loose, elbow-length sleeves and a bloused bodice, then pulled her hair back and tucked it into a white net pinned tightly at her crown. Wearing only one petticoat under the dress and no corset, she felt ready to do a good day's work.

Work. She had to begin somewhere if she were to prove her independence from Justis and remain in Gold Ridge. Surely the army wouldn't carry off a Cherokee who had a livelihood in town.

She went downstairs and out the hotel's back door. A short breezeway connected the main building to the kitchen, and that kitchen, lit by large oil lamps, bustled with the preparations to feed ten boarders at breakfast. Noah stirred corn mush in a big ceramic bowl and Lilac sliced bread. Both grinned at her sleepily.

Katherine received only a scowl from Cookie, a tall, angular slave with toffee-colored skin, coarse brown hair, and the temper of a bilious mule. "I don't want nobody else in my kitchen," she said as soon as Katherine stepped across the threshold. She rattled a massive skillet atop the kitchen's wood stove, as if in warning.

Cookie had been a special wedding gift to the Kirklands from Sam's grandfather, and she was proud of it. She worshipped Rebecca, merely obeyed Sam, bossed Noah and Lilac, and just tolerated everyone else. "Scat," she ordered.

"I came to find Mrs. Kirkland."

"She's outside easin' her stomach."

Katherine went out the kitchen door and through an herb garden. Rebecca sat on a bench under the well shed, wiping her face with a damp cloth. She smiled wanly as Katherine sat down beside her.

"I have a female illness," she said.

Katherine nodded solemnly, though excitement coursed through her. "When will the babe arrive?"

"Late next fall."

This was a wonderful turn of events! "Before long you'll need more help around here . . . and at the store."

"Yes. I've already mentioned that to Sam."

Trying to appear calm—she didn't want to sound like a beggar—Katherine said slowly, "I'd like to apply for the job, please. All I require for pay is room and board here at the hotel plus a dollar a week for spending money."

Rebecca looked at her with wide eyes. "Katherine, I mustn't. Justis would be furious—and he is our partner. It's not that he tries to run the hotel or the store, but . . ."

"Please." Katherine looked away, her hands clenched tightly in her lap. "I'm not asking for handouts. No one will work harder for you than I will." She faltered for a moment, then continued, "I know you must be thinking about the stockade outside town, that I'll be sent there with the other Cherokees. I *can't* think about it, Becky. I have to believe that I'll be allowed to stay. But on my own terms, not as Justis's charity woman."

Those last words galvanized Rebecca. She straightened, full of authority. "You should have a fighting chance. The job is yours."

"Becky, bless you!"

Rebecca wilted a little. "He'll rage when he hears this," she said worriedly. "He'll throw a conniption."

Katherine smiled grimly. "I shall throw it right back."


WORD TRAVELED QUICKLY after her arrival at the store that morning. Justis walked in less than two hours later. Katherine was kneeling beside a wooden bin filled with cornmeal, concentrating on catching the mouse inside it.

Gazing up at Justis, she realized how the poor trapped mouse must feel.

Justis looked like a large panther approaching cornered prey. His eyes were narrowed under a frown that gave him a cruel look; his long legs moved in a slow and measured gait as he wound his way through barrels, bins, and tables. A ruddy-faced girl, barefoot and wearing a coarse homemade frock, trailed behind him, looking terrified.

Katherine stood unhurriedly, but her heart pounded. He stopped in front of her and asked in a low, deadly tone, "Where's Rebecca?"

"She's not feeling well. She's resting in the back. Don't you dare bother her."

His eyes flickered with warning. "I brought her a new helper. Somebody who *needs* the job." He pointed a finger at Katherine, then jerked his thumb toward the door. "You get back to the hotel. Right now. You're fired."

"Rebecca can fire me. Not you."

He spoke between gritted teeth. "Don't talk like you got a choice. I said *get.*"

It was the way he would have dismissed a dog, she thought. There was no respect in it, just the bitter command of master to servant. She dug her fingers into her skirt, trembling with such fierce fury and humiliation, her stomach twisted.

Threats were on the tip of her tongue. She'd leave town this minute even if she had to walk, she'd never forgive him, she'd demand that Sam and Rebecca have a say in the matter. Katherine let the words die in her throat and subdued an almost hysterical urge to laugh. Nothing would stop him. The menace in his expression suggested that he'd drag her out by the hair if she didn't obey.

Silently, her back taut and head up, she walked past him. Outside, she went down the porch steps into the dusty street and glided blindly along, hardly breathing, feeling as if she might explode with rage.

*He always treated me like an equal before. Not now. It hurts. Oh, how he hurt me.*

She stopped, lost in the grim knowledge that she felt wounded more than anything else. He had betrayed the friendship they'd shared over the past three weeks. He had treated her as if she were truly a slave, an *a-tsi-na-Ha-i*. She couldn't let him have this much power over her anymore.

She whirled about, then headed down an alley between the store and another building. The strain of recent weeks played havoc with her reason, and she recognized the danger of that. But all she wanted was to hurt Justis, to make him see that she had the courage to be free no matter what the price.

She cut across the back alleys, sidestepping chickens that were picking at the tobacco spittle on a sleeping drunk, ignoring the coy calls from a lawyer who stood outside his back door urinating in a clump of grass. She walked with long, forceful strides, refusing to think about her mission.

A few minutes later she reached a narrow street lined with everything from shanties to fancy two-story buildings with glass-paned windows. She picked a two-story one that had flower boxes beside the front door. When Katherine knocked, the door opened enough to let a stout woman in a low-cut gown peek out.

"My gawd," she said, slack-jawed. "What do you want? Aren't you Justis Gallatin's doxy?"

The word hit Katherine like a slap. Apparently she'd earned herself a prized place in town, whether she liked it or not. After a second she managed to fake a smile. "No, not anymore. And I'm looking for a job."

JUSTIS FORCED HIMSELF to wait several hours before he rode over to the hotel to see her. He knew it wouldn't be easy to explain how crazy she made him, not without explaining how much he cared for her, which was something she didn't need to know—and didn't want to hear.

Lilac, her expression so down that it was almost comical, met him by the front door. "Miss Katie won't come out of her room. She won't even talk to me."

"I'll soon fix that," he told her gently.

Frowning, he took the stairs two at a time. At Katherine's door he knocked briskly. There was no answer.

"Katie. Let's talk." He waited. "Katherine." Again, no response. "Dammit, come out and have your say at me. I'll listen. I couldn't let you work at the store. You don't need to be independent." A thread of alarm wound through him when that brought no reply. Katie Blue Song was not a woman who sulked, pouted, or played other such female games. It was one of the reasons he craved her.

"All right, I'll break the damned door down." But he tested the latch and found it unlocked. Justis shoved the door open and stepped into her empty room.

He'd stopped by the store on his way over, so he knew

she hadn't defied him and gone back there. Rebecca was
fiercely upset with him, and Sam hadn't looked too
happy either, but they had finally agreed to let him wrestle with Katherine's pride in his own way. As far as they
knew, she had gone to the hotel.

Justis swung about and left the room. God, what had
he caused her to do? He ran for the stairs, feeling the cold
bite of fear.

THE DAY HAD been brutally long, and the sweet
night air coming through the open window was almost
enough to make Katherine forget that she was sitting on
a bed that smelled of lavender toilet water and sex, in a
room outfitted with only the bed, a small table, and a
washstand, in a brothel.

This, she knew with bitter satisfaction, was the only
way to destroy Justis's interest in owning her. He
wouldn't want to wed or bed a whore. For as long as he
thought that's what she was, she'd be free.

She left a lamp burning on the table because she
couldn't bear to feel the room's darkness around her yet.
It was bad enough just to close her eyes. When she did
she heard every sound more clearly—the tromping of
feet up and down the hallway as Mrs. Albert's girls took
clients to their rooms, the repetitive thumping and creaking of beds when the clients were particularly vigorous.

Katherine shivered and fought tears of shame. She refused to indulge in self-pity. Justis wouldn't give her
enough money to start a new life on her own, he
wouldn't let her work to earn it, and she knew without
asking that he wouldn't even allow her to go west when
the Cherokees were removed. With her own people at
least she would have had dignity. So, because she had no
decent options, she had stoically accepted an indecent
one.

Looking around the bare little room, Katherine hoped

she would be safe in it. Somehow she'd get her belongings from the hotel. She'd clean this filthy room tomorrow and decorate it as soon as she had some money.

That would take time. Doctoring prostitutes wasn't going to make her rich. But they needed her, and it was a job, and she had her freedom, and as soon as Mrs. Albert quit eyeing her greedily, she could relax a little.

Katherine craned her head to double-check the flimsy wooden latch on the door. It wasn't meant for protection, just privacy, but Mrs. Albert had promised that she could have a real lock on her door tomorrow. Katherine didn't trust her, and she'd angled a chair under the doorknob.

She removed her dress and arranged it over the bedpillow. Settling down on top of the smelly covers—there was no way she'd get under them—she eased her head back. Trembling, she stared at the plank ceiling through a haze of tears. Exhaustion won out, and she dozed. She hoped that the ache in her chest from thinking about Justis would ease by the morning.

HE PROMISED HIMSELF that he wouldn't kill anyone right away. Justis stepped into Mrs. Albert's red-on-red parlor and joined the laughing, excited group of men who surrounded the madam.

"Attention, you mud-turkles!" she bawled, and raised arms that had flesh the color and consistency of buttermilk. "All right, let's start the biddin'. Most of you have seen the girl in town over the past few weeks, so I don't have to tell you what you'll be gettin'. But if you haven't seen her, just take my word for it—she's one of the prettiest pieces, white or Injun, that ever spread her legs in Gold Ridge!"

"Ten dollars!" someone called.

Mrs. Albert clutched her ample, mostly uncovered bosom in disbelief. "This is her first night at work, boys! She's new to the business! And pure-blooded Cherokee

Injun—you know what kind of things a savage will let a man do. I cain't let this momentous occasion pass for less than twenty dollars."

"Twenty-two!" someone said immediately.

Justis listened in sick horror. He couldn't believe that Katherine knew what she'd gotten herself into, that she was eagerly waiting upstairs for the top bidder to use her as he pleased. But a friend of his had seen her knock on Mrs. Albert's door this morning and go inside.

He almost choked on disgust. He knew he'd bullied her, that he'd spent the past three weeks circling her like a randy stallion, scaring her, trying to intimidate her into agreeing to do what he thought was best. He'd seen the pure anguish in her eyes this morning, as though she finally knew that she was losing her fight with him.

He'd been a bastard. He admitted that. But what kind of lady would take up whoring rather than accept a respectable offer of marriage?

"Twenty-sish," a pot-bellied miner with a mouth full of tobacco gurgled. "I'll pay twenty-sish to have her."

Justis pulled one of his pistols from his belt. He angled through the crowd and stopped directly in front of Mrs. Albert. When she saw him she reeled back two steps and gasped loudly. "Mr. Gallatin, she said she didn't belong to you no more. I'll get the sheriff if you cause trouble."

Justis leveled the pistol at her head. "No trouble. I'll give you fifty dollars gold for her. For the whole night."

"You're the winner," she said weakly.

"Where is she?"

"Upstairs, last room on the left."

She nearly collapsed with relief when he lowered the gun and turned away. The crowd parted quickly, and though there were some angry mutterings, no man was fool enough to hinder his departure.

Mrs. Albert's girls had been watching the action from the staircase, and they scattered wildly in front of Justis. He strode along a narrow hallway where colored lamp globes cast flickering red shadows. When he reached the last door on the left he raised a foot and kicked it open.

A chair clattered to the floor and the door latch hit the room's far wall. He stepped inside and slammed the door shut behind him. The scene on the bed made him groan with fury and disgust.

Katherine, wearing only her sleeveless undershirt and petticoat, her hair streaming over her like a curtain, scrambled upright and stared at him in shock. Then her eyes darkened with fury. "Get out! I'm free of you, you hear? I have a place to live and a job to pay my way!"

"What kind of lady are you? What kind of lady turns herself into a whore just out of spite?"

"A desperate one," she retorted. "And it's no worse than what you wanted me to be—a slave in a loveless marriage, a doxy with a wedding certificate!"

"A *what*?" He cursed viciously, then flung a hand out in a violent gesture. "This is what you'd take instead? This is what your damned pride tells you to do?"

She got to her knees and shook her fists as if ready to do battle. "*Your* pride drove me to this! Your pride and vanity and lust! Now, get out! I won't take your orders anymore, sir!"

His chest heaving with anger and frustration, Justis started forward, then halted, thinking. He'd planned to drag her back to the hotel and lock her up. But then what? Keep trying to gentle her with words? Hellfire, the heartless cat would spit in his face.

He smiled an evil, victorious smile. "You'll take my orders for the rest of tonight," he told her. "Whether you like 'em or not. I bought you."

She froze, speechless, her dark eyes wild. "You couldn't have."

"What? You weren't plannin' to work on your first night in the house?" He tossed his hat onto the washstand. "Well, Mrs. Albert has other plans. She just auctioned you off downstairs. I was the high bidder. Fifty dollars."

She sank back on her heels, her hands rising to her throat. "I completely misjudged her."

"Better get used to being lied to. You're gonna hear a lot of lies in this place—most of 'em while you're layin' on your back."

"You *paid* for me," she whispered grimly. "You bought me so that you wouldn't have to pretend to be gallant anymore."

"That's right." He threw his weapons on the washstand, then whipped his belt off and slung it so violently that the heavy gold buckle cracked the handle on the washstand's pitcher. "Cheer up, Katie. If I'm the first man to ride you, at least you'll get broken in easy."

Her eyes were wells of torment. Suddenly she dropped her hands from her throat and braced them on the bed, leaning forward like a panther in a crouch. "Take me," she said in a low, fierce tone. "Take your fill, and then you'll let me go."

"Maybe you'll beg me not to."

"This is nothing but business to me. A way to show you how little I care what you do."

He scanned her belligerent expression, and his mouth curled in disgust. "I think I believe you." He pulled his shirt over his head and dropped it to the floor. "I'm ready. I want a damned good time for fifty in gold."

"You're not taking off your trousers or boots?"

He smiled sardonically. "Not for the first round. I'm in a hurry."

For a moment she hesitated. Then she slung her hair back and climbed off the bed. Justis watched as she reached under her petticoat and untied her drawers. They fell to the floor and she kicked them away. She sat on the edge of the bed and looked at him calmly.

"Do you want me to remove my stockings?"

"No. But take off the undershirt."

She nodded, then stared blankly at the floor, her mouth set in a tight line. But she couldn't hide the tremor in her fingers as she untied the drawstring around the scooped neck of her shirt.

Justis bitterly ignored the sympathy that threatened his resolve. She had planned to do this for other men. Why should he feel sorry for her now? But his sorrow refused to be ignored, and he cursed the lack of readiness between his legs. Dammit, he wanted to take her in anger, shoving himself into her like a weapon, but his body betrayed him.

"Hurry up," he said impatiently. He crossed the room to her, grabbed the loosened undershirt, and jerked it down her shoulders.

She caught a whimper in her throat and glared up at him as the shirt settled around her waist and elbows. He saw fear flicker in her eyes and made himself study her without emotion. Stepping back, he appraised her slowly.

Blood hammered in the pit of his stomach, and his body couldn't help but harden at the sight of her jutting, darkly nippled breasts, their bronze skin gleaming in the lamplight. By fashion's standard she was much too slender in the arms and waist, but that delicacy made her breasts seem all the more voluptuous.

"You'll do," he said gruffly. "Lie down."

Her expression a mask, she pulled her arms from the shirt, leaving it hanging about her waist, and slowly stretched out on the bed. She stared at the ceiling without blinking and laid her arms by her sides. He noticed that she clenched her fingers into her petticoat.

"Do your business," she said in a tortured whisper.

Justis ground his teeth in frustration. He told himself that this was the only way he'd ever dominate her, that she'd be forced to notice him after this. He was also relatively certain that she'd feel bound to him afterward, whether she'd admit it or not.

"It'll hurt your first time. There's nothing I can do about that." He shoved her knees apart and knelt between them.

She continued to stare at the ceiling. "I don't care."

*Katie, for God's sake, care.* He bent over her and flattened his hand on her stomach. "You might as well get used to men touching you," he said grimly.

She shivered as he slowly moved his hand over her, between her breasts, over each shoulder and down each arm, then back up. He turned his hand over and stroked the same areas with the backs of his fingers.

Her chest rose and fell harshly. It was from fear and distaste, he thought, but then he watched her nipples harden into dark peaks. He shuddered. Her body had betrayed her too.

With both hands he began to touch her breasts, drawing his fingertips over them in feathery strokes, moving closer to the nipples each time but not touching them.

"I thought you were in a hurry," she said in a tear-soaked voice, swallowing hard. "I imagine that few of Mrs. Albert's customers take this much time."

"You oughta thank me for it," he said fiercely, trying not to reveal the knot in his own throat. "I'll learn you things your customers will like."

"Teach you," she corrected him, her mouth trembling. She never stopped staring at the ceiling, but a tear slid from the corner of one eye.

Justis looked away and fought a desire to shake her until her teeth rattled. He wanted to cry too. He wanted her to say that she felt something for him, even just a little.

"Some men will probably want to do this to you," he said bitterly. He bent over her and took one of her nipples in his mouth. He sucked it gently at first, then harder, taunting it with his tongue. With a despairing sound she arched under him, pushing her breast farther into his mouth but just as quickly pulling away.

"You make me disgusted with myself," she said between gritted teeth, her breath coming in little puffs. "If it is so easy for me to react to a man I don't want, then I am well suited to a whorehouse."

"You want me."

His hand surrounded her other breast and squeezed it upward. He raked the nipple with his teeth, then apologized with slow, wet strokes of his tongue. She made a mewling sound and raised her hands to his naked shoulders, trying to push him away.

"I've heard Mrs. Albert's girls talk. I know the customers don't tempt them like this!"

"How is it different, then?" He drew the tip of his tongue down the center of her stomach. She squirmed, and her fingers dug into his skin.

"They're not gentle. They don't try to give pleasure."

"You want me to treat you like a whore?"

"Yes." Her tone held angry determination. "That's what I plan to be."

Tenderness left him. "Damn you, Katie." He unbuttoned his trousers with violent speed, then pushed her legs farther apart. In one coordinated movement he shoved her petticoat to her thighs and lowered himself atop her. "Draw your knees up and put your arms around my neck," he ordered. "And look at me while I take you."

She cried out and shook her head. "I can't look at you." Her arms encircled him and she pressed her face into the hollow of his shoulder. He felt her tears slipping down his chest. "Do it," she begged. "I hope it hurts so much I can hardly stand it. Then maybe I won't want you anymore. Dear Lord, I hope I won't."

Her words sank into him like a knife, slashing his bitterness in two. She wanted him, wanted him so much that she'd go through this because she thought it would rid her of the wanting. Slowly he drew back and looked down at her. His hands lay on either side of her head on the pillow; he realized that he had wadded the pillow's covering into his fists.

She shut her eyes and cried silently. "Don't stop," she urged. "I don't need your pity."

"Give me an honest answer to one question. Do you want to stay here and be a whore?"

She looked up at him miserably. "That's not the point."

His angry tugging had drawn the pillow covering completely out of place. Justis realized abruptly that the covering was her dress. "Look at this," he said sarcastically, pulling it from under her. "You don't even want to put your head on a dirty pillow. How can you work as a—"

He stopped, words dying in his throat when he noticed dried bloodstains on the skirt of the dress. "Who did this to you?"

She grabbed for the dress. "That's not your concern!"

He dropped it on the floor, then sat back and pushed her petticoat all the way up. "Who hurt you? Why didn't you say so? What bastard tore you open like that?"

He slipped his hand between her legs and she wriggled desperately. "Leave me alone! Don't! Justis!"

He held her down with one hand while he probed gently with the other. She quivered with anger and humiliation as he studied her thighs and stroked his fingers over the thatch of black hair between them. Finally he looked at his fingers. "You're not bleeding."

She twisted her head aside and shut her eyes. "I'm a whore now, bleeding or not. I . . . I took two customers this afternoon."

"That's funny," he said in a dry tone. "What I had my fingers on was still tighter than an old maid who'd sat on a lemon."

Her eyes flared with fury. "No matter. I've already been bedded by someone else!"

"You prissy little liar."

She tried to scramble upright and slap him with both

hands at the same time. He caught her wrists and she hung from his grip, making fierce sounds that reminded him of a trapped animal. "Finish what you started!" she commanded. "What do you care if I'm bleeding or not, hurt or not, virgin or not!"

"I don't want to hurt you more!" he yelled. "I don't need to prove I'm a man that way! If you've been bedded by someone else, I'll doctor you and kill him!"

The unselfish words stunned her. With a groan of exasperation and sorrow she collapsed back onto the bed. "Impossible," she muttered, shaking her head. "Impossible to know what to do when you say something like that." She drummed her heels on the bed in frustration, then admitted, "It's not my blood on the dress. I've not taken any customers."

"Whose blood is it?"

"I delivered a babe for one of Mrs. Albert's girls. That's what I spent all of today working at. I intended to be a whore, but I just couldn't bring myself to do it."

He groaned with relief. "Katie Blue Song, you're more cantankerous than any other woman in the world. Why did you stay here?"

"I was going to work as a doctor instead. Mrs. Albert said she'd give me room and board if I'd tend her girls and those at the other houses. The old biddy lied to me."

"Katie, oh, Katie. You crazy, proud gal. I drove you to desperation, and I'm sorry. I sure don't want our first time to be like this—you scared, mad, and laying on a whore's bed with tears in your eyes."

"The *first* time? Justis, don't expect—"

"Shhh. You're upset. Save the arguin' for later."

He pulled her upright and held her tightly. After a moment, working together, they got her legs from around him. Justis buttoned his trousers, then helped her settle her undershirt back in place.

"Thank you," she murmured, still a little stunned and breathless. She gazed straight into his eyes while he fumbled with the tie string. "Though I believe that you wanted to strangle me when you came into this room."

"I don't always go about things the right way. Like this morning at the store. I was wrong to talk to you that way."

She ducked her head. "I suppose you're trying very hard to do your duty to my family."

"Yeah. I owe 'em."

"You mean it when you say that you can't let me go off into the world alone, even with a lot of money. I believe you're sincerely concerned about protecting me, not just about keeping the Blue Song gold."

"Yeah." His fingers increasingly awkward, he guided the shoulders of her undershirt into place. "I reckon you're beginning to see why the world's not a safe place for a gal like you alone."

He was startled when she clasped his face between her slender, gentle hands and looked at him tenderly. "You're a fine man."

He felt the breath stall in his throat. "Then you'll marry me."

"No." Her eyes clouded with sorrow. "Your sense of duty will ruin us both. No more talk of marriage. For white and Indian to mix would only bring grief. I know it's been done before—my grandfather was a half-breed, remember—but he was born when the *A-ni-Yu-wi-Ya* ruled the world. You and I would have been accepted by that world, but not by this one."

Justis sighed. The *A-ni-Yu-wi-Ya*. The Principle People. They would have adopted him into Katie's clan and treated him like a native born. "The offer stands, Katie. I want to marry you."

She stroked his jaw and looked as if she might cry some more. "No. It would take a great deal of love to make a marriage like ours survive. We have friendship, but it's not enough. Neither can we build a marriage on duty and lust." She left the obvious point unsaid—that she couldn't love him.

"I reckon you're right. I won't mention any more about it," he muttered. "It was a fool idea."

A careful shield dropped over her face. She drew her hands away. "I understand why you offered, and I'll always be grateful."

He patted her knee. "If I leave you alone, will you promise to stay in Gold Ridge and live at the hotel? As a guest, I mean. Not like you were beholden to me, or anything. I'll do what I can to help you."

"Then I promise. You have my word that I won't try to leave town." She paused, then smiled at him. "I know that one day you'll give me my fair share of the Blue Song gold. I am beholden to you, and always shall be."

"That's nice." *Beholden,* he thought grimly. He wanted much more from her than that.

Her gaze dropped to his bare chest. She stared at it wide-eyed, as if seeing it for the first time, which, in a way, she was. This was the first calm moment they'd had together. Justis couldn't read her eyes, but he doubted that he looked like the kind of dandy she favored.

"That feller in Philadelphia," he said as casually as he could. "I guess he's hard to forget."

She kept staring at him and said in a distracted tone, "He certainly confirmed my doubts about marriage in general and marrying white men in particular."

"But he was pretty good-lookin', huh?"

Her eyes filled with memories, but she frowned. "He was blond and rather pink. He didn't go out in the sun much. I saw his bare arms once and they hardly had any color at all. Or much hair." She shrugged lightly. "He was very fashionable."

Justis glanced down at himself. "I'm right big and furry," he admitted, as much to himself as to her. "And I've been out in the sun until I look like old leather. Plus I've got all sorts of scars."

She nodded, then looked away. He figured that she couldn't stand the brutish sight any longer. "You can put your shirt back on, sir. And I'll slip into my dress."

*Sir.* So the intimacy was over. Frowning, he got up and went to the washstand, turning his back to her so that she'd have privacy. "I'll go on downstairs and have a word with Mrs. Albert."

"No!" she cried.

Justis pivoted. She was stepping into her dress. Now she halted, bent halfway over, to gaze at him. "Wait for me," she told him. "If you go alone, you might get into trouble on my account. I wouldn't want you to break any heads and land in jail. Or to get your hard head broken."

Her concern made him smile. He stared wistfully at the soft, luscious tops of her breasts, which in her current position bulged over the neck of her undershirt. "I wish I'd talked less and stroked more a little while ago. Fifty dollars would have been a bargain just to look at you."

She almost smiled back—but hurriedly pulled her dress up. "If I hadn't admitted the truth to you, would you have gone through with our, umm, business together?"

"Would you have wanted me to?"

For a long moment they simply looked at each other. Justis smiled wider as he saw the unmistakable blush rising in her face. At least there was one thing she'd never deny.

"I think we'd be content together in some ways," he told her.

She looked flustered but said softly, "I think you're right."

He set his hat on his head and tugged the floppy brim over his eyes at a jaunty angle.

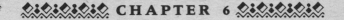 

## CHAPTER 6

OVER the next few days Katherine went back to work at the store, though it was just a way to occupy her time now that Justis had agreed to her independence. She knew he'd give her a fair share of gold as soon as her future was decided, but that wouldn't happen until they heard the governor's decision.

Justis hadn't come to see her since the escapade at Mrs. Albert's. He had learned the recklessness of his involvement, Katherine thought, and now wanted to retreat. Her relief was overshadowed by a sorrow she couldn't deny.

What a blustery scoundrel he was, so full of himself and so proud. Yet he wasn't a vain man; he was shrewd about his shortcomings, even amused by them. He was brutal to his enemies but also to himself, because he never expected mercy. Yet he was capable of offering it, of treating anyone in need with extraordinary compassion. She no longer doubted that he had the heart and soul of a true chevalier, no matter how crudely he expressed that nobility at times.

She would never forget the night at Mrs. Albert's. He'd threatened to run the madam out of town for her scheming, and Mrs. Albert had been reduced to tears and begging, much to Katherine's unholy delight. But she hadn't wanted him to make the threat good, and to her surprise, he had agreed.

"If I run her off, her girls will suffer for it," he had explained afterward.

"You did the right thing by her, and by me," she'd assured him. "I've got my revenge. I escaped that miserable place. She never will."

Justis had gazed at her as if she were something rare. "For a woman, you sure see things in a practical way."

"For a man," she had replied dryly, "you certainly have a tender heart."

Being accused of tenderheartedness apparently had perturbed him, because when he brought her back to the hotel he said good night rather abruptly, and left. She told Sam and Rebecca what had happened, leaving out the most lurid parts, and they angrily vowed that the days of Gold Ridge's brothels were numbered.

Now, after a little time to think about it, Katherine saw the brothel problem from a different perspective. The girls at Mrs. Albert's were treated little better than property. Most were in poor health, suffering from all sorts of maladies.

One evening Katherine formed a secret plan. If she weren't forced to leave Gold Ridge, she would offer her doctoring skills to the town's prostitutes, though on her own terms, not Mrs. Albert's. She would never forget how the girls had showered her with gratitude when she delivered their friend's babe. They knew the value of compassion, even the compassion offered by someone unlike themselves.

So she'd be their doctor—if she didn't have to leave

with the other Cherokees. As a May twilight settled around the hotel and the boarders finished supper, she walked to the front veranda alone.

From the trees beyond the hotel a whippoorwill sang its heartrending call. Katherine's throat tightened. She lived with a constant heaviness inside her, a despair that colored everything she said and did. Her chest ached with bittersweet sorrow—a sense of homesickness even though she was home. The magenta shadows that were fading over the forests and distant mountains seemed like shadows of doom.

She hugged herself and leaned against one of the veranda's slender wooden columns. When customers came into the store they stared at her with a mixture of fear and curiosity, and some muttered that it would be bad to have a Cherokee right in their midst when the uprising began. A sizable number of townspeople were certain that the Indians planned to wage war rather than be removed.

Katherine shook her head wearily. Her people had given up war many years earlier and settled, more or less happily, into a life of hunting and farming. There were no fierce, battle-hardened warriors left, and no war chiefs. Her parents had spoken of knowing such men— and women, for in the old days Cherokee women had held great power in war as well as in peace—but now even the most traditional Cherokees embraced peace.

Yes, they would go without resisting, because they'd become civilized. Katherine trembled with disgust. This was the value of civilization, to suffer betrayal despite all efforts to live peacefully, because the missionaries had said that the old ways were sinful.

What would her future be if she were allowed to stay in Gold Ridge? A small portion of the townspeople would undoubtedly befriend her, but the rest would always consider her inferior, someone to be pitied or distrusted. Even with all her gold she wouldn't be a citizen; she'd have no legal defense if she were cheated or robbed. She would never be able to buy property, not even the Blue Song property.

She slipped her fingers across the back of her neck and rubbed muscles that throbbed from too much anxiety and despair. No one knew the depth of her anguish—not even Justis. Especially not him. He must never know how much she needed his strength.

She went to the veranda's steps and sank down, glad that the darkness hid her distress. Justis. Living in Gold Ridge would mean forever fighting the emotions he stirred inside her. It would also mean that one day she'd see him marry—for love, not duty—one of his own people.

Katherine gazed sadly into the beautiful forest that lay just beyond Gold Ridge's sprawling growth. She should simply disappear into the ancient woodland that had held no fear for her as a child. She should forget her promise to Justis and vanish into the night.

Shakily she rose to her feet, caught in the spell of memories, tormented by visions of the future. She slipped one foot off the steps, her breath short with indecision, her hands clenched.

"Katie."

She grasped the wooden railing beside the steps and stared into the darkness. Justis climbed the slight rise of the yard, his long strides carrying him silently up the trail from the square. He stopped a few feet away from her in a faint patch of light from the parlor window. His shadowed mystery, the handsomeness of his rugged face and tall, work-honed body, made her touch her throat lightly in awe.

He was dressed in his usual work trousers and a loose white shirt, and the gold nugget over his heart reflected the lamplight like a beacon. Transfixed, Katherine realized that she'd dropped her hand to her own chest.

"How are you?" he asked, and pulled his hat off belatedly.

"Startled." She shook the odd mood away and managed a strained laugh. "You walk more quietly than any white man I've ever known."

"You looked like you were in a trance."

"No. Just . . . thinking."

"I brought you something." He stepped up to her and held out a letter. "I'd like you to carry this whenever you go out of the hotel. It's just something I wrote. It says that you're in my care. In case anyone wants to know why you're not penned up with the other Cherokees."

He paused, then added gently, "The army finished buildin' the stockade today. Tomorrow the patrols and state militia start roundin' up your people. They'll go into the hills and find all the families who hid out. I reckon they'll bring in four, maybe five hundred folks over the next few days."

"Will you take me to see them at the stockade?"

He inhaled harshly. "Katie, it'd only make you feel bad. The place—I went to look at it today. It's just a big pen in the middle of a field. No shade, and the closest water is a good quarter mile off. I wouldn't shut an animal in it, much less humankind."

She looked up at him desperately. "How long will the army keep them there?"

"I don't know. At least the government's brought in plenty of supplies. Blankets, flour—"

"People won't take those things! They'll have too much pride! And the flour—Cherokee women cook with cornmeal. They don't know how to use anything else!"

He grasped her arms and stroked them soothingly. "I'll talk to Sam. We'll send food from the store."

"That's how I want my share of gold used. I'll buy supplies from you."

"All right, gal, all right."

"And I want to visit the stockade."

"Dammit, Katie, no."

"You forbid it? Are you forgetting that I'm your *guest*, not your servant?"

He let go of her and stepped back. "No, I hadn't forgot. But I don't want you near that damned stockade."

"If you won't take me, I'll find someone else."

"I'll thrash the skin off any man who takes you there without my permission."

She cried out in frustration. "Nothing has changed between us. I am *a-tsi-na-Ha-i*. A slave! You make me dread the sight of you."

His chin rose slowly. "If you crave to see misery," he said between gritted teeth, "I'll be glad to take you to the stockade. I'll come for you at the store tomorrow afternoon."

He turned without another word and disappeared into the night.


THE SUN WAS too hot for late May, and Katherine's head was damp under her black bonnet. Red dust swirled under the feet of the buggy horse, and even the saw grass looked thirsty in the fields on either side of the road.

Coming up on the left was the stockade, a large square structure built of logs. It had a guardhouse at the top of each corner, and catwalks along the walls. She was close enough to hear the sentries swearing about the heat.

Beside her, Justis pushed his hat back, drew a handkerchief across his forehead, then slapped the buggy reins lightly. "We're goin' there." He pointed as he swung the horse into a pine thicket off the road. "You'll have a good view, but the trees will hide you. Keep that bonnet on."

Those were the first words he'd spoken to her since he'd come for her at the store. There were stern grooves on either side of his mustache, and his eyes glinted with alertness. Lying on the floor of the buggy was a loaded rifle.

"You have to promise me something, sir." With that formal prelude she laid a hand on his arm. Through the light cotton of his shirt she felt corded muscles flex at her touch.

"I'm not much good at promises today," he said grimly.

"If any of the soldiers notice me—if any of them come over here and see that I'm a Cherokee, and tell me to go to the stockade—you must promise me that you won't try to stop them."

He pulled the horse to a halt, then dropped the buggy reins and climbed down, his face turned so that she couldn't read his expression. The determined set of his big shoulders worried her. "Do you want me to let them put you in that hell trap?" he demanded, gesturing toward the stockade.

"No, but I don't want you killed or thrown in jail because you fought them."

He swung about. His gaze searched her face until she looked away. The anger slipped from his tone. "I'll be on my best behavior," he said gravely.

"Such vague reassurance." She gave him a solemn look.

"After the governor sends your exemption, I won't worry so much."

She nodded, but she knew as well as he that there was no guarantee she'd win the governor's support. "If the worst happens," she said as calmly as she could, "I'll survive. You certainly know how ornery I am. I'll be all right in the stockade."

He shook his head slowly, his eyes cold. "I'll never let them keep you there. Or send you west. I promised your pa I'd take care of you."

Duty, she thought sadly. "Papa wouldn't expect you to do more than you already have."

"He wouldn't want you left in that pen with strangers."

"They won't be strangers. I'd be safe with them."

"No Cherokee man ever raped a Cherokee woman?" he asked bluntly. "No Cherokee ever stole food or water from another?"

"Not very often."

He shook his head. "Your people have new vices now. Drinkin' is one of 'em. Rape and thievin' go hand in hand with the liquor. Don't count on bein' safe among your own kind."

They fell silent, watching the activity around the stockade. The troops had set up rows of canvas tents outside the structure. Those who hadn't gone on patrol were bustling about, exercising their horses, unloading wagons full of supplies, and staring fitfully down the road as if expecting Cherokees at any moment.

Townspeople began to arrive, some walking, some in wagons or on horseback, and soon it looked as if half of Gold Ridge had come to see the first group of Cherokees enter the stockade. The atmosphere was almost festive. Katherine winced at the shouts and laughter, at the frequent passing of jugs and bottles, and especially at the firearms the men waved with glee.

"I see dust down the road!" someone yelled. "They're a-coming!"

Justis leapt into the buggy and helped Katherine to her feet. Where the road curved out of sight into the wooded hills, she could see the first mounted soldiers appear, shrouded in dust. The spectators whooped with glee, but their elation soon dimmed, and a few muttered angrily.

Katherine heard one man call to his friend, "Don't look like they're escortin' dangerous Injuns to me! Lots of women and children! Ain't quite right, seems like!"

The crowd had now formed two lines leading to the gate of the stockade. Katherine twisted toward Justis and

gave him a hopeful look. "If I could only get closer . . .
Couldn't we stand just behind the line on this side of the
gate?"

"Wait a few minutes. Let's see how the crowd acts."

She nodded and strained her eyes toward the approaching column. Soon it reached the outskirts of the
field, and even through the dust she saw the marchers
clearly.

"Where are their belongings?" she asked in bewilderment. "So many of them are empty-handed. They
wouldn't leave their homes without packing everything
they could carry."

Justis gripped her elbow tightly. "Unless they weren't
given a choice."

She covered her mouth in horror and watched as
about one hundred Cherokees, flanked by cavalry,
walked wearily toward the stockade. Most of the men
wore thigh-length hunting shirts cinched with colorful
woven belts. On their heads were turbans of bright cloth,
some bearing a feather or two. Their legs were covered in
fringed leggings or cloth trousers tucked into knee-high
moccasins.

The women were less exotic, dressed in loose print
skirts and blouses, with scarves tied over their hair. Even
so, there was an almost biblical look about the group—
they might have been some Old Testament tribe being
herded into captivity.

A cursed tribe. Children screamed. Old women buried
their heads in their arms and wept as they shuffled along.
Several of the men were obviously drunk, and they
hurled curses at the spectators in broken English.

Those who had packs on their backs staggered under
the load. An ancient man, little more than a copper-hued
scarecrow, wavered under a tall bundle tied to his shoulders by coarse rope. When he fell to his knees a pair of
white men stepped from the audience and helped him
up.

That galvanized many of the other spectators, and a hush fell over the scene as they silently offered assistance. A burly blond man lifted two Cherokee children to his shoulders and carried them toward the stockade. Several women went to the aid of a young mother who limped along leading one child and carrying another.

Katherine realized that she was crying and that Justis had put his arm around her. "Please, can we go closer?" she asked. "The crowd's not mean."

"I reckon you're right."

When they reached the spectators Katherine ducked her head so that the bonnet would shield her face from all but the closest inspections. Everyone was looking at the marchers, anyway. Justis put a hand between her shoulder blades and guided her through the mob. They reached the front and she watched anxiously, looking for familiar faces.

Her gaze kept returning to the scarecrow. His turban was askew, half covering one eye, and his face was caked with dust. But she saw pride in the set of his mouth, and the pleated skin of his face couldn't completely blur its past strength.

Recognition came to her abruptly, and his name left her lips like a plea. *"Tsa-yo-ga!"*

A white man near them whooped drunkenly and fired his pistol. The gun blast spooked one of the soldier's horses and it careened into the prisoners, bucking wildly. One of its iron-shod hooves lashed into the chest of the frail old man, Tsa-yo-ga.

Katherine darted into the melee and caught him as he slumped to the ground, blood already bubbling from his mouth and nose. His pack slid off and he fell sideways against her, his blood spattering her gray dress.

She cradled his head in her lap and bent over him to block the sun from his eyes. "Tsa-yo-ga," she whispered tearfully. His turban had fallen off, and coarse gray hair tumbled about his face and shoulders. She stroked bloody strands of it back from his mouth. "I'll save you as you saved me once."

His eyes flickered, and the proud mouth drew up a bit at the corners. "Me-li!"

"Me-li's daughter," she said hoarsely.

"Ah. So many . . . years." The words gurgled from his throat. "Today. This is very bad."

"I'll take care of you."

His lips moved weakly. "Is this one the daughter Me-li named She Sees Dreams?"

"It is she, yes." She brushed her tears from his wizened face. "And this one will always be grateful that her *e-du-tsi* saved her from the rattlesnake."

His eyelids fluttered. He whispered, "Ah! Glory! I remember!"

The old eyes focused directly on hers, and life faded from them. Kathcrine cupped the ancient face between her hands and began a soft chant in Cherokee.

Rough hands grabbed her by the shoulders. "Fool woman! The old coot's dead!"

She gasped. Justis's hands. His voice. Vicious. He put a boot on Tsa-yo-ga's body and shoved it from her lap. Then he twisted her around to face him, yanked her up angrily, and grabbed the back of her bonnet.

"I'm damned if your crazy ways will shame me!"

He pulled her head to his shoulder and held it there brutally, nearly suffocating her as he swept his other arm behind her legs. She clawed at his shoulders and face as he jerked her close to his body and picked her up. She screamed with rage, but the sound was muffled against his shoulder.

Angry mutters came from the spectators. "Don't blame her for showing Christian charity," Katherine heard one say.

Justis gave a terse answer and carried her through the line of people, walking very fast. His hold on her was painfully tight. She tried to gulp air into her lungs and made a sound of sheer loathing.

Finally he reached the pine thicket and climbed into the buggy. He sat down, breathing in shallow bursts as he held her in his lap, his hand still mashing her face against his shoulder. She fought wildly and he squeezed her until she gasped in weak surrender.

"Why?" she wailed.

He anchored a hand in her bonnet and the hair bundled underneath, then drew her head back. Between ragged breaths he said, "The soldiers coming. Had to do something, quick. Hide your face from them. Sorry. Sorry I hurt you."

Stunned, she saw the red welts her fingernails had left in his jaw. His left earlobe was bleeding. She crumpled with misery and put her arms around his neck. "Justis, oh, Justis."

They held each other tightly. Katherine listened to the continued sounds of the Cherokee procession. Shame choked her. She should be with her people, not here crying silently in a white man's embrace, her head resting against his bloody jaw. When she heard the soldiers close the stockade's heavy wooden gates, she knew her future was sealed inside them.


AMARINTHA PARNELL WAS a mystery Justis had never been able to figure out. When he'd met her, six years before, she had been just barely past the gawky stage that follows childhood, but even then she'd had the look of a grown woman in her eyes.

Those eyes—they were an odd shade of blue, dark and wounded, the color of a bruise. He didn't understand why they repelled him, because it was no secret that other men in town found Amarintha and her odd eyes fascinating.

In a way, he did too. She was soft and fashionably

plump, and her affinity for wearing pink gave her the appeal of a strawberry pudding. She had a beautiful, fine-boned little face, and its maze of freckles only drew attention to its charms. One of her admirers had confided to Justis during an inebriated moment playing cards at the saloon that Amarintha looked like a white cat with a calico mask.

The year she'd turned fourteen she had cornered Justis at a Fourth-of-July barbecue and said firmly that she intended to marry him on her sixteenth birthday. He'd kissed her just to see what kind of steel lay behind the girlish sass. It had only been a teasing peck on the lips, that kiss, but something akin to horror had risen in her eyes. She'd backed away and spat on him, and then, to his complete bewilderment, she'd smiled as if nothing were wrong.

He'd known then that he'd never get near Amarintha again, no matter how enticing her soft pink sweetness seemed. There was craziness in her, some kind of torment.

In the years since then plenty of men and boys had courted her, and to Justis's great relief she seemed interested in all of them. Her sixteenth birthday had come two years ago, but she never said another word to him about marrying. Still, she always made it clear that he was her favorite.

He'd kept her at arm's length all this time, and he couldn't understand why she didn't marry someone else. He'd heard rumors that the judge chased off any man who got too cozy with Amarintha, but that kind of wild tale was probably the result of the old lion's reputation for meanness.

Justis grimaced as he rode to the judge's house. He hoped Parnell could be persuaded to help with Katherine's problem.

He tied Watchman to the split-rail fence that surrounded the yard. The judge's white clapboard house was situated just off the square under a pair of huge oak trees, sad evidence that the town's namesake ridge had been covered with such kingly trees until a few years before.

Amarintha opened the door before he finished knocking. She removed a frilly white cap from her red curls and brushed her hands over a white and pink work dress. "Goodness, I was cleaning house. But how nice to have a visitor."

"You're lookin' mighty good today." He tried not to sound impatient. "Is the judge in?"

She smiled widely. "No. He's ridden over to Auraria." She grabbed his hand. "Do come visit, though." Justis let her lead him into the parlor. She took his hat and waved delicately toward an upholstered chair. "I'll bring you a cup of tea."

"No, I'll come back later—"

"I've been planning to talk to you," she said, and the smile vanished. She wrung her hands and gave him a sweet, pleading look. "I'm concerned about your activities of late. I don't want you to suffer any ill treatment because of them."

He studied her shrewdly as she settled on a footstool, twisting his hat between her pink fingers. "You're kind to worry about me."

"Oh, I do worry, I do! Please sit down for a moment."

He lowered himself into the armchair. "I know folks are talkin' about Miss Blue Song and me. I'd appreciate it if you'd pass the word that she's a lady and that I've treated her that way. There's nothing between us but friendship."

"But, Justis, why are you sending supplies to the stockade every day? Lots of us are trying to help the poor Indians, but you—you're practically turning into one of them!"

"Miss Blue Song is buying those supplies with her own gold."

"But that's the problem. People say that you're just

encouraging trouble, giving her that gold. It's not rightfully hers. The state says so."

"Then it's my gold, and I can use it any way I please."

"Justis, folks say that if you let one Cherokee parade around like she's going to stay here, then the other poor wretches will think they can stay too."

"Anybody got the gumption to tell me that to my face?"

"No. But they're after Captain Taylor to arrest her."

"Why are you warning me? I've seen the way you look at her when you come in the store. You'd like to see her get carted off."

"Why, I feel sorry for her. I don't want to see her humiliated by a public arrest."

Justis leaned forward and took his hat from her. His eyes narrowed. "What's your bargain, Amarintha? What do you really want?"

"I just want you to get the respect you deserve from folks here in town. You'll lose that if you associate too closely with Miss Blue Song. Though she's certainly a fine lady who deserves a fine home—in the Indian territory out west."

She paused, looked down demurely, and added, "But if you insist on helping her, I'll understand."

"Good. I want to ask the judge to swing it where she can visit the stockade without gettin' in trouble. I've written the governor about exempting her, but he hasn't sent an answer yet. Meantime, she can do good for her people. She's got some doctorin' skills."

"But the army has a doctor for them. I heard so."

His mouth curled in disgust. "One doctor to serve hundreds. They've been in the stockade only a week, and a dozen have died."

"I thought Indians were a hardy race."

"They are. If they weren't, even more would be gone by now. Katie—Miss Blue Song is frantic about it."

"Why do you think my father can keep the army from arresting her?"

"Come on, Amarintha. Everybody knows that the judge is tight with Cap'n Taylor."

She tilted her chin up and smiled at him under half-shut eyes. "I have more influence with the captain than my father does. I'll be glad to talk to him about Miss Blue Song's plight." She hesitated, still smiling.

"What do you want in return?"

"Just for you to take me to the dance at Mrs. Warner's this Saturday."

Justis smiled but cursed her silently. "That'd be my pleasure."

"And promise me that you'll not be seen with Miss Blue Song anymore. Either in public or by visiting her at the hotel. Not at all." Her gaze fluttered over his incredulous expression. "It's for your own good," she assured him.

KATHERINE STACKED BOXES of quinine tablets on a shelf in the store's back room. The quinine, along with liniments, salves, and various other medical supplies, had arrived by wagon just an hour earlier.

She'd run out to the loading dock and excitedly helped the teamster carry the precious packages inside. "I can accomplish a great deal with these medicines," she'd told Rebecca. "If Justis can just get permission for the army to leave me alone."

Now she carefully arranged the supplies so they'd be ready to pack at a moment's notice. Out in the store Rebecca called, "Noah's returned."

Katherine glanced out of the storeroom as Noah trotted toward her. He came to a breathless halt, his brow furrowed with concentration.

"I told Mr. Justis you said the medicines had got here. I told him you says thank you for ordering 'em. I told him you missed him something awful the past three days and wondered where in tarnation he'd got off to."

She gasped. "That's not what I said. I said for you to ask him when he was coming to dinner at the hotel."

"Uh-huh. He says he cain't come. They cut into a new vein at the mine and he's up to his, up to his—he cain't come any day soon. And Miss Amarintha was there, and she said—"

"Noah, quit jabbering," Rebecca interrupted. She handed him a piece of molasses candy. "Scoot back to the hotel and help Cookie clean rooms."

Katherine stopped him. "Miss Amarintha was at the mine?"

"Yes'm. She come by to visit Mr. Justis. They're goin' to a dance on Saturday."

Rebecca burst into activity, darting a sympathetic look at Katherine and shooing Noah with both hands. "Take yourself to the hotel this second, you chatterbox. Before I swat your behind."

He escaped out the door, his eyes twinkling with mischief. Katherine returned to the storeroom and slammed a box of quinine tablets on the shelf. Damn the man. Damn him for making her care.

## CHAPTER 7

THE AFTERNOON of the dance Katherine went to Sam and Rebecca, who were playing cards in the small parlor of their private rooms.

"You can keep no secrets from me," she told them. "Because I've won Cookie's friendship, and Cookie knows all."

Sam eyed her askance. "Tell me how you persuaded that cranky creature to bestow her favor on you."

"She had a spell of stomach trouble. I gave her a cathartic for it."

He snorted. "So that's the secret. Cookie trades friendship for a happy bowel."

Rebecca blushed and covered her face. "Sam!" Her voice vibrated with restrained laughter.

Katherine gazed at them both reproachfully. "She says you've been invited to Mrs. Warner's dance but you're not going, on my account. You must go. Please."

Rebecca shook her head. " 'Tis just a dance. There are lots around here in the springtime."

Katherine wouldn't relent. "Go. You're very dear to feel sorry for me, but don't sit home to keep me company. I don't expect to be included in the social life hereabouts, not ever. Besides, how could I go in good conscience while my people are suffering at the stockade? I'm ashamed of my freedom and good fortune as it is." She hesitated. "I'm not hurt by Mr. Gallatin's actions."

Rebecca's eyes teared. "I'll never forgive Justis for deserting you!"

Katherine looked at her proudly. "He hasn't deserted me. He's fulfilling his duty without personal involvement, which is exactly what I asked him to do."

"You can't tell me that you wish it weren't so!"

Katherine faltered, unnerved by Rebecca's bluntness. "I might as well wish to be blond and blue-eyed," she said finally. "And I'd never do that. So why mourn something that can't come true?"

Easy words to say, but they lay heavy in her chest as she left the room.


CHEERFUL LANTERN LIGHT filled the Warner barn along with cheerful music—the scratchy, high-pitched duet of the county's best fiddlers. Judge Parnell stood in front of them, calling the steps to a square dance, his voice less stern but no less commanding than when he sentenced men in his courtroom. Justis stood in a shadowy corner, avoiding the whirl and stomp of the dancers, his hands shoved in the pockets of a long black coat.

Amarintha nestled against him, holding his arm. "Don't glower so," she said, sighing. "The world is set right. Your Indian friend can visit the stockade as much as she pleases. She'll be safe. And you needn't accompany her at all."

She waited for a show of gratitude that never came. Finally she said in exasperation, "Justis Gallatin! You've always told me that you intend to be a respectable citizen, and I'm only trying to help!"

"I don't like bein' forced into it." Disgust boiled inside him, and it was all he could do to be civil. "You've got a mighty selfish way of bein' helpful."

"Sometimes the only way to get sense into a stubborn mule is to hit him over the head!"

"And hope he doesn't bite your hand off."

She cried a little and dabbed her eyes with a handkerchief. "All I intend is to save your reputation from ruin. You simply have to stay away from Miss Blue Song from now on."

He slowly removed her hand from his arm. "We got a bargain. You just make sure you keep Cap'n Taylor happy. Save your sugar for that."

She glared at him as he walked away. Justis stepped outside and strode through a moonlit June night, heading for the corral, where Watchman waited among the other guests' horses and wagons. He needed to ride and think until he couldn't think anymore, until he was so tired that he couldn't see Katherine's face or hear her voice inside his mind.

"Hullo! That you, Justis?"

He heard raucous laughter from the farm's smokehouse and looked over to find a man hanging on the open door, silhouetted by lantern light. Justis recognized him as the owner of a small mine north of town. The man swayed crazily.

"Set down, Billy, 'fore you fall down."

Billy chortled. Then he plunged face forward onto the hard, grassy earth. Justis ambled over to him as several other men staggered out of the smokehouse and gazed down at their fallen comrade.

"Didn't hurt a bit," Billy said enthusiastically, rolling over on his back.

Justis studied the man's bloodied nose and giddy smile. "What are you possum farts drinkin'?"

"Not drinking, friend." Billy pointed up at a stranger in the group. "We're having an ether frolic. Peddler here is selling the stuff."

"What's ether?" Justis eyed the peddler warily.

The man reared back and grinned. "Just a harmless product of nature, sir. Sulphuric ether. Why, even ladies have ether frolics. Perfectly moral and clean, it is. You just take a few whiffs of ether gas and you feel exhilarated. Soothes aches and pains too."

Justis thought all of that sounded good, especially considering his bad mood. "What's your charge?"

"A quarter for five minutes of sniffing. Dollar if you want your own bottle."

Justis reached into his pocket, then flipped a small gold nugget to the man. "Gimme two bottles."

KATHERINE WOKE FROM a light, troubled sleep, and her heart skipped. Someone was trying to unlatch her door.

She scrambled out of bed and fumbled in the darkness for her wrapper. There was no time to hunt for her scalpel or even light the lamp. In a streak of moonlight she saw a thin knife blade slip through the fine crack between the door and its facing. It flicked upward and popped the latch.

Her heart racing, she threw herself forward just as a hand grasped the facing, slamming her shoulder into the door so that it trapped the invading hand's fingers. To her amazement, the intruder didn't struggle or scream in pain.

"I bet that's gonna hurt like a sonuvabitch tomorrow," a drawling, unmistakable voice observed solemnly.

She swung the door open and watched in distress as Justis tucked his knife back into its scabbard, then raised his hand close to his face and studied it, his expression grave. Moonlight fell on his slowly blinking eyes and nonchalant frown. His hat was shoved back crookedly, and when he lowered his hand he gave her a lopsided smile.

"You're drunk," she said, and sniffed. "I don't smell liquor, but it's obvious."

"I'm not drunk." His words were slightly slurred. "I just wanted to visit you."

"You came to do more than that, I'd say. Sneaking into my room!" She struggled not to cry with rage. He was ashamed to visit her in public now. She furiously tied the neck and waist strings on her wrapper, as if warning him not to touch her. "I'll not be your secret entertainment, sir."

"Shhh." He wavered a little, looked up and down the dark hall with exaggerated care, then gazed back at her. "Don't worry, I can't bother you," he said in a low, utterly sincere voice. "My pecker's numb."

She gasped softly. "You are *very* drunk."

"Come outside and dance with me," he said, taking her hands.

"No!"

"Shhh. Don't wake everyone up." His expression darkened as he added sarcastically, "Think of my reputation."

She tried to pull her hands away. "You've had enough dancing for one night."

"Not with you, I haven't. Now, totter on outside with me, or I'll yell like a Cherokee on the warpath."

He led her down the hall to a back staircase, where he stumbled more than once during the descent. She grabbed one brawny arm and tried to hold him steady. "You'll kill yourself!"

"Nope. Already fell off m'horse. Didn't hurt a bit."

"What's wrong with you?" she cried in a bitter whisper. They reached the back door and lurched outside to the porch. "Why did you do this to yourself? Didn't the evening go well with Amarintha?"

"Hmmm. Damn well. She gave me everything I

wanted. My reputation's at stake because of you, see? She'll save me."

Katherine jerked her hands away and walked into the moonlit backyard, hugging herself. Oh, this was agony. He had no idea how much his honesty hurt her. "I see your predicament," she said acidly. "You regret taking me in, and you had to get drunk to say so. *Coward.*"

He threw his head back and cursed loudly. "I'm not drunk and I'm not a coward!" He came after her, swaying, and grabbed her by one arm.

"I just won't be coming to see you anymore. That's what you wanted—no more of that damned Gallatin hangin' around you. *Say it.* That's just fine with you, isn't it, by God?"

"Yes," she retorted, her voice vibrating with emotion. "All I need is the gold you owe me. I wouldn't care if I never laid eyes on you again."

He stared at her for a moment. "That's a bald-faced lie."

She shook her head fiercely. "Good night."

She pulled her arm away and started back to the porch. Her pulse was thready. She heard his boots crunching the loamy soil with what sounded like long, unsteady strides. Following her! When she stepped onto the porch she pivoted to rebuke him, then squealed as he clamped a folded handkerchief over her mouth and nose. She inhaled a pungent gas that tickled her throat.

Justis circled her shoulders with one arm and pulled her against him, holding her gently but firmly while she struggled and swallowed huge breaths filled with the fumes. Her bones seemed to fall apart. When she slumped against him, he took the handkerchief away and asked, "You ever been to an ether frolic, Katie?"

"Ether," she repeated groggily. "Dr. Ledbetter experimented with it. Painkiller, he thinks. You b-blackguard."

"I need to kill a lot of pain tonight," he whispered in her ear. "Figure you do too."

His legs buckled slowly and he leaned against a porch column, sliding downward still holding her. He put the handkerchief over her nose again, until she clung to his shoulders weakly and began to giggle.

"You're d-despicable."

"I reckon that's bad."

"Bad."

He half sprawled on the porch with her lying across his thighs. They helped each other haphazardly until he was upright and she was seated on his lap, her left arm draped around his neck. She rested her forehead against his and knocked his hat off in the process. "Sorry, blackguard."

"Katie, I got it all set for you to go to the stockade. To doctor folks, I mean. You can start tomorrow."

"That's nice." Her head felt as though it were floating. She patted his cheek, stroking the healing red welts left from when she'd struggled with him at the stockade a week before. "How did you accomplish it?"

He shook his head. "Don't matter."

"*Doesn't* matter."

"Either way." He sighed and hugged her gently. "I'll be around if you need me. I'll send one of my men to take you back and forth every day."

Her head drooped onto his shoulder. "Justis?"

"Hmmm?"

"I never thought . . . you'd be ashamed . . . to be seen with me."

He groaned. "Katie, *no.*"

He ought to explain about Amarintha's manipulative little bargain, though he hadn't wanted to let Katherine know how much pride he'd swallowed on her account. No, Katherine didn't want sentiment or sacrifice from him. He dipped his head close to hers and listened to her soft sounds. She was asleep, but crying.

* * *

KATHERINE ROCKED A sick baby in her arms and prayed for a breeze to stir the heat. Under a cloudless sky the stockade seemed cast adrift from the rest of the world, a huge ship on a sea of filthy ground. The soldiers kept the gates open, thankfully, because they'd learned that their captives stayed quieter if they could glimpse the outside world.

Captain Taylor, an idealistic young officer whom Katherine had grown to like during the past six weeks, said that the Cherokees wouldn't start the march west until September, more than a month away. As brutal as captivity was, the drought and lack of supplies would have made traveling worse. So all over the Cherokee Nation, in stockades such as the one at Gold Ridge, Indians waited under a broiling sun.

Katherine laid the baby next to its mother, who was also sick. Their only shelter was a lean-to made of poles and canvas; it was nearly identical to those built by the other several hundred captives. People spent most of the days stretched out beneath the crude tents, venturing into the sun only when necessity demanded it.

The soldiers weren't heartless, and they tried to help. Every day they escorted groups to the river, but the brief sanctuary of running water, so sacred to Cherokee rituals and so necessary in the heat, was barely enough to make a difference. The inadequate food, the contamination from human waste, and their heartbreaking grief were simply too much for some captives to survive, especially the elderly and the children. Every week the graveyard beyond the stockade grew larger.

"Will he go to the Dark Land?" the sick mother asked Katherine, laying a feverish hand on her child's head.

"I don't know. I'll leave more medicine for him."

"The shaman says your medicine does no good—but your strong spirit scares away the witches. He tells others not to look at you with black eyes."

Katherine nodded gratefully. "They still talk about me . . . because I'm free?"

"Yes. But many understand why that's best. Don't worry. The things you bring are much needed. Some are calling you Beloved Woman."

A pang of remorse shot through Katherine. "No. There are no more Beloved Women. It was a great honor. My mother earned it only after many years."

"Still, that is what some are calling you."

Katherine hung her head. "But many say I'm a traitor."

"They are bitter toward everyone. I know who they are. They take your gifts anyway, so don't feel too bad."

Katherine cupped her hand into a bucket of tepid, dirty water and smoothed the liquid over the baby's forehead. "Keep him cool and give him the medicine. I'll come back to see him tomorrow. And you."

The woman pulled the baby close to her breast and smiled at Katherine. "You'll find us still living in the Sun Land. We're strong."

Katherine smiled as she rose to leave, and ignored her intuition about the baby's prospects.

She made one last round for the day, her moccasin-clad feet moving wearily, her satchel dragging at the end of her arm. She wore a print skirt and light blouse during her visits to the stockade, and kept her hair in a doubled-up braid that hung to her lower back. People accepted her better now that she dressed more Cherokee than white.

She finished her work and went to the gate. As usual, one of Justis's men waited patiently under a canopy, where he was playing poker with several off-duty soldiers. Sorrow tugged at her throat, as it had many times during the past few weeks.

She hardly ever saw Justis anymore. Occasionally he came by the store when she was there organizing her supplies for the stockade, but he never stayed long. The strange night with the ether was still unclear in her memory. When she had awakened the next morning, she was back in her bed, and the escapade seemed like no more than a vivid dream. But she remembered enough to know that Justis no longer thought it wise to associate with her.

Well, he had done his duty more kindly than any other man would have, and she knew he'd always be her defender if she needed him.

Her wounded pride would never let her need him again.

RUPERT MORGAN ESCORTED Katherine to the stockade regularly, so he'd learned to expect Justis's interrogation every evening after they returned.

"Yes, sir, she looks just fine. A little thinner than last week, but gawd, she works in that heat all day without stopping, so she's bound to lose a bit of meat."

"Are some of 'em still cursin' her because she's free?"

"Not many, no. It's hard to cuss an angel, even if you hate her for bein' able to fly."

"From now on you make sure that she stops for an hour in the middle of the day to rest. Make sure she eats while she's at it."

"She won't cotton to that, Mr. Gallatin."

"You tell her it has to be that way, Morgan. I say so."

"Yes, sir."

After Morgan left the mining office, Justis slumped in the chair behind his desk, head in hands. This was the kind of thing that drove men crazy. He couldn't think of anything but Katie. He couldn't sleep, he barely knew what he ate, and worry gnawed at his stomach until he drank to stop it. He'd been this way for weeks.

But at least she was carrying out her mission at the stockade in safety, and Amarintha had kept to her word about Captain Taylor's support. All he had to do was stick this madness out until the governor sent that exemption.

He was asleep with his head on the desk the next morning when Sam arrived.

"Justis? Did you stay at your desk again? Dammit, friend, you're making yourself sick."

Justis eyed him morosely. "What's that you're carryin'?"

Sam raised a letter stamped with the state seal. "It's from the governor."

KATHERINE HAD BEEN at work for only an hour. The sun was barely above the stockade; the dew still lay on the tufts of grass that grew near the walls.

"Beloved Woman, the men are coming toward you."

The words were spoken in a soft, warning whisper by her patient, an elderly woman with swollen sores on her arm. Katherine looked up from putting a salve on them and saw her escort, Mr. Morgan, winding his way through the stockade. Captain Taylor was with him. Both men looked unhappy.

She stood, feeling a knot of dread tighten in her stomach, and suddenly she saw the sentence, written neatly in a prim, official hand: Miss Blue Song is not exempt from the Cherokee removal.

When they reached her Taylor removed his blue cap, ran a hand over short blond hair that he never mussed otherwise, and cleared his throat roughly. "I've some bad news, Miss Blue Song."

"I'm to be a prisoner now," she said flatly.

"Yes."

Morgan slapped his hat against his leg. "I'll tell you who done this to you, miss. It was that sour-faced Amarintha Parnell. She brought the letter from the governor—drove out here herself and gave it to the cap'n a few minutes ago."

Taylor stiffened with anger. "I won't have you talk that way about Miss Parnell. She was just delivering a letter that came to her father. She was in tears over it."

"Tears of joy," Morgan retorted. "Are you a fool, Cap'n? Don't you know better than to set your sights on that Parnell piece? The only man she wants is Justis Gallatin, and Miss Blue Song was gettin' in the way."

"I assume that Mr. Gallatin also received a letter from the governor," Katherine murmured, lost in tortured thought. Now Amarintha would have Justis all to herself.

"Clear out, Morgan. I mean it," the captain said fiercely. "Or I'll have my men throw you out."

Katherine stepped forward and laid a trembling hand on Morgan's arm. "Thank you for your concern, but I'll be all right. Would you go over to the hotel and have Mrs. Kirkland pack my things? Then will you bring them to me here?"

"Miss, no. I bet the boss doesn't know you've already been arrested—"

"Mr. Gallatin can't counteract the governor's decree," Taylor interjected. "I'm sorry, Miss Blue Song. I wish that weren't so."

"There's nothing Mr. Gallatin can do," she told Morgan. "And nothing I want him to do—except to keep sending supplies for my work here. I'm not his concern anymore."

Morgan gaped at her, then shook his head. "Miss, you're his only concern, and if he *don't* know that you been arrested, I gotta tell him. Otherwise he'll skin me alive and fry me for lunch." He turned and hurried away, almost running.

IT TOOK THREE soldiers and a loaded pistol against his temple to keep Justis from going inside the stockade. "Let that man up!" Captain Taylor commanded, strid-

ing over from the small cabin that served as his headquarters.

Justis lay sprawled under the bruised and bleeding
soldiers, who'd decided the only way to subdue him was
to sit on him. They gazed at the captain worriedly.

"He can't be trusted, sir! He's damned wild."

Justis spat blood and dirt out of his mouth and glared
up at the captain. "I have a right to see Katherine Blue
Song."

"You have no rights at all," the captain shot back.
"This is a military post and I'm in charge. Give me your
word that you won't cause trouble, and I'll have my men
release you."

"You've got my word."

The soldiers moved off him and Justis got up,
drenched in dirt and sweat from the fight and his furious
ride to the stockade. He jerked his head toward the enclo-
sure. "She doesn't belong in there."

"None of the Cherokees belong in there. But I can't go
above the governor's order."

"Who can?"

Taylor exhaled wearily. "General Scott could, since
he's in charge of the whole removal and he reports only
to the President. He'll be stopping by this station in a few
days. I'll get you in to see him."

"A few days?" Justis stared inside the gate at the pitiful
lean-tos and dejected captives. The place reeked of human waste and sickness. "Why can't I at least go to see
her?"

"If you'll give up your weapons, I'll let you. But you
better understand this—if you try to take her out of here
by force, I'll have you shot."

Justis smiled thinly. "Amarintha's got you by the
balls, I reckon."

The captain pounded a fist in the opposite hand. "I'll
horsewhip the next man who blackens Miss Parnell's
name! Goddammit, Gallatin, if you want to see Miss Blue

Song, shut your mouth." Justis nodded immediately and began handing his arsenal of pistols and knives to a timid-looking soldier.

When he finally found Katherine she was on her knees under a lean-to, holding the sweat-soaked head of a young man as she dribbled dark liquid down his throat from a tin mug. Justis recognized her, though she had her back to him and was dressed like most of the other women, in a loose skirt and blouse with a colorful kerchief over her hair.

His throat tightened at the sight of her proud, graceful posture and the deft gentleness of the hand that lowered the man's head back to a dusty blanket. He knelt near her and touched her shoulder. "Doc, you look a mite overworked."

*"Justis."* One hand flew to her face as she swiveled toward him; the other reached for him desperately, then halted.

He made a garbled sound and grabbed her, staring at the bruise she tried to cover on one cheek. "Who did that to you?"

"Be careful. You're hurting my arm."

His gaze went to the bloody strip of cloth under his fingers. Breathing raggedly, he let go of her. "What happened?"

She shook her head. "I'm all right. I have many friends here, and they'll make sure no one bothers me again. A few bitter women tried to show their joy over my captivity." She smiled grimly. "But now they know that I wield a sharp scalpel."

Justis wanted to yell with fury. The idea of her penned in this place, fighting like an animal to protect herself, was more than he could stand. The way she looked at him—proudly but with shivering restraint, as if she could barely keep from hugging him—made his hands tremble.

"I'm gonna get you out of here," he told her. "In two

or three days, when General Scott comes. If he won't listen to reason, he'll damn sure listen to gold."

"No!" She lost her pride and grasped one of his hands. Her eyes glittered with tears. "Justis, as ugly as it is, this is where I belong, where I'm respected and needed. My life is with these people."

"Your life is with me."

"Because of a promise you made my father? No, you've paid your debt. Don't jeopardize your standing with your own people any further. Go back to town and just make certain that supplies are still sent to me."

"I can't walk away from my promises that easily."

"Why are you such a dedicated fool?"

He groaned in disgust. "My loyalties ain't ever gonna be decided by what other people think. To hell with 'em." He met her gaze fiercely. God, he thought, in one way she was just like other women. She might not care for him very much, but she sure wanted to know that he was arse over teakettle for her. He wouldn't give her that pleasure.

"You and me are stuck with each other," he said flatly. "We didn't ask for it, we may not want it, but it's done." He reached for her doctor's satchel sitting on the ground nearby. "Don't waste your time trying to figure me out. I swore I'd take care of you, and I never break my word. Just get back to work. I'll help you."

His harsh words made her stiffen. She let go of his hand and sat back on her heels. "You're right. We're stuck with each other. And I can use your help."


HAVING JUSTIS BESIDE her for the rest of the day gave Katherine a deep sense of happiness she couldn't deny. She tried not to think about him leaving.

He joined her in the dirty, hot work without much comment but with great effect on her patients. They stared at him at first—the ultimate insult in a culture where it wasn't polite to look at someone directly—and muttered to Katherine that they didn't want the hands of a hairy *a-Yu-ne-ga* on them.

But they couldn't resist his gentleness or his lack of qualms about doing whatever was needed. Nothing repelled him, not blood nor vomit nor worse, and by the end of the day word had spread through the stockade that this *a-Yu-ne-ga* was a good man.

An elder, lying weakly on a pallet of blankets, motioned for Katherine to bend her head close to his. He nodded toward Justis, who was holding a poultice on the man's arthritic knee. "That one watches you with sad eyes," he whispered in Cherokee. "He is longing for you. You stand in his soul."

It was wrong to correct an elder, so she merely smiled.

When the sun sank behind the stockade walls and long shadows began to ease the heat, Katherine's heart twisted with bleak anticipation. Justis sat with his back against one of the walls, holding a child who was sick with fever. He patiently let the little boy tug at his mustache.

How could she help but want him? she thought wistfully. She shook the idea aside and went to him, kneeling down and holding out her arms for the child. "Let me take him. You should ride back to town before dark comes."

"I'm not goin'. I've decided to stay with you until General Scott gets here."

"That could be several days!"

He glowered at her. "I reckon you need my help even if you don't need me. Now, don't jaw at me. Go find me some supper."

His bluster worked well. She was able to nod brusquely and leave without kissing him.

## CHAPTER 8

SAM AND Rebecca drove a wagon filled with clothes and supplies to the stockade the next morning. After it was unloaded they received permission to take Katherine to the small river nearby, with a soldier's accompaniment. Justis went along, taking the fresh clothes and shaving gear Sam had brought.

Katherine welcomed the chance to wash, even if it was accomplished in icy water while Rebecca held a blanket around her. Justis simply called, "Turn your eyes, ladies," stripped off everything, and waded into a waist-deep pond with a bar of soap in one hand.

Katherine ducked her head behind the blanket and laughed. "I suspect he wouldn't have been so inhibited if you weren't here," she told a blushing Rebecca. "He'd have dared me to look at him."

"Would you have?"

Katherine felt a rush of sensation through her breasts and stomach that had nothing to do with the scrubbing she'd given them. "Probably."

After they dried and dressed, Katherine watched in amusement as Justis sat in the sun-dappled shade beneath a willow tree and tried to shave himself without a mirror. "You'll whack your mustache off if you're not careful, sir," she called. "Horrors! You might look civilized."

One of his chestnut brows arched wickedly. "The mustache stays."

She sighed and sat down beside him. "I suppose I've grown used to it, anyhow. But here, let me have that razor before you need my stitchery on your throat."

With a small flourish he handed it to her. "I reckon you can be trusted. It's not as mean a blade as you're used to."

He tilted his head back and shut his eyes. Katherine got on her knees and bent over him, chuckling fiendishly but scraping at his beard stubble with great care. Rebecca claimed female illness and went off to sit at the river's edge with her bare feet in the water. She told Sam, in a firm voice, to come with her. The soldier stayed back by the wagon, lolling in the cool haven of the trees.

Katherine was greedy for the private moment, knowing that another busy, brutal day lay ahead. She put sorrows aside and enjoyed the excuse to brush her fingertips over Justis's skin and to study, up close, his boldly drawn features.

Looking at him always stole her breath, but she'd never thought of him as handsome. That description was reserved for sleek-faced men with aristocratic noses and delicate mouths. And yet she wouldn't change him. He was like the gold nugget that lay over his heart—unpolished, birthed from harsh elements, and incredibly special.

"This crease beside your mouth could be called a dimple," she said as she eased the razor over it. "I thought only dandies had dimples. There. Done."

He made a comical sound of disgust and opened his eyes. "I guess you like it, then, since you like dandies."

She was very close to him, and his taunt made her reckless. His head was still tilted back, his lips slightly parted. She lowered her mouth to his and kissed him slowly, catching him so much by surprise that he simply sat still and let her savor him with little flicks of her tongue.

She nuzzled his mustache and drew away just enough to break contact. Her pulse raced. "Thank you for yesterday," she whispered, gazing down into his heavy-lidded eyes. "And everything else."

He blinked languidly as she sat back. "I must be addled. I couldn't think fast enough to grab you."

She laughed, but when he leaned forward and his face came into a streak of sunlight, she grew quiet and frowned. "Let me look at you." She caught his chin and turned his face fully into the light. "Oh, it's just my imagination," she said finally. "I thought your skin was a little pale."

"I'm a paleface."

She shook her head. "Tanned like a nut, you are. But stay healthy, or I'll pour a foul-tasting tonic down you."

"I do feel a little strange," he said dramatically, laying a wrist on his forehead. "Put some tonic on your lips and I'll kiss it off like honey. Put it somewhere else and I'll—"

"You're most definitely not sick!" Laughing, she got up and hurried away.


KATHERINE WOKE UP with dew on her face and the unpleasant sense that something was wrong. She turned over on her blanket and studied Justis, lying next to her with an arm flung behind his head.

Like her, he was fully dressed, and the night was too hot to warrant any other covering. Moonlight showed that he had pulled the tail of his shirt from his trousers.

In sleep he had wrenched the shirt up, revealing a swath of bare skin above his belt. She watched the rise and fall of his stomach.

The rhythm was abnormally fast, she thought. She eased her hand onto the lean, muscled terrain covered in soft hair. His skin was damp, but whether from dew or sweat she couldn't tell. Worried, she slid closer to him and laid her hand on his forehead. He jerked awake and grabbed her wrist, twisting it in a deliberate attempt to hurt.

"Let go, it's Katherine!" she said in his ear.

"Katie." He brought her mauled wrist to his mouth and kissed it. "Sorry." Then he exhaled with a long, weary sound. "Strange dreams. Can't remember 'em."

"Do you feel all right?" She touched her fingers to his forehead again, then to his jaw. The skin was cool.

"Yeah. Sure." Abruptly he slid an arm around her shoulders and pulled her close. "Now I feel even better."

Katherine debated for a few seconds, then gave up and rested her head on his shoulder. But she tucked her uppermost arm between his side and her breasts and kept her legs pinched together at the knees and ankles, not touching his.

He chuckled, the sound rumbling warmly under her ear. "I'm gonna sleep a helluva lot better than you do, unless you relax."

"Oh, be quiet, scoundrel." She sighed with disgust but draped her arm over his chest and edged one knee atop his thigh. Then she sighed again, this time with pleasure. Nature must have designed women to sleep next to men this way, she mused, because it was perfect.

Barely three paces from them a husband and wife stirred sleepily. Katherine could see them without raising her head. She lay in breathless dread as they nuzzled each other and whispered love words in Cherokee.

The woman lifted her skirt and the man pushed his trousers to his thighs. He got to his knees and raised the hem of his hunting shirt. Katherine could see the dim outline of his jutting arousal. He stretched out on his wife and she circled him eagerly with her legs as he thrust into her, groaning softly.

Katherine trembled. She wasn't shocked—there was no privacy in the stockade, and people were forced to love as well as die in public. It was also true that no matter what the missionaries had taught them, Cherokees simply weren't prudish about sexual matters. Men and women were meant to enjoy each other.

No, she wasn't shocked, but she wasn't certain this was a wise thing to watch with Justis. He was likely to think the pastime worth copying.

She would not, she told herself, take him with her back against the hard earth and hundreds of people around them. Not for their first joining, at least.

Katherine bit her lip. Oh, no, no. She couldn't think in hopeful terms such as those. They were a dream with no future, even if General Scott said she could stay in Gold Ridge. She was sure Justis had rethought his impulsive offer of marriage, and she couldn't bear to become his mistress while knowing that one day he'd take someone else as his wife.

Even if he did make his reckless, dutiful offer again, she wouldn't take it. A white man could never be fully accepted by his own people as long as he had an Indian wife. Justis's devotion might turn to regret as time passed. That possibility was too tormenting for her to risk it.

The husband curled his wife's hands above her head and held them as he arched into her faster. Her cry of delight was muffled against his shoulder, and he buried his face in her hair as his body curved in one last, nearly violent lunge. Then he slumped atop her, and she stroked his shoulders affectionately.

Within a minute they lay side by side again, asleep. Katherine realized that her hand was stroking Justis's chest through his shirt and that her leg had inched farther across him. She was rubbing her thigh against his.

She raised her head to look at him. To her amazement he was asleep, too, though he frowned harshly and his breathing was still too fast. Even in the moonlight his face looked drawn with fatigue, and when she felt the moisture on his forehead, she knew this time it was sweat, not dew.

Don't let him fall sick with a fever, she prayed. She moved up and put her arms around him, then cradled his head against her chest. He stirred, burrowing his face into the soft valley of her breasts. She fell asleep holding him that way.

KATHERINE WAS TOO frantic to ask anyone's permission. The guards lazed on the ground in the broiling afternoon sun, but as soon as she strode boldly through the gate they leapt up and surrounded her.

"I need to see Captain Taylor immediately," she told the lieutenant in charge.

"He's gone to town, miss. He probably won't be back until after dark."

"Mr. Gallatin is very ill," she said as calmly as she could. "I thought I could treat him here, but I can't. He needs to be taken out of the heat."

"I can't authorize that until the captain returns."

She drew her chin up and gave him a commanding look. "Do you want one of Gold Ridge's leading citizens to die in a Cherokee stockade because you refused to help? What will General Scott say when he hears how you've treated a white civilian?"

The lieutenant paled beneath his sunburn. "I'll send a messenger for Captain Taylor right now."

Katherine went back inside the stockade and wound her way among the lean-tos until she reached the one she'd rigged, with the help of friends, for Justis. He lay sleeping restlessly in the sparse, hot shade, his face flushed an unnatural color.

He'd insisted all day that he felt fine, despite the fact that he had no appetite and was noticeably tired. Stubborn! she thought now, sinking to her knees beside him. Her throat clogged with tears.

He'd followed her around the stockade, doggedly helping her as he had during the other days, until finally he'd leaned against a wall, remaining there until he had slumped to the ground, half conscious.

Even then, when men were carrying him to a shady spot, he kept muttering that he wasn't going to leave her. Katherine cupped her hands into a tin bucket and smoothed water over his forehead. His eyes fluttered open.

"What's wrong with me, gal?" he asked.

"Oh, not much," she said lightly. "You're a white man who's caught an Indian fever, that's all. As soon as I get you back to town you'll be fine."

"Feel like I'm roasting from the inside out."

She clenched her teeth. The damned captain had better hurry or she'd show his men how much war a Cherokee woman could wage. She bent over Justis and wiped sweat from his neck. "I'm going to undress you. Nobody here will care whether you're clothed or not, and at least you'll be cooler."

He smiled weakly. "So I have to get dog-pukin' sick to make you undress me?"

"I'm a doctor. I'll try not to gape."

"Go ahead. Gape."

She removed everything except his shirt, which covered him to mid-thigh. "I'll leave you some dignity."

"Hope you're impressed."

She glanced down at long, muscular legs and thought of the soft but amazingly large bulge her hand had brushed as she unbuttoned his trousers. "You'll do." She touched the fiery skin of his face. "I'm going to rinse you off. You'll feel better."

He shut his eyes and nodded. "Couldn't feel worse."

She dipped a rag into the bucket and wiped his head and neck, then did each leg from thigh to foot. When she was through she sat back on her heels and gazed at his cotton shirt for a moment. If he didn't mind, why should she? She lifted the shirt hem to his waist and quickly covered his groin with a cloth.

"Well, that's no howdy-do," he mumbled, his voice faint. "Didn't you like the looks of it?"

She laughed miserably. She hoped his bawdy teasing meant he was stronger than he seemed. "I've not had anything to compare it to, but I'd say you deserve your vain Cherokee name, Stud."

"It's a prizewinner."

"Here, lift your arms so I can get the shirt off." When it was a struggle for him to obey, she felt like crying. She finally got the shirt and wiped it across her damp eyes. "You are indeed the hairiest *a-Yu-ne-ga* I've ever seen. But it's a very beautiful pelt."

She smoothed a wet rag over his chest and stomach, watching their erratic movements as he breathed. Water pooled in his navel and in the slight indentations of several small scars on his abdomen. She brushed it away with her fingertips.

"Playin' in my fur, are you?" he murmured, his eyes still shut.

"How did you get these?" she asked, touching the scars.

"Man tried to carve me with a rusty old sword."

"I assume you broke the sword and the man's neck."

He managed a faint look of amusement. "Nope. I was only half growed at the time. Maybe eight years old."

She fought the whimper of anguish that rose in her throat. "Rest," she whispered. She sat down by his side and fanned him with a paddle made of reeds from the riverbank. "I'll have you out of here soon."

"Don't let 'em steal my heart and eat it," he said, his voice trailing away in sleep. "The Cherokee witches."

She cried and smiled. "I'll keep it safe. I swear. I've got my hand over it."

IN ALL HIS weeks of watching Katherine Blue Song wrestle with death and sickness at the stockade, Captain Taylor had never seen fear in her eyes. But now he saw it —stark, almost wild. And mixed in with it, as she looked up at Amarintha Parnell in the wagon Amarintha had hastily commandeered, was hatred.

"He's no good to you dead, Miss Parnell," she said fiercely. "The doctor in town doesn't know half what I know about treating these fevers."

Amarintha pursed her mouth and fluttered a hand over her heart. "You want your freedom, and this is a very convenient way to demand it, isn't that so? Well, Justis will be perfectly fine as soon as someone other than a heathen Indian woman is caring for him."

Taylor shifted awkwardly as Miss Blue Song shot him a desperate look. Damn, he was hot for Amarintha— even if she had her eye on Gallatin—but he hated to play the villain. He could probably let this determined squaw go back to town with Gallatin; he could overlook the governor's orders under the circumstances and no one would care, not even the general. Well, no one but Amarintha would care.

"I'm sorry," he told Katherine. "You can't leave the stockade. But I assure you that Mr. Gallatin will get the finest attention. In fact, wouldn't you feel better if a real doctor looked after him? If he died while under your care, there might be trouble."

"He'll die under that fool's care in town!"

"I'm sorry, Miss Blue Song," he said again, watching

her warily. She seemed very close to violence. "You can discuss your case with General Scott tomorrow." Taylor motioned to several men. "Go get Mr. Gallatin and bring him to the wagon."

She latched a hand onto the wagon and looked up at Amarintha. "You're jealous for no cause. I'm not interested in Mr. Gallatin for personal reasons. He's been a good friend to me and I don't want him to die. You can *have* him, Miss Parnell, after he's well. I'll be going west. But please, please, don't take him out of my care right now."

Amarintha sighed as if thinking. "Captain, excuse the bad language I'm about to use." She bent down so that her face was inches from Katherine's and asked softly, "Don't you think I know the kind of nasty things you savages do with men? You can't keep your hands off them; you'd just as soon lay down for this one as the next. Mr. Gallatin is not just your friend, you lying squaw. He's like any other man—he'll take whatever's easiest to get, be it white or Indian. Well, you may have gotten him into your bed, but I won't let you ruin him for decent society."

She sat back and smiled with unnerving ease. "I'm waiting, Captain."

Taylor glanced toward the stockade gate and saw his soldiers carrying the unconscious Gallatin out on a blanket. Though another blanket covered him, it was obvious he was naked.

"What have you done to him, you female devil?" Amarintha demanded. "You're filthy, *filthy*!"

Katherine grabbed a buggy whip from the wagon seat and drew it back to strike the mules. "Hold on, Miss Parnell, because you're going for a ride straight to hell." She swung the whip.

Taylor reacted as he thought any gallant ought to, given the threat to his lady. He leapt forward and landed a fist in Katherine's temple. She fell against the wagon and slumped to the ground while soldiers grabbed the reins of the startled mules.

"Oh, this is the most dreadful thing!" Amarintha cried. "Please, let's take Mr. Gallatin away from this awful place."

Breathing heavily, already ashamed of what he'd done to the woman who lay at his feet with her incredible black hair strewn around her in the dust, Taylor yelled, "Load that man in the wagon, dammit!"

The soldiers put Gallatin onto a mattress in the back. He moved his head weakly and frowned. Taylor climbed into the seat beside Amarintha and took the reins. "Carry that woman to her friends and see that they look after her!"

Taylor felt justified but sick as he drove away with Amarintha's small hand patting his arm soothingly. He looked back and saw one of the soldiers dragging Katherine Blue Song's limp body into the stockade.


KATHERINE SAT IN a shady spot by the stockade wall, her head back and eyes shut. Her temple ached this morning, but not as badly as it had during the night. No, today she had a clear mind, and all she could think about was Justis. She heard running feet and looked up to see Sam dashing across the crowded compound toward her. His eyes filled with distress at her disheveled appearance and swollen face.

"God in heaven! How are you?" He squatted beside her and she grasped his arms.

"How is Justis?"

He exhaled wearily. "Not good. Amarintha has him hidden away at her house and I couldn't get in to see him until this morning. The damned doctor keeps bleeding him."

She wailed softly. "That's no help! It will only make him weaker! Sam, get me out of here."

"The general's arrived. Let's go see him."

He helped her up while she anxiously tried to straighten her hair and clothes. "I don't look very impressive, Sam."

"Just be yourself. I think the general will be smitten."

General Winfield Scott, a tall, imposing veteran who favored long sideburns and fine uniforms, very much deserved his nickname, Old Fuss and Feathers. As Katherine sat across from him in the rough little cabin that served as the stockade's headquarters, she was shocked to learn that he was sympathetic to the Cherokees' plight, and hers.

"I'm willing to let you go about your business in town," he told her, stroking his sideburns, "as long as Mr. Kirkland here will be responsible for you."

"Yes, sir," Sam said quickly. "My wife and I will look after her."

"Thank you, General," Katherine added.

He shook his head. "But I can't allow you to stay permanently. When the others go west, you'll go with them."

She nodded. "I'm just happy to be free for the moment."

"What is this Mr. Gallatin to you? Common-law husband?"

"No. A dear friend."

"Let me warn you, I'm tired of white families trying to sneak their Cherokee in-laws past me. If you've got any idea of marrying him so that you can stay here, it won't do you any good. If you marry him, he'll have to go west with you."

Katherine gave him a pensive smile. "I understand. I have no intention of marrying Mr. Gallatin."

The general studied her shrewdly, then nodded. He crossed the small room to a crude plank desk. After a minute of careful writing he handed a sheet of paper to an orderly waiting nearby. "Put my seal on that and give it to Miss Blue Song."

General Scott bowed to her. "That order will keep your freedom for you until the march begins. I wish you well, Miss Blue Song. And I hope you're able to do some good for your friend."

She curtsied. "I hope so, too, sir. Thank you." She turned and ran for Sam's buggy.


AMARINTHA STOOD IN the door to her home like a fierce pink tiger.

"Mr. Kirkland, I will not let that woman in this house!"

Katherine tried to step around Sam, but Rebecca shoved past them both and confronted Amarintha nose to nose. "My dear Amarintha, do you know how many times I've seen you take liberties with the merchandise in my store? How many times I've said nothing when you've tucked a packet of pins into your sleeve or hidden a ribbon under your bonnet?"

"I have never!"

"You most certainly have! And if you don't let Miss Blue Song upstairs to doctor Mr. Gallatin, I'll send your father a bill for everything you've stolen!"

"Sweet baby?" a booming voice called from the back of the house. "Do we have guests?"

Amarintha's eyes glowed bitterly as she stared past Rebecca at Katherine. "Yes, Daddy, we do."

The judge strode down the hall, smiling, and asked what the problem was. Sam explained, and Amarintha's face took on a shuttered, almost fearful expression. The judge looked down at his daughter thoughtfully.

"You've grown too fond of Mr. Gallatin, dear. I think you're being overly concerned for his health." He looked at Katherine. "Young woman, he's called for you more than once. That's the only reason I can absolve myself of responsibility for his well-being. You may work your Indian medicine on Mr. Gallatin if you like. But if he dies, remember this—you'll be liable for a murder charge."

Katherine nodded brusquely. "He won't die. Where is he?"

Amarintha was shivering with a strange combination of fear and anger. "Well, come along, then, squaw," she said, and pivoted grandly. "Follow me. He's upstairs."

Katherine pushed ahead of her and took the stairs at a run. When she reached the landing she headed instinctively for the one door that stood open. Stepping into the shuttered, airless room, she gasped at the smell of sweat and stale air.

Justis lay in the center of the bed, unconscious, his arms and chest bare above several heavy quilts. She dropped her satchel on a chair and went to him, throwing back the suffocating quilts until there was only a sheet left.

She put her hands on his face and groaned at the feel of dry, hot skin. Glancing at the marks left by the leeches the doctor had placed on his arms, she cursed out loud.

His eyes flickered. "Hullo, Doc." His voice was a rough croak, but he almost managed to smile. She sat beside him and took his head between her hands. He looked up at her with such welcome that she kissed him.

"Don't spread your lustful poison in my house," Amarintha said from the doorway. "I'll be watching you."

Katherine stared at her. "Get out of this room and stay out, or Miss Blue Song will sing merrily."

Amarintha's eyes narrowed as she realized Katherine meant that she would tell Justis every detail about the scene at the stockade. Her spirit crumpled visibly and she looked, to Katherine's surprise, like a child who'd been whipped. "No need to sing," she said in a dejected tone, and left.

Katherine forgot her immediately and gazed back at

Justis. "I'm going to take care of you now, you scoundrel. And you're going to get well."

He struggled for a moment with parched, tight lips before he whispered, "And then you're going to marry me."

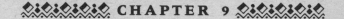 

## CHAPTER 9

I<small>T WAS</small> nighttime, Justis decided, though he was too tired to turn his head toward the windows Katie had opened. He could smell the cool, green earth scent of darkness, and when he opened his eyes he found himself squinting at a bright, blurry shape on the night table. The shape became a flickering oil lamp.

"I didn't mean to wake you."

Ah. Katie's voice, low and soothing. Her hands, strong, gentle, rubbing something cold on his chest and belly, something that made him feel less like a rock heating in the sun. But her voice hadn't always been soothing, nor her hands gentle.

More than once during the day she had scolded, bossed, even yelled at him, calling him names—lazy and a coward and a stupid, stubborn ox—whenever he refused to open his mouth for another awful concoction. Her abuse made him so mad that he took the drinks just to end it.

And the cat had used her damned claws on him! Each

time he had tried to shove her and her piss-sour drinks away, she had pinched one of his ears until the pain penetrated his feverish haze.

It was only now, as his mind began to clear a little, that he remembered all the sweet apologies she had offered after he did as she ordered. He frowned as he felt the night air on his legs and groin. She had uncovered that part of him to rub the blessed cooling ointment on every inch of his skin.

"Don't like it," he muttered, trying to lift his head. "You seein' me so ugly, helpless. Unmanly."

"Shhh. Helpless, yes. Ugly or unmanly, no. You're very handsome. *Très beau.*"

"Speakin' French. Must be the truth." His tongue felt swollen. "Talk to me. Tell me. Real name."

Her hands paused on the thick muscles of his thigh. "My Cherokee name? That's powerful medicine. Not many people know it." She paused, then added in a hollow tone, "Most of them are dead."

"Must be bad luck, your name."

She gasped with surprise, then realized he was teasing. Her fingers pressed warmly into his leg. "You're feeling better. Thank God."

"Hmmm." He managed to crane his neck and squint at her. Words, confused and emotional, tumbled through his hazy mind. "I'd like to eat you."

"You'd get a mouthful of dirt and sweat."

He let his head fall back on the pillow. "Com'ere. Lemme taste."

"Shhh."

His strength had grown enough that he could grasp her arm and hold on tightly. "Here, gal."

"All right," she said in exasperation. She moved closer and he pulled her arm to his mouth.

He licked the skin and gazed at her woozily. "Hmmm. I like that. Do you like that?"

"Yes," she admitted sadly. Slowly she bent down and

kissed his cheek. Her lips brushing his ear, she murmured, "Katlanicha is my real name. It means 'She Sees Dreams.' "

"Katlanicha," he repeated, his throat making the name sound hoarse and raspy. "Thank you."

"Don't use it to conjure spells against me. I'm your *a-tsi-na-Ha-i*, your captive, already." Again the sadness radiated through her words.

He held the back of her hand against his cheek and shut his eyes. Damn the world for putting so much trouble between them, he thought. He struggled sleepily for a way to express his frustration. "I wish you were white. Everything would be so easy if you were white."

He drifted off as she slid her hand from his grasp.

KATHERINE HEARD FOOTSTEPS on the stairs and stiffly raised her head from the back of a thinly upholstered chair. Her neck still ached from the force of Captain Taylor's blow.

Amarintha came to the open door and stopped, peering inside at Justis, who slept fitfully. She clutched a ruffled pink robe over a matching nightgown. Her red-gold hair streamed from under a pink nightcap. She had cried so much that her face matched her outfit.

"Is he better?" she asked in a small, timid voice.

Katherine stared at her. Did this mean-spirited creature feel sincere concern? "His fever's lower, I think."

"May I come in?"

Katherine wanted to say no, but the expression in Amarintha's eyes was pitiful. Bewildered by this new side of her, she nodded. "Of course."

Amarintha padded inside and sat on the footstool near Katherine's chair. She gazed at Justis woefully. "He can't die. Please don't let him."

"I don't think he will." Jealousy churned in Katherine's chest, but she knew she had to ignore it. "Do you love him?" she asked.

Suspicion clouded Amarintha's eyes. "I'll not tell my feelings to you."

"Tell. They'll be a secret between us. What would be wrong with saying that you love Mr. Gallatin?"

Amarintha thought for a moment. Her gaze darted to the open door, then she said in a low voice, "My father forbids it."

"Loving Mr. Gallatin? Your father isn't wise, then."

"No. Loving anyone."

Katherine was startled. She watched Amarintha twist knots in the ruffles of her robe. "What about Captain Taylor? Isn't he in favor with your father?"

A tight, desperate laugh burst from Amarintha's throat. "The captain hasn't the gumption required. No man has." Her eyes hardened. "Except Justis."

"Doesn't your father want you to marry?"

"Oh! Oh, certainly!" Her hands wadded the material with malicious intent, but she smiled. "What a fool you are to ask such a question."

Katherine wondered at the strange contrast between Amarintha's smile and her nervous, angry hands. She recalled how Justis had said the fourteen-year-old Amarintha had spat on him and smiled.

Now the pink face became sad again. "I'd have married Justis long ago, except for those women of his." She cut her eyes at Katherine. "He took up with two of your kind, you know. Over at the Talachee village. Daddy said he was as good as married." She paused. "But now the dirty squaws are gone."

Justis groaned and passed a hand over his eyes. Katherine rose and went to his side, welcoming the excuse to get away from Amarintha. The girl's control seemed brittle, and her cruelty held a puzzling amount of fear, as if it were self-defense. Katherine stroked the thick chestnut hair off Justis's forehead, and he grew still. He was sweating a little—a sign that his fever was breaking, she hoped.

Amarintha came to the foot of the bed and watched as Katherine smoothed his shaggy hair. "Is he big?" she asked, scanning the form of his body under the thin sheet. "You know—his nasty man-part?"

Katherine studied her in quiet shock. It wasn't the question that perturbed her, it was the tone of loathing. Suddenly she wanted to protect Justis from this woman's less-than-admiring scrutiny. She casually pulled a blanket up to his waist. "You should ask him yourself."

"No decent woman can ask a man that. Tell the truth. Does he hurt you with it?"

Katherine swallowed her nausea. Amarintha's curiosity had a perverse edge. "I've never lain with him. I swear it." Downstairs a clock chimed three times. "It's near morning. Go back to bed and try to rest. Your wits are shaken by worry, I think."

"No." The pink mouth curled sardonically. "If he hasn't stuck it in you yet, he will. I know men. But he won't marry you just to get between your legs. He'd be a fool to marry an Indian."

Katherine grimaced. Was there no way to get rid of this odd, disturbing woman? "I agree," she said brusquely. "And he may be reckless at times, but he's never a fool. Besides, I wouldn't marry a white man. I won't bring half-breed babes into the world to be scorned by both sides."

"Not even if you loved the man something dreadful?"

Katherine winced inwardly. Amarintha would probably act even more strangely if she suspected the truth. "I don't love Mr. Gallatin, and I never could. I want a man with education and sensitivity, someone who appreciates the finer things, not some backwoods scalawag. Oh, Mr. Gallatin is very kind and likable, but he's not my type at all."

"Well, I declare, you certainly take on airs. Justis is better than you deserve."

Good, Katherine thought. She was defending him now. "Then you may have him. Later. For now, go back to bed before our chatter wakes him up. He's resting better than he has all day."

Amarintha nodded. Her blue eyes held a hint of respect along with the dislike. "Good night."

After she left, Katherine took the blanket off Justis and straightened the sheet. She ached to slip into bed beside him and hold him close.

"Sleep well," she murmured. "In an hour you get another dose of medicine. For me there's another dose of cold coffee waiting downstairs—right this second." Exhausted, her knees so weak that she stumbled, Katherine walked from the room.

Justis opened his eyes and watched her go. Her conversation with Amarintha rang bitterly in his ears.

KATHERINE LAID HER book down and turned from the afternoon sunlight as she heard Justis shoving his covers around. "Stop that," she commanded, going to him quickly.

He cursed in a sleepy voice that was growing stronger by the hour and pushed the heavy quilts down his chest. "What are you tryin' to do—boil me now that I'm done roastin'?"

She pried his hands off the quilts and held them snugly across his torso. He was drenched in sweat. "Your fever is breaking. I want you to perspire—and I don't want you to catch a chill."

He quieted, panting a little because he was still very weak. "Let go. All right. I'll stay covered." She rearranged the quilts. "Leave me alone. Go on with your damned fancy readin'. You've done enough."

Surprised by his anger, she gazed at him in bewilderment. "I don't mind."

"You look like a hag. Big ugly circles under your eyes. Hell, what are you doin', sleeping on one side of your head all the time? Looks like one side's swollen."

She backed away from the bed, shocked by his mean temper. "I think the fever fried your brains a bit."

"No, I just don't want you killin' yourself to take care of me. You don't owe me that. There's no bond that strong between us."

"Oh, I see. After all that you've done for me, I'm not supposed to return the favor."

"Have I ever asked you to hang over me like I was your dearly beloved?"

After a startled second, hurt and anger welled up inside her. "No."

"Then don't."

"Fine. I'll ask Amarintha to feed you dinner, and I'll go back to the hotel for a while."

She heard him sputtering as she went out the door.

Katherine waited until nearly dark before she left the hotel and hurried back to the Parnells' house. She encountered a flushed, disheveled Amarintha at the entrance.

"What did you do to him?" Amarintha demanded angrily. "He tried to kiss me! When I bent over to wipe chicken broth off his cheek he grabbed my hair and pulled my mouth nearly to his! If I hadn't knocked the bowl of broth onto his—his person, he would have had me!"

She whirled without waiting for an answer and fled to the judge's library at the back of the house. The judge, thankfully, was out drinking for the evening. Katherine marched upstairs, frowning while anxiety settled heavily in her chest.

Justis sat upright in bed, his face flushed with exertion as he wearily tried to wipe broth off his chest with the corner of a quilt. When he saw her he attempted to look nonchalant. "Didn't expect you back so soon."

She grabbed a small towel and wet it at the washstand. Her mouth grim, she went to him, pushed his fumbling hands away, and began to wipe up the broth. Under the thick reddish-brown hair his skin was ruddy from being burned.

"I guess Amarintha told you what happened."

"She said you tried to kiss her." Katherine went back to the washstand, rinsed the cloth carefully, and returned to him. She continued her cleaning without another word.

"You don't care?" he muttered.

"I care that you're being a first-rate jackass for some reason I don't understand."

"I'm just a lot less needy than you think. I don't have to have one woman in particular."

"Well, grand. Now you've got no woman, no dinner, and a scalded chest." She threw the towel on the nightstand and began checking the covers. "And you've got broth all over your sheets. Well, I'd meant to change them anyway. If you're strong enough to pester Amarintha, you're strong enough to get out of bed for a few minutes."

"I don't feel like it."

She whipped the covers back and haughtily surveyed his nakedness. "Phew. *U-ne-gi-li-di*. Ugly. I'll get a quilt to hide the sight of all that hairy skin."

The language that came from his mouth was more scalding than hot broth ever could be. Trembling with weak rage, he shoved his feet off the bed. When she came back with the blanket he snatched it out of her hands and drew it around his waist. He was panting for breath.

"Go ahead, make yourself sick again," she said bitterly.

"You cold-hearted hellion!"

He braced his feet and used one hand to give himself a violent push upward. He stood, swayed dizzily, and immediately careened backward against the tall bedstead. As he slid to the floor, Katherine cried out in dismay and caught him by the shoulders. His teeth began to chatter.

"Oh, Justis, damn you for making me be a jackass too." She dragged a quilt from the bed and put it over his shoulders. He gave her a disgruntled look, but she knelt and slipped her arms around him anyway. "Be still. Rest a minute," she whispered hoarsely. Defeated by his illness, he muttered an oath, then laid his head on her shoulder.

They didn't speak anymore. She got up finally and changed the bed, then helped him back into it. When he was warmly covered she sat down beside him and wiped a last bit of drying broth from his chest. All the while she was aware of him watching her with hooded, unhappy eyes.

"I'll bring you some more dinner," she told him.

"That silliness with Amarintha. Didn't mean nothing."

She looked at him firmly. "What are you trying to prove to me? Why are you angry?"

"I'm tired of gibbering with you over what's best to do. I've got no more sweet talk, Katherine. Let's get down to brass tacks."

"This is very serious," she said pensively. "You called me Katherine."

He nodded. "You've got something I want—culture and education—plus some basic attractions that I reckon I don't have to describe in detail. I've got something you want—Blue Song gold—plus some basic attractions that you're pretty familiar with after the past couple of days."

"All right. We've discussed this before."

"No. We've talked about marriage. I don't want to marry you anymore. I offered in the first place only 'cause it's what your folks would have liked. It's pretty clear that you aren't ever gonna want to marry me, or love me, so I don't feel guilty for takin' the offer back. White and Indian together brings too much grief. Are we agreed on that point?"

"Yes." She looked away, dying in slow degrees while she managed a neutral expression by biting her tongue until it bled. "And so?"

"So you go to New York with me. You teach me what I need to know about fancy manners, help me impress the business nabobs up there, and you'll walk away in a year or two a rich woman. Owned by nobody but yourself."

"You're asking me to be your mistress?"

"That's right."

"And what if we have a child from this arrangement?"

"We won't, if I can help it. I don't like the idea of raisin' a half-breed any more than you probably do." He looked at her grimly. "There's a way of being careful. All I have to do is keep myself under control until—"

"I understand." She managed a semblance of a smile. "I'm a doctor, you know."

"Then you're agreed?"

"What if I say no?"

A deadly stillness settled in his eyes. "Then you'll never get your share of gold. You'll always be my charity case—and I'll get you into my bed sooner or later, to boot."

"I suppose I accept, then."

She laughed. She bent over and touched her head to the covers and laughed until it became a soft wail. She began to choke, and tears slid down her face. He made a sound of distress and moved over enough to pull her onto the bed alongside him. His arm over her, he held her as tightly as his returning strength would allow. As she quieted, he kissed the top of her head, and his words were muffled in her hair.

"I was raised havin' to fight for everything I wanted. To fight dirty, to steal, to hurt other people without thinkin' about it too much. I know some of that's still in me. I don't care if you don't love me—I'm gonna have you anyway. This deal isn't what you want, but I swear to God that I wouldn't force you into it if I didn't think it'd serve you best in the long run."

She wiped her face. "I owe you so much. You've been kind in so many ways. I suppose you really do think this is kind too."

"You'll be happy." He exhaled in relief. "I'm glad you don't hate me."

They lay there quietly and she felt his chest move slower against her back. His breath cascaded onto her neck, warm and regular. He was exhausted, and she suspected he'd sleep soundly for hours now that the fever was gone.

She got up and very carefully slipped the leather necklace and its gold nugget from around his neck. She put the necklace around her own neck and hid it under her shirt. Then she kissed him gently on the mouth, taking care her tears didn't fall on his face.

"You're a scoundrel, but I love you dearly," she whispered. "Good-bye."

AMARINTHA KEPT GAZING about furtively, and Katherine knew she was afraid the judge would ride up at any minute. From the front porch of the Parnell house, she and Amarintha watched the doors of the square's brightly lit taverns and gambling halls.

"Oh, botheration," Amarintha said nervously. "Let's go ahead and get it over with."

They left the porch and walked a short distance from the house, to where the road narrowed and the forest began to close in on civilization. They turned off the road, their shoes crunching on dried leaves.

Katherine halted after a dozen paces. "I'll be hidden well enough here. Tell Captain Taylor to stop his buggy near the big walnut tree with the bent trunk." She set her valise and doctor's satchel down, then pulled her cloak tighter around her shoulders. "I'll be waiting."

Amarintha gasped when an owl screeched nearby. "I'll tell him." She peered at Katherine in the darkness. "You'd better be pleasant to him. This is a great favor he's doing."

Katherine laughed bitterly. "Dear girl, I'm doing *him* the favor. Since I'm leaving town, Justis will never find out that the captain struck me. I'm sure Captain Taylor is happy to escape the worst beating of his life."

Amarintha had known Taylor would be in town playing poker. She'd sent for him, and when he'd learned what she wanted, he had definitely looked pleased. No, he didn't want anyone telling Justis Gallatin about the scene at the stockade.

Katherine studied the nervous woman beside her. "I appreciate your help."

" 'Tis my pleasure."

"I'm sure. I knew that no one else would be so eager to get me out of town."

"You're very right."

Desperation made strange companions, indeed, Katherine mused. Amarintha had gone to the hotel and stuffed a valise with some of Katherine's clothes and personal items, plus a small pouch of gold coins. She'd explained to Sam and Rebecca that Katherine would be staying at the Parnells' for several days, while Justis recuperated.

"Remember what we discussed," Katherine warned. "In the morning you're to tell everyone that I was in Justis's room reading a book when you went to bed. You don't know where I disappeared to after that."

"Don't lecture me, you arrogant savage! Of course I'll remember!"

Katherine fought for patience. Through the trees she glimpsed a lamp burning in a window of the Parnell house. She was torn apart by the knowledge that Justis lay sleeping in that house and that she would never see him again.

She spoke to Amarintha as pleasantly as she could. "I just want you to realize that Mr. Gallatin will track me down if he has any idea where I've gone. Not because he cares for me but simply because he considers me his property and his responsibility. If you let slip where I've gone, and he finds me, it won't do a bit of good for your romantic designs, will it?"

"You regard your charms too highly. I'm sure he'll be relieved to be free of you."

"Don't risk it."

Amarintha thought for a moment, then said peevishly, "Well, go farther, then. Don't stop in Tennessee."

"I have to find what few relatives I have left. They'll probably be at one of the stockades there. Don't fear, Amarintha, I'm not coming back. I'll head west with the rest of my people."

Suddenly Amarintha's curiosity exploded. "I don't understand why! Why are you giving up? If it's a trick, I'll—"

"It's no trick," Katherine retorted. "And my reasons are none of your business. You want me to go, and I'm going. Let that be enough for you."

"Be sure you never come back!" Amarintha whirled toward the road. When she reached the edge of the woods she turned and stood braced as if for battle. "I'm going to marry Justis Gallatin! You needn't doubt it! I'll be his wife and no one will ever cause me misery again!" Then she fled toward home as if the forest had been listening.

Katherine slumped to her knees, trembling inside her cloak. Justis would marry someone, but it wouldn't be strange little Amarintha Parnell, who could barely stomach a man's touch.

She looked again toward the light of the Parnell house,

and her hands clenched in hopeless sorrow. Her family was gone, her home was gone. Though the land remained—and she believed it once more would be hers someday—that was no consolation now. All she could take with her were memories of an outrageous and unique man who'd captured part of her soul.

*No-wu, ge-ga,* one said politely, when it was time to leave. *Now I am going.*

*Hwi-lo-hi,* the host should answer just as politely. *Go, then.*

She gazed at the lamplight desperately. When it faded away, she was surrounded by darkness.

AH, KATIE WAS moving about the room. Justis could hear her. His eyes still shut, he took a deep breath of warm morning air full of sunshine, and it made him feel good. Today he'd get more of his strength back. Today he'd try to soften the blunt words he'd spoken last night.

He and Katie would be grand together—her infernal pride just wouldn't let her admit it. Eventually she'd cuddle up to the idea of marriage and half-breed babes and everything else. Maybe she'd even love him someday. He just had to coax her. By force, it seemed.

"Com'ere," he ordered, and lolled one arm out of bed. He curled his forefinger in a beckoning gesture. "See? I'm keepin' my eyes shut because I trust you won't take your scalpel to me after what I said last night. You want to, I know."

She had stopped moving. The ornery cat was standing across the room, he figured, trying to test his patience, as usual. "Dammit, you she-fiend, if you don't come over here I'll come get you. Do you want to see me bounce my nekkid ass on the floor again?"

Katie Blue Song would never have uttered the frantic gasp that answered his threat. Justis frowned and opened his eyes quickly. Amarintha tottered toward him, her eyes wide with distrust, her hands pressed to her mouth.

"Where's Katie?" he asked.

She stopped a safe distance from the bed and began to cry. "It's the most dreadful thing," she said in a choked whisper. "She's run away. Back to Philadelphia."

## CHAPTER 10

Autumn was magnificent in the misty blue Tennessee mountains, the *Tsacona-ge*, Place of the Blue Smoke. Katherine remembered them from her childhood, when her father had brought the family to great council meetings. The summer's drought hadn't weakened the mountain forests enough to dim their brilliant fall displays of red and gold, and the first autumn rains had swept the dust from them.

Now they looked like beautiful patchwork quilts draped over the mountains' rounded summits. Above them the sky was a crisp, clean blue dotted with puffy white clouds. Gazing up at them from the valley of the Hiwassee River, Katherine shivered with emotion. Their serene grandeur was a tragic contrast to the chaos around her.

The road was lined with wagons and ox carts as far as Katherine could see in both directions, and this was only one contingent of marchers—one of thirteen that had been organized within the tribe, each numbering about a thousand people. The rough lean-tos and huts of the now-empty prison camp had been set on fire. Embers and flames rose high in the air, eyed nervously by livestock that threatened to bolt at any moment.

Katherine wanted to cover her ears against the noise. Dogs barked; naked children ran squealing among the horses, then dodged their hooves; people shouted at one another, and a few swung fists. Those who had bartered their food rations for cheap whiskey were the worst offenders. One man stumbled drunkenly through a crowd, bellowing orders at a child he pulled behind him by the child's long braid.

People yelled at the small company of cavalry soldiers who would accompany them on the march. The soldiers, who understood little Cherokee, answered with rough shoves and vigorous oaths. The tribe had finally been allowed to take over supervision of the march, so the road was also clogged with mounted Cherokee police. Their long hair streamed from under their turbans as they galloped back and forth, trying to bring order so that the trek could begin.

The first contingent had left for the west at the beginning of the month. Several more had gone since, each following a few days after the last. People were gloomy but stoic. Most were just glad that the torturous days of imprisonment were over. Rumor had it that hundreds of Cherokees had died in the camps during the summer.

Today, for a few hours at least, people were too busy to think about death. They milled around the wagons, trying to decide who should ride and who must walk, since the army had been able to provide only one wagon for every twenty people. Katherine looked down at her dirty brogans. She'd bartered an ivory hair comb for them a month before, when her shoes wore out. She hoped the brogans would survive a thousand-mile walk.

Gone was the pretty calico dress she'd worn the night she left Gold Ridge; gone was the other dress Amarintha had packed in her valise; gone were her delicate white stockings and ruffled petticoats and drawers made of batiste. She'd kept two things—her doctor's satchel and the gold nugget she never took from around her neck. Everything else she'd traded for necessities—cooking utensils, blankets, and a skirt and tunic of coarse butternut-colored material that could withstand any hardship.

She smiled thinly. The tunic was cinched at her waist with a wide woven belt, a present from someone she'd doctored. Tucked in the belt was her most prized possession—a deadly sharp hunting knife. More than one enemy had backed away from its wicked steel blade.

In her first weeks at the huge Tennessee encampment she'd been alone among thousands of strangers, but, like before, word had soon spread about her doctoring skills. In September the Gold Ridge stockade had been emptied and its prisoners brought to Tennessee to await the big march with everyone else. The Gold Ridge Cherokees had greeted Katherine with great warmth, and soon she was known as Beloved Woman to others besides them.

Fame had its advantages. No one dared harm the Beloved Woman. Even the shamans, her professional competition, gave her respect. These days she rarely needed the knife for protection. But an honorary title hadn't won her a lighter backpack, she thought wryly, shifting the heavy bundle tied to her shoulders. She was often tired and hungry, but at least her sense of humor remained.

Above the squalling of babies and shouts of people she heard a small, stern voice. "The Beloved Woman did not wait for me!"

Katherine squinted through dust and sunshine at the child stomping toward her. His hair was gathered in two long plaits. He wore nothing but a long deerskin shirt that ended above his knees, and moccasins.

Squirrel was the son of traditionalists. He didn't speak English and had encountered very few white people before the soldiers came to drive his family from their farm in the mountains. He was of the Blue clan, so he was a distant cousin of Katherine's.

"I did not run away," she assured him. "I told your mother I would stay right here. You went to play and forgot about me. Where is your mother?"

Squirrel jumped over a small rock and bounded to a stop beside her. He tilted his head back and grinned. "She sits in the woods to nurse my sister. A soldier said he would let her drink from his bottle as long as she let him watch. So she is not hurrying."

Katherine kept her expression calm, while distaste soured her stomach. Walks Smiling was a drunk, and had been since her husband had sickened and died two months before. Katherine understood the need to escape pain—too many nights she slept in her own tears, thinking about Justis—but if Walks Smiling kept up this kind of behavior, she wouldn't live to reach the Indian territory beyond Arkansas.

Katherine took Squirrel's hand. "You wait with me."

A few minutes later Walks Smiling ambled out of the woods, her toddler, Little Bird, tucked in the crook of one arm. A young soldier followed, adjusting his britches in a way that told Katherine he'd done more than watch while Walks Smiling nursed her daughter.

"He will carry my pack," Walks Smiling called, pointing at the soldier. She was a small, pretty woman, still a little plump despite weeks of poor food. Her baggy woolen dress didn't hide the sensual sway of her hips, now accentuated by the whiskey.

Katherine said nothing. Grief had etched lines around Walks Smiling's eyes, and the shaming words of a kinswoman would only make those lines deeper. Walks Smiling waved to the soldier as he went to his horse and tied her bundle on its saddle.

"You should find one of those," she told Katherine, winking. "An *a-sga-Ya* who wants to carry your load."

Katherine shook her head. Thoughts of Justis burned

inside her. What had he done after she'd run away? Certainly he had looked for her, but by now he would have given up. Perhaps he had a new woman, maybe several women, to ease his anger and disappointment.

Her throat tightened. Today she would walk farther away from him, and every day afterward, for weeks and months, until she crossed the big river and left him behind in the Sun Land.

A chief rode down the line, his white-haired head lifted high as he held his pony to a slow, dignified walk. A plume of feathers bobbed in his turban, and below his hunting shirt he wore fringed leggings rather than army-issue trousers. Several young men rode behind him.

"Make ready to go!" they called. "We lead the way!"

Along the line people climbed onto wagons or took their children by the hand to walk. Soft wails went up from men and women alike. Shamans began to chant. Walks Smiling sank to the ground and drew her children to her, sobbing.

Katherine turned toward the southeast and the ancient mountains. Tears ran down her face. She thought of her family, of her home, and of Justis. *Good-bye, my beloved*, she said to all.

As the line began to move, thunder rumbled in the distance, though the sky was bright. It seemed a very bad omen.

REBECCA STOPPED ROCKING and laid her needlework down on her stomach. "You make a very fine table," she told the babe inside. "But I hope you come out soon."

The harsh patter of rain made her glance at the window in dismay and hitch her chair closer to the fire. A week before the weather had been beautiful, but now the dreary autumn rains had settled in for good. A cold wind whipped them, moaning under the eaves of the hotel. An early dusk darkened the already gray afternoon.

She pulled the lamp on the table beside her nearer, then resumed her work. Soon she would have to go check on Cookie's progress with supper. They had a full house tonight—ten boarders—so the table would be sagging with food.

Rebecca bit her lip. Nearly a full house. One room was never used anymore—Katherine's room. Her trunks and clothes remained there, just as they had been when she left three months before. As he had ridden off to Philadelphia, Justis had asked that they be kept that way. He had followed her as soon as his recuperation allowed, less than two weeks after her departure.

He had yet to return.

Rebecca put her needlework down once more and rubbed her forehead wearily, remembering his fury. It had frightened her, more so because it contained so much pain. Sam had told her privately that Justis had used terrible language about Katherine, and then had sworn he'd bring her back to be his doxy, just out of spite.

It wasn't spite, it was the most desperate kind of love, she'd told Sam. The kind that couldn't give up even when there was no hope. If Justis came back without Katherine, he'd be a ruined man. Sam had said pshaw to that notion. There wasn't a tougher hide around.

"I'm not talking about hide," she muttered now, as she had then. "I'm talking about *heart.*"

HE WAS HOME, not that it made a damn bit of difference to him, no more than the blood dribbling down the side of his face made a difference, nor the blood covering his knuckles.

Justis staggered out of the Gallatin-Kirkland Saloon, leaving a wake of awed miners, five of whom—the ones who had intended to beat him up while he was stinking drunk—lay on the floor groaning in pain. He *was* drunk, so drunk that he knew he wasn't going to care when he threw up.

Cold rain hit him in the face as he reeled off the saloon's porch. He patted Watchman's wet, muddy shoulder and cursed himself loudly for letting the weary stallion stand there loaded with gear. After all the weeks of travel, Watchman deserved better than that.

Justis held on to the saddle and bent forward, clutching his stomach. After he'd emptied it of half a bottle of whiskey, he sat down in the mud by Watchman's legs and looked around the town square.

Gold Ridge appeared the same as when he'd left. To hell with it. He wished he were anyplace else, and if he could think of a better place to be miserable, he'd go there.

"Got to start over," he said out loud. Dimly he realized that the crowd in the saloon had filtered outside to watch him. In fact, people had come out of the adjoining establishments to watch him.

Someone splashed through the rain and the mud toward him. "You organized your own welcome home party, I see," Sam yelled, bending over him.

Rain dripping in his eyes, Justis looked up his partner. "I didn't find her. Not nowhere, not any of the way between here and the whole goddamned state of Pennsylvania. That doctor in Philadelphia hasn't laid eyes on her since she left to come here. She's hid out. She knew I'd look for her."

"Come on, get out of the weather, friend." Sam ordered gently. He and another man helped Justis up.

"Don't mess with me. Take care of m'horse."

"I'll send Noah after him. Let's get you to the hotel."

Justis swayed. "That damned room," he said in a deadly soft voice, as new bitterness and pain washed over him. "That room full of her things. Yeah."

Now he knew where he could go to be even more miserable.

* * *

THE WEATHER HAD remained rainy for the past several weeks, and now that the march was so much farther north, sleet mingled with the rain. Katherine had gotten used to hearing her teeth chatter and to struggling through mud that made her feet feel like lead blocks.

When they made camp for the day she helped Walks Smiling get the children settled under a wagon, then went on her rounds, wearing a piece of heavy blanket wrapped around her head like a scarf and another blanket around her shoulders as a coat. She had given her gloves to a child, and she stopped frequently to warm her fingers over the cooking fires.

She could only dole out what few medicines the government made available, and those were only what the suppliers could scrounge from towns near the trail. Fevers and pneumonia were epidemic. A crew was kept busy digging graves each time the marchers camped for the night.

Katherine tried not to think about the fact that the journey was only a third finished. November had not yet ended. Thanksgiving, a holiday she had enjoyed while living in Philadelphia, had come yesterday. No one had noticed.


THE SOFT KNOCKING at the cabin door woke Justis from a groggy sleep. Fully clothed—the way he slept most nights because he got drunk before he got undressed—he rose from bed, shoved an untouched plate of biscuits onto a table, and carried his whiskey bottle to the door with him.

"Who the hell is it?"

A timid female voice answered. "It's a . . . a gift, Mr. Gallatin."

He swung the door open and glared down into the

fearful eyes of a dark-haired young woman. Lamplight cast her small shadow toward a black, windswept night. "Who sent you?" he demanded.

"Friends of yourn over to Pearl's house. They p-paid Pearl already. She sent me over fer the whole n-night. They says you n-need some cheerin' up r-real bad."

"Come in 'fore you shiver to death."

She stepped inside, hugging herself through a heavy shawl that covered a low-cut cherry-red gown. Justis slammed the door and she jumped. He eyed her angrily. Women. More trouble than they were worth. And this one was just a little bony nip. But a pretty one. She tried to smile. At least she had all her teeth.

"Don't be scared of me," he told her.

"I heerd that you got a bad temper."

"Not the kind that hurts women."

"Oh." She dropped her shawl on a chair, then surveyed the place with furtive glances. "It's sure warm and cozy in here." She stared at logs scattered around the stone hearth and whiskey bottles lying about the floor. "A mite messy, though."

"What's your name?"

"Franny."

"Well, Franny, I'm drunk. And I haven't had a woman since last spring. So maybe you're the best present anybody ever gave me."

"I'm sure good at my work. You wanta see?"

He squelched an urge to shrug, and nodded instead. Then he went to his bed in one corner and sat down with his back against the rough log wall. She removed her gown and stood by the fireplace wearing nothing but red slippers, black stockings, and red garters.

Justis directed her to turn around, to walk across the cabin, to stroke her breasts and thighs. She complied without the least bit of shyness and began to sway sensually under his intense, slit-eyed gaze.

All he would have to do was give a few more simple

orders and she'd be lying on the bed with her legs around him. He waited for the impressive hardness to grow between his thighs, and he cursed it when it didn't. This was what Katherine had reduced him to, Katherine and the liquor he drank every night to keep her face and voice out of his mind.

"I heerd that the Injun women used to call you The Stud," Franny said, and winked.

"Not anymore." He threw the whiskey bottle against a far wall and it shattered. Franny screamed. "Get dressed," he told her. "Don't go bug-eyed—I'm not turnin' crazy. Here." He reached into a trouser pocket and removed a five-dollar gold piece, which he tossed on the red heap of her gown. "You've a grand-lookin' pair of tits, Franny, but I'm too tired."

"You're what they says you are," she murmured in a frightened tone as she jerked her gown on and threw the shawl around it. "You're *cursed.*" She left the cabin without looking back.

Justis put his head in his hands and laughed cruelly.


"BELOVED WOMAN, my son needs you quick!"

Katherine felt a hand shaking her shoulder. For a second she fought the cruel intrusion of reality into her dream. She was safe in a world she'd never seen before, a world of balmy winds and treeless green hills dotted with cattle that were being herded by horsemen outfitted in the Mexican style. Justis was there—somewhere—if she could only find him.

"Beloved Woman, wake up!"

The coldness came back, mantled in freezing December wind. Katherine sat up, shivering. Her whole body ached from sleeping on the icy Kentucky ground. Squirrel and Little Bird were bundled next to her in the better blankets; Little Bird twisted fitfully and coughed. Walks

Smiling, her face no longer plump, curled herself against the toddler and cooed to her.

Katherine held two thin blankets around her shoulders and squinted at the woman who bent over her. Even in the shadows of the waning campfires the woman's face revealed terror.

"My baby," she said hoarsely. "He is jerking all over."

Katherine licked her lips in the hope that the chapped skin wouldn't break when she spoke. "Mother, I can do nothing but hold him and speak a sacred formula. I have no more white medicines and no more herbs."

"Your touch alone heals sometimes, Beloved Woman. I have heard people say so. Please come."

Squirrel stuck a small hand out of his blankets and grasped Katherine's hair. "Your helper will go too."

She kissed his grimy, chapped fingers. "My helper will stay and keep his mother and sister safe."

That flattery satisfied him, and he burrowed inside his blanket once more. Katherine stood weakly, giving her head and her empty stomach time to adjust to the new position. The wind seemed to push icicles through her worn skirt.

"*Hena,*" she told the woman gently. "Go."

Katherine followed her through the darkness of the sprawling camp, treading gingerly so that the blisters and cuts on her feet wouldn't start to bleed again. The brogans had fallen apart, and her crudely made moccasins were poor protection from sharp sticks and rocks. The woman who'd summoned her limped noticeably.

They reached an old wagon. In the light of the campfire beside it sat a squat man with skin the color of leather. His dirty turban was askew and his eyes were swollen slits. In his lap he held a toddler wrapped in the filthy remnants of a blanket. As Katherine watched, the child's eyes rolled back and its body convulsed violently. Its mother began to whimper.

"Greetings . . . Beloved . . . Woman," the man said

in a thick, slurring voice. He grinned at her as she knelt beside him and reached for the child. The odor of rotgut whiskey swept over her.

"Poor little one," she crooned to the child. She cuddled it to her chest and sat down close to the fire. Rocking back and forth to distract herself from the bitter cold and the pain in her chapped hands, she began to chant. A few seconds later the child relaxed, and its eyelids fluttered together.

"Thank you," the mother said softly.

Katherine closed her eyes for a moment, willing away a weariness that made her dizzy. She knew the convulsions would return, but she didn't say so. Instead, she handed the feverish child to its mother. The father rolled sideways and stretched out to sleep, his shoulders hunched under his thin coat.

"If the jerking comes back, rock the child as I did. The charm will keep working, and the jerking will go away soon."

"Thank you, thank you," the mother repeated. She handed Katherine a cold chunk of boiled bacon. Katherine accepted it and hobbled away.

A man called to her as she shuffled along. "Come here, long legs, and keep me warm." She looked straight ahead and kept moving. She wished she hadn't left her knife at her sleeping spot. "Come here!" he yelled louder. She heard someone shush him. "It's the Beloved Woman," the person said. "Be quiet."

"Forgive me," the rowdy called. She nodded and didn't slow her pace.

Squirrel's dark eyes gleamed at sight of the bacon. Walks Smiling shook her head—she vomited blood these days, and food had little appeal to her. Little Bird was too young to chew the meat and too feverish to want it. Katherine pulled Squirrel onto her lap and handed the precious bacon to him.

He tore into it. Grease ran down his chin and onto his

thin chest. She held him close while he fed her several pieces of the salty pork. "Enough," she told him. "You eat the rest."

"Did the Beloved Woman make the babe well?"

Her eyes stung. She knew that he'd seen too much death to be fooled. "No. The babe will travel to the Dark Land, just like the others."

"Do not cry," Squirrel said anxiously. He put his arms around her neck. "I forbid it."

She laughed raspily. "You give silly orders. You are truly becoming a man."

The next morning Katherine dug a trench in the icy ground a little distance from the road. Walks Smiling sat limply beside the shallow grave, holding Little Bird's body in her lap. Squirrel cut his long braids off and laid them across his sister's chest.

"Fly now, Little Bird," he whispered as Katherine wrapped the toddler's blanket around his shoulders. He limped away, his face wet with snow and tears.

His mother smiled. Blood rimmed her lips. "Her spirit has gone west. And we are following."

NOAH AND LILAC, both crying, huddled in bed with Rebecca. She kept one arm around their shoulders and cradled her sleeping babe in the other. Cold December sunlight filtered through the room's heavy drapes.

Her throat dry with fear, Rebecca listened to the clomping sounds of boots on wooden floors, then the door to their private parlor opening and closing. Sam walked wearily into the bedroom, bringing cold air with him as if it clung to his coat. She had never seen his face look so drawn and colorless.

Lilac wailed. "Did they whup Mr. Justis for shootin' that man?"

He nodded. Lilac wailed again and Noah snuffled noisily. Rebecca shut her eyes and murmured a prayer. Then, fighting tears, she shooed the children from the room. Sam took his daughter, grown restless from so much noise, and placed her in the cradle near the bed. He slumped into a chair and stared, hollow-eyed, at the floor.

"Was Justis lashed badly?" Rebecca asked in a choked whisper.

Sam nodded again. "But flogging's meant to humiliate a man more than it hurts him." He rubbed his eyes. "There was a good-size crowd. Men, women, even some children. The judge came to watch his sentence being carried out." He raised his head slowly to look at her. "Amarintha watched too."

Rebecca gasped. "What kind of heart does that creature own?"

"I don't know." He stared at the floor again, swallowing roughly. "She cried the whole time—but she never took her eyes away. It was almost as if the pain and blood fascinated her."

Rebecca covered her mouth in horror. "How did Justis get through it?"

Sam sighed. "Without a sound. They took his shirt off and chained his arms up—" He stopped abruptly, hearing her gag. "Forgive me."

She took a deep breath. "He just stood there silently through it all?"

"Yes. And he managed to walk back to the jail without help. A lot of people cheered him."

She made a small, broken sound. "What will become of him, Sam? He's gone to wrack and ruin."

"I don't know." His voice was a rough croak. "Thirty lashes and sixty days—maybe it's the only way to make him change."

She shook her head and said tearfully, "There's only one way to do that. Get Katherine to come back. And that won't happen."

*  *  *

AMARINTHA CREPT INTO the austere bedroom and padded to the massive bed that was its focus. The lamp beside it cast dancing shadows on the rumpled covers.

"Daddy?" she said sweetly.

The judge put his book down and looked at her in pleased surprise, his expression showing how rarely she visited his room. Usually she forced him to go to hers.

"Are you lonely, sweet baby?"

She pouted girlishly. "Yes." Settling beside him, she curled her feet under the hem of her pink robe. "I have to ask you a favor, Daddy."

His hand stretched out and idly stroked her arm. "Yes, baby?"

"I want you to let Mr. Gallatin out of jail."

"Sweet baby! He nearly killed a man."

"But everyone says it was self-defense, Daddy."

The judge chuckled. "But 'twas a senator's brother."

She laid a hand on his stomach and tugged playfully at his nightshirt. "People are saying that Mr. Gallatin is like an Indian. That he'll die if he's kept locked up."

"Bombast."

"Daddy? Couldn't you just . . . umm, order him to leave town for sixty days, until the gossip cools down?"

The judge snorted. "Justis Gallatin would rather die than skulk off like a whipped dog."

"I could talk to him." She crawled upward on the bed, pulled the covers back, and slid under them. Snuggling to the judge's side, she put her head on his shoulder. "I bet I could talk him into leaving town. Would you let me try?"

"Well, well," the judge murmured as her hand began raising his nightshirt. "This is a pleasant change of routine."

"Yes, Daddy? Please?"

He drew a soft, groaning breath. "I suppose I can't fault you for being an angel of mercy. All right, sweet baby, if you can talk sense into that sinner, I'll have him set free."

As her hand began its well-trained work, she smiled.

WIND SIFTED THROUGH spots in the cell's log walls where the chinking was poor. Justis shifted painfully on the rough straw mattress of his cot and cursed in disgust. Why didn't somebody just cut a window in this drafty grave and be done with it? At least he'd be able to see out while his arse froze off.

Two days gone. Fifty-eight left. Christmas, two weeks away, would find him here with nothing but the rats and a mean-tempered sheriff's deputy for company. Not that he was eager to celebrate the holiday. It would only make him wonder where Katherine was celebrating it. Probably in Philadelphia.

He hoped she'd been forced to go to the dandy for money. He hoped the dandy had made her suffer to get it. That'd be a right proper revenge—Katie Blue Song, who'd been too proud to accept a backwoods miner, forced to spread her legs for a dandy who wouldn't treat her half as well. He hoped she regretted what she'd given up. He hoped she choked on her Christmas pudding.

"Visitor," the deputy called. He swung the heavy plank door open and quickly peered inside to make sure Justis's booted foot was still chained to the wall.

At the sound of soft crying, Justis raised his head. Amarintha swept into the tiny cell, her voluminous pink skirt making her look like a human bell. She dabbed a handkerchief to her nose, and one gloved hand plucked nervously at a fur-trimmed cloak.

"I have fretted so because of you!" she exclaimed.

He sat up slowly, his back throbbing, and removed his hat. "I appreciate your worries, but I think you'd best go. If the judge—"

"He knows that I'm here. He agreed to it. I . . . I

have a negotiation to make." She came to him and laid a folded sheet of paper on the bed, then stepped back and clasped her hands together. "You know how deeply I hold you in my affections."

He cleared his throat. The last thing he wanted was crazy Amarintha mooning over him. "I've given up on bein' respectable. I'm done with it. You better look elsewhere for a husband."

"Oh, no, I won't do it! You can be saved, I'm certain." She shifted awkwardly. "If you'll demonstrate that you have a humble spirit, my father will reconsider your sentence."

Justis looked at her warily. "How so?"

"Would you agree to leave town? To be, in effect, banished for sixty days?"

"Hell, no!"

She shook her clasped hands at him. "I implore you. That paper I gave you is a decree written by my father. It says that you're to be released from jail if you agree to leave town temporarily. Go to Auraria. Or go down to Terminus and watch people build the railroads. In two months you can come back."

"And have every man in town say that I was too soft to serve my time in jail? No."

"But—but you'll not be fit for anything if you stay in this place!" She flung her hands about her. "You'll just keep moping until bitterness ruins you for decent pursuits! You might even die!"

He settled back on the mattress. "Good-bye, Amarintha. Come see me again sometime. Bring me some Christmas cookies. Don't put no poison in 'em."

Her frustration exploded. "You still lust after that Indian squaw! Oh, don't look mean-eyed at me. I know it's true!"

"Go home."

"You'll do anything to have her back, even if she despises you. You still want her!"

He slammed a fist into the mattress. "I'll not talk about her. Now, get on home."

"You wouldn't be ruining yourself over her if you thought every man between here and the Mississippi had used her by now! You'd forget her if you figured that she was walking the trail like all the other filthy Indians, taking handouts and lying on her back to barter for more!"

The stillness that settled within Justis simmered with a raw energy waiting to rip it apart. His heart pounded, but he leveled a quiet, killing gaze at Amarintha, whose mouth opened in speechless horror at what she'd revealed.

"Do you know where Katie went?" he asked, his voice soft and deadly. "Have you known all along?"

"She—she made me promise not to tell! She said awful, ugly things about you! She hates you!" Amarintha gulped for breath. "She said she'd rather die than be with a stupid white man such as you!"

He rose, his hands clenched. "Did she go west? Is she on the trail with the other Cherokees?"

Amarintha made a high-pitched sound of utter fury. "Yes!"

Justis turned toward the door and bellowed, "Deputy!"

"I'll tell my father! He'll change his mind about your sentence!"

Justis swiped the decree into a hand that trembled with impatience. "I'll be halfway to Indian territory 'fore he gets the chance."


"MOTHER, MOTHER," Katherine heard Squirrel whimpering as she awoke. He tugged at Katherine's hand. "Mother."

Katherine thought he was half asleep and confused about her identity. After all, she and her blankets were covered with a soft layer of snow that had fallen during the night. "Come here, sleepy cousin. I love you. Snuggle and be quiet."

"Mother," he insisted. She frowned when she noticed that he wore no blanket. His thin body was shivering fiercely with nothing but a ragged woolen shirt and pants to cover it.

"Squirrel!" She lifted her blankets with one arm. "Come here!" She gritted her teeth as a blast of frigid air made her own shivering more violent. The snow beneath her put ice in her veins.

Squirrel threw himself into the frail warmth of her embrace. A hard, racking cough spasmed his body. Fear surged through Katherine and she stared blankly at the cold blue Illinois sky. *This little one won't go to the Dark Land, God. Please.*

"M-Mother," he whimpered again.

"Shhh. Go back to sleep."

"She has f-flown away."

Katherine sat up quickly, pain stabbing her stiff muscles, and looked behind her at Walks Smiling. She lay on her side, her blankets half off, one hand frozen to the snow in a grasping gesture. Frost jeweled her eyelashes. The first rays of morning sun glimmered on the frozen pool of blood near her mouth.

"M-Mother has flown to the Dark Land," Squirrel whispered, wheezing. "I want to g-go too."

"No!" Katherine pulled her top blanket over them like a hood so that she and Squirrel were hidden from the horror beside them. "No!" she wailed this time, a hysterical tightness in her chest. "It's Christmas morning!"

She hunched forward, rocking both Squirrel and herself in silent desperation. How much longer before dignity and hope were gone?

TRUE TO CHEROKEE custom, the young woman standing before Justis didn't raise her eyes to meet his. He watched snowflakes settle on her filthy black hair and the blanket she held around her emaciated body. Behind him, Watchman and a pack horse stamped their hooves, frustrated by the never-ending delays and the cold.

The Cherokee man who'd brought the woman from the line of people and wagons seemed to sense that Justis's patience was as short as the horses'. He shook her arm.

"This one is the Beloved Woman," he told Justis. "You pay me now."

"To hell with you. This is a scarecrow."

"All women on the trail look like her."

"This isn't Katlanicha."

"You pay," the man repeated. "Or else." The army had taken most of the Cherokees' weapons and wouldn't return them until the tribe had crossed the Mississippi, but this man was a member of the tribal patrol. He had a rusty pistol in his belt, and Justis saw his hand twitch toward it.

Justis grabbed him by the throat and almost lifted him from the ground. "Get outta my sight, you sneaky bastard."

The man stumbled away, clutching his neck. Justis turned his gaze to the woman again. She backed away, terror in her eyes. "Here," he said quickly. "Take a gift."

"You want me to lay with you?"

"Nah. It's just a gift." He reached inside one of his coat's big pockets, fumbled with the leather pouch there, and retrieved a gold coin. He held it out on the palm of his hand.

She snatched the coin away. "You are kind. Thank you."

"Go on now. Before you get left behind."

As she limped off, Justis cursed wearily. A week earlier he'd arrived in Kentucky on a cramped keelboat. Watchman and the pack horse had been sore from constantly fighting the boat's pitch and roll. He'd had to push them hard to catch up with the Cherokees this quickly.

"Wait! Wait!" Justis heard a frail voice calling as he started to mount Watchman. He saw an old man hobbling across the snowy ground toward him. The elder stopped and stared up at him shrewdly, his dark eyes nearly hidden in folds of skin.

"You search for the Beloved Woman? I remember you from the stockade. You put medicine on my leg. You looked at her with sad eyes. I told her that she stands in your soul."

Excitement made Justis want to grab the old man roughly. He jammed his fists into his coat pockets. "Have you seen her on the trail?"

The elder's jaw clenched tight. "What do you want with her?"

"I mean to make sure she's safe. But no one will tell me how to find her."

The old man ruminated on this information for several minutes. Finally he pointed a bony finger at Justis. "She is in a group far ahead of this one. But I have heard stories of her. When her own back is cold, she refuses a blanket so that someone else will have it. She goes hungry so children may eat. You find her. You make sure the Beloved Woman lives. She deserves to live."

Justis fought the sickness rising in his stomach. The scarecrow woman, gaunt and filthy, flashed through his mind. He remembered all the graves he'd seen in the past week, some of them no more than piles of rocks that barely covered the bodies. What kind of hell had Katie suffered while he lolled in Gold Ridge, drinking himself into a stupor and cursing her?

"Good," the elder said sharply. "I see the sorrow in your eyes. Now even a white man understands."

Justis gave him a blanket from the pack horse's bundle. "Thank you for helpin' me. What is it I understand?"

The elder wrapped himself in the gift and shut his

eyes. "What we call this journey. *Nuna-da-ut-sun-yi*. The trail where they cried."

THE PEDDLER WAS pop-eyed with terror. "I traded for it! I swear! When I met up with a tribe of Cherokees 'bout a week ago!"

Justis pushed the tip of his knife closer to the man's Adam's apple. With his other hand he jerked the man's leather necklace across the blade. Justis wound the leather into his fist and held it so that the gold nugget dangled in front of the peddler's eyes. " 'Fore I cut your windpipe, you best tell me who sold my gold piece to you."

"A woman with a sick youngun! She was desperate for medicine!"

"What'd she look like?"

"Dirty, half starved, half crazy! Hell, all I remember is that she spoke fine English and knew how to barter!"

Justis gave an evil smile that made the peddler sway noticeably. "Where was her group headed?"

"Toward G-Golgonda! On the Mississippi! They're likely camped there by now! Can't ferry across the Miss too easy in January! Have to wait for the ice to bust a little. You could catch 'em if you hurry!"

Justis lowered the knife. "Peddler," he whispered, "you just rescued your windpipe."

KATHERINE KNEW WITHOUT looking up that a crowd had gathered around her. A man squatted and shook her gently by one shoulder. "You gave your word."

"Yes," she admitted dully.

"We have made camp. Now it is time to rest."

She pulled her blanket tighter around herself and Squirrel. "I am sitting down. I am resting."

"Does the Beloved Woman break her word?"

Katherine dipped her head close to Squirrel's. "He is no trouble. I will keep him here."

"He does not need you anymore. And you are no longer strong enough to take care of others."

"Then it is time to die."

He stroked her hair slowly. "Keep your word, Beloved Woman. Rest."

She felt someone tugging her blankets open. "Let go," the person murmured. "You have carried him all day. Let us bury him now."

With a soft sound of despair she allowed Squirrel's body to drape into another's hands. An owl hooed softly in a nearby thicket, then crossed the twilight sky with a startling flutter of wings. People gasped.

"His spirit is leaving," someone said in awe. "It waited until the Beloved Woman let go of him."

Katherine touched the spot on her chest where Justis's gold nugget had lain. "I will die soon," she murmured. Everything that had given her strength was gone now. She watched the owl as it faded from sight on the western horizon. She knew, in the peculiar way she sometimes dreamed, that she would never reach the Indian territory there.

"HER NAME IS Katlanicha," Justis told the grim-faced Cherokee matron. "But she goes by the name Katherine too. I just want to find her. I don't mean the gal no harm."

He squatted by the campfire and pushed his wide-brimmed hat back so that the woman could study the honesty in his eyes. She stared hard into their green depths, then cast a scowl at the luxury of his heavy fur coat and warm wool scarf. Without hesitation he pulled the scarf off and handed it to her. She ignored the gift.

"You call her Beloved Woman," he said, speaking slowly so that she'd understand his poor Cherokee. "Everyone on the trail has heard of her. She knows white medicine and white ways."

"I hear nothing of such a one. Go away."

Justis stood wearily, his shoulders slumped. Tonight he was nearly beaten by frustration and worry. Dully he noticed a lanky young man hurrying toward the campfire.

"Mother! The Beloved Woman won't eat! And she's gone to sit beside the big river alone!"

The woman gasped. "Be quiet!"

Justis ran for his horses. Behind him he heard the woman yelling for help.

KATHERINE SWAYED AS a gust of wind swept off the wide, ice-choked river. She leaned forward, placed both hands on her blanket, and braced her arms. Her hair floated behind her as she tilted her face up toward the high, cold moon. She felt its silver fingers running over her.

This same moon was shining on Georgia, blessing her family's graves and the Blue Song land. Katherine's head swam and she shook it groggily. *Always mine,* she told herself. *Home.*

She cried out sadly. *Justis.* They were one and the same.

Staring blindly across the water, she at first didn't hear the thudding of horses' hooves racing up the river bluff. When she did, she lurched to her feet, staggered, then caught her balance and looked wildly toward the sound.

The moon silhouetted the dark figures of a tall rider and two big horses. The horses were only a few strides from her, and the rider reached out for her.

"I fight!" she warned in a voice too weak to hear. Her hands fumbled uselessly for the knife she'd traded days earlier for food.

She couldn't even manage a scream when the horse's

shoulder bumped her. She started to fall, then felt the
rider's hand winding into the neck of her ragged tunic.
The material ripped as she tried to struggle.

"Katie gal, calm down!"

*Justis.* Stunned, dreaming, she went limp, and he
pulled her in front of him on the saddle. His arm went
around her waist. She sagged against him, her hands digging into his furry coat, her face burrowed in his shoulder.

Her hazy grip on consciousness told her only that
hope had come back into the world. She couldn't understand the distant sounds of men shouting and horses galloping. Justis held her tighter and clucked to his mount.
It went into a smooth, rocking lope, following the riverbank north.

Katherine tilted her head back and tried to look at
him in the moonlight. Shock and happiness confused her
until all she could manage to say was a plaintive
"Home?"

"Someday. Thank you, God. Thank you." He bent his
head to hers and brushed a kiss over her forehead.

## CHAPTER 11

THE WARMTH woke her, the delicious warmth after months of shivering. Katherine moved a tiny bit and sighed. She was wrapped in a cocoon of soft, thick blankets. The mattress under her was lumpy, and it made a rustling sound. It was stuffed with coarse hay, she decided. But compared to cold, hard ground, it felt luxurious.

How had she gotten there? Vaguely she recalled being wrapped in warm blankets and carried on horseback through the night, the horse rocking under her like a cradle, protective arms holding her with strength and comfort, a much-loved masculine voice urging her to rest easy, to forgive, to live.

She heard the crackling of a fire nearby and turned her face toward its wonderful heat. Her eyes still shut, she inhaled and felt light-headed when the aroma of roasting meat filled her. Pangs cramped her stomach, and she made a keening sound of hunger.

Callused fingertips stroked her cheek. "Katie?"

The drawling bourbon-and-cigar voice caressed her name and brought her fully from sleep in a whirl of groggy emotion. She opened her eyes and cried out in recognition. Justis bent over her, frowning. His face was drawn and tired, his hair ruffled, his mouth set in a grim line. "You," she said raptly, trying to smile. "You." Pain stung her chapped lips.

"Shhh. Don't do that." He reached for something, brought it to her mouth, and rubbed gently. "You're bleedin'." She dimly felt soothing grease on her lips. Lost in gazing at him, she smiled wider. His expression darkened. "Stop it. Dammit, stop. You're hurtin' yourself—"

"Justis. Never thought . . . I would see you again. *Justis.*"

Her fervent, happy tone snapped his restraint. With a soft groan he cradled her face and rested his forehead on hers. She breathed raggedly, loving the scent of his hair and skin, knowing that the fragrances of woodsmoke and tobacco would always remind her of this moment.

"Christ, I was afraid you'd never wake up," he whispered. "Could you take some food?"

After months of constant hunger, the irony of that question overwhelmed her. "Food?" Tears slipped from the corners of her eyes. "You have food?"

He drew his head back and gazed at her. His mouth worked for a moment without forming words. Finally he spoke in a low, barely controlled rasp. "Just lie still."

"Where are we?"

"A little place I found last night. Owner's out beyond the barn—what's left of him—with a pile of kindlin' scattered beside him. Must have been sick, dropped dead while he was toting firewood. Probably been dead for months. Bad luck for him, good luck for us. This place is way off the road. I found it only because I was tryin' to lose your little private posse of Injuns."

"I n-need some good luck."

He cupped her cheek with his warm palm. "You got some now, gal."

She watched him wistfully as he moved away. Her hazy mind finally realized that they were in a cabin of squared logs chinked with clay. The place was so little that Justis could probably lie down and touch one wall with his fingertips, the other with his toes.

*Justis.* She drank in the sight of him while he knelt in front of a crude stone fireplace and lifted a black iron kettle from a hook above the flames. Firelight played on his strong, big-knuckled hands and shot red-gold streaks through his hair.

He wore a heavy wool shirt, and trousers held by leather braces. The arms of white long johns showed beneath the shirt's rolled-up sleeves and in the V made by its floppy lapels. His face was thinner than she remembered, and older. It no longer held a hint of youthful smoothness. His wavy chestnut hair was ragged, and so long that it brushed his shoulders in back. And the mustache—it badly needed a trimming.

She thought him more handsome than ever. *"Très beau,"* she whispered. *"Tu es très bien."* Almost crying with happiness, she added hoarsely, *"Je t'aime,* Justis. *Je t'aime beaucoup."*

He hurried to scoop some sort of stew into a wooden bowl. "Aw, it's nothin' good enough to speak French over. It's just rabbit mixed with cornmeal." He carried it to her and sat down on the bed, a narrow structure of rough-hewn wood built into the cabin's corner. After placing the bowl on the cabin's dirt floor, he slipped his arms under Katherine's shoulders. "Can you sit up, gal?"

She nodded, not caring whether she could or not. She stared devotedly into his worried eyes. "Still as green as new leaves."

"Shhh. Your mind'll be all right soon as you eat something." He lifted her to a sitting position and moved around behind her on the bed.

"I want to look at you," she protested weakly. "See your mustache."

"Katie, please. Just try to eat."

He reached for the wooden bowl and set it on her blanket-wrapped lap, then lifted a small strip of meat to her mouth. She lunged for it with sudden, single-minded desperation, swallowed it whole, and licked his fingers like a grateful dog.

"Oh, God," he said in pained shock. "Easy, now, easy."

Trembling, she whimpered again. "More. More."

He made a gruff, sorrowful sound and brought the food to her mouth as swiftly as she could eat it. "Slow down. You'll be sick." She ignored him until he grabbed the underside of her jaw and held it firmly. "Slow," he ordered.

She forced herself to chew each bit of meat a few times. When her stomach stopped begging for more, lethargy took over. Between one bite and the next her eyelids grew heavy and her head drooped forward.

"Katie!" He tilted her head back and looked at her anxiously.

"Sleep," she murmured, turning her face toward the crook of his neck. "Warm. Strong. You feel so good. Hold me. Have to sleep again."

He almost sagged with relief. "You sleep all you need," he said in a low, shaky voice. "I won't ever let go."

"I should have known that," she murmured, her voice trailing off. "Should have known."


A TINY DRAFT of cold air curled between the cabin's chinking and touched the tip of Katherine's nose. She groggily pushed a blanket down and opened her eyes. On the opposite wall a line of dawn light shone at the bottom edge of a window covered with a deerskin. The fire was no more than a bed of weak embers, and her breath made white mist in the air.

She looked at her chapped, aching hands in bewilderment. They were covered with grease. She touched her lips. The same. He'd oiled her as if she were a rusty gun, she thought with giddy amusement.

She burrowed into the lovely heat under the blankets and the wall of warmth that cupped her back, hips, and thighs. The wall shifted, curving closer against her, and she sighed with pure, uninhibited pleasure. Justis. His long, rock-hard arm was draped over her waist, and as she lay there smiling, he slid it farther around her. It pulled sleepily, fitting her hips into the angle made by his belly and thighs.

Katherine plucked at the long, heavy shirt she wore and realized that it was one of his. She was too exhausted to feel any embarrassment that he'd changed her clothes. In fact the only thing that did bother her was her ugliness. What a sight she must be, all bony and sunken.

She shifted swollen, overused feet and discovered that they were covered in coarse stockings—obviously another of Justis's belongings. Moving her legs closer to his, she sighed with delight at the feel of his soft long johns against her bare skin.

She stroked the arm he'd wrapped around her, ignoring the pain in her sore, cracked fingertips. Finally she determined where the sleeve of his long johns ended and his thick, hairy wrist began. She slipped her fingers downward and curled them around his hand. With another sigh, infinitely peaceful, she grew drowsy again.

His face was buried against the back of her neck— apparently he'd gathered her hair into a nest there—and his deep, even breathing cascaded onto her skin. But just as she was about to drift off he mumbled incoherently, then flexed against her.

She blinked in slow surprise as he grew hard, his robust stiffness fitting neatly against the cleft of her hips, its size impressive even when obscured by clothing. His breathing quickened, and he arched languidly a few times. His arm slid from around her and she felt him fumbling with the material that covered his groin.

She was too weak to be aroused but not too weak to be curious. Justis wasn't the kind of man who'd take her in her helpless, unresponsive condition. She sensed that strongly. But what did he intend to do?

Slowly he pulled her shirt up in back. She felt his hand caress her bare hip—gently, more like a loving pat than a touch designed to excite. Then he grasped himself and stroked slowly. Her eyes widened in amazement as a satiny, rounded surface rubbed up and down on her hip. He stroked faster until his whole body tautened and he groaned softly. Warm fluid tickled the small of her back.

He wiped it away with the hem of her shirt, then eased the shirt back down and fastened his long johns. His arm slid over her again, snug and possessive, and he nuzzled his head closer to hers. "Oh, Katie," he murmured. "Katie."

The tenderness in his voice made tears crest in her eyes. He hadn't tried to find her right away, but he *had* searched for her eventually. Why? To salve his lust and anger? To make her sorry for breaking their bargain? To force her to accept it? Maybe all of that, but his stubborn pursuit held a world of affection, too, a sort of love.

Months of hardship had left her feeling vulnerable and confused, her emotions wrenched by losing Squirrel, Walks Smiling, Little Bird, and so many others. She didn't have the energy to analyze, to scold herself, to hold back her feelings. They flooded her with the truth. It didn't matter why Justis had tried to find her, why he wanted her, or for how long. If he asked, she would never leave him again.


JUSTIS HUNG THE turkey carcass on a peg outside the cabin door, leaned his rifle against the wall, and stamped snow from his boots. "Katie? It's me," he called loudly.

He'd given her one of his pistols, and he figured it wasn't wise to startle a fighter such as she.

There was no answer. He shoved the door open. The cabin was empty, but the fire blazed as if recently tended. His pistol lay on a table by the door. She'd barely had the strength to sit up while he fed her breakfast—how could she have left? He turned and plowed hastily through foot-deep snow, cupping his hands to his mouth. "Kath-er-ine!"

"Over here."

The cabin and its small barn were surrounded by woods. Behind the cabin a small stream wound among the straight white trunks of a poplar grove. Her voice had come from there.

He ran to the grove and halted. She was huddled on the ice-banked edge of the stream, holding a blanket around herself with one hand. With the other she lifted her hair from the frigid water and turned to look at him.

"I'm washing up. I found a crockery jar with some soap in it. I'm done now. You may help me back inside."

His language could have melted all the snow in Illinois. He finished scalding the air about the time he reached her. "I didn't save your skinny behind so you could freeze it off for vanity's sake!" he yelled, jerking the wool scarf from his neck. He wrapped it around her head, slinging the dripping hair to one side. "Crazy! Crazy woman! If you get sick I'll—"

"I'm accustomed to the cold," she protested, swaying under his hurried ministrations. "I've spent many nights sleeping on frozen ground. And I've always washed in creeks like this. There's been no other way."

"I don't care if you're used to dancin' nekkid in a blizzard!" He grabbed her by the shoulders to lift her up. His grip jerked the blanket, and she fumbled for it as it slid in a heap around her waist. He saw her bare, wet back and nearly exploded with anger. "You took off my shirt!"

"Well, sir, I couldn't wash very much of myself with it on, could I?"

He muttered fierce oaths and snatched the blanket back around her. She clamped her lips tightly together, offering no protest when he scooped her into his arms, but her hands shook as she clasped the blanket to her chest.

After he got her inside the cabin he laid her on the bed and got a towel from his bundle of supplies. He came back to her and shoved her hands down. The blanket fell open and she crossed her arms instinctively to shield herself.

"I've seen it all before," he said in disgust. He was too scared and angry to be gentle. Only by the grace of God had he found her on the trail before she was beyond saving. He wasn't going to lose her now.

"Prissy, proud, stubborn woman," he muttered. He toweled her roughly, hurrying to get done and get her dressed warmly again. "At least those tits still look grand —smaller, but grand. Hmmph. Arms like sticks, ribs all showin', belly sunk in like an empty pond. But you think you're healthy, sure, healthy enough to go prancin' outside nekkid and soak yourself in ice water. So high and mighty!"

She yipped with anger when he rolled her over and toweled her back. "Backbone like a starved dog," he continued. "And an ass so flat I could serve tea on it."

"You didn't mind this morning," she wailed. "I wasn't so dreadfully ugly to you then!"

His hands hesitated. "Dammit to hell. I thought you had gone back to sleep."

"I knew what you were doing! My flat a-ass suited you *then.*"

"If what I did upset you, why didn't you say so?"

"I thought you were paying me a compliment! Now I understand—I'm good enough to use for stimulation even if I'm horrible to look at."

Quickly he flung dry blankets over her and removed the damp one. She turned her face into the pillow, her body quivering as he pulled the wool scarf from her hair. "It was a compliment," he said gruffly. "Sorry if I hurt your feelings."

Startled, she was silent. Then, sounding bewildered, she asked, "What do you want from me? I can't do you much good in or out of bed. I feel so broken and used up."

He turned to the table and fumbled with the shirt and stockings she'd left there on her way outside. Was she no more willing to put up with him now than she'd been in Gold Ridge? When he'd looked into her eyes yesterday, hadn't he seen so much welcome that it had choked his throat with happiness?

"You ran out on your agreement with me," he said. "I can't let that kind of insult pass."

"What penalty do you plan for me, then?"

"I figure you suffered it over the past few months. Reckon it's settled. Now you see that stickin' with me wouldn't be the worst thing you could do."

"How did you discover where I'd gone?"

"I finally sweet-talked Amarintha. Her tongue slipped." No point in telling her the grim truth about that day in the Gold Ridge jail.

"You must have promised her something—otherwise she'd never have told my secret. You're not going to marry her, are you? She's not suitable for you at all."

"I'll not be marryin' Amarintha or anybody else."

"Not until after you're done with me, at least."

He slung the shirt and stockings on the bed. "You sorry I came after you? You think you'd a-lived to reach Injun territory?"

"I don't know. I feel so . . . lost. I wonder if I'll ever be strong again."

"You will." He brusquely pulled the blankets down her back. "Here. Get into this shirt." He helped her sit up. She faced the wall and stubbornly covered her breasts. He slipped his huge wool shirt over her head.

As it settled into place, covering her thinness, he wanted to tell her that she stirred the heat in him with a lot more than just her body. He wanted to tell her how he'd searched all the way to Philadelphia and back, then nearly driven himself to ruin, all because he'd lost her. But those were things that would only give her more power to hurt him, and would probably make her think he was a fool.

"Turn over," he commanded. He wrapped the towel around her hair and helped her settle comfortably on the mattress with its one lumpy pillow under her head. He flipped the bottom of the blankets up to reveal her feet. Christ, he thought. Her tattered moccasins must have let every stick and rock on the trail leave their mark. "Don't know how you shuffled along on these. What'd you do, traipse on 'em the whole way from Tennessee to Illinois?"

"Yes," she said grimly, staring hard at the ceiling.

His stomach twisted with anguish. "Fool thing to do."

"Sorry. I traded my royal coach for a cooking pot."

Justis took a moment to dump his coat and hat by the hearth. Then he picked up the pottery bowl that held the crude salve he'd made from pork fat and liniment. He didn't speak again until he was seated on the bed with her feet in his lap. As he carefully rubbed salve onto them, he asked, "So you traded the royal coach for a pot, huh? Why didn't you trade my gold nugget for a horse to ride?"

She jumped a little. He looked up at her and saw that she'd shut her eyes. "I wanted a memento," she told him. "Something from the Blue Song land. That's why I took it."

Damn her. Why couldn't she say that she'd wanted it to remember him by as well? "I got it back." She opened her eyes, craning her head to stare at him. He slipped the leather necklace from under his shirt and let the gold nugget catch the firelight. "From a peddler who said you bought medicine with it. Said you had a sick youngun with you. Want to tell me about it?"

"No." She let her head fall back and swallowed harshly. "You have your gold piece again. And you have me. In your own way, you've been kind and wonderful to me. You probably saved me from dying on the trail. I shan't ever betray your trust again. You have all my gratitude—and all my loyalty."

He gazed at her in amazement. She offered so much, more than he'd expected, and it made him happy. "You can depend on me, Katie. I don't take without givin' equal measure back. You can share how bad you hurt, and what makes you cry, and everything ugly that's happened to you."

"There's nothing to tell." Drawing her knees up, she lay on her side and stared resolutely at the wall, clenching her hands under her chin, withdrawing into a private sanctum where he wasn't welcome.

"Can't you talk to me as a friend?"

"I don't know if I'd call what we share *friendship*. Perhaps it would be better if we tried to treat each other like . . . umm, partners. Yes. Like that. Polite but formal."

"Well, fine," he said bitterly, hurt by her refusal to share her deeper thoughts and feelings. "We'll be partners. As long as I get what I want, I don't care."

She gave him a wary look. "What exactly do you want?"

"What I've always wanted—what you agreed to give me before. Help with society folderol, book learnin', and a damned good time in bed. Rest up. Get yourself healthy. You owe me plenty of service for all the trouble I went through to save your pretty red hide."

His harsh words seemed to drain her. "I wish you hadn't saved me," she said dully. "I was prepared to die. I wish that I had."

"I can grant that there wish in a big hurry!" He would call her bluff and teach her to regret saying such nonsense just to get sympathy. He grabbed the pistol off the table, whirled toward the bed again, and bent over her. He jerked the hammer back and pressed the muzzle to her temple. "You want to die? The idea of carryin' out your deal with me is so damned awful that you'd rather have your brains blown out? Really? Then say your good-bye prayer!"

He saw her pulse beating swiftly in her throat, but her dark eyes met his with tragic calmness. He stared at the despair in them and realized that there were more painful memories inside her than he'd ever imagined.

"I think I'll just let you suffer," he said with a show of disgust. He drew the pistol away and tried to look unconcerned, though his hands trembled. "Go to sleep, you conniving hellion. You can't get out of our bargain that easy."

She turned away, pulled her blankets a little higher, as if trying to escape his scrutiny, and shut her eyes. "I will honor it, sir," she said bleakly. "But for now I want only to rest."

"Rest, then." He watched with growing concern as she fell asleep almost immediately, her face slipping into a sorrowful expression so poignant, his chest ached. He laid a hand on her damp hair and stroked gently. "You'll be good as new," he murmured. He wanted to believe that, but wasn't sure that he did.

"MY WIFE'S A Cherokee Injun, and if you don't want her here, say so now. I won't have her insulted."

His problem stated bluntly, Justis waited for the innkeeper to reply. The way the dapper little man and his stout wife kept staring at his mustache, he figured it was as much an oddity to them as him having an Injun wife.

Folks in this part of Illinois weren't used to either mustaches or Injuns, he decided.

"I thought the Indians had all been removed," the wife said.

Justis nodded. "We were headed west with 'em," he explained, "but my wife got poorly and we decided to drop out. We'll be leavin' for New York soon as she's fattened up some." He opened a pouch full of coins and showed it to them. "Gold. Georgia gold. None purer."

"Well, that settles it," the innkeeper said quickly, his eyes gleaming with surprise. "We'll be glad to have you both. Got a nice big room upstairs with a fireplace. No lice, no bedbugs. A real window. And the missus sets a fine table three times a day." He cut his eyes toward her considerable girth. "Your wife'll be healthy in no time."

Relieved, Justis went out to the narrow porch, where Katie sat wrapped in blankets. Four hound dogs and two young boys stood in the snow, gaping at her. She seemed oblivious.

"Got us a fine room," he said.

She looked up, her eyes shadowed with fatigue from the day's ride. "Us? Do they know we're not husband and wife?"

"Nope. Come along, Mrs. Gallatin."

He lifted her into his arms and carried her inside. The innkeeper and his wife ran a tavern in the main room downstairs. They came out from behind its bar and approached Katherine timidly. "Me Mr. Martin," the innkeeper said in a slow, patient manner, pointing to himself. Then he pointed to his wife. "She Mrs. Martin. Mar-tin."

Katherine extended a hand gracefully. "I'm quite pleased to meet both of you, I'm sure. I'm Katherine Blue Song . . . Gallatin. Mrs. Gallatin. Thank you so much for accommodating us."

Their jaws dropped. For the first time in months Justis

wanted to laugh. He bit his lip and hoped the droop of his mustache hid his smile.

When they were safely inside their room with the door shut, he placed her on the bed and began to chortle. Even Katie managed a smile. "Me tired," she muttered. "Heap sleepy."

He unwrapped her and pulled the covers down. "Got to see about getting you some clothes. You can't wear my shirt all the time."

"Hmmm. Whatever you want." A look of weary pleasure on her face, she settled under the clean flannel sheets and fluffy quilts.

"I'm tired of hearin' you say that. It's gettin' to be the only words you know."

"Since I want only to sleep, everything else is truly up to you."

Justis worried about her lack of enthusiasm, but told himself that she'd been off the trail for only a week. It would take a little longer for her spirits and strength to improve. He glanced around the room with approval, hoping she'd be pleased with his choice of inns.

"Washstand, good towels, good-size fireplace, rugs on the floor"—he sat down on the foot of the big four-poster and bounced slightly—"and a mattress that makes a man hate the idea of gettin' up. What do you think? Will it do?"

"Since we'll be sharing it, I'd like to know how soon you expect to use my—my person for your pleasure. I have, after all, agreed to be your mistress. I will fulfill that duty whenever you ask."

Her martyred attitude infuriated him. Back in Gold Ridge he'd seen the fire in her too often to believe that she didn't want him as a lover. "You're a mite dangerous right now," he said blithely. "I wouldn't want to jab myself on your hipbones. I'll wait."

"Thank you."

She said it without sarcasm, as if she'd taken his words

seriously. He gazed at her in dismay as she slid farther under the covers and snuggled her head into a huge feather pillow. Shutting her eyes, she grew very still.

He couldn't stay angry with her, not when sadness shimmered around her like a dark aura. It hurt that she expected him to use her like a piece of property. It hurt even more that she thought he'd thrust himself into that frail, tired body of hers without a bit of guilt. He *did* crave her, and if she had wanted him in return, he'd have loved her with all the gentleness in his soul. But she didn't want him—or anything, really, except to sleep, eat, or stare into space.

Justis stood up and looked at her, frowning. "I've got to go see about the horses. You rest good, you hear?"

She was already asleep. He reached out and touched the back of her hand where it lay atop the covers, the fingers unfurled as if there were no fight left in them.

MRS. MARTIN LOOKED upset as she pulled Justis out of his room. Katherine had just fallen asleep after gazing dully at several nightgowns and other articles he had purchased for her.

"She's lost her heart, Mr. Gallatin," Mrs. Martin said. "I've seen it before. My sister got that way after measles took her family. Her spirit died, and she followed."

"My wife's not gonna die! She just needs to rest!"

"You let her sleep that way all the time and she'll rest permanently."

Justis paced the hall, jamming his hands through his hair. He didn't believe that Katie's invincible spirit was gone. He *wouldn't* believe that her listless sorrow came from dreading their future together. Not entirely, anyhow.

Had she been raped on the trail? Had she fallen in love with some man from her own people and then lost him to sickness? Had someone hurt her some other way? Every question tore at him, mingling protectiveness with jealousy and anger because she wouldn't let him inside her private, grief-filled world.

What would make her happy? He halted, gazing at Mrs. Martin thoughtfully. "You got any books to read, ma'am?"

"Sure do. All sorts."

"Can I borrow a stack of 'em?"

"Certainly. I'll send one of the boys up with them. But, Mr. Gallatin, how is that going to help your wife if she refuses to read them?"

Justis smiled wickedly. "She'll read."

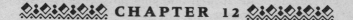 

## CHAPTER 12

K ATHERINE frowned as sleep gave way to a dull headache. Her muscles ached from staying in bed so
much, but she couldn't think of any reason to get up.
Justis left her alone except when it was time to eat, and
then he watched her carefully until he decided she had
swallowed a hearty amount of Mrs. Martin's food.

A blunt finger poked her in the shoulder. She woke
enough to realize Justis was propped up in bed beside
her. "Sleepy," she protested. "Don't."

"I'm gonna read to you."

"No."

"Wake up. I'm damned tired of sitting downstairs playing cards and drinkin' while you snore."

"I do not snore."

He cleared his throat. " 'Love, whose month is ever
May, Speed a bloosum passing far—' "

"Stop." She groaned in weary dismay. "What book are
you trying to massacre?"

"It's a Shakespeare. *Love's La-bour's Lost.*"

Katherine turned over and looked up at him. He sat on top of the covers, fully dressed, and he had a cigar tucked above one ear. His eyes met hers solemnly. "I'm not embarrassed to sound dumb as a jackass in front of you, gal."

Her heart melted. "You don't sound dumb. Would you like some assistance with your reading?"

"Yeah. If you feel like it."

She pushed herself upward. He planted the pillow behind her, then casually draped his arm around her shoulders. Even in her lethargic state Katherine enjoyed being close to him more than she'd ever admit. He didn't know that she watched him every time he moved around their room, or that she often lay awake at night, contentedly admiring him.

"Warm enough?" he asked.

"Yes, thanks."

She glanced around. He'd built a fire and lit a lamp beside the bed. Outside, a snowstorm was already dimming the day's light. The room was a cozy, cheerful haven. She settled closer to his side. "Why don't you begin the passage again?"

"Sure." He held the book up rigidly. " 'Love, whose month is ever May, Speed—' "

"Spied."

" 'Spied a bloosum—' "

"Blossom."

" 'Spied a blossom passing far—' "

"Fair."

He put the book down and sighed. "I'm glad we got lots of time to practice this while you stay in bed. I really want you to learn me—I mean, teach me to read better."

"I'm afraid I'm still too tired to do much."

"That's fine. I'll read to you and you don't have to say a thing." Placing the book where she didn't have to look at it unless she wanted to, he continued. " 'A blossom passin' fair, playin' in the one-ton—' "

"Oh, I can't help myself. It is *wanton,* not *one-ton.*"

" 'Wanton are—' "

"Air."

" 'Wanton air. Through the vel-vet lives—' "

"Velvet leaves."

" 'Velvet leaves the wind, all insane—' "

"*Unseen.* Justis?"

"Hmmm?"

"Would you mind if we did this later? I'd like to change into one of my new nightgowns and brush my hair. Afterward, perhaps you'd enjoy it if I read to *you* for a little while."

"You feeling better, gal?"

"Yes, I believe so." *Anything to escape this reading lesson.*

She looked at him. He grinned and stuck his cigar between his teeth at a cocky angle, almost as if he were pleased with himself.

From then on it was read or be read to, and the former was less tiring than the latter. So over the next few days Katherine found herself dressing in her robe and sitting in a chair by the fireplace, a book in her lap, while Justis sat cross-legged on the hearth by her feet.

At first Katherine barely paid attention to the words she spoke; her mind was dull and preoccupied, though she tried to concentrate. Images from the trail kept haunting her, and she used much of her strength to suppress the emotions they fostered. But as time passed, the reading forced her to concentrate. It guided her mind into soothing channels, and she began to look forward to it.

Justis sat utterly still at her feet for hours at a time, his droopy green eyes hardly ever looking away from her. His devotion gave her quiet hope. If he enjoyed even these simple, unexciting pastimes with her, perhaps he cared about her in a deeper way than she expected.

"I will trim your hair if you like," she announced one morning in an attempt to be friendly.

"You feelin' that much better?"

"Yes, I am. Reading to you has been good for my attitude."

He grinned and gave her a lopsided squint, looking self-satisfied for some reason she couldn't fathom. He ran a hand over his shaggy locks, which were beginning to curl luxuriously on his shoulders. "All right, I'll take a trim. Not too short. I don't wanta look like a sheared stallion."

Mrs. Martin sent up a comb, scissors, and a mirror. Justis sat on a stool by the fireplace. Katherine stood behind him and speared her fingers into his burnished hair. "There's enough mane here for two stallions, sir."

"Don't turn into a savage and try to steal my purty scalp."

"Oh, it's much handsomer attached to its owner than it would be hanging from my war lance."

She started at his temples and stroked her fingers down through the curls to untangle them, brushing her fingertips along his neck as she did. The intimacy of it surprised her. She hadn't thought such an ordinary contact would make desire wind through her veins. She hadn't thought anything could make her feel human and female again.

The skin of her hands, now well healed, seemed alive with sensation. She loved the caress of his silky hair as she combed her fingers through it again and studied the longest strands, trying to decide how best to cut them, debating the wisdom of curling herself around him for a kiss. She warned herself to be patient, that she still didn't have the strength or the beauty to please him in bed.

Breath feathering in her throat, she moved in front of him. "I'm trying to see how the hair wants to fall," she explained. " 'Tis best to cut it that way."

"Hmmm."

Her belly tightened at the low erotic pleasure in his tone. She was suddenly aware that she had stepped between his casually spread legs and that her knee was brushing the inside of his thigh. He sighed deeply, and his breath stirred a bit of decorative ribbon on her robe, directly over her breasts.

She glanced down and saw that his face was nearly touching her. His eyes were half shut, but there was no doubt that he was admiring the view in front of him. And no doubt that her breasts ached for a repeat of the gentle sucking he'd given them that tempestuous night, so many months before, at Mrs. Albert's house.

Her hands shaking, Katherine stepped back to collect herself. "Perhaps I should trim your mustache first."

"Nah, I'll do it myself, thanks."

The sensual languor in his expression made her knees weak. She laughed softly, the sound strained. "You are always so protective of it. I truly like the furry thing, Justis. I won't damage it, I promise."

"You like it?" he echoed in amazement.

The surprise and delight in his gaze nearly undid all her caution. She sidled around behind him to escape the compelling sight. "Yes. I can't imagine you without it." She sighed. "But I warn you—if you want to look more gentlemanly, you ought to shave it off."

"I'll just have to look less gentlemanly, then." He reached back and grasped her hand, then brought it to his mouth. "Feel."

Her stomach dropped as he guided the tip of one finger under his mustache. Again, an ordinary contact created an extraordinary reaction in her pulse. He drew her finger along the firm swell of his upper lip, then to the coarse ridge running parallel above it. "A *scar*?" she exclaimed.

"Yep. Got it in a knife fight." He slowly pushed her hand away. "Guess it's kind of a brand. I like to hide it."

"A brand? How do you mean?"

"It tells the world that I'm no good, that I grew up fightin' with trash and won't ever be anything but trash myself."

She exhaled raggedly and slid her arms around his neck. Pressing her cheek lightly to the top of his head, she murmured, "You are a hellion, a rogue, and quite often the most infuriating man I ever hope to know. But you are also the finest kind of gentleman."

"Aw," he said gruffly, and added a less polite word.

She kissed his hair. "Give me that hand mirror before you fumble it onto the floor." She took the mirror and started to lay it on the washstand behind her, but caught a glimpse of herself and froze. "Dear God," she whispered, and hurriedly turned the mirror facedown on the stand.

"Katie?"

Justis followed her as she stumbled to the bed, hugging herself. She curled up on her side. When he sat down and bent across her, she shut her eyes. "What is it?" he demanded urgently. "You upset because you look so thin? Hell, you look wonderful compared to how you were two weeks ago. And in another two weeks you'll be beautiful again."

"I never realized how everything that happened to me shows on my face," she said in a small, choked voice. "I knew that others on the trail had an awful look of horror in their eyes, but I thought I could hide my own torments."

He gripped one of her hands. "Tell me what happened to you."

"I can't . . . nothing. The way to fight your troubles is to push them out of your mind. If you act as if you're strong, you *will* be strong."

"Or you'll sleep all the time to keep from thinkin' how much you hurt inside," he rebuked her gently.

"No! I'm just tired! I'm tired now. Really, just let me take a nap. I'll trim your hair later."

"No, Katie. I want the truth." He squeezed her hand, and his voice was troubled. "What kind of things happened to you?"

"I'm perfectly fine!"

"I won't care . . . I'll still want you . . . even if you did some things you're ashamed of. Or if somebody did things to you against your will. No matter what happened."

She rolled onto her back and searched his gaze. "You truly mean it," she whispered in awe.

He laid a hand on her belly. "Things can still be good between us, even if you've been hurt that way. When you're strong enough to want me, I'll show you how sweet a man can be to a woman."

She reached up and caressed his face. "I think you're already showing me that."

"What happened to you?"

"Not what you think." She told him how people had protected the Beloved Woman. "Perhaps if terrible indignities had been done to me, I would feel less sad."

Bewilderment filled his eyes. "Why?"

"Here I am, safe and well cared for, while so many others are buried along the road from here to Tennessee. Why am I special? Why do I deserve to live?"

"You deserve to live because you fought to live! You fought to help others live!"

"But I couldn't save them, not one."

"What? You saved some—you did the best you could."

"My family, I mean."

"What family?"

Her throat constricted. "Cousins. Two children. Their mother. If I could have saved them, at least saved my relatives . . ." Her voice trailed away and tears pooled in her eyes. "Do you know what that means to a Cherokee? Our families are everything to us."

"You're not alone. You have me." He took her by the arms. His eyes were full of sympathy. "Me! I'll be your family. Are you . . . the way you look sometimes, like you don't care what happens to you . . . is it because bein' with me makes you miserable?"

She gazed at him, then slowly shook her head. "Sometimes I wonder how much torment we will bring to each other before we're done, and it makes me sad. I tell myself to think of you as just a partner and not a friend. But then you do or say something that is entirely kind, and I have to admit that we *are* friends." Her voice faltered. "No, I'm not miserable with you. I need your friendship. I need . . . I need you to be my family."

She sat up abruptly and hugged him. He put his arms around her and rocked her, surprised and very, very relieved by her answer. "Gal, for better or worse, you've just adopted me."

"Welcome, kinsman. What relation are you?"

He thought a moment. "A kissin' cousin."

For the first time in months, she laughed.


KATHERINE WOKE UP in pitch darkness and didn't know where she was. Flinging her hands about in terror, she contacted hard muscle covered in soft hair. "Dream. Bad dream," she said, panting. "Help." She patted her hands about, finding broad shoulders and long arms. The arms reached around her.

"Katie, shhh."

She exhaled with shaky relief as Justis pulled her thin, trembling body close to his. He had never come to bed without his shirt before. The silky hair of his chest was more wonderful than even her best imaginings, and she nuzzled her face into the center of it.

He stroked the length of her back as she slowly recovered from her dream. "What was it?" he whispered, his voice a soothing rumble.

"On the trail. My hands, bloody." She struggled to regain her breath. "Birthing a babe. It died. Mother died too. Had to leave them for men to bury. A snowstorm. Snow everywhere. Looked back. Dogs. Dogs after the bodies. Whole world was . . . white and red."

"Oh, Katie." He brushed hair from her forehead, tilted her head back, and placed small kisses across her face. His mouth touching hers, he murmured, "Go on back to sleep. It was just a bad dream."

A ragged sound caught in her throat. "No. It happened about two weeks before you found me."

"The way you told it?" he asked, stunned. "Like in the dream?"

"Yes."

Drowsiness washed over her, not the sweet, relaxed drifting that precedes happy sleep, but the thick fog of escape she craved. In the last moment before oblivion, she was aware of Justis rising on one elbow to look down at her. "It's a good sign, you talkin' about the sad things that happened. Tomorrow you'll tell me the rest. All right?"

"No. Nothing much left to tell."

"You'll tell," he ordered, and wrapped her in his arms.


KATHERINE WATCHED HIM warily the next day and hoped he'd forget his vow. When he left to take Watchman to a blacksmith over in town, she sighed with relief. She was seated by the window reading when he returned. She stared at the paper-wrapped bundles he tossed on the bed.

"Clothes for you," he said. "Probably a little too big, but the way you've been eatin', they'll fit before long."

"Oh, thank you!" Pleased, she got up and padded barefoot toward the bed. It would be wonderful to trade her nightgown and robe for a nice dress. She even thought her feet were healed enough to take shoes. "Let me see!"

"Nope." He blocked her way and stood with his fur coat shoved back, hands on his hips, long legs braced.

"Not until you agree to tell more of what happened to you on the trail."

She halted. Damn the man! "Why must you hear all that? It's over with."

"Not as long as you have nightmares and cry over it every night."

"I had one nightmare, and I do not cry every night." She huffed loudly but crumpled inside. It was no use lying. He had heard her sniffling like a child at night! Humiliation burned her face. "I thought you were asleep!"

"Every night," he repeated, nodding. "And even though you're not sleepin' most of the day anymore, half the time you just sit starin' into space. Might as well be asleep. How can I take you to New York and get any good out of you if you stay like that?"

"I see. Your concern has to do with my worth to you." She waved a hand toward the gifts on the bed. "Take your bribes straight to hell, sir."

"You're goin' downstairs tonight and eat at the table with the other boarders."

"Not in my nightgown and robe, I'm not."

"You'll go nekkid if you have to, but you'll go. Best if you put on a nice dress and some drawers, instead."

"I will. Get out of my way."

He pointed toward her chair by the window. "Plant yourself over there and start talkin'."

"About what?"

He threw his head back and yelled in exasperation, "About the things that make you act like a broody old hen!" His gaze leveled on hers, hard and demanding. "Did you fall in love with some feller on the trail? Is that what you're sorrowful about?"

"Fall in love?" The idea was so absurd, she laughed. How could she fall in love with anyone else when she loved Justis with all her heart and soul? She had nothing left to give another man.

"Stop, dammit," he said fiercely. "Forget I asked. The notion of lovin' a man that much is so strange to you that you don't know what I mean."

She grew quiet and gave him a grim look. "No. I couldn't fall in love with anyone on the trail. I was too busy trying to keep me and mine alive. And I did a terrible job of it. I lived and they didn't."

"Stop feelin' sorry for yourself!"

"This is not self-pity! It's the truth!"

His mouth curved sarcastically. "Why am I alive?" he mimicked her in a high-pitched voice. "I don't deserve to be alive. Why, I want Justis to think I'm sorry to be alive." His voice dropped. "Bullshit. You're tickled silly to be alive. You just feel bad about admitting it."

Katherine wavered, fury flooding her until she felt weak with it. *He was right.* She tried to say something in her defense, sputtered, then finally groaned in disgust. "Leave me alone." She went back to her rocking chair and sat facing away from him, her back rigid and her hands clasped in her lap.

He strode to her, grabbed the arm of the chair, and swung it around to face him. "Tell me about those cousins of yours."

"They all died! That's all there is to know!"

"How did they die?"

"The youngest died from fever, the mother died from a stomach ailment, and the other child—" She stopped, her throat closed.

"The other? Yeah?" He glared down at her, his eyes intense as he scrutinized her stricken face.

She beat her fists on her knees. "Squirrel died. He had a cough and he simply died! Leave me alone!"

"How did he die? Is he the one you wanted the medicine for when you bartered my gold piece?"

"Yes."

"Then you did all you could do for him."

"I killed him!"

She buried her face in her hands. Justis knelt in front of her and grasped her arms. "What happened?" he asked in a low, soothing voice.

"I told you. I killed him."

He shook her lightly.

"How?"

She made soft choking sounds. "I gave him too much of that worthless medicine."

"How do you know that?"

"He kept coughing. He couldn't sleep, he coughed so much. There was blood in his spittle. He cried and begged me to make his chest stop hurting. I gave him an extra dose of medicine to help him sleep. That's all it was good for, to make him sleep. But I gave him too much, because he never woke up. I killed him."

"Aw, Katie, shhh." He pulled her into his arms.

She knelt on the floor, clutching his coat as tears ran down her face. "I'm no doctor. He trusted me and I killed him. But I lived. I was rescued. I'm alive and safe now. Why?"

"He would have died anyhow. You just made it kinder."

"I don't know that. He was dear to me—bright and loving and courageous."

Justis stroked the back of her head. "What can I say to you to ease this blame in your mind?"

"I keep thinking that perhaps he might have gotten well if I hadn't used the medicine."

"Katie," he said in mild reproach. "You're a doctor— think like one. Use your smarts instead of your grief. Did he have the whooping cough?"

"Yes."

"And how many children live through that?"

"Not many, but—"

"And him with no place to rest out of the cold and wet, probably worn down from hunger . . . How far did he make the trip? No more than halfway, I bet. He wouldn't have lasted till you got to the western territory. If the cough hadn't taken him, something else would have."

She drew her head back. Tears streamed down her face. "You don't understand," she whispered. "He was strong. He'd come almost the whole way. We were at the Mississippi. *He died the day before you found me.*"

"Oh, Katie." He cupped her face in his hands and kissed her, then held her cheek against his. "I'm sorry, gal. I see now. He nearly made it. That's what hurts the most."

"Yes. And I don't understand why I couldn't save even him."

"I'll never be able to answer that one for you, gal. I'm a selfish son of a bitch, and all I care about is that you're safe, and you're gonna be just fine"—his hands tightened —"just *fine*, Katie Blue Song. You can't bring nobody back from the dead, but you sure can make the living happy." Guiding her head to his shoulder, he raised one of her hands and held it in front of her eyes. "Look at that. There's a whole lot of doctoring left in that pretty paw. Think of all the lives it'll save."

"I need to believe that."

They were quiet for a moment, holding each other in companionable sorrow. Finally he moved to the rocking chair and pulled her onto his lap. Katherine curled an arm around his neck. Together they gazed out at a clean, snow-covered world.

"It'll be spring before long," Justis said.

"New beginnings. Good."

"That's right. Try to think of it that way. Try real hard." He cleared his throat. "I want you to be happy."

She tugged at one end of his mustache. "Is that an order, sir?"

"Yeah."

"I'll do my best to carry it out." She looked at her hand

thoughtfully. "I suppose I do have some good doctoring skills left in my 'pretty paws.'"

"Believe it. Think of the lives you'll save and the babes you'll help birth." He added after a second, "You cared for Squirrel like a mother for a son. You love children—that shows it. You'll have your own someday."

Katherine stiffened. Why did he have to make such a callous remark? She'd have her own children—with some man besides him, he meant. She'd never forget his words that last night in Gold Ridge. *I don't want any half-breed babes any more than you do.* She trained her anger on a dash of snow along the windowsill and half expected to see it melt under the heat.

"You sound so certain of my future," she said.

"Well, I have to be the practical one, I reckon. All you do is argue."

"You'll take charge of the whole procedure, then?"

He studied her, his brow furrowed in concentration as if he were trying to figure out something new about her. "If you want me to," he said carefully, watching her reaction. "Birthin' babes is pretty hard work, I figure, and it's easy to see why a woman wouldn't look forward to it. But if you have the right man to look after you, and encourage you, and help care for the babe after it comes, well, *that* would make a difference, wouldn't it?"

"Good heavens. You've planned this all out, I can see. What do you think I am, a mare you must be responsible for breeding? Will you pack me off to the broodmares' pasture when our partnership ends, then select a stud for me? I can picture you interviewing prospective fathers on my behalf. Thank you, no. Perhaps I'm not suited ever to become a mother. And what makes you think I'd want children with some other white man if I don't want them with you?"

Dead silence filled the room. Katherine didn't know what to make of the sudden tension in his body. She was only stating the situation as he had outlined it. He pulled her arm from around his neck. His expression might have been carved from ice created by the chill in his eyes.

"Maybe you can find yourself a rip-snortin' redskin stud and he'll give you the kind of younguns you can be proud of. You and me won't be together forever."

She lifted a hand to her head, dizzy from the strain of their conversation. "I can't tell what I'll do so far in the future. I can't think that far ahead right now." How could he care for her so tenderly one moment and the next talk bluntly about turning her loose to find another man?

He set her off his lap and stood up. She looked at him and found an almost cruel gleam to his eyes. "You don't have to think any further than New York," he told her. "We're leavin' for there in the morning."

He walked out of the room without looking back and slammed the door behind him.


JUSTIS HELPED KATHERINE across the inn's snowy yard to a private coach he'd hired for the long trip east. She wore her new dress, a lovely blue wool with draping sleeves and a voluminous skirt, and a matching cape lined with satin. The dress and all her underthings were almost comically baggy, but she was so proud to have decent clothes again that she didn't care.

"I'll be ridin' right behind," Justis told her as he closed the door to the compartment. "If you need me, just tell the driver to stop."

"We've got weeks of travel ahead of us. Surely you're not going to ride Watchman the whole way?"

"We'll see," he said, and walked off.

She distractedly pulled a lap robe over her knees. What had she done to anger him? He'd been cool since that strange scene in the room the day before, when the subject of babes arose. He'd stayed downstairs playing cards most of the night, and when he had come to bed he'd kept to his side. During all their preparations to leave he had been polite but not friendly.

*You and me won't be together forever.* She felt as if she'd been struck whenever he said something such as that, something to remind her that friendship and loyalty were hardly the same as eternal love.

Katherine stared out the coach window at the long road winding through barren winter fields in the distance. The bittersweet emptiness inside her was a good thing, she decided. She would fill it with the excitement of living in New York. She would fill it with helping Justis turn Blue Song gold into a fortune. She would be the perfect partner, companion, and teacher for him.

But she would build herself a separate life as much as possible, so that when their partnership ended, she could walk away with at least a façade of dignity.

THEY COVERED 150 miles in the first week, with five or six times that much to come, and a March thaw turned the roads into slush. As they reached yet another stagecoach inn, Justis climbed stiffly down from Watchman's back while the driver pulled valises from the carriage. Twilight was broken only by a yellow stream of light coming from the door of the inn.

Exhausted, Justis slogged through mud and snow to the coach door. From the darkness within, Katherine glanced at him as she wearily tucked books and a piece of needlework into the small valise by her feet. Justis knew Mrs. Martin had given her the needlework materials as a good-bye gift. The fact that Katherine liked doing stitchery had surprised him. It was a side of her that he'd never seen before, a nice, ordinary, domestic talent that ought to show how easily she'd fit the role of wife and mother. If only, he thought grimly.

"Yes?" she inquired in a voice drained of energy. Riding in a cold, lurching coach all day was hardly an easy way to travel. She was much stronger, but she still looked gaunt. He would have given anything to pamper her at night, to rub her sore muscles and brush her hair for her, but he was determined not to let devotion make a fool of him any longer.

"I'm gettin' us separate rooms from now on," he said, "so you don't have to pretend to be Mrs. Gallatin anymore. 'Least not until we get to New York."

"All we do is fall into bed after supper and sleep like logs. It would be wasteful to pay for two rooms."

"I've got money to waste. What difference does it make to you?"

"None," she retorted. "But would you explain what this change of attitude means, sir?"

He hated being called sir. It was her best way of reminding him that she preferred to keep their relationship formal. "Means I'm tired of spendin' all night beside a woman who's still too frail to service me."

She straightened regally. "My disability has never stopped you from servicing yourself whenever you thought I was asleep."

"But now I'll have the privacy to grunt and kick the bedcovers. Really enjoy it."

That bit of crude banter stunned her into silence, and he rebuked himself for talking to her that way. She brushed his hand aside when he tried to help her from the coach. "I shall take dinner alone in my room," she informed him. "Good night, sir."

He stood by the coach and stared bitterly after her as she swept through the inn's door. When they got to New York he'd break her of this arrogance once and for all. Love him or not, she'd learn what it felt like to need someone so much that it hurt.

## CHAPTER 13

KATHERINE stood in the midst of the opulent hotel room, trying to look as if she were accustomed to such grandeur. Each time Justis glanced at her she nodded reassuringly. After all, he was counting on her to guide him through this elegant New York world. She couldn't tell him that it took her breath away. She'd never seen anything like it in Philadelphia.

From the outside, their hotel looked like a palace. It was five stories tall, its windows decorated with ornate cornices, its entrance flanked by marble columns. Inside on the ground level were dining halls, parlors, all sorts of shops, and a magnificent lobby with a vaulted ceiling. On each floor upstairs were mazes of hallways lit by lamps that burned some type of gas. She'd heard of such innovative lamps but had never seen them before.

The room Justis had ordered was actually a small suite. One entered the enormous sleeping chamber through a parlor furnished with richly upholstered chairs, marble tables, and Oriental rugs. Off the sleeping chamber was a dressing room outfitted with hot water faucets and a bathtub. That room was the stuff of fiction and fantasy.

"Sure'n you'll be wanting to use our grand hot water system," the head porter said proudly, his Irish brogue so thick that Katherine could barely understand him. "Steam-pumped, it is. Just turn a knob and there it comes. Glory, there's not another hotel on Broadway that has such a luvly thing. If you got any questions about it, ring downstairs for your faithful servant, meself."

He bowed, doffing a red velvet cap that matched both his hair and his livery. "Thomas." He turned and shooed a crew of maidservants out the open door to the hallway. "They'll come runnin' at your every whim, or they'll be tellin' meself why not."

"Thank you, Thomas," Katherine said quickly, smiling as if she were entirely familiar with armies of servants and miracles such as pipes that produced hot water on command. She turned to Justis, who stood by a tall window studying the street below. Broadway, it was called.

"God damn," he said in awe. "I've never seen so many buildings and people jam-packed so close together in my whole life."

Katherine was glad to find him distracted. She needed distracting, too, not only from the amazing surroundings, but from the tall, plush bed that stood between large windows along one wall. The bed, a four-poster with a canopy, was indecently sensual. There must have been three feather mattresses stacked under its satin covers and enormous pillows. The long side drapes were made of embroidered silk and pulled back to the head posts with tasseled velvet ties. The bed whispered provocatively to her.

She was healthy now; during the weeks of travel she had gradually gained weight and strength. Her clothes almost fit. There was no longer any reason not to begin the intimate phase of her agreement with Justis. Tonight.

In this chamber. In that bed. These days he was not in a mood to be patient.

"My dear," she called smoothly, though her heart thudded hard, "do you have some coins?"

He looked at her in bewilderment until she cut her eyes toward the expectant Thomas. "Ah! Hell, yes." He grinned and threw several to the porter.

His first lesson in hotel etiquette, she thought with hidden amusement. She glanced at the bed. He would undoubtedly teach lessons of his own in return.

The man bowed low. "Thank you, sir! I'll be taking me leave now."

"Hold on. I'll walk down with you," Justis said abruptly. "Got to see about havin' my horse stabled."

"Yours truly can help with that, too, sir!"

Relieved and disappointed that Justis was leaving, Katherine tugged nervously at the fastenings on her cloak. The maids had built a fire in the sleeping chamber's fireplace and set another going in the parlor's, but the suite would need some time to grow warm. Early April in New York City was cold and blustery.

Justis followed the porter toward the door, but halted as he came by her. She met his eyes and found them both somber and challenging. "Get everything warm before I come back," he ordered.

She gave him a deceptively nonchalant look. "I've grown accustomed to the cold."

"Better get used to bein' hot. I want it that way from now on."

Thankfully he left the room before her face began to burn. Yes, a new phase of their relationship was about to begin.

Justis waited to speak until he and the porter were halfway to the stairs. "Thomas," he said casually, "that lady isn't my wife."

If that news shocked the porter, the shock didn't

show. "What would she be, sir? Some kind of Indian fancy woman?"

"Yes. Cherokee." Justis pulled a heavy gold coin from his coat pocket. "And she thinks it's beneath her to marry a white man." He turned the coin over a few times, glancing at the porter's face to see if he had caught his attention. He had. The man could barely keep from staring at the gold piece.

"Thomas, I want that lady to be my wife. I want a legal weddin' with a real preacher and a fancy weddin' certificate. I got an idea as to how I can accomplish that."

"Yours truly is at your service, sir."

He tossed the coin to him. "If I get married tonight, you'll get another one of those in the mornin'. Savvy?"

"Yes, sir! You're the devil's own beloved, Mr. Gallatin, sir." The man grinned. "I know an old-country name when I hear one. Just tell me what you have in mind, and the leprechauns will be makin' all your wishes come true."

Justis clapped him on the shoulder and said tautly, "Right now I'd just settle for a damned weddin'."


KATHERINE DROPPED HER book onto her lap and stared at Justis. She couldn't read, she couldn't think, and she could barely sit still. When they'd gone downstairs for supper she had struggled merely to sample the dozens of dishes that a regiment of waiters had paraded in front of her.

Now Justis sat in a plush chair across the parlor table from her, his long legs stretched out to one side and crossed at the ankles, a glass of cognac near his stack of cards. Lamplight played lovingly on his relaxed features. He seemed utterly content to sit there enjoying a game of solitaire.

Every time he shifted she almost jumped, expecting him to make some coy remark that would tell her what he had in mind. The man looked ready to start for bed at any moment—his shirt was unbuttoned halfway down his hairy chest, his braces hung off his shoulders, he'd kicked his boots into a corner, and his eyelids had a heavy, sensual droop that was either fatigue, desire, or both.

"I suppose," she said primly, raising her book again, "that after weeks of virtually ignoring each other, some rearrangement of our attitudes will be necessary. I suppose it will take a few days to resettle them."

"I never ignored you," he said. He studied his cards with calm, deliberate attention and didn't look up at her. "I can tell you what your favorite victuals were, what books you read, how you did your hair, and how many times I caught you lookin' at me like you wanted to be undressed."

She started guiltily. "If I truly looked that way, you would have taken advantage of it. I've been nicely recovered from my ordeals for at least two weeks."

"I didn't want to bed an ornery woman worn out from travelin' all day."

"Ornery? Need I remind you that you haven't encouraged the least bit of friendship between us since the day we left the Martins' place in Illinois? What was I to make of that?"

"I let you simmer so you'd be good and ready for me."

She slammed her book shut. "Well, what if I'm not ready now? What if your self-serving manipulations have gone awry?"

"You're ready," he said, his attention still on his cards. "Otherwise you wouldn't be squawkin' and squirmin' like this. Your eyes have been as bright as black buttons all afternoon and you've got a blush even a blind man could see. You keep lookin' toward the bed and sighin'."

"Oh! You! You! Why don't we get it over with! It's going to be mere heartless entertainment to you, I can tell!"

He looked up then, his expression full of quiet anger. "Isn't that the way you want it?"

"No! I care so much—" She halted, watching the flare of interest her reckless words provoked in his eyes. She struggled for composure. "I want it to be kind, and friendly, and beautiful. Surely that's not too much to ask, even if we don't love each other."

A muscle throbbed in his jaw. His eyes narrowed. He looked angry again, but also sad. "I'll do my best."

Someone knocked loudly on the door. "I'll see to it," Justis said. He vaulted up from his chair as if tension had been coiled inside him, waiting for this moment. Katherine patted her hair and absently checked her dress as she watched him pull the door open.

A stocky, well-dressed man stood there. A constable stood beside him. "Mr. Gallatin?" the man said in a stern, formal tone.

"Yeah."

"My name is Mr. Gordon and I'm the manager of this hotel. I understand that your wife is an Indian?"

"Hell, yes. What of it?"

"Nothing of it, sir. But I want to see a marriage certificate."

Katherine's blood froze. "This is outrageous," she said in her most regal tone. She stood and glided gracefully to the door. "You are maligning my honor, sir."

He bowed. "I beg pardon, ma'am, but if I don't see some proof that you're married to this gentleman, I'm going to have you both arrested for fornication."

"What?" Justis bellowed. He raised a fist. "Any man who tries to cart my wife to jail will get his face knocked in."

Katherine grabbed his arm. "We are married, Mr. Gordon, I assure you. I've never heard of such strict adherence to propriety. I doubt that many of your guests carry their marriage certificates with them everywhere they travel."

"Pardon me," the manager replied, "but most of my gentlemen guests don't look like they walked in straight off the frontier, and most of my lady guests are lily white. If you don't have a marriage certificate, you'll have to get one."

"Well, find us a preacher," Justis said.

Katherine gasped. "Wait, oh, wait. Can my husband and I have a moment in private?"

The manager nodded. Justis shut the door and turned to her. "Guess we're trapped," he said, and shrugged. "Makes no difference to me. Let's do it. We need to be respectable, you know. All it takes is a bit of paper with some words on it."

She stared at him in dismay. "It's much more than that. It's a lifetime pledge. It's an oath before God."

"It's a way to stay out of jail."

She hugged herself and paced rapidly. "I need time to think! Overnight. A day or two. There must be some other way. We could switch to another hotel—"

"Where we'd probably get insulted again. Let's tie the knot and be done with it."

"I can't give up easily!"

"You sure ain't doing *that*," he said dryly. "Just gettin' you to live with me has been the toughest work of my life. You've fought a good battle over what's wise and what's not, but it's time to give up and get hitched."

She whirled on him.

"You sound almost pleased about this! Do you want to be married to me even after we go our separate ways? For the rest of your life?"

He shrugged. "It's just a piece of paper. I can probably go to court in a couple of years and bribe some greedy judge to nullify it. Besides, bein' married makes me sound like a solid citizen, whether I got a wife to show for it or not."

Katherine wanted to cry. He didn't care why he married her, so long as he accomplished his business goals.

But wasn't that kind of practical attitude the best? If she built her own separate life, what difference would a marriage certificate make when he no longer wanted her? Marriage didn't mean they'd be together forever, but at least it was a step in the right direction. And if it meant that he owned her, well, he had demonstrated over the course of nearly a year's acquaintance that owner or not, he was inescapable and irresistible.

"I don't want to go to jail," she said dully.

"Good. Let's get married and go to bed. I'm sleepy."

"You don't look sleepy."

"You don't look married. Yet." He swung the door open again. Mr. Gordon and the constable gazed at him expectantly. "Get us a preacher," Justis told them. His gaze met Katherine's. "What kind?"

She sank down in a chair, defeated. "Presbyterian. At least we'll be solemn about it."


LONG AFTER THE minister had left, Katherine continued to stare at the wedding certificate he'd bestowed on them. She stood in the middle of the bedroom and read it as if it would never make sense. Justis moved around the suite, turning lamps down one by one and banking the fires.

"Real pretty, huh?" he said, coming up behind her. He looked over her shoulder at the scrolled gilt letters and the blanks where the minister had filled in their names, the date, and the witnesses—Mr. Gordon and the constable. "Not so scary, huh? Just a pretty piece of paper."

She numbly laid it on a table. "I'll change into my nightclothes."

Justis caught her arm and swung her to face him. "No," he said gruffly. "You won't need 'em."

Her stomach dropped as she saw that all the levity was gone from him. The image of the carefree rascal had been a complete ruse. In his grim, strained face she found a year's worth of waiting, a year of wanting her and not having her.

"You've run out of patience," she whispered.

"Yeah."

"I think you look forward to hurting me a little."

"God, no. I look forward to making you want me so much that you forget to despise me."

*"Justis."* She said his name half in rebuke and half in shared desperation. It was hardly out of her mouth before he pulled her to him and kissed her. Her knees buckled as he slowly moved his mouth over hers, goading her with rhythmic shoving motions of his jaw, retreating a fraction to let her take a quick breath, then sinking his mouth onto hers again and using his tongue to part her lips.

She moaned, exploding inside with a reckless mixture of nerves and desire. In the back of her mind a tormented voice reminded her that their forced marriage was a terribly sad thing that could bring her only more heartache. She was married to a practical man who would never love her the way she loved him. But still— she was his wife. *His wife.*

She broke away slightly. "Let it be, then. I can't help it. I can't help anything anymore. But, dear man, *I don't despise you.* If I were given a chance to choose where I might go in the world and who I might go with, I would freely choose you."

"Why?" he asked, stunned.

"We—we seem to be fated to torment each other for the time being."

"You want me," he whispered fiercely. "Say it. No matter what happens, no matter about love, tonight you want me more than anything or anybody else in the world."

"No matter." Tears slid down her face. "No matter. You're everything I want."

With a low groan of satisfaction he kissed her repeat-

edly, and she found herself lapping her tongue across his
lips to learn every essence and texture of him. She clung
to him, lost in the shattering, heart-draining possession of
their kiss, while he unfastened the back of her dress with
hands that fumbled and finally ripped off buttons violently.

"You're beautiful," he told her as he pushed aside the
gaping back of her bodice. "And you were beautiful even
back when you were so hurt and thin."

He ripped her undershirt, then pulled the remnants of
it and the bodice down her shoulders. His roughness excited her, and she cried out in delight when he shoved
the tight material beneath her nipples. As her breasts
slipped free he bent and took one in his mouth, sucking
with such a perfect blend of skill and ferocity that she
cried out again and grasped his head to urge him closer.

"Please let me see you," she begged, jerking on the
collar of his shirt. "Please let me touch you too."

He straightened, his strong arms circling her waist and
pulling her up on tiptoe so he could study her eyes
closely. The primitive flush of desire on his face made her
dizzy with anticipation.

"Tell me the truth—the truth now, you hear?" he said
in a gravelly voice. "Am I too hairy for an Injun to admire?"

A disbelieving laugh rose in her throat until she saw
his stern, worried frown. "I adore your hairiness," she
murmured. She wrenched the collar of his shirt apart
and angled her head so she could nuzzle the thick pelt
she'd exposed.

He staggered a little and growled hoarsely with amazement. His hips flexed in response to the sudden addition
of her tongue to the nuzzling. She caught his leather
necklace in her teeth and dragged it out of the way, then
speared it with a fingertip and flipped the gold nugget
over his shoulder. "I want no distractions." She curled

her fingers into his chest hair. "How wonderful it is to pet."

"I don't look like your damned Philadelphia dandy. I'm not pink and hairless."

"You're entirely too talkative, that's what you are." She tilted her head back and gazed at him, her eyes sultry. "I think you have the most beautiful hair and scars and leathery skin. I don't want you to look a bit different. I've seen all of you, remember? And I want to see you again."

"Oh, God. I never thought I'd hear you say anything like that to me."

"Is it shocking? Do you think a lady ought not to be so open about her admiration?"

"I think," he murmured, sinking his mouth onto hers for a moment, "that you're the perfect kind of lady just the way you are."

She unbuttoned his shirt and he stripped it off, then she pressed her hands to his shoulders. She slid them slowly down his chest, melting at the feel of him, the entrancing combination of hair and muscle swelling repeatedly under her fingertips.

Justis carried her to the bed and placed her in the midst of the huge, extravagant pillows. He knelt beside her in shadowy lamplight and undid her braids. "I've got to see this spread over you. Later on I've got to see this spread over *me*."

She reached up and caressed his face with quick, almost frantic touches. "You said once, a long time ago, that we would burn each other up. You were right."

Her back arched as he feathered long strands of her hair across her naked breasts. He raked it over her nipples and down her belly, then gathered it close to the crook of her neck and burrowed his face there. She shivered with pleasure as he nipped the tender skin under her ear. He bit her like an animal enticing its mate.

"That makes me go limp," she whispered.

He chuckled, the sound torn with desire. "That's not what it does to me."

"Then you would like it too?" She turned her face toward his neck and nibbled in return, tasting his skin with little sucking movements of her mouth.

"Oh, yeah." He dug his hands into her arms and shuddered. "Before tonight's over I'm gonna bite you in places you never thought a bite could be."

The images that filled her mind were so overwhelming, she moaned. Her thighs felt damp and relaxed; inside she ached with a pulsing emptiness that begged to be filled. Justis got to his knees and quickly finished undressing her. She lay there in quivering silence, so aroused that a mere look from him made her skin tingle. His gaze moved over her slowly and thoroughly, as if he'd never seen her naked before.

She still wore white stockings and the garters that held them above her knees. He placed his palms just above them, on the insides of her thighs. Katherine thought she'd die from the exquisite feel of his blunt, calloused fingers slipping down her sensitive skin. He caught the garters and stockings and pulled them off her legs in a maddeningly unhurried way that turned the simple act into a lurid caress.

She felt open and vulnerable as he circled her bare ankles and began the same slow journey again, this time upward. Sensations cascaded along her skin ahead of his stroking fingers. Unseen forces urged her to spread her legs widely and welcome every sensation to the aching center between them.

She panted for breath and curled her hands to her mouth. His eyes met hers, and their hunger seared her. Slowly he reached the tops of her thighs. He pulled them apart a little. "This'll feel good to you," he promised. "So good. Like this."

He stroked her between the thighs, his fingers slipping deep into the folds there, then rising over the mound and rubbing the swollen nub it guarded. "You are so ready for me." His voice was a throaty murmur. "I know how to make it even better."

She wanted to protect her dignity, make some witty remark that would let him know she was aware of how helpless and adoring she must look with her legs opening eagerly. But she only moaned with desire as she saw the approval in his eyes. His fingers continued their slow rubbing motion.

She tossed her head from side to side as his other hand gently pinched her nipples and squeezed her breasts. Her hair tumbled across her, across his hands. "More. More of everything," she begged.

"Say my name."

"*Justis.*"

The happy rush of his breath warmed her belly as he bent over and kissed it. His hands never stopped their sweet torture. She muffled a high-pitched keening sound against her knuckles as rhythmic pleasure poured into her womb. In the midst of it Justis took her with his fingers, and her body surrounded them eagerly, adding new fervor to her delight.

Dazed, Katherine realized that she was nearly crying as she reached desperately for him with both hands. He groaned—ragged, demanding sounds in the back of his throat—and began to kiss and suck her breasts.

She protested with a whimper when he stopped touching her, then watched him unfasten his trousers and shove them down. The sight of his large, jutting arousal signaled some deep part of her to relax rather than fear it. "It won't hurt," she said in soft awe. "I'm certain."

He kicked his trousers onto the floor and knelt beside her, one hand resting reassuringly on her belly. "Aw, Katie, Katie, I hope it won't."

He lay down next to her, and she molded herself to his side. The unhurried atmosphere of a moment earlier was lost in a whirlwind of swift, bawdy caresses. His hands roamed over her. Finally he manacled her against him with one arm and pulled her topmost leg over his thighs, while he kissed her roughly, his mouth open and utterly without inhibition. She rubbed her leg up and down on his. When she put a hand on his arousal he threw his head back and shut his eyes.

"You got no qualms about pleasurin' a man there?" he asked hoarsely.

"No. Is that bad?"

"Good. Katie. I can't believe anything could be so good."

She carefully stroked one thigh, then the other, marveling at the size and strength of his body, the lean, ropy muscles and their soft covering of reddish-brown hair. She raised her hand and slowly rested it on his arousal again. "So smooth," she murmured, barely breathing. She ran her fingertips along the shaft, then explored the taut pouch beneath it. "Does it feel good when I do this?" she whispered.

"Like I died and went to heaven."

She pressed small kisses to his shoulder and neck. "When my sisters and I were little, we saw two people from the Talachee village lying together in the woods. So we watched. We thought all the odd things they did to each other were *very* funny." Her fingers brushed up and down his belly. "The woman did something to the man that I never understood. Until now."

Trembling, not knowing what he'd think of her boldness, she quickly sat up and leaned over his thighs. She kissed the tip of his arousal, then feathered several more kisses down the shaft. The taste and texture were a primitive enticement that made her want him even more.

His low moan of shock and delight told her she'd done the right thing. He grasped her head and pulled her toward him. His hooded, starkly sensual gaze sent fire through her blood. "Have you no shame, woman?" he teased hoarsely.

"Not where you are concerned. And"—she studied him closely for a reaction—"I wasn't raised to be delicate, as a white woman is."

He stroked her hair, wound his hands into it, and said between gritted teeth, "That's why I want you. Not just in bed, either."

She kissed him happily. "We will be grand together, then."

"Katlanicha." He whispered the name across her mouth. "Katlanicha."

They traded slow, damp kisses. She copied everything he did and measured her success by the small, thrilling noises he made. He rolled her on top of him. "Just let me see the need in those black eyes."

"See it?" she murmured, emotion nearly trapping the words in her throat. Her eyelids felt weighted, her face warm.

"Like a promise." His thumbs moved over her cheekbones, then slid to her mouth. She kissed them, then sucked the one that he slipped between her lips.

She straddled him because it was a very pleasant way to remain where she was, but as soon as her knees sank into the soft mattress she settled atop his arousal. The tip was so close to entering her, it tantalized her silky, swollen flesh and made her hips move languidly.

"Be still now," he crooned. "You'll loosen up real good if we play awhile. Then I'll put you on your back and take you gentle and slow. Lord, it's hard for me to wait too."

He slid his hands down her spine and cupped her hips. She looked at him with bittersweet adoration. *I love you.* "For you," she whispered.

"No, Katie!"

His hands dug into her buttocks to stop her, but she slid herself swiftly onto his thick shaft. He grabbed her shoulders as she cried out in distress. She bit her lip to keep from whimpering again, but the stinging pain made tears pool in her eyes. She tried to smile.

"Sweet, stubborn gal," he muttered. He folded her close to him and stroked her back. "Lie still."

She burrowed her face into his shoulder and drew long, shaky breaths. "I'm glad I did it, but, oh, it hurts." She felt as if everything inside her were stretching to accept him.

He molded his big, gentle hands to her and massaged her from neck to hip, crooning soft sounds in her ear, tickling her cheek with his mustache. "That'll learn you to listen to my advice."

"*Teach* you."

He slapped her rump lightly in rebuke, then rubbed the slapped spot. "*Teach* you." He added in a growling voice, "I sure will teach you."

As he slowly flexed his hips under her, she squeezed her eyes shut and waited for the torturous pain. But he slid back and forth gently, nudging her deep inside with such care that it didn't hurt anymore. She exhaled in relief and slowly began to squeeze his sides with her knees.

He kissed her until she could barely think, and his thighs flexed upward at a faster pace. She gazed at the slumberous, primitive heat in his eyes and knew that it was matched in hers. Pleasure, like before, made her ache. This time he stroked the ache in a different way, with even greater effect.

Her hands kneaded his chest in a quick, mindless rhythm, and she circled her hips, discovering realms of pleasure she hadn't even imagined. Her eyes shut, she gave her senses to the feel of Justis's powerful body thrusting into her, his belly tightening with hers, the musky, exciting scent rising from their joining, the guttural sounds he made in the back of his throat.

In the midst of a sweet daze she heard him caress her

with her own name. Its effect was so potent, she kissed him in rough, greedy response. Then she felt him begin to lift her off his thighs, to withdraw.

"No, no," she begged. "Justis, don't go yet. Oh, Justis."

He cursed helplessly as she enclosed him again and cried out long phrases in Cherokee, their meaning evident in her tone of praise. She clung to him and writhed as sensation crested inside her. His back arched like a tightly drawn bow and he plunged into her deeply, then held her as he quivered with release. A fierce growl of pleasure and defeat rushed from his throat.

They looked at each other in silence, catching their breath. Katherine felt the creamy flood of his seed slip down her thighs. She searched his troubled gaze and saw a frown growing on his face. Her head drooped to his shoulder.

"My fault," she whispered. "I didn't realize why you were trying to stop me."

"Shhh. I was so crazy for the feel of you that I didn't think right. I was the teacher—I knew what was happenin' better than you did." His hand rose to her head and he stroked her hair. The other hand he slipped around her shoulders to hold her snugly. "No more recklessness, Katie. I promise."

"It was wonderful," she said with a happy sigh.

After a moment he sighed in agreement. "Better than anything." They lay there, sweaty, still joined, emotions shimmering between them until she could barely tell whether the heart beating steadily against her rib cage was hers or his. *You will always stand in my soul,* she told him silently.

"Katie Gallatin," he drawled in a languid, thoughtful tone, his hand still caressing her hair. "Katlanicha Blue Song Gallatin. We're gonna have ourselves a helluva time together."

She hugged him until her arms ached and prayed that it would never end.

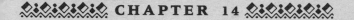 

## CHAPTER 14

IF KATHERINE weren't a happily married woman, she was sure doing a fine imitation of one, Justis decided over the next few weeks. She seemed to enjoy her roles as teacher and partner, and he had no doubt that she enjoyed her role as lover. She treated him with unreserved affection and a wanton desire that matched his own.

During the day he let her go her own way, though he was eager to be with her. She seemed to want her time alone, and he tried not to wonder if she craved his company a great deal more in bed than out.

He spent his time meeting with men who had plenty of ideas on how to spend someone else's money. His personal banker, who for the past several years had managed the accounts for the three hundred thousand dollars made from Blue Song gold, had helped Justis make some contacts in the shipping business. Chances were good that the Gallatin name would be on a pair of handsome freight brigs before spring ended.

When he got bored with businessmen's claptrap, feeling restless in their stuffy offices and elite dining clubs, he slipped away and walked the city. Even with all of Katherine's instructions on etiquette, he still felt awkward with the silly rules of society. He was at his best when he could find a good fire and join in the fighting of it with a group of the city's volunteer firemen. They were nearly all Irish, and for the first time in his life he saw his heritage as something worth having, something to be proud of.

At the end of each day he and Katherine discussed the business deals he had investigated. He knew it was odd—some might even say sinful—to talk business with a woman, but Katherine was smarter than other women and most men. She read all of New York's newspapers and used the information to give him sensible advice. With her patient help he improved his own reading by practicing on the stories she considered most important.

She was more relaxed than he'd ever seen her before. New Yorkers weren't a problem the way people had been in Gold Ridge; they tended to be genuinely fascinated by her, not scornful. Still, when they were out in public he tried to shield her from the curious stares of strangers, and God help anyone stupid enough to ask her a rude question about Indians within his earshot.

She surprised him with the circle of well-to-do lady friends she'd already made. Katherine didn't cultivate them for their idle gossip and prissy devotion to matronhood, but with an eye toward making business contacts. Many of her new acquaintances were the wives of important men—merchants, lawyers, bankers, businessmen of all sorts—and through their dinner invitations Justis had already begun several promising deals.

Katherine said her lady friends were merely titillated by the notion of having an exotic in their midst. Justis suspected she was right, but he told her they were damned lucky to have her anyway, and he meant it. He was glad for her friends, no matter what their motives, because with them she could safely attend female lectures, visit museums, and shop.

And shop she did. She outfitted herself in tasteful and elegant style, and he almost burst with pride when he took her out walking. She also supervised his wardrobe with glee, dragging him to tailors and hatmakers and all kinds of fancy specialists until he had more clothes than he'd ever have needed if she hadn't insisted on variety.

Justis leaned back in a parlor chair, tossed several shipping trade reports aside, and pulled a gold watch from his vest pocket. The watch was a gift from Katie. He smiled. The lovely she-cat had pinned it to her drawers. He'd found it one evening as he was hurriedly undressing her.

He was checking the time impatiently when a key rattled in the hall door. He leapt up to let her in. She stepped over the threshold, smiled, and held out her arms expectantly. She wasn't a bit surprised when he pulled her bonnet and cape off as he was shutting the door, and removed the rest of her clothes as he led her toward the bedroom. She was too busy undressing him.

As he took her into his arms he prayed that she'd never leave.

KATHERINE FOUND IT helpful to sit and daydream these days, lost in warm memories and warmer anticipation, pretending that Justis loved her dearly. Lounging in a tall, upholstered armchair in the hotel's parlor for ladies, a stack of magazines lying unread in her lap, she shut her eyes and smiled.

After two months of marriage she could almost believe they would be together forever. If Justis regretted their forced marriage, he never said so. She was certain he was happy with her, *when* he was with her. He stayed out every day during the week, and often on the week-ends. He dined out several nights each week with men from his growing circle of business acquaintances.

She hid her loneliness and made certain to look preoccupied with her own duties, which included studying real estate possibilities for him and keeping an eye on all the financial news carried by the newspapers. Maintaining her resolve to build her own life, she made few demands on his time. She rarely asked him to accompany her somewhere just for entertainment, and insisted that he go to business functions even when the invitations didn't include wives.

He must be pleased with their separate schedules, she mused, because he never complained, and when he was with her he seemed utterly content. They shared their daily happenings, they cheerfully argued the fine points of his business negotiations, and they spent long, blissful hours in bed.

Katherine gazed out a hotel window pensively. They never spoke any endearments or made any reckless vows about the future, but they filled those hours together with a wondrous brand of passion that mingled affection and respect with bawdy lust. Surely that meant something special to him. Surely.

A small hand tugged at the sleeve of her dress. "*Señora* Gallatin."

She looked down at an impeccably dressed youngster with olive skin and dark hair. "Felipe! How are you today?"

Before he could answer she was surrounded by six more children, all expensively clothed and dark-complected. The eldest was a teenaged girl, Leanor; the youngest was Felipe. They chattered their hellos in heavily accented English and tried to tell her all at once about their visit to an ice cream emporium.

A wiry little woman arrived in a rustle of blue satin. An entourage of nannies and personal maids hovered behind her like dull-colored chicks following a peacock. "Silence!" Francesca Adela Mendez ordered.

Her dark Spanish eyes gleamed with friendship as she gazed at Katherine. "Reading again! Bah! You are truly an American woman! A Californio would never sit still so long!"

Katherine laughed. "Good afternoon. Would you like to go to tea with me?"

*"Bueno.* And I have a dinner invitation for you and your husband. Tomorrow night. My brother-in-law Vittorio returns from his trip to Boston. I want you to meet him. He reads too much, like you. You will have much to say to each other, yes?"

"Yes. Thank you. We accept." Katherine nodded toward one of the children. "How is Juan feeling today?"

"Perfect! I had Anita mix the medicine as you said. *Gracias."*

*"De nada."*

Adela clapped her hands in delight. "I will make you into a Californio yet!"

"Could an Indian become a Californio?" Katherine asked, smiling drolly.

"Oh, yes. We have thousands of Indians!"

Katherine glanced at the short, swarthy maids. "Are they all servants trained by the priests?"

Adela arched a brow at the innuendo. Then she swept her hands out in an exuberant, dramatic gesture and looked around in mock horror. "No! There are still many wild, free savages who make war on our people!" Her eyes snapped with humor. "And there are many Indian wives among our men. So you see? Come to California! For you all the handsome rancheros would fight each other! What excitement!"

"What flattery." Katherine stood up and they traded smiles. They made an odd pair of friends—Cherokee and Mexican-Spanish, Protestant and Catholic, outcast and aristocrat. But Adela Mendez was the only one of Katherine's new acquaintances who inspired true friendship and trust. In Katherine's world, haunted by an uncertain future and a lonely present, it was a great prize.

"THERE. DONE. A finely tied cravat, if I do say so myself." Katherine stepped back and admired her handiwork.

Justis held out his hands and arched one chestnut brow. "A fine-lookin' man," he coaxed.

"A fine-looking man."

He turned around slowly, his hands still out in a look-at-my-handsomeness gesture. She drew a slow breath of admiration. His big, rangy body with its broad shoulders and lean hips was hardly fashionable, but the way New York ladies stared at him, she doubted a fashion critique was uppermost in their minds. She always clothed him in conservative colors—mostly tan, black, or white—because a magnificent rooster didn't need to gild his plumage.

For tonight's supper party at the Mendez apartments upstairs, he wore tan trousers and a crisp white shirt with a black silk cravat. He had not yet donned his black vest and fitted black coat.

"A good, strong back," he hinted.

"I've admired it a few times, I admit."

"Sturdy legs. Muscled haunches."

She laughed happily. "A handsome mule."

He turned around and gave her an exasperated look. "Mule? No mule has what it takes to fill the front of these trousers."

She was giggling now. "Indeed. He'd need a very large opinion of himself."

He strode to her and grabbed her around the waist. She yipped as he swung her around. When he halted, grinning, she ruffled his hair in mild rebuke. "You shaggy hellion."

"My hair and mustache are gonna stay uncivilized. I like 'em that way."

"All right." She sighed as if horribly defeated, but looked up at him with glowing eyes. She never wanted to see him clean-shaven or close-cropped. Nothing was more provocative than the feel of his mustache damp with sweat and kisses, or his hair disheveled by her excited caresses.

"I have a present for you," he told her. "Cover your eyes."

She did as he asked, thoroughly intrigued. She heard him moving about the parlor, then coming back to her. He'd already given her several pieces of beautiful jewelry.

"Look," he whispered. "On the table."

She withdrew her hands and gazed at a sleek black satchel. Breathless, she opened it and gazed down at a complete array of doctor's implements and medicines. She caught a soft sob in her throat. "Oh, thank you, thank you."

"Now you're a full-fledged doc again."

She slipped her arms around his neck. "You are as dear sometimes as . . ." She struggled to find praise that wouldn't complicate their unsentimental brand of affection. "As a real husband would be," she finished.

His expression changed only a little, but the subtle tightening made it go from tender to grim. "Maybe you'll find one of those someday. A real husband."

She winced. "I thought I was complimenting you."

"I know." He sounded weary. "I'm glad you like it. I just didn't want you to lose your doctorin' skills. You bein' an independent woman and all. Someday you'll be on your own again."

So much for sentiment, she thought in silent despair, and stepped back. "It's truly a wonderful gift. Thank you again. I suppose we'd better be going upstairs. It's impolite to be late to a private meal."

"I'll add that to my list of rules to live by."

Both of them subdued, they turned away.

ADELA'S BROTHER-IN-LAW was a dashing figure who seemed suited to the richly ornamented backdrop of the Mendez hotel suite. Vittorio Salazar was dressed all in dark colors except for the startling white of his shirt, which set off his dark complexion to perfection. His features were elegant, like his tall, graceful frame. He made Katherine think of a black swan.

Gray feathered his hair at the temples, and he had a look of quiet sorrow. He was a recent widower, Adela had explained at tea. His wife—the sister of Adela's husband—had died in childbirth after years of barren frustration, taking their child with her. This trip to New York was his idea, a way to escape the memories at his rancho.

Adela had gleefully snatched the opportunity to sojourn in New York with him as chaperon. She had kissed her husband good-bye at their rancho and told him not to let his mistresses grow too fond of running her casa. Then she had rounded up her children and her servants and happily followed Vittorio aboard a ship bound for the east.

Salazar's mournful eyes were huge and rimmed with upswept girlish lashes. When he bowed deeply to Katherine, murmuring in a melodic Spanish-tinged voice, "What ethereal loveliness. I hope you will favor me with your presence often," she felt as though a tragic poet were offering his soul.

Which was all well and good and interesting in a melodramatic sort of way, except that Justis was not the kind of man—loving husband or not—who wanted another man to admire his wife so boldly. Katherine glanced at him and saw seething disgust in his expression.

Anger burst into a stubborn flame inside her. What

right did he, who didn't love her, have to glower? She was still no more than a possession to him. Even a possession deserved to enjoy compliments.

She thanked Vittorio in slow, careful Spanish, and he smiled at her as if she'd said something important and very private. She watched with quiet victory as the Californio introduced himself to Justis. Her husband was chewing the inside of his cheek, a sure sign that he was trying to control his temper.

There were several other couples at the supper party, all people who either lived permanently at the hotel or were in New York for a lengthy visit. Adela's maids served a ten-course meal catered by the hotel's staff of French chefs.

It should have been a marvelous event. For Katherine it was torture. Justis ignored her and most of the food, opting instead to drink outrageous amounts of the various wines and liquors that accompanied the meal. He turned his attention to the guests near him, including Adela, and soon had them entranced with wild tales of the frontier, most of which Katherine recognized as inventive lies.

She regretted her part in antagonizing him and began to worry about the consequences. Vittorio, though seated at the far end of the table from her, managed to direct most of his conversation to her, and she knew Justis had an ear tuned to every word. Vittorio was well-read, impeccably sensitive to the arts, and he gave fascinating accounts of the Californios' lazy, regal life-styles on their immense ranches.

Justis managed to maintain an air of indifference until the after-dinner liqueurs were served. When Vittorio spent several minutes describing the European liquors he imported and the time he spent developing vineyards, Justis turned to him slowly and said, "Sounds to me like you Californios just sit around piss-drunk with your grapes hangin' out to dry in a warm wind."

The women gasped and their husbands sputtered with consternation. Adela unfurled a large fan and laughed merrily behind it. Vittorio rubbed a long, smooth finger across his lower lip and looked thoughtful, as if pondering the image of his personal grapes drying in a warm wind.

"I do not understand the insult very well, Señor," he said at last. "I also do not understand why a gracious and intelligent lady is married to a man who seems intent on ignoring and then humiliating her in public."

"She's used to it," Justis shot back. "She's an Injun."

Katherine hoped that years of rigid self-discipline kept her face from showing her devastation. *How could he talk about her that way?*

Two of the couples coldly excused themselves, thanked Adela for her hospitality, and left. Katherine drew her chin up and looked at Adela, whose expression was carefully nonjudgmental. Mustering all her training in decorum, Katherine said in a calm, conversational tone, "I believe my husband is attempting to compliment me. He means, I believe, that my peculiar status in life has taught me to overlook trivial slander."

To Vittorio she said, "My husband would never deliberately humiliate me, Señor. I respect him and he shows me the utmost respect in return. Your defense is noble, but misguided."

"No, the bastard's right," Justis said.

Stunned, Katherine pivoted to look at him. His eyes were full of a bitterness she didn't understand, but when he took the hand she'd clenched in her lap, his touch was infinitely gentle.

He kissed her hand, stood up, and bowed to her. "Forgive me." Then he turned and left the apartment.

When Katherine returned to their suite a short time later, he was standing, his arms crossed, in front of a window in the dimly lit sleeping chamber. The slow stiffening of his posture was the only sign he gave that he'd heard her come in. He might have been riveted to the never-ceasing activity of Broadway.

"I wish I could cut my tongue out for what I said about you," he told her. "Something ugly came out in me that I couldn't stop. God help me, I didn't mean to hurt you."

She went to him and leaned her head against his shoulder. "Vittorio Salazar is nothing. Why be so angry at him?"

"He's everything I'm not. Educated. Got good manners. Knows how to say the right thing—in at least two languages. Hell, he's even kinda dark, like an Indian."

"Oh, for goodness' sake . . ."

"You were taken with him from the second he spoke to you. I could tell."

She groaned in despair. "Justis, how could you—"

"You're not to see him again, you hear? I won't have you trailin' after that Spanish dandy. You and me got a deal. You may not like bein' my wife, but you better act the part. I expect you to be faithful."

She backed away, her hands clenched. "How could you ruin all the friendship and trust between us by accusing me that way?"

"I'm not accusin'. I'm warning."

"It's the same thing." She was so hurt and angry, she could barely breathe. Shivering, her breath coming in short gulps, she said tightly, "I will see whom I please. I would enjoy talking to Señor Salazar about art and literature."

Justis turned slowly, his body and face rigid with restraint. "I'll dump you out of this hotel with nothing but your smile for a meal ticket."

She straightened proudly. "Never offer an ultimatum to me, sir. I thought you learned that long ago. Goodbye." She turned on one heel and headed toward the parlor. " 'Tis July. I'll get by with nothing warmer than my smile."

A few seconds later she was kicking and flailing as he carried her back to the bedroom. He wrestled her onto the bed and stripped off every stitch of her clothes, then used her stockings to tie her wrists to the headboard. Standing over her with a patient expression on his face, he listened until she ran out of virulent insults in both English and Cherokee.

"Good night, wife," he said sardonically, and pulled the covers over her.

"I am not an *a-tsi-na-Ha-i* anymore! I will never be your captive again!"

"Doesn't look that way right now, does it?"

"You will pay for your distrust," she said bitterly, crying with humiliation. "We were friends. You have taken that away."

He uttered a concise obscenity. "Don't talk nonsense."

He slung his clothes off as he went to the lamps and turned them down. Katherine jerked on the tethers that held her hands and turned her back to him as he got into bed. The darkness crackled with silent tension. Finally he thumped a fist onto the mattress as if in frustration, then slid close to her and arranged her pillows so that she'd be comfortable.

"There. You'll sleep without misery."

She exhaled raggedly. "You think I'm a dog who will forget a beating if her master pets her."

"I didn't beat you!"

She groaned in disgust. "You will never understand. Go away."

"Fine." He moved to his side of the bed and didn't say another word.

Katherine quivered with anger and disappointment. His stubborn determination to make her do his bidding was born of pride, not love. Now he had let it ruin the lovely camaraderie that had given her so much hope for the future.

Before they had abandoned their traditions for the

more complicated dicta of white law, her people had regarded revenge as a good and necessary thing. It was the accepted way to rebuild honor and peace between enemies. She wanted revenge.

She pretended to sleep. Sometime later Justis slid close to her again. He untied her hands and rubbed the wrists gently. Tears pooled behind her eyelids as she felt him kiss her hair. *Scoundrel!* Why did he confuse her so? He sighed as if exhausted, then went back to his side of the bed. Within a few minutes she heard his breathing fall into the deep, even cadence of sleep.

She waited for more than an hour, until she knew he was settled firmly in his dreams. Then she tiptoed from bed and got her new doctor's satchel. *Revenge.*

JUSTIS STRUGGLED TO wake up. His arms and legs felt weighted, and his mind was groggy. It was puzzling but not unpleasant. He stretched and dragged a hand up to rub some life into his face. With any luck he'd be able to force his eyelids open.

There was something odd about his face, something different. He yawned and rubbed a knuckle over an itchy spot along his upper lip. His hand froze.

His mustache was gone.

With a bellow of disbelief he pushed himself upright and squinted painfully as morning sunshine struck his face. His throat was sore and his voice came out a deep, brutal rasp. *"Kath-er-ine!"*

"I'm right here." She rose from an armchair near the fireplace and walked to the bed. She looked regal in a white dressing gown with her hair in a neat braid around the crown of her head. Her expression was troubled but stoic. Her dark eyes held no victory. "I didn't run away after taking my revenge. There would be no honor in that."

"Revenge," he echoed hoarsely. "Honor."

"I couldn't live with you otherwise. I couldn't bear it, after the way you disgraced everything good that we've shared. Now I have my revenge. If you accept it, we can go on together. If you don't . . ." She looked at him sadly and waited for his response.

Speechless, he slung the covers back and rolled out of bed. He staggered to the dressing room and stared at himself in the mirror over the washstand. Years had passed since he'd last seen the scar on his upper lip. It was a distinct white ridge that ran just above the corner of his mouth to a little past halfway across. It made him look evil.

She had shorn the hair on his head to a uniform inch in length, all over. The luscious waves were gone. It was straight and so short on top, it bristled. He felt like an ugly cur dog with its hackles up.

To add insult to injury, she had shaved his chest hair off. Justis looked down in horror. His pubic hair was gone too. He braced his arms on the stand. His head drooped and he shut his eyes, then he cursed softly, viciously.

"It is a severe revenge, I know," she said, watching him from the doorway. Her voice was low and anguished. "And I know you may do something terrible to me in return. But I would rather suffer that than be forced to leave you. At least I can stay with honor now."

"You did this because I tied you to the damned bed?"

"The bed? Hah." She dismissed that indignity with a wave of one hand. "No. Because you accused me of disloyalty. I *will* be friends with Vittorio Salazar and any other gentleman I wish to cultivate. But I will never be unfaithful to you. I've never given you any reason to think that I would."

He gripped the washstand fiercely. "No, you haven't."

"Then why distrust me?"

*Because you don't love me and I can't stand the thought of losing you to some other man.* "What kind of hellion are you? I knew you were different from other women, but I'll be damned if I expected this."

"I won't be owned. I won't be treated like an *a-tsi-na-Ha-i.* Do you finally believe that?"

"By God, I guess I do after this."

He gazed at her, frowning. It was either take her on her terms or not have her at all. Before she had come into his life he wouldn't have been capable of such a compromise. In the brutal world where he'd grown up, compromise meant defeat and humiliation. In her world, compromise meant honor and trust.

He looked into the mirror again. "You've changed me a helluva lot."

"You still look handsome. The scar . . . I don't mind it."

He hadn't been referring to his hair. He had meant the way she'd changed his attitudes, making him less selfish and more willing to negotiate. It was amazing. Right now, despite the disgusting stunt she'd pulled, he felt himself falling even deeper in love with her.

"I'll be growin' all of my hair back—includin' the mustache."

"If you want." She hesitated. "Are you going to do something violent now?"

He grunted. "What'd you think I'd do after I woke up this morning? Hit you? Throw you out?"

She gazed at him, her eyes calm and confident. "No. You're not that kind of man. I wouldn't be with you if I thought you were."

"What kind of man am I?"

"One who has a terrible time trusting anyone but himself, yet who wants very badly to trust. One who thinks only fools are kindhearted, but who can't resist being a fool. One who hides his fears and doubts because the world has never been merciful with him."

"So—if you're right about me—is it good or bad?"

"Good." She came to him and slipped her arms around his neck. "You look confused."

"I ought to be so damned mad at you that I can't see straight. I ought to tie you to the bed again and keep you there until you promise not to get within a mile of that cocky Spanish nabob."

"But you're not. And you won't."

He sighed and put his arms around her. "Be friends with the devil. I won't say a word."

"Dear Lord," she whispered. "I can't believe it."

"I don't want to wake up with something more important than my mustache missin'."

"I'd *never* harm that."

He jerked her to his naked body and ground his hips against her. "I'm still a little numb. What did you use on me?"

She smiled tentatively. "Ether. While you were sleeping I held it under your nose."

"An ether frolic and a shaving party. You must have had fun."

Her smile faded. "No. I felt sorry for you."

"But not sorry enough to leave my mustache alone."

She kissed him and ran her tongue over the edge of his lip. "Hmmm. It will be different. Interesting. Though I do want your mustache back."

"I'm starting to tingle."

Her voice became sultry. "All over?"

He picked her up. "Where it will do us both some good."

He carried her to the bed. He was still fuzzy-headed, and she took advantage of it to make him forget the ludicrous indignity she'd done to him. When she finished her seduction, he lay on top of her in a languid daze. She licked and nuzzled his naked lip, and promised that he wouldn't regret trusting her.

He nibbled her neck to hide his frown. He trusted her, but he would never trust Vittorio Salazar.

## CHAPTER 15

Delmonico's was a place of fantasy, a romantic Italianate dream with gilded mirrors, marble tables, and waiters who were so formal and elegant that they seemed as elite as the diners they served. Katherine was torn between watching them and studying the menu, an artistic masterpiece that listed dozens of dishes, all described in French.

Even Adela, usually unimpressed by everything, was wide-eyed. Only Vittorio seemed perfectly at ease. He leaned toward Katherine and rested a hand on her forearm. She glanced down, startled. His hand was slender but strong, and it looked somehow unnatural and too commanding against the figured white material and blue lace of her sleeve. Katherine politely said nothing but wished that he would not touch her as often as had become his habit. She didn't fear his motives—he was an exquisite gentleman—but she feared Justis's reaction if he ever saw such familiarity between them.

A month had passed since the tempestuous night

when she'd shaved Justis in revenge, and since then he had tolerated, even joked about, her association with Salazar. She didn't want to endanger his newfound trust. Also, she would prefer that he not strangle Vittorio. The Spaniard was a charming escort and a wonderful conversationalist.

"Ladies, do you know who we're sitting near?" he asked. "See that heavyset gentleman at the table of honor?"

Adela peered over her menu. Katherine glanced delicately to one side. "Yes?"

"That is William Astor. The son of John Jacob. You are looking at the heir to the richest fortune in America."

"He is a very ordinary hombre," Adela commented. "Like a fat frog."

Katherine smiled. "But his money makes the waiters love him. See how they pamper him."

"Ah, love," Vittorio said. *"Cras amet qui nunquam amavit; quique amavit cras amet.* My Latin is poor—do you understand it?"

Katherine nodded. " 'May he love tomorrow who never has loved before, and may he who has loved love tomorrow as well.' "

"Do you believe in love, Señora?"

"Certainly."

"And does your husband?"

She laughed, feeling uncomfortable and more than a little sad. "You'll have to ask him that question."

"Surely he expresses his love for you?"

"I am quite content with him."

"Ah, the lady parries my question."

Adela interjected drolly, "She may stab you with it if you persist."

"Never," Katherine assured him. "I would lose my only chess partner."

He smiled directly into Katherine's eyes. "I believe in love, Señora Gallatin. I love all beautiful things."

Katherine clasped her heart dramatically. The man was a harmless flirt. "But do they love you in return?"

As a waiter approached their table, ending the discussion, Vittorio leaned close to her and whispered, *"Aut viam inveniam aut faciam."*

Katherine felt a twinge of warning, but she laughed as if he'd made the merriest joke in the world. *Where there's a will there's a way.*


IT WAS THE most glorious feeling. He was sweaty and filthy, with his shirt torn, hand blistered, and forehead bleeding where falling glass had struck it. Justis lifted a glass of whiskey to the three equally disreputable-looking men who sat around the parlor table with him, their muddy boots propped on the marble surface.

"To Ireland," he said solemnly.

That produced a chorus of bawdy agreements, and they all swallowed another round of the hotel's best stock, then immediately refilled their glasses. "To his fine self, Mr. Justis Gallatin, our host," one man announced.

"Who will be a fireman yet!" another added.

"Who risked his own ugly hide to pull a pair of wee tots from a terrrrible burning hoose!"

"I thank you," Justis said. He downed the liquor, and they followed suit.

He wasn't drunk, just pleasantly relaxed, and just loose enough to whoop when he heard Katherine's key in the lock. He went to the door and slung it open, saying loudly and cheerfully as he did, "Come in, wife! I've got meself an Irish toothache, and soon as I kick these boys out, I'll explain what that is!"

She stood there looking at him warily. Beside her, Adela Mendez dissolved into chortles. Vittorio Salazar appraised him with a slight, cool smile.

Katherine frowned at the blood on his forehead. "You're injured!"

"It's nothin'." He stepped back, all humor gone, and gestured stiffly. "Looks like we both have guests today. I thought you were gone till after supper."

"We spent all afternoon at Delmonico's. We decided to forego supper and play cards."

His three dirty, bloody, drunken friends staggered to their feet as Katherine ushered Adela and Vittorio into the parlor. Justis silently cursed the timing and Salazar's patronizing expression. "Katie. Katherine. Mrs. Gallatin." *Damn introductions!* "I'd like you to meet three of the finest lads in New York." He waved toward the trio. "Mr. Gilhooly, Mr. Flannigan, and Mr. Connery."

"Sirs." As Justis had known she would, she smiled graciously and held out a hand to each of them. They nearly fell down trying to bow over it. She kept a pleasant expression on her face, but Justis recognized disgust in the hard set of her mouth.

"Gentlemen," she said, "I'm very glad to meet you. These are my friends, Señora Mendez and Señor Salazar. They're visiting from Mexico. The California area."

"Mex'cans," one of the men muttered darkly. "I was with Sam Houston when he whipped the murderin' bunch in Texas. California's next."

Justis grimaced at the insult and hitched a thumb toward the door. "Time to go, lads." But he couldn't send them packing as if he were embarrassed to be with them. He'd spent too many of his early years ashamed to call himself Irish. Not anymore. He grabbed the battered, wide-brimmed hat he'd brought all the way from Gold Ridge and refused to throw away. "Come on, fellers. I'll spring for supper down at one of the oyster cellars."

He held the door for them and they doffed their caps to Katherine on their way out. After they were gone, Justis looked at her and saw the questions and insinuations in her eyes. "Is that the kind of business you usually devote yourself to during the day?" she asked. "Brawling and drinking? Where did you meet that bunch—at a saloon on the wharf?"

His intended words of explanation faded behind a defensive sarcasm he had honed since his days as a no-account Irish kid, the one who fought insults with insults. "Nah. I met 'em at a whorehouse," he told her, and walked out.

HE CAME BACK well after midnight, sober and exhausted but still burning with a sense of betrayal. She had stood there and insulted him while that damned Salazar watched like a smirking shadow behind her.

The sleeping chamber was pitch dark. Justis dropped his clothes on the floor and got into bed, sensing her presence even though he couldn't see her. He lay on his back and frowned into the blackness, too tense to sleep. He could smell the delicate cologne she used and feel the heat of her body only inches away.

With a soft rustling of the covers she shifted closer to him. Her hand settled gently on his shoulder. "Why didn't you tell me they were firemen? Why didn't you just say that you'd been helping them? I heard the truth from Thomas. His brother saw you at the fire."

Justis frowned. He'd have to talk to the hotel porter about his damned wagging tongue. "What difference does it make? You took one look at me and made up your mind to the worst."

"I'm sorry. I truly am. But you've never bothered to tell me that you've taken to fighting fires for sport."

"I don't tell you everything. Just like you don't tell me what you and Salazar do together."

"You never ask."

"You wanted your freedom and privacy."

"But I never meant to exclude you. I wouldn't mind if you inquired politely—"

"I don't feel like *inquiring politely*. I see the happy look on your face after you've been with him. It tells me all I need to know."

"Perhaps I look that way because I'm glad to see *you.*"

"Hell." He rolled toward her and explored with impatient hands. She was naked. "You're glad to see me in bed."

"Oh, Justis. *No.* It's not only that."

He tossed the covers back and found her belly with his mouth. As he kissed it roughly he pulled her legs apart. "Be quiet and let me do what you want."

Her hands tightened convulsively in his hair as he lowered his mouth between her thighs. "I am proud of you for saving those children today," she whispered in a choked voice. "Very proud, no matter what you think."

His fingers dug into her thighs as bittersweet emotion twisted his throat. "Shut up."

She whimpered. "All right. This is the only way you know how to say that you forgive me."

"I don't care what you think of me. There's nothing for me to forgive."

"Shhh."

He took her with his mouth and tongue until her pelvis writhed upward and she trembled with release. As she collapsed, panting in the aftermath, he rested his head on her stomach, feeling weary and sad. She had assumed the worst about him today; it had shown him what she really thought.

She licked her fingers and gently smoothed them over the scratches on his forehead. "I am proud of you," she whispered again. "And very sorry that I hurt your feelings."

"Hurt my feelings? Hell, all you did was make me mad. Women get their feelings hurt. Younguns get their feelings hurt. I'm a grown man." He moved away from her and turned his back. "Good night."

"But I am truly—"

"Good night."

He heard her exhale softly, defeated. "Good night, then," she said, her voice ancient. "It's no use."

IF THERE WAS one luxury he had grown to crave, it was the copper bathtub that sat in the dressing room. Justis got up shortly after dawn to soak his sore muscles in hot soapy water. As he lounged in the wonderful contraption with his eyes shut, Katherine burst into the room, her robe half drawn and her mane of black hair tangled around her.

"Excuse me," she murmured, and grabbed a towel from the washstand. She pressed it to her face and retched for a moment, then leaned heavily on the washstand and rinsed her mouth with water from the drinking pitcher.

Justis sat forward and watched her. Lingering traces of anger were pushed aside by concern. "Katie?"

She dabbed cold water on her face and kept her back to him. "What you said about the whorehouse. You've never gone to one of those with your friends, have you?"

He settled back in the tub, assessing her with shrewd eyes. "That notion been chewin' at you?"

"Yes."

"I ask no less of myself than I ask of you. I've not been unfaithful to you."

"Good."

"Why do you care? 'Fraid I'll give you a whore's disease?"

Her sharp gasp turned into a hiss of anger. "Your nasty temper is matched only by your vulgar mind."

He reached out and grasped her wrist as she started out of the room. She jumped and wouldn't meet his gaze. "Bein' mad at me doesn't usually turn your stomach. What else is wrong with you this mornin'?"

"I'm just worn out." Finally she looked at him. "I think my flux is coming on, that's all."

"Oh." Women's monthlies were a mystery he'd never pretended to understand. "Why don't you go back to bed? Maybe I'll bring you some tea."

"No, no. Go on about your day's appointments. I'll just sleep late."

He let go of her wrist with an abrupt little shove. She didn't want coddling, but sometimes he forgot that. She didn't want him around any more than she could help.

"Get on back to bed, then," he ordered. "And give yourself a rest from that damned Salazar."

She laughed shortly, her voice cracking, and fled out the door. By the time Justis finished dressing, she was curled on her side under the covers, sound asleep. He stood next to the bed and watched her in miserable uncertainty. She was unhappy. It was more than just the problem they'd had yesterday, something much more.

*Salazar.*

OVER THE NEXT few days Katherine felt Justis watching her closely, and she put on a good show of acting as if everything were fine. As in months past they had an understanding—she would tell him when her flux ended, and until then they would just hold each other companionably at night, warm and intimate in a different way, a way that always made her feel secure and happy.

But not this time. Worry gnawed at her. She avoided Adela by pleading headaches; above all she avoided Vittorio. She found it necessary to nap often, not for the kind of escape she had needed after Justis had rescued her from the trail, but because she was more tired than ordinary.

Finally she was forced to admit the truth. After Justis left one morning she rushed into the dressing room and threw up in the basin. She removed her nightgown and stared at herself in the mirror. Already her breasts felt swollen. She hadn't had her flux this month, nor the last one. How much longer before the changes became obvious?

She braced her arms on the washstand and leaned toward the drawn, hollow-eyed face in the mirror. "I'm carrying a babe," she whispered tearfully. "And even if Justis believes it's his, he won't want it."

THOMAS MET HIM in a quiet alcove off one of the main halls. "You'd be wantin' to see me, Mr. Gallatin, sir?"

Justis nodded. "You know everything that goes on in this hotel and half the what-all that goes on in New York."

The porter grinned. "That'd be true, sir."

"What do you know about Vittorio Salazar, the Mex upstairs?"

Thomas shuffled his feet and looked awkward. "The one who squires your wife about?"

"Yeah." Justis gritted his teeth. "That's him."

"I've never seen anything improper-like pass between them, sir, I swear it. I would have told you for sure if I had." He paused to pull a plug of tobacco from one pocket. He kept his eyes on it as he fumbled with a pocket knife, trying to cut a piece from the plug. Almost sheepishly he added, "I know a lot about his habits, sir. So I didn't worry about your wife bein' seduced. You shouldn't either."

"What do you mean?"

"Salazar's the kind what likes to be seen with a lady but beds only a whore."

Justis looked at the porter closely. "Has he got himself a doxy or two?"

"About a dozen, sir. I've snuck 'em into the hotel for him."

"What makes you so sure he wants only the hired pieces?"

The porter's face turned dark red. "He's got strange appetites, sir. Some of the whores won't go back a second time. He's not wantin' the kind of pleasure a lady would give."

"How so?"

A look of revulsion settled in Thomas's eyes. "He ties 'em up and beats 'em."

"I'll be damned." Justis leaned against the wall and crossed his arms, waiting for the nausea to settle in his stomach. He tried to comprehend Salazar's sort of pleasure. He'd heard of men who liked that kind, but he'd never run across one before.

"I wouldn't be tellin' my wife, sir, if I was you. The Mex is fine with ladies—I'd swear on a stack of Bibles to that. In a way you oughta bless him for bein' an odd sonuvadevil. No need to worry about him askin' your wife to lay down with him. Beggin' your pardon for even the thought of it, sir."

Justis tucked a coin in the fancy braided pocket of Thomas's livery jacket. "What else do the doxies tell you about his habits?"

"He, umm, he never does anything but the beating. Uses a little leather whip. Never even takes off his clothes, they say. His favorite girls are the ones who cry and beg—the more they plead the more he likes it. He told one of 'em that he was born and raised in Spain, sir, but a scandal drove him to the Californias as a young man. He never let on what the scandal was, sir, but meself suspects that his family found out about his cruel streak. So now he's careful to hide it."

Justis mulled over the information for a moment. Katherine might love the sly bastard, but she'd never get anything except fancy talk and companionship from him. In the long run that wouldn't suit her, not with her fiery passion in bed. He recalled that Salazar was a widower whose wife had died in childbirth—her only childbirth despite many years of marriage. He'd bet gold that the Mex's dislike for normal relations had been the reason.

Relief washed over him, and he slapped Thomas jovially on the back. "You've set my mind at ease. God bless you, you ugly Irishman."

The porter laughed. "I bless you back. We ugly Irishmen have to be stickin' together, sir."

THIS INDECISION WAS the worst kind of torture, Katherine thought. She dressed, did her hair, and forced herself to accompany Adela to lunch. When she returned to the suite she felt better, and hoped she'd have a respite from the sickness and fatigue. She had to ponder her problems while she was strong.

How would Justis react when she told him about the babe? Would he take a moment to remember the times when they hadn't been careful, when one or both of them had let passion rule common sense? Those times had been few, but with a man who radiated potency as Justis did, even one would have been more than adequate.

Or would he accuse her of unfaithfulness and say that her condition was proof? She had known Vittorio for nearly two months and had, of her own free choice, seen him almost daily.

She stared out a window in the sleeping chamber, gazing at the rainswept sky of early fall. The world was bleak both inside and out. She wanted the babe. God help her, she'd have to refuse if Justis asked her to rid herself of it. She knew how to expel it—there were medicines available that even married women could use quite respectably. Sometimes they were dangerous and half the time they didn't work, but with her knowledge of drugs she could make certain of success.

No. She shook her head and hugged herself tightly. She'd have the babe even if Justis ended their arrangement because of it. He would leave her anyway, eventually. At least this way she'd keep a bit of his soul with her.

There, then. She was still miserable, but at least part of the problem was decided. Now all she had to do was convince Justis that he was the father. Otherwise his pride and vanity would demand frontier-style revenge. She choked at the thought that he'd go to the gallows for killing Salazar if she failed.

She jumped when she heard the parlor door opening. "Katie, gal, are you back there?" Justis's deep, drawling voice rang through the suite with more good cheer than she'd heard in days.

"Yes?"

"We've got a letter from Rebecca and Sam!"

She ran into the parlor. He tossed his hat and long frock coat onto a chair and stood there, looking outrageously handsome in snug black trousers, a gray silk vest, and a white shirt and cravat. His hair and mustache were nearly back to their handsome, wickedly shaggy selves.

Overcome by all the emotions churning inside her, she threw herself into his arms. "I'm glad you're back."

He lifted her off the floor and kissed her. "I've been gone only since the mornin'."

"I know, but—"

"I bet your flux has ended. You're too happy to see me." He looked resigned but not angry. "That blue dress suits you, Mrs. Blue Song Gallatin. It's your color. Are you feelin' more sprightly today?"

"Yes."

"Want to read this letter to me?"

"Yes!"

The mail between New York and the Georgia frontier

was neither reliable nor fast. She'd written Rebecca and Sam only twice, once as soon as she and Justis had arrived in New York, to let them know Justis's whereabouts and plans, then again later, to assure them that everything was going well. Rebecca had written once to bless her for saving Justis's life—a comment Justis refused to explain when she mentioned it to him—and to say that all was well in Gold Ridge.

Katherine took the packet of paper from Justis's hand as he set her down. He stretched out on a sofa and crossed his booted feet on the arm. "Let's hear the news."

Her fingers trembling, she broke the seal and unfolded several pages filled with small, neat script. "It's Rebecca's writing. 'Dearest Justis and Katherine, we are desperately in need of your help—at least, we must have Justis back for a short while. Poor Katherine, I know you cannot return to Gold Ridge. Can you spare your man for the sake of mine? Sam was pinned when his wagon turned over last week, and only yesterday did the doctor offer hope that he would live. We think he may not be back to health for at least four months.'"

Dazed, Katherine stopped reading and looked at the date. "This is only three weeks old. She must have paid someone to carry it up the coast by ship."

Justis was already up and pacing, his hands on his hips. "Read the rest."

She continued, but it was all just elaboration on the first shocking part. Sam was nearly crippled right now, but in time he'd recover fully. He had assistants to run the mine and the other businesses, but they were an uninspiring lot.

"I'll have to go, then," Justis said. He halted and looked at her grimly. "But you'll go with me."

"No." How could she travel, nauseated and tired half the time, without him realizing the truth right away? If she stayed in New York, at least she would have a temporary reprieve from telling him. Plus Vittorio and Adela were going back to California in two or three months. Perhaps they'd be gone by the time Justis returned.

"No?" he echoed, frowning.

"I can't go back. I'm a Cherokee, remember?"

"You can go to visit."

"And be scorned." She went to him and pried his hands away from his hips, holding them tightly. "I'll simply wait here for you. Let the people in Gold Ridge think you've been in New York alone all this time."

"You want to be rid of me. Say so."

She jerked on his hands. "Damn you! Nothing I can say will make any difference to you. I want you to come back. I'll be waiting. And in the meantime I'll keep track of your business dealings. I can do it very well—you know that—if your associates don't faint at the thought of working with a woman and an Indian!"

"You've got no one here to keep an eye on you. What if you get sick or something?"

"Adela won't be leaving until after New Year's. Surely you'll be back before then." She cupped his face between her hands. He looked as unhappy as she felt. "I think you're worried about your investments, not me. They'll be fine under my care."

He swore viciously. "And you'll be happier left alone. What's been wrong with you lately? Why are you moping?"

She stepped back, her hands clenched. Fear demanded a quick bluff. "Sir, you have never expected me to be satisfied with this life, any more than I expect you to be. I will never stop missing my home and grieving for my family. There are days—such as lately—when they are all I think about. Don't you ever think about going home to Gold Ridge?"

"All right, I do. I miss it damned bad sometimes."

She nodded sagely, but his admission frightened her.

He'd never said anything before about wishing he could go back to Gold Ridge. "Being a New York businessman galls you terribly? I've suspected as much."

His expression became guarded. "I'll make a go of it. Don't write me off."

Katherine trembled inside. "I'm not. But tell me the truth. You'd like to go back to Gold Ridge for good, and as soon as you accomplish what you want here, that's where you'll head. Is that right?"

He watched her carefully. "What difference does it make to you?"

"I just want to know how to plan my future once we separate." She knotted her hands together behind her back and squeezed until her knuckles hurt.

"Fine, then. Yeah, I'll be goin' back to Georgia to stay."

"Will you live on the Blue Song land?"

"The *Gallatin* land. Probably. I'll never sell it, I know that much. No harm'll come to it."

Tears stung her eyes. Katherine knew that the changes in her pregnant body were putting a strain on her emotions, and she struggled to keep them in control. She whirled, her manner brusque, and crossed to the writing desk in one corner of the room. "You'll enjoy this visit home, then. I'll send a letter with you, for Rebecca. She'll like hearing about life in New York. Perhaps it will take her mind off her worries about Sam."

Katherine sat down and busied herself setting up her writing supplies, but she could feel Justis gazing angrily at her. Suddenly he strode across the room. "Damn you," he said, and dragged her out of the chair. He held her arms in a harsh grip, nearly pulling her off her feet as he scrutinized her tear-filled eyes. "After all we've been through together, don't you care a little that I'm goin' away for only God knows how long?"

She made a ragged, anguished sound. *More than you'll ever know, my love.* "I shall miss you," she whispered, her voice choked. "Please come back."

Amazement tinged his eyes. His hands tightened. "I will," he promised hoarsely. "You don't know how I—" He struggled for words. "We have a deal, remember? I've always kept my word to you."

"Your word. A deal. Yes." He would honor their agreement whether he wanted to or not. She put her arms around his neck and hugged him. "Thank you."

He picked her up. Katherine knew that signal—it invariably meant he would carry her to their bed, where he could show her affection but disguise it as desire. She had come to understand that much about him during their months together, and it made her kiss him desperately, begging for every bit of affection he had for her.

Much later, when they lay satiated and still in each other's arms, she gazed into his troubled eyes. "I think you'll miss me too."

"As much as you'll miss me," he said wearily.

She rested her forehead against his and shut her eyes. If only that were true, she thought.

The next morning he dressed in his old clothes—a worn wool shirt, coarse trousers held up by braces, and heavy boots—and packed others in a valise. A subdued Thomas carried the valise downstairs, where Watchman was waiting outside. Justis planned to take the stallion aboard a steamer bound for Charleston, on the coast of South Carolina. From Charleston the ride to north Georgia would be relatively easy and quick.

While Justis made his preparations, Katherine hurriedly dressed and fixed her hair. "You goin' out somewhere?" he asked, frowning.

She swallowed a knot of sorrow in her throat. He had never understood that she wanted so much to please him. "No. I just didn't want your last image of me to be a sleepy-looking hag in a dressing gown."

"Not a hag," he corrected her gruffly. They walked to the door together. He turned to her and slipped his arms around her waist. A muscle worked in his jaw. "Still the most beautiful woman I've ever known."

"I shall certainly miss your flattery." She leaned against him and pressed her face into the crook of his neck. His body was like hers—taut with restraint. He probably felt embarrassed, she decided. "Take care of yourself," she said lightly, nuzzling him.

His lips brushed her temple. Slowly he slid a hand under his shirt collar and withdrew the gold nugget. "An early Christmas present," he said as he eased the leather necklace over her head. "Since I may not be here to give you one."

She laughed shakily. It was the only sound she could make without bursting into tears. *Come back. Dear God, please let him come back.* She'd be swollen with their babe by then, and she'd tell him why she wanted it, half-breed or not. If forced, she'd admit that she loved him. Perhaps he wouldn't mind.

"Well, there's no point wastin' time," he said, and stepped back with a formal attitude.

"No. Of course not." She helped him into a heavy wool coat and retrieved his battered, beloved hat from the parlor sofa. "Ugly thing," she muttered, but her hands lovingly brushed a bit of dust off the wide brim.

He set it on his head at the jaunty angle she had seen so many times, and she wanted to dissolve onto the floor with longing. She casually pressed a hand over her stomach. If she didn't have their babe inside her, she would forget caution and go with him to Georgia.

Justis opened the door to the hall. Then he caught her chin in one hand and lifted her face to his for a slow, thorough kiss. She stroked his cheeks with her fingertips and feathered one over his mustache as he drew back. "Let no harm come to this."

His gaze was somber, but he almost smiled. "Stay well and safe," he murmured.

Their eyes met and held. Katherine felt as if he were

searching for something, then realized she must look the same way to him. Finally he turned away. His hand still cupped her chin. He trailed his fingers over her lips, and was gone.

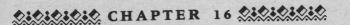 **CHAPTER 16**

*And so we were married our first night in New York
rather than end up in jail, as the hotel manager threatened. I expressed grave doubts about the legality of his
stance, but Justis said we had no choice but to comply.
Oh, Becky, I am bound by a fate I never confessed to you
before. I love Justis. He does not know that, and probably
does not want to. But he is wonderful to me, and I think
we can be happy.*

AMARINTHA folded the much-read letter carefully and
hid it back in her bureau drawer. Then she dressed
in her prettiest winter dress, a dark pink with tiny roses
embroidered on the bodice. She parted her hair in the
center and fixed it in masses of long red-gold ringlets over
each ear.

Bundled in a short white cape and matching muff, she
marched out of her father's house without bothering to
glance toward the square to see whether court had let

out. Let her father wonder where she'd gone. His tyranny didn't matter anymore. She had confidence for the first time in her life.

She climbed into the hired buggy and told the driver to take her to the Gallatin mine. Once she arrived, she told him it wouldn't be necessary for him to wait.

She knocked firmly on the door of the cabin that served as the mine's office. When Justis answered the door, looking surprised and disgusted to see her after all these months, she breezed past him with only a curt hello. He was sickening, like all men, and she didn't have to pretend otherwise anymore.

She fluffed her skirt, eyed him in haughty silence, and lowered herself into the chair he brought her. "Welcome home," she said finally.

"Just visitin'," he told her. He went back to his desk, which was covered in paperwork, and dropped into its big leather chair without much show of patience. "I've got no time to talk to you and no reason to want to."

"You'll make time and you'll find reason. Or you'll lose everything you own, including your wife's land."

He stared at her in silent shock. Fury crept into his eyes, though he tried to appear nonchalant. "I don't know what you're talkin' about. I'm not married."

"Oh, stop it," she ordered. "I have a letter she wrote to Rebecca Kirkland months ago. I was at the courthouse the day it arrived in the mail. I offered to carry it over to the hotel. Then I kept it, of course, and read every word. It's very frank and quite detailed about your marriage. Your wife's handwriting is excellent. Her full signature is at the end. 'Katherine Blue Song Gallatin.' How proud the squaw must have been to take a white man's name. All in all, she provided me with a very tidy legal document."

Justis settled back in his chair and eyed her with loathing. "What kind of bribe do you want this time, Amarintha? What'll it take to keep your mouth shut?"

She smiled. Years of waiting had finally paid off. "Marriage." The color drained out of his face. Good. She loved this kind of power. It was so new, so thrilling.

"You're crazier than I thought you were," he said, staring at her in horrified disbelief.

"I don't care what you think of me. Either you marry me or I'll have my dear, deranged daddy nullify every contract and deed you ever signed in the state of Georgia. You'll lose everything because you married an Indian. That makes you an Indian, and Indians have no legal rights. My daddy despises you—you're the only man he can't humiliate. He'd just *love* to ruin you."

"Let him try. Damn you to hell, you pitiful, scheming lunatic. I couldn't marry you even if I wanted to. I'm already bound to a wife." He jabbed a hand toward the cabin door. "Get out of my sight."

Amarintha sighed. She'd let him have his rage. She would enjoy it, in fact. "No one knows about your first marriage but me. No one else will ever know it. I won't tell. You won't. We'll marry, we'll set up housekeeping for a few months, then you can go back to your squaw and never give me a second thought. But I'll be Mrs. Gallatin —the only Mrs. Gallatin as far as Gold Ridge is concerned. I'll expect you to build me a nice house and set up a generous bank account in my name."

He got up, kicked his chair across the room, then bent over his desk toward her. Was he capable of hitting her, she wondered idly. The thought didn't bother her a bit. She was adept at dealing with much worse threats.

"I've already got a wife," he repeated.

"She need never know you've got another one."

"I'd rather geld myself than share a bed with you."

"I wouldn't care if you sliced off the whole ugly business. I don't want your filth inside me."

"Dear God, what do you want from a husband, then?"

"Escape," she retorted. "A home of my own. A new name. A name for my child."

"Your *child*?"

She nodded curtly. "I'm just a month along. We'll be married right away, and no one will pay much attention when the babe's born a month early."

"Who's bastard would I be givin' my name to?"

"That's none of your business."

He looked as if he might explode with fury and frustration. "Do you think you can lead me around like a bull with a ring through his nose? I've got enough money stashed in New York to keep me rich even if I lost everything I own in this town."

"Yes. But what about your partner? What will happen to poor, half-crippled Sam and his family if somebody takes over your holdings?"

"I'll look after Sam. He won't suffer."

"Hah. Liar. I see the worry in your eyes, you arrogant fool. Besides, no matter what you arrange for Sam, there's one thing you most certainly can't help but lose. The Blue Song land."

He slammed a fist onto the desk. His voice came out low and lethal. "Nobody'll take that land from me."

Amarintha smiled. "The law says you're a Cherokee now. Go out to the Indian territory if you want to own land. My daddy can turn the law to your ruination and have the Blue Song property auctioned off. Believe me, he's got important friends in this state who'll help him. He got the governor to put your squaw in the stockade last year."

She laughed, watching different expressions cross her husband-to-be's face. More fury. Despair. Distraction. And finally a grim look that drained all the life out of his eyes.

"You love that savage so much, you'll do anything to keep her land for her," Amarintha said happily. "That's what I was counting on."

\* \* \*

DEAR WIFE. *Have arrived safely in Gold Ridge. Sam has both legs broke, ribs cracked, neck hurt. Looks like a dog run over by a wagon. A long time to get well, but he will make it. Don't expect me back for two, three months. Write me about all business with our investments. And about yourself, if you have an extra minute.*

YOUR LOYAL HUSBAND, JUSTIS.

DEAR HUSBAND. *I'm very glad to know that you're loyal. I am loyal also, and now that your business associates have recovered from their shock over me, we are accomplishing a great deal. To sum it all up, you and I are now a bit richer thanks to several real estate negotiations of which I am quite proud. As for myself, I am well and gaining weight. You'll be pleased, I'm sure.*

YOUR BUSY WIFE.

KATIE. *Sorry not to have written for so long. Work all the time. Sam is not healing as fast as hoped. How was your Thanksgiving? You keep asking what is happening here. Nothing new. Nothing. Think of you often. You must think I forgot you. Will come back, I promise. Visited the B. Song land again last week. I know why you love it. I swear I do. It's everything to you.*

JUSTIS.

DEAR LOYAL HUSBAND, *who writes very distracted-sounding letters, Thanksgiving was quiet here. I spent the day with Adela and Vittorio. My Spanish is excellent now, thanks to Vittorio's teaching. He is also teaching me about his country's food. I love a Mexican pancake he calls tortillas. Goodness! I'm still gaining weight! Don't be surprised if I'm fat! When are you coming home?*

YOUR HUNGRY WIFE.

WIFE. *Got your letter about the shipping deal. You could be an Astor. The first Cherokee Astor. Don't ever think I'm not proud of you. Ever. I'm still working hard. Sam not improving too fast. Sorry—looks like I won't be back for one, two more months. Could tell from your last letter that you are puzzled. You should trust me. Please. Saw your land under a snowfall yesterday. Made me feel good. So pretty. It will always be yours. Really. All of your letters say how fat you're getting. I think it's time you stopped eating so much.*

HUSBAND. *Spent the New Year's playing cards with Vittorio and Adela. They are leaving for California soon. I hope not to miss them too badly, especially Vittorio. It surprises me that you never ask about him. Ah, well, you trust me—or have forgotten me. Rebecca writes to say that Sam is well. What am I to think?*

YOUR PARTNER, KATHERINE.

WIFE. *I hope to head back to New York next month. Am settling last problems here. You accuse me of forgetting you because I don't ask about his Mex royal highness. I trust you, remember? We agreed on that. You trust me too. And you always can.*

JUSTIS.

KATHERINE SMILED AND patted her stomach as she felt the babe kick. She loved the feeling of companionship from having it nestled inside her. Adela and her large brood, plus Vittorio, were leaving for California in one week. After they departed she'd have too much time to sit and wonder why Justis hadn't returned yet. She hoped the babe kicked often—she needed the distraction.

She was six months into her pregnancy and could no longer hide it under cloaks and shawls. Propriety dictated that she disappear from public view until after the babe was born, and she dreaded spending her days in her room growing bored and anxious.

Someone knocked on the door to the suite. She put a

stack of financial reports down and, drawing a large silk shawl around her, hurried to answer. Thomas smiled at her and bowed, then held out a crumpled, dirty packet.

"I've another letter from Georgia for you, ma'am. Looks like this poor thing has been a bad, slow route, but at least it's here."

After he left, Katherine studied the unfamiliar hand that had addressed the letter. The script was a haphazard scrawl, as if the writer had been excited or upset. *Something awful had happened to Justis and a stranger was writing to tell her.* Terrified, she quickly ripped the seal.

Katherine frowned in bewilderment as she unfolded a front page from the *Gold Ridge Gazette*. The poorly typeset little weekly had been a source of some amusement to her. But who would send her a clipping from it? No one knew where she was except for Justis, Rebecca, and Sam, and this wasn't from one of them. And the clipping was several months old. Bewildering. Then her gaze lit on a somewhat smeared headline halfway down the page:

TWO LEADING CITIZENS ARE MARRIED
Town's Biggest Wedding Yet!

Beside it was written in that strange, unnerving hand: "Your husband is coming home—or is he? His white wife is carrying his child."

Sometime later Katherine was under control enough to make her way upstairs to Adela's apartments. When the sturdy little Californio saw her face she gasped and came forward, her arms out. *"Querida,* what is it?"

Katherine dropped to her knees and buried her face in Adela's flowing black skirt. "My husband has died," she whispered.

BITTER JANUARY WIND whipped Katherine's cape and stung her face as she stood on the deck of the big square-masted brig watching New York slip away behind her. Vittorio laid his arm around her shoulders in a companionable way.

"Come below, Catalina," he called against the rush of wind and snapping of sails. "Adela is worried about you. Mourning is very hard on any woman, but for one who is going to be a mother—"

"My child will be strong," Katherine said. She dug her mittened fingers into the deck's railing. "Strong and perfect."

"Yes, yes. In California your *bebé* will grow up strong and perfect. We will have a priest christen it with a good Spanish name—"

"A priest?"

"Of course! Your child must be a Catholic and a citizen of Mexico, as you must be. You will have a new life, a new home. Try to look toward the future. The ship's safe is full of your gold. You will be a wealthy Californio and live at my rancho as an honored guest."

"I have told you already. I cannot live permanently as your guest. I must make my own life."

He took her by the shoulders and jerked her around to face him. Katherine was numb inside—except for the occasional movements of the babe, she would have felt completely hollow. The roughness of his touch provoked only a dull curiosity in her, and she puzzled over the cool command in his eyes. She had never seen him look or act this way before.

"Your life is going to be very different now," he said loudly, and she couldn't tell if he was yelling merely because of the wind. He had changed since hearing that— as she continued to explain to everyone—Justis had been killed in a mining accident. Now Vittorio was too sure of himself with her, almost imperious. A small, still-alert part of her brain warned her to be wary of this new side of him.

"We have a journey of six months ahead of us," he

told her. "It will give you time to contemplate your new position and adjust to it. When we reach California you will have stopped grieving for your husband. You will have the *bebé* to care for. You will be ready to do what you must."

"What I must?" she asked, frowning.

He shook his head. "No more talk. You should go below to your cabin and rest."

"I want to stay here until the coast is out of sight. Alone." Anger flared even under the smothering mantle of her despair. She would not be controlled by any man ever again.

Vittorio saw the implacable defiance in her eyes. He stepped back and bowed politely. "As you wish. For now."

After he left her she turned toward the fading coastline, her teeth clenched. *For now?* Forever. She was free, finally free, and she would raise her child as she pleased, in a place where there were fewer rules—or at least different rules—and an enterprising woman with plenty of gold could have her own rancho. Perhaps in California an Indian and her half-breed child might prosper.

Katherine sagged as a new wave of sorrow tore at her resolve. She needn't worry about Justis pursuing her; he had bound himself to a new life. He had betrayed and deserted her in a disloyal, dishonorable way that she could never have imagined, and she couldn't understand how she had misjudged him so much.

The coast became a blurred line hung with blue-green mist, a color that reminded her of the mountains back home. *Home. The Sun Land.* She was leaving it very far behind this time. She was going so far toward the sunset that she would never come back. She would no longer exist except in the memory of a man who was now dead to her. Because he would always stand in her soul, she was dead too.

\* \* \*

JUSTIS HELD HIS letter—the letter that had arrived at the hotel a week after Katie's departure—in his hand.

KATIE. *By now you have gotten the damned newspaper story about the marriage. I found out that Amarintha mailed it to you two weeks ago. Forget it. Burn it. I swear I can make you understand. I have never broken my word to you. There are reasons for what happened. I have never spent one night in her bed. Am leaving for Charleston today. Will take a steamer up the coast. See you soon. Believe. Trust. Still Your Loyal Partner—and Husband,*
                                                            JUSTIS.

Thomas continued to stare at him as if a phantom had just strode into the hotel's grand lobby. "Glory, sir, she told me you were dead," the porter said for the fifth time. "The poor lady was so despairin' in the way she acted that I never thought she'd be tellin' me a lie. Sir, let me bring you something hot to drink before that Irish blood of yours turns to ice. You're shiverin' like a two-bit sinner. What did you do, sir, run all the way from your ship? And it sleetin' like a bitch outdoors!"

"I wasn't dead," Justis said grimly, staring at the letter. "But as good as dead."

"She looked like a grievin' widow, sir. I swear it. It was such a change in her. She'd been so kind of, well, she'd had sort of a glow in the past months."

*Had she fallen in love with Salazar?*

"But after she got the letter that day—the one that upset her—she took so poor that Mrs. Mendez moved her into the suite with herself. I think that's when they talked about your wife goin' to California, sir."

Justis groaned inwardly. Whether she loved him or not, her pride had been devastated. She had wanted to be free of him all along, and his so-called marriage to

Amarintha had given her a legitimate reason to break their bargain. Still, she must have been sick with hatred for him after reading the newspaper clipping. If he let her go for good, let her start fresh without him, he'd be giving her the most loving, unselfish gift in his soul.

"What about Vittorio Salazar?" he asked suddenly. "Where was he durin' all this?"

The porter turned and vehemently launched a stream of tobacco juice into a spittoon. "Right beside your wife, sir, bein' the dearest gentleman friend in the world—but still beatin' up whores at night."

Katherine was headed to California in the company of a man she thought she could trust, a man who might see her as something less than a lady now that she had no protection. A man who liked to use women in a way that Justis could picture all too easily at the moment.

Thomas grabbed his arm. "You look like you've met the devil and he's about to carry you off to hell, sir. Come sit down."

Not himself, he thought. Katherine. The devil had her, and she didn't suspect. "I'm all right," he told Thomas. "I want to see what personal things she left behind."

Thomas shifted awkwardly. "She didn't take much with her, sir. The rest—includin' all of your clothes and things—she gave to me. Told me to enjoy what profit I could from 'em. I'm sorry, sir. They're sold."

"Did she give you a gold nugget hung on a leather necklace?"

"No, sir."

She'd never give up her memories of home. He had done the right thing by accepting Amarintha's god-awful blackmail, and maybe Katie could forgive him for wounding her dignity. After all, the land was the thing she loved, the only thing.

"You'll be takin' a room at the hotel, sir?" Thomas asked.

Justis shook his head. She would hate him, hate him

even more than she did now, but he couldn't let her go without eliminating Salazar's danger from her life and explaining the reason behind his marriage to Amarintha. He couldn't let her go even then. He'd have to see for himself that she hated him and that nothing he could say or do would ever change that.

He clasped Thomas's hand in farewell. "I'll be takin' the first ship I can get for California."

THE WHOLE WORLD was a swaying, creaking nightmare filled with pain. Caught in a squall in the middle of a moonless night, the brig lurched from side to side. The maids staggered about Katherine's tiny cabin, trying not to fall down with their lanterns. Adela and one of the children's nannies kept bumping against the wall. They protested in terse Spanish and crossed themselves fearfully.

Kneeling on a blanket on the floor beside her narrow bed, Katherine watched the chaotic scene through a haze of exhaustion. She was more aware of her own body than anything else at the moment. Her hair felt enormously heavy hanging in several braided loops between her shoulder blades. She was naked except for a nightgown she'd drawn up beneath her breasts and tied in a knot. Sweat ran from under it and tickled the tight, hypersensitive skin of her swollen belly.

"Holy saints save us!" one of the maids screamed as the ship rolled again.

"Amen!" Adela said as she careened off a wall.

Katherine swayed but remained securely in place. She gripped the bed's sideboard as another contraction stabbed her.

"This will be the one!" she said between gritted teeth as she stretched her head back in agony.

Adela toppled beside her and reached between her

legs. "Yes! Push hard! Push hard! Ah! It is here! The little one is here!"

Katherine collapsed backward as the nanny knelt and caught her. Propping herself up with the woman's help, Katherine panted for breath as she looked at the blood and gore between her legs. In the center of it, moving weakly in Adela's hands, was a tiny, wrinkled baby girl.

"She is so beautiful," Katherine murmured. Love poured through her, and she was filled with a sense of awe. She had been so professional until this point, so much like a doctor observing her own delivery. Now she was purely a mother, and the sight of her blood-slicked babe with black hair and light eyes made tears slip down her face.

"Justis," she moaned softly. "This is our *daughter.*"

After the storm finally quieted, Adela and her servants got Katherine and the baby cleaned up and into bed. As Katherine watched her daughter nurse, she vowed to make a wonderful home for the two of them. She would never let anything happen to this miraculous little angel. All the love she had wanted to give Justis was here, cradled close to her heart.

The next morning Vittorio came to her cabin to visit. He carefully studied the baby sleeping in her arms. "She will be fairer-skinned than you. And her eyes are so blue! Those eyes will not turn dark, like yours. What color were the father's eyes?"

"Green." Green as new leaves, she thought with a swift tugging in her chest.

"I predict that the babe will have her father's eyes."

She wouldn't say the words to anyone, but deep inside she hoped so. It would be a measure of comfort to look into her daughter's eyes and see Justis there. But Vittorio's tone of voice bothered her. "You sound as if you're glad she won't look so much like an Indian."

He nodded. "We must accept the facts, Catalina. The Californios will never consider you an equal, but your half-caste daughter may fare well, especially if she is pretty. Perhaps she will even be able to make a good marriage."

Katherine frowned. "What would she do instead? Do you think my daughter will become some Californio's mistress? She will marry a fine man—if she wishes to marry. Perhaps I will encourage her to take a husband from my own people, someone who will not congratulate himself for being noble when he marries a half-breed woman."

Vittorio's slow, patient smile annoyed her. She was finding him less likable these days. Once they reached California she would organize her future and relegate him to an insignificant part in it.

"What have you decided to name her?" he asked.

Katherine sighed happily, her pique forgotten for the moment. The babe's real name would be Dahlonega. It was the Cherokee word for gold. "I am naming her after my parents," she told Vittorio. "Mary Jessica." She swallowed a lump in her throat. "She will be Mary Jessica Gallatin. I shall call her Mary."

He nodded. "Maria. A fine name."

"Not Maria. Mary."

"Catalina and her daughter, Maria. Yes. I like the sound of those. They will serve me quite well." Vittorio left the cabin as she stared at him with slowly dawning concern.


JUSTIS DESPISED BEING cooped up on the schooner, and he vowed that if he ever reached California, he would never leave again, at least not by ship. The problem at this point, however, was that the damned schooner had taken a lot of storm damage off the western coast of South America after rounding the Horn. The captain had barely gotten it to a safe harbor.

Now he and the other passengers were marooned in a

tiny village while they waited for a passing ship to take them on to California. By Justis's calculations, Katherine's ship must have arrived there within the past month. Even if he got another passage right away, he would be more than three months behind her.

He had never been much for praying, but now he spent a considerable amount of his time asking God to protect her from Vittorio Salazar.

## CHAPTER 17

THE FIESTA at Rancho Mendez was like nothing Katherine had ever seen before. After several days of near-nonstop festivities it continued in full force, with picnics, bullfights, dances, horse races, and a dozen other entertainments that ranged from genteel to wildly bawdy. The families and guests of every rancho within a two-day ride had come to the event, along with many of the Yankee traders from the coastal village of Yerba Buena and the village of Sonoma to its north.

Adela's husband, Miguel, a sturdy, dark-skinned patriarch of medium height and cheerful, rounded face, had organized the fiesta in honor of his wife's homecoming. Katherine had expected to be treated pleasantly by her open-minded California hosts, but Miguel Mendez's old-world courtesy surpassed her highest hopes. Judging by his sincere and formal manner toward her, she might have been a Mexican aristocrat.

Don Miguel, as everyone respectfully called him, was typical of the men who commanded the huge cattle-and-sheep estates of the balmy northern California wilderness. Flamboyant by American standards, he decorated his clothes with colorful braid and gleaming studs of gold and silver.

He wore fancy ruffled shirts under short jackets, and snug vests that displayed his rotund physique; his trousers flared from knee to ankle, and the insets were ornamented. He frequently and boisterously waved a wide-brimmed hat the Californios called a sombrero, and when the air grew cool at night he draped a bright-colored serape over his shoulders.

He rode his equally ornamented horses with fascinating grace, looking more like a centaur than a man. Everyone—men, women, and all but the tiniest children—rode in California, often at nothing less than a fast gallop. Horses were plentiful and spirited, like much else to be found in the region where cattle flourished untended and fortunes could be had simply by shipping the hides east.

Katherine found the California women just as exotic as the men. For the fiesta Adela excitedly outfitted her in their style, and each time she looked into a mirror Katherine was amazed by the change in her appearance. No corsets for these women—they let their curves jiggle and their waists grow. And no solemn colors. Today Katherine wore a bright blue shawl over a scoop-necked white blouse with puffy elbow-length sleeves. The blouse tucked into a gay print skirt and rustling red petticoats. On her feet she wore delicate blue slippers; on her head she wore a white lace mantilla.

Head to foot she was a California woman now, she told herself. It was a heartening notion, though she wasn't sure whether the future promised more happiness than the past. The Californios had various social castes, just as any group of people did, and she couldn't predict what position they would assign to her.

It was true that the ranchos existed almost entirely on the labor of her kind—Indians—and mestizos, mixed-bloods. But the workers, everyone from house servants to the rowdy vaqueros who herded cattle, were employees, not slaves, and they mingled with their *patróns* in a way that hinted at respect, if not equality. Among the rancheros Katherine had seen one or two who had wives who were obviously of Indian ancestry.

That gave her hope. Her new home wasn't perfect, but at least it bore signs of being hospitable. *Hospitable.* She thought of Vittorio. Lately he had returned to his more accommodating, reliable behavior, and her reservations about him had faded.

"If you are not happy at Vittorio's home you must come straight back here," Adela told her during the fiesta's fifth and final night. "It is only a day's travel."

Seated in the cool adobe grandeur of the great room in the Mendez hacienda, Katherine smiled. She felt comfortable and optimistic. "I'm sure he'll be an excellent advisor and host while I acquire my land grant from the governor."

"He will. Do not let my husband's opinion worry you. They have always disagreed on everything."

Miguel Mendez was decidedly cool toward his deceased sister's husband. Judging by Miguel's cheerful tolerance of everyone else with whom she saw him, Katherine couldn't understand his distaste for Vittorio. "What does Vittorio do that angers Don Miguel so often?"

"My husband accuses Vittorio of being too harsh with his vaqueros, but I think it is just that they manage their workers in different ways. Vittorio's methods are not Miguel's or my own." She took Katherine's hands and laughed. "But you are a guest, not a cow herder, and you will be treated very well indeed. I will visit you often, and you will always have the company of many fellow guests at Salazar's home. In California the wilderness would swallow up travelers if we did not take them in. Vittorio is kindhearted that way. You will meet many fascinating people."

That night, as she lay in bed with Mary asleep at her breast, Katherine allowed herself the luxury of memories and tears. Ten months had passed since her last day with Justis in New York. His betrayal hurt just as much now as it had when she'd learned of his marriage.

She dreamed about him that night; she saw him so clearly that he seemed within reach of her arms, and she ached to hold him again. *Don't go with Salazar,* he told her. *It's not safe. Trust me. I love you.*

Katherine woke up crying. He didn't love her and never had. The dream's warning must therefore be just as much a lie.


ADELA'S DESCRIPTIÓN HAD been accurate—there were fascinating people at Vittorio's beautiful rancho. The impressive two-story adobe hacienda overflowed with interesting travelers, some of whom Katherine had met at the Mendez rancho during the fiesta. At most times of the day or night she could look out the small window of her upper-gallery bedroom and see people strolling in the courtyard or conversing around the fountain at its center.

The estate provided wonderful food and wine, thanks to the labor of several hundred workers who cultivated the orchards and vineyards that covered its gentle hillsides. The guests, who included the governor's cousin, a pair of burly Russian fur trappers, and a Mexican merchant traveling to Santa Barbara with his family, enjoyed a life of carefree overindulgence. Much as did Vittorio, Katherine quickly discovered.

With her gold in his safe and her presence guaranteed at his side, he was in no hurry to discuss the business of helping her acquire a land grant. After two weeks of growing impatience, she wanted no more of his silky evasions.

One evening after the other guests had gone to bed she

stayed up to play chess with him in his private library. In the light of a small table lamp she watched boredom flicker across his handsome, patrician face. Now was the moment, she decided.

"Would you mind discussing my plans for the future?" she asked pleasantly. "With fall coming on, I think I should start investigating the land hereabouts. I understand there are some beautiful valleys farther inland."

"Our fall is hot and dry. There is no hurry."

"I want to start planning a house. Can you at least find a craftsman to discuss the design with me?"

"Catalina, this is a rough land for a woman by herself. How would you fare with a large house and many servants to manage? Who would command your vaqueros and take your cattle hides to market?"

"I'm going to concentrate on farming, not ranching. I want to start orchards and vineyards. The inland valleys are perfect for that, from all I've heard."

"But you have everything you need here."

"Except a sense of *home*." She smiled at him wistfully. "I have to create my own future in my own home."

"Hmmm. You are insistent. Then it is time we talked seriously about your future. Yes."

"Thank you. You don't know how much I appreciate your compassion."

Abruptly Vittorio rose and went to the library door. Katherine watched in bewilderment as he shut and locked it. He cut a dark, commanding figure in his tight jacket and trousers. Silver spurs clinked on his boots as he crossed the room to an ornately carved cabinet. His black hair had grown long during the ocean voyage; in the style of his people he wore it pulled back in a queue.

From one of the cabinet drawers he retrieved several black silk scarves. "Hold out one of your hands," he said as he turned to her, smiling a little. "Before we talk I want to show you an entertaining trick of mine."

Katherine sighed in exasperation but did as he asked.

He bent over her hand and quickly knotted one end of the scarf around the wrist. "Now let your arm rest on the arm of the chair. Yes. Like that."

He tied her wrist to the thick wood. She shifted impatiently on the upholstered seat. "If there were a fire, I would certainly roast, sir. I couldn't drag this heavy chair one inch. Hurry with your parlor trick."

"Be calm, *querida*. I have much to show you."

He tugged on the big chair, sliding it around on the red-tiled floor to face him. "Your other hand, please."

She frowned as he secured it to the chair's other arm. "Aha," she said. "These are some sort of magician's knots. If I pull a certain way, they'll come free."

"No," he said softly. "I'm certain that they won't."

His game struck a chord of alarm in her as he slipped a scarf around her ankle. "Let's forego this silliness and talk business," she said as he tied her ankle to the chair leg. "I have to check on Mary soon. I don't like to leave her with the servants too long—"

"Just a moment more."

He tied her other ankle to a chair leg, then rose, studying her intensely. Her throat went dry as she saw a flush darken his olive complexion; his eyes burned with a fervor that seemed almost sexual. "Untie me," she ordered as fear raced up her spine. "This is an undignified game."

"You will learn to like it. I promise."

Suddenly he rested his fist against her mouth and shoved hard. She gasped, and he jammed his knuckles so far between her teeth that her jaw stretched with painful pressure. She stared up at him in utter shock and struggled against the chair's bindings. With silent rage and terror she cursed her naiveté.

Her blue silk dress had a wide, rounded neckline. Vittorio sank his free hand into the front of it and tore the material open. She screamed uselessly and bit into his knuckles.

His low moan of pain and pleasure horrified her. Dark

eyes glittering under half-shut lids, he casually ripped her undershirt down the center and jerked the torn halves back on either side. She made a high-pitched keening sound of fury that changed to distress when he twisted the nipple of one milk-swollen breast.

"Now listen to me, Catalina," he murmured. His fingers went to the other breast and repeated the torture. Sweat broke out on Katherine's forehead and pinpoints of light danced in her vision. "Listen, my beautiful Catalina." His chest moved swiftly. She groaned with more horror when she noticed the thick bulge straining at the front of his trousers. She bit into his knuckles and tasted his blood, then bit harder.

He shivered in his strange, delighted way but squeezed her breast so viciously that tears came to her eyes. "I will bruise you until you cannot nurse your child," he promised. "Enough biting. A lady does not bite."

She relaxed her aching jaw and gazed at him with hatred. He shook his head. "You must depend on my influence now, Catalina. You are alone in a foreign place. You are nothing but an American—and not even a white American. It is not legal for Americans to settle here, but our government ignores the law to encourage trade. The law, however, can be enforced if we wish."

He slid his hand back and forth on her naked shoulder, stroking so roughly the skin burned. "Adela would never believe you if you tell her about tonight, so do not think of it. You should not risk insulting one of the few true friends you have. I know that you are shocked, but that will pass. Besides, you don't really want to leave me. You and your beautiful daughter. You love her very much, don't you, Catalina, and would never want to see her hurt. No. We will enjoy a very amicable relationship, Catalina. Very beneficial for you."

He put his hand on one of her wrists, caressing the black scarf with his fingertips. "This is the only kind of pleasure I will ask from you. I will never use you in the ugly way other men demand of ladies. You will learn to appreciate the honor I am doing you." He hesitated. His gaze was tender as it moved over her. "You are so special. Such a fine lady, and yet you have the needs of a savage. How do I know?"

He smiled and raked his fingernails down her chest. "No woman of delicate sensibilities would have married a man as low and coarse as your husband. Oh, Catalina, I revere the contradictions in your nature. From the very first I knew I would never find another woman with such a perfect blend of desire and control."

She twisted her head and struggled to keep from gagging. He ground his fist deeper into her mouth and crooned soothing words. She willed herself not to panic. A mind such as Vittorio's was capable of rationalizing any cruel deed. She had to remain calm enough to bargain with him. She had to remain calm for Mary's sake.

What if he were telling the truth about Adela's reaction? Perhaps Adela had known about his sick nature all along—perhaps she even considered it normal. That didn't seem likely, but Katherine couldn't trust anyone but herself at the moment.

"I adore you, Catalina," he whispered. "I will treat you as if you were my wife. Better than that, even, because I never shared these honors with my wife. Do you understand how precious you are to me? Does that please you?"

Katherine's stomach roiled. She gazed up at his utterly gentle eyes and forced herself to nod. When trapped, she would play by his rules. When free, she would plot her escape—and her revenge.

"No hysteria?" he asked, watching her closely. "If I remove my hand? No indelicate screaming?"

She nodded again. Slowly he pulled his fist from her mouth. Her jaw had been growing numb; now shards of sensation ran through the joints like knife pricks. "You drive an interesting bargain, Vittorio," she finally managed to say.

He laughed. "I should have known you would not be offended. Your Indian blood makes you more difficult to hurt. You are strong." He stroked her face with the back of one finger. "That will make our games more interesting."

"Are we finished for tonight?"

"Yes. I know you have much to think about. I also know that my kind of pleasure is particularly exhausting. Go and rest." He brushed a fingertip over her mauled nipples. "I will not hurt you in this way again until after your daughter is weaned. I am not a cruel man."

She nearly choked. As she stared at him in shock, he untied her. When she was free she made herself move calmly, though her hands trembled as she pulled her torn clothes back together. Vittorio watched with a pleased expression.

"I see your fear and doubts," he murmured hoarsely. "They do honor to the more sensitive aspects of your nature. I treasure them."

"You are . . . remarkable. *Buenas noches.*"

He bowed, then went to the door and unlocked it. Katherine walked numbly from the library. When she reached her bedroom she ignored the servant girl's curious stares and took Mary from her without a word. After the girl left, Katherine sat by the window and gazed at the sleeping baby, holding her in a streak of golden moonlight.

"Your father would kill the madman for this," she whispered brokenly. "No matter the consequences. If I didn't have you to consider, my love, I would do the same. Tonight."

She cradled Mary to her shoulder and rocked. Her mind churned with escape plans, but all of them posed too much risk. If anything went wrong, Mary would suffer.

Toward dawn Katherine lay down with Mary nestled against her side. She shut her eyes and prayed softly. She would wait. Until the time was right to strike back she would do whatever Vittorio asked.

OVER THE NEXT few days Vittorio acted as if nothing odd had passed between them. His manner was courtly, his smile genuine. Katherine felt as if she were balanced on the edge of a precipice waiting to be shoved to her death. The distress affected her milk, and Mary protested with hungry wails. Katherine was forced to request a wet nurse from among the servants.

Vittorio sent a note to her as she was dressing one morning. *I will come to your room tonight, my love. You seem ready.*

It was all she could do to sit at the breakfast table with him. Only the presence of a dozen other guests saved her from revealing her fury and fear. With a determination that drained all her energy she focused her attention on a newcomer. "Did you arrive yesterday, sir?"

The man, a lanky Mexican in clothes still dirty from the trail, nodded. *"Sí.* I am guiding a group of settlers to the Valley of the Sun."

"Where is that, señor?"

"Two days' ride east of here. It is a place for farmers. The valley lies too many miles from the coast for the taste of the rancheros. Who wants to haul cattle hides so far to market?"

"Who named it Valley of the Sun?"

"The Indians. Many years ago they had a village there —before the priests built missions and offered civilization to the people."

"The farmers, where are they from?"

"They are Americans," Vittorio interjected. "Too many Americans. But I will not protest as long as they mind their own business."

*Her own countrymen.* Katherine could barely wait until the meal was finished. Carrying Mary, she went outdoors and made her way through the outbuildings until she found the settlers' camp in the shade of an oak grove. Their group consisted of six solemn, worn-looking families who shared five rickety wagons and five pairs of gaunt oxen. Katherine introduced herself, and as soon as they got over their shock at meeting such an unusual compatriot, they asked her to sit with them and talk.

"We came by ship from Boston and put every penny we had left into provisions for an inland journey," their leader told her.

He was a tall, gray-haired pillar of a man with an orator's voice and a New England accent. What dream would make such a man travel so far, Katherine wondered.

"You wouldn't be missionaries, would you?" she asked cautiously. The furtive looks he and the others gave her confirmed her suspicion. "Your secret is safe with me. What church?"

"Presbyterian," a nervous young man whispered.

"The mission board funded us," the leader told her stiffly. "We will start a good Protestant community here."

She thought their naive piousness spelled trouble, but she told them about her training at the Presbyterian girls' school in Philadelphia. The growing interest in their eyes made her heart race.

Trouble or not, they were her only hope. Katherine hid her desperation and said casually, "You need someone with you who knows the Californios and has friends among them. They're not going to be happy with such a large group of foreign settlers taking root in their country. When they figure out that you're here to convert good Catholics into good Protestants, they may go hard on you. Perhaps I can prevent that. Also, I have money to contribute to your cause. Gold."

Several of the group whispered excitedly. Katherine

held up a warning hand. "But you must take me with you. And my child."

Their leader gave her fine clothes a stern appraisal. "Are you prepared to share the work and suffer hardships?"

She bit back an ironic laugh. "Oh, yes," she said. "I am sure I can adjust."

VITTORIO CAME TO her after dark. She had piled pillows in one corner of her room and put Mary there, safely out of the way. When he knocked she swallowed nausea and went to the door with a nonchalant expression on her face. Her nerves felt as if they might break into tiny pieces.

He stepped inside and shut the door softly behind him. In his hand he carried a short, thick quirt of rawhide. "You are ready?" he inquired politely, glancing toward the corner where Mary lay sleeping.

Katherine couldn't make herself speak words of agreement. This horror will end, she thought. I must simply wait. I will have revenge. "What do you want me to do?" she asked tersely.

He smiled. "I will show you." He grabbed the heavy braid bundled at the back of her head. She shut her eyes and said a silent prayer as he jerked her toward the bed. "Strip to the waist, please."

LATER, HIS CLOTHES soaked in sweat and the scent of his arousal, Vittorio sat on the floor beside the bed and stroked the quirt over the welts on her naked back. "These will sting for only a few days," he assured her.

Shivering, Katherine fought an urge to scream into the pillow beneath her face. Oh, if only Justis were there! What she would give to watch him strangle this sick creature with his bare hands! Then he would carry her and their daughter someplace safe, where he would treat them tenderly and say words of grief and apology.

She stifled a groan of despair. No more fantasies! Justis had deserted her to take a respectable white wife. She had to be strong all alone. She would never have his help again. She could not kill Vittorio yet, so she would continue to play the game.

"Vittorio?" she asked, raising her head to look at him. The satiated expression on his face hinted that he might be generous at the moment.

"Hmmm?"

He lazily flicked the quirt over her shoulders. She struggled not to jerk with pain. "I would like a small portion of my gold, please. I feel sorry for those silly American farmers. I want to give them a gift. A few hundred dollars, that's all."

"Certainly. I approve of your kind spirit." He sighed. "I will be away for a short while. Tomorrow I am leaving to visit a friend in Monterey. He is getting married."

"Oh?" Excitement hammered in her stomach. "How long will you be gone?"

"Several weeks." He stood, snapped the quirt down on her back one more time, then yawned. "I will send a boy to your room in the morning with the gold."

She sat up, her flogged back to him, and straightened her clothes with as much dignity as she could. She heard him open the door to the gallery. He paused there. "You never cried or begged," he said thoughtfully. "Amazing. I haven't even begun to hurt you."

The next morning a servant boy brought her a pouch filled with gold coins. She held it to her lips for a moment, praying that the missionaries could be persuaded to hide her and Mary when Vittorio came looking.


IN JUST OVER two weeks the missionaries marked off a valley for their small community, designating a pretty glen nearby for their church site and a spot next to a creek for their school. Each family had a hurriedly built but sturdy cabin, and the tiny home they'd constructed for Katherine at the far end of the valley was secure, if not particularly comfortable.

She had already proved to them that she could work as hard as they, though her enthusiasm was fueled by dread of Vittorio rather than a grand desire to bring civilization to a barbaric Eden. The more settled she was there, the more the missionaries considered her an asset and a compatriot, the less likely they'd be to give her up without a fight when he tracked her down.

If the missionaries wanted heaven on earth, they'd found it, Katherine mused one day as she sat on a warm, grassy hilltop. She curled her legs under her and rocked Mary, who had fretted all night and most of the day.

"Poor love," Katherine crooned to her, stroking her head. "I promise that you will have strong white teeth when all their growing is done. You'll be the most beautiful little girl in all of California." The contrast between the baby's black hair, fawn-colored skin, and green eyes already made for surpassing charm.

"I wish your father could see you," Katherine whispered. "How could he resist such a combination?" She bent forward and, shutting her eyes, touched her forehead to Mary's. Had it really been a year since he'd left for Gold Ridge? Would she ever stop listening for his voice when other men talked? Would she always hurry to meet strangers, hope warring with bitterness?

Mary's soft cry of dismay made Katherine look at her closely. The baby gazed up at her with unhappy eyes, appearing almost comically put out. "You angry little fox," Katherine teased. "I know I haven't had much time to hold you lately. I've been helping to build us a home. A fine log shanty with pretty mud between the cracks. Nothing fancy, but we'll be outdoors most of the time anyway. The weather is so pleasant here."

She raised her head and swept a loving gaze over the countryside. The hills wore ever-changing patterns of emerald grass dotted with groves of oaks; the sky was a rich blue, and the September breeze that curled out of it was deliciously hot. A creek flowed through the shallow valley in front of her, shaded by sycamores. This secluded paradise looked more like the pastoral estate of a king than a wilderness.

The missionaries were a stern, complaining lot who never took time to admire the land. Instead, they worried over how to tame it and attract heathen Indians to their ministry. Still, Katherine lauded their hard work and determination.

Mary made a mewling sound that carried a more serious note of distress. Frowning, Katherine unwrapped the light blanket that covered her and probed her velvet-skinned stomach with quick, expert hands. "You've not got the colic, have you? Well, I'll fix you some tea that will help that. You'll be just fine. Yes, my love, my sweet little Dahlonega."

She whispered a medicine chant in Cherokee, then, gathering Mary in her arms, walked down to the valley settlement, humming contentedly. By evening a terrible scarlet rash covered Mary's body. By dawn her fever was so high, she suffered convulsions. By noon the light began to fade from her beautiful green eyes. At sunset she whimpered softly and died in Katherine's arms.

"BRING SEÑORA GALLATIN to me, please," Vittorio commanded, jabbing his mount's sides with his spurs until the palomino lunged forward, nearly crashing into the group of worried Americans. He jerked a gloved hand toward the vaqueros waiting with rifles resting at lazy alert on their thighs. "I do not wish to use force, but I will if I must."

"A moment of patience, please, Don Salazar," the

Americans' leader asked in a nervous voice. "The woman is not in a frame of mind to—"

"Vittorio!"

He turned to see her running up to him. He didn't notice the primal smile that was not a smile at all, or the lethal gleam in her eye, because he was staring at her once-magnificent hair. It whipped around her shoulders in a chopped, ragged mass.

"You have nothing to threaten me with now!" she screamed, and threw herself at him with the ferocity of a rabid beast. Silver flashed in the sun as her hand swung. Agony slashed from his hipbone to his knee as he spurred the palomino away from her.

Her countrymen and their wives grabbed her and wrestled her to the ground. A scalpel fell from her grasp. Caught by their restraining hands, she spat at Vittorio with frustrated violence. "You will pay for your betrayal and cruelty," she promised. "I will kill you the first chance I get."

"Her babe died two days ago," a man explained. "Took some kind of sickness and passed away quick. She's near out of her mind."

Vittorio stared at the half-mad beauty and pressed a hand against the long gash in his leg. She didn't know how much her maddened fury excited him. He would bide his time and let her hatred simmer into something even more deadly, even more wonderful to tame. "I will come back for you, Catalina, but first I will give you time to find your senses. My poor angel. I promise not to forsake you."

"Good," she retorted, her eyes vivid with murderous lust. "Come back. I'll cut your throat and watch you strangle on your own evil."

He gestured to his men to follow him. Then, tipping his sombrero to her, he whirled his blood-flecked horse and rode away.

* * *

Justis had taken to working with the ship's crew out of necessity. He was sick of the ocean, but more than anything else he was sick of lying in his bunk sweating over Katherine's fate. Several times he had thought he heard her voice. Worry and impatience were addling his senses, he feared. He'd be no good to her that way. So he spent his time on deck.

"Raise tacks and sheets!" the captain called.

His face stinging in the briny wind, his bare chest wet with ocean spray, Justis copied what the sailors beside him did, letting heavy rope slide through his gloved hands. As usual, he forgot his worries for a few minutes as he concentrated on the swift litany of commands yelled by the captain in his booming voice. When everything was done, the calls came back from the crew— "Cross-jack yards all well!" "Well the mizzen-topsail yard!" and others.

"Give the call, Mr. Gallatin!" a grinning sailor urged.

Justis threw back his head and called, "Well all!"

As he coiled the rigging, the captain came to his station and clapped him on the shoulder. "Your wait is about done, sir. I'll be sorry to lose you, but I hope you find your wife."

Justis grabbed his arm. "Are we near?"

The captain pointed. Justis swung to his right and gazed desperately toward the shimmering blue line on the horizon. "We'll be putting in near the Presidio de San Diego," the captain told him. "It's hundreds of miles south of where you're headed, but it's California land. We'll be harbored there for a month or more."

"I can't sit and stew for another month. I'll go ahead on horseback."

"But that would mean weeks of hard travel, sir. The Mendez and Salazar ranchos are up beyond the mission at San Francisco de Asis."

"Doesn't matter," he said softly, searching the coast as if he could already see Katherine. Nothing mattered but finding her.

KATHERINE GREW ACCUSTOMED to being by herself, buried in her grief. She ventured into the missionaries' lives only when they needed her doctoring skills or when she needed to replenish her food supplies, to which she was entitled by the money she'd given them.

Otherwise, in the weeks following Mary's death she became a hermit. October passed; November arrived and brought cool, rainy days. She spent much of her time beside the primitive mud-and-rock fireplace in her cabin with a shawl hanging loosely around her shoulders, or she went to the crude log church in the glen, where one tiny grave marked the cemetery.

That grave, surrounded by the stumps of trees, was where she carried out her two most important duties in life. First she sat on a stump beside the grave and spoke as if Mary could hear, telling her Cherokee legends, stories about the Blue Song family, and loving anecdotes about Justis.

Then she took out the long, slender knife she'd bartered from one of the local Indians who came regularly to trade with the missionaries. She honed the blade a little finer each day and waited for Vittorio to return. Out of all she had lost—her family, her home, her husband, her child—she would have only one victory. But it would be sweet.

A COOL, MISTY dusk had settled into the slopes of the hills. Justis reined his horse to a halt on a rise that gave him a long view. He squinted in the failing light at log cabins scattered on the valley floor. Smoke rose from their chimneys and mingled with the fog rising from the nearby creek. Across the valley, one tiny cabin sat off to itself. No smoke curled above its pole-and-thatch roof.

The pulse pounded in his throat. Katherine lived there somewhere. She had left Salazar's rancho for unknown reasons almost three months earlier according to the servants he'd bribed to talk. He had wanted to confront Salazar, but the Californio was away on a hunting trip. No matter. If Salazar had done anything to hurt her, there would be time for killing him later.

Justis urged his tired horse into a lope and entered the valley. A small boy rounded the corner of a cabin, carrying firewood. He dropped his load and stared in fear as Justis slid the horse to a stop.

"Hello, young feller. Don't be scared of me."

"You're dressed like a Californio but you sound like a Yank."

"Yeah. I'm a Georgia Yank. I'm lookin' for a Injun lady named Katherine Gallatin."

His eyes still wide, the boy pointed toward the end of the valley. "Beyond the trees there. She always stays by our church building until dark."

"Thanks for the help." Justis put his horse in a walk, though he could barely keep from kicking the animal into a sprint. He didn't want to go tearing up to Katie in the shadows and scaring her half to death. *Katie*. After more than a year. He felt like a man about to enter battle —excitement pumping through his veins, every nerve alert to the fullest, emotions stretched taut under a calm veneer.

"Mister!" the boy called. "Be careful! My pa says she's got a devil on her shoulder!"

Justis almost smiled. And another about to come back into her life.

KATHERINE TILTED HER head toward the faint sound of hooves on wet ground. The shadows were so deep she could hardly see past the clearing to the narrow trail that led to the settlement. The hooves came closer, moving fast, sucking into the soil. Now she even heard the soft clink of the rider's gear.

She leapt up from her sitting place by Mary's grave and ran to the church. She hid behind a back corner and watched carefully, her breath short. Slowly she withdrew her knife from the sheath in her belt, then pulled her shawl over her head like a hood, draping the ends down her back where they wouldn't hinder her arms.

The man who rode into the clearing was a dark, indistinct form in the dusk, but his height and the outline of his wide sombrero were enough to confirm her suspicion. *Vittorio.* Who else would come so boldly to her sacred place? This was no missionary.

Her hand tightened on the knife's handle as she watched him halt his horse and sit very still, only his head moving as he surveyed the church and the dark woods on the hillsides that formed the small glen. Ghostly white mist swirled around his horse's hooves. He climbed down, and by the angle of his head she knew he'd spotted Mary's grave. He knelt on one knee by the roughly carved wooden marker.

Strength and rage surged through her. Good, she thought. Let the monster read the epitaph for her child. *Mary Jessica Gallatin. Beloved Daughter of Justis and Katherine.* Let him enjoy one last cruel laugh before she killed him.

His face was hidden by the tilt of his sombrero, but he seemed transfixed by the marker, even tracing the letters on it with his fingertips. Katherine moved forward quietly and raised the knife. She would wait until he heard her and jerked his head up in surprise. Then she would plunge the knife into a vulnerable spot above the neck of his brightly striped serape. Nothing would save him after a throat wound such as that.

She crept to within a few feet of him. Still he stared at

the marker. Slowly he reached up and grasped the brim of his sombrero. *Now,* she screamed silently as he removed it and let it fall on the rain-soaked ground.

"*Die,*" she commanded in a ringing voice. She lunged at him and thrust the knife downward just as he raised his face in the twilight.

## CHAPTER 18

KATHERINE screamed and tried in the last second to tuck the knife under so that it wouldn't hit home. It sliced across the front of his serape as he jerked back from her assault. He grabbed her wrist and she fell to her knees in front of him.

Wrapping his other arm around her waist, he trapped her against him from thigh to chest. Together in that tight, stunned embrace, they stared into each other's eyes. Katherine's hand went limp, and the knife fell to the ground.

"You hate me enough to kill me, gal?" he demanded, his voice low and hoarse.

The sound of his dear, deep drawl brought him to life in her shocked senses. *Justis.* He was no ghost conjured by love and memories. After fourteen months, after traveling thousands of miles, he was holding her in his arms. And she had nearly killed him. She saw anguish in his eyes.

"Not you," she whispered. "I didn't know it was you. I swear that."

He searched her face for a second, then his grip slowly relaxed on her wrist. "Katie." His tone was filled with relief.

Finally she noticed the tears on his face. They had been there when he raised his gaze from their child's grave. She lifted a trembling hand to the rugged features she knew by heart and caught the wetness on her fingertips. She had never seen him cry before.

"Justis?" she asked in desperate confusion.

"We had a daughter? And she died?"

Katherine nodded, stunned. *He had been crying for Mary.* "Oh, Justis!" Her arms went around his neck. He gasped in surprise, then dragged her even closer. He held her as if he could make her a part of him. They stayed that way for a long time, clinging to each other silently, arms tightening into quick hugs, then relaxing, then holding on fiercely again.

Darkness grew around them and Mary's grave just beyond their feet. Justis reached out with one hand. Katherine twisted, her head against the crook of his neck, and saw him rest the hand on the mound of dirt. Tears slid down her face.

"I was carrying her when you left for Gold Ridge. She wasn't part of our agreement, so I didn't tell you."

"My *daughter.*" His voice was hoarse. "And you kept it from me."

"I planned to tell you later. You never came back."

"I came back. You just didn't wait long enough. You didn't want to wait."

"You married Amarintha Parnell."

The silence stretched between them, full of tragedy. He held her tighter. "Yeah, I did," he said wearily.

She reeled inside. Hearing him admit that he had betrayed her brought all the pain rushing back. She inhaled the scent of him—tobacco, leather, sweat. Warmth. Kindness. Laughter. Good memories. All she had left. Despair caught in her throat. "Why have you followed me again?" she asked bitterly. "I thought you were done with me."

"You can't rid yourself of me that easy. When was our daughter born? When did she die? How?"

Katherine told him. Then, her voice cold, she added, "You almost sound as if you wouldn't have been ashamed of her. As if you wanted her."

"Did you?"

The question sank too deep for pretense. She groaned softly. "Oh, God, yes."

"But you said you didn't want a half-breed."

"You said the same."

"But I would have—"

"If you could only have seen her, Justis! She was beautiful! Dark, like me, but her eyes, oh, she had your eyes, the most amazing shade of green." She dug her hands into his damp woolen cape. "I did everything I could to keep her well and safe. I tried so hard."

He slipped a hand under the hood made by her shawl and cupped her head gently. She felt his lips brush her forehead. She whimpered in defeat, needing his tenderness too much, and turned her face upward. He kissed her. His hand slid down her hair and jerked to a stop at the end of the braid, just a little below her shoulders. He tugged the shawl off her head and lifted the pitiful remnant of her long tresses.

She sensed his shock and bewilderment. "It was all I could do for her," she said, her voice breaking. "I couldn't put her in the ground without something of myself to keep her . . . keep her from being so cold and alone. I wrapped my hair around her."

He groaned and rested his cheek on her head. His big hand knotted around the short braid, caressing it. Katherine sagged against him. "What now?" she asked. "Our partnership is over. I don't understand your curious brand of determination. Your lack of honor destroyed even the friendship and affection we shared."

"Then why are you so close and quiet in my arms? Why did you hug me? Why did you want to be kissed?"

She clenched her teeth together. "I crave a fire's heat but I won't ever let it burn me again."

He drew back and looked at her. Though her expression was hidden by the growing darkness, he seemed to sense every confused emotion running through her. "Who did you want to kill? Salazar? Why aren't you livin' with him?"

She crumpled inside as the truth struck her. "Now I understand. You crossed a continent simply to punish me, because you thought I deserted you for Salazar. You had to take revenge even though *you* deserted *me* to marry a crazy woman who could barely stand your touch. A respectable white wife who had neither my intelligence nor, probably, my passion in bed. Your ambition warranted that sacrifice, I suppose. But this—this holy grail that has brought you clear to California—it is made of more vanity and pride than I ever imagined!"

"God damn your tongue," he said fiercely. "I came to make certain you were all right."

She wavered for a second. "I am *quite* fine."

"Liar! Hiding behind a shack in the wilderness with a knife in your hand, waiting like a wild she-wolf to murder somebody! Who? Salazar? What happened? Did you love the Mex sonuvabitch, but he wouldn't have you? What?"

She dug her hands deeper into his serape and tried to shake him. "I won't listen to your accusations! Not by our daughter's grave!"

He muttered a curse and rose to his feet, pulling her with him. She didn't have time to protest before he picked her up and strode with her to a massive black horse that looked strong enough to carry easily its heavy Spanish saddle weighted with saddlebags and other travel gear. He set her sideways on the saddle, then, holding the horse's reins, led it close to Mary's grave.

He scooped the knife up and handed it to Katherine. "Your scalpel, Doc."

The gentle taunt loosed a flood of emotion. Her hand shaking, she slipped the knife into its sheath. Nothing made sense right now. But Justis was here, here with her. He had come thousands of miles for revenge, but he had cried for their lost daughter, then offered both strength and tenderness. So many questions, so much to say. She could not trust him, but for now she had to be with him. "I live in the cabin at the near end of the valley."

"The one off by itself."

"Yes."

"I figured the lonely one was yours. If you've got room, I'll make a bed on the floor."

"For how long?"

"Until you and me get some things settled." He stood by his horse, almost lost in the darkness, but she felt his eyes searching for her reaction.

"All right."

"Good. Good, Katie." He turned and looked down at the little grave, fading into blackness now, with only the ugly stumps to keep it company. "I would have loved her. I love her now."

Katherine cupped her shawl over her mouth and cried silently as he led the horse away.

HIS PRESENCE FILLED the tiny one-room cabin. Katherine was still in shock, and she was silent as she built a fire. Justis had hobbled his horse on a patch of grass outside and now arranged all his gear by the wall near her bed. She kept her back to him as she put a kettle of coffee among the flames.

He dropped his hat and serape on the thing she called

a table, though it was only a wide slab of redwood with legs made from the small limbs of an oak tree. Standing in the center of the cabin, he frowned at it, the dirt floor, and her rudimentary bed—a pile of dried grass in one corner, covered with a blanket.

A sense of humiliation fueled her dull anger. She snatched her only mug from a nail. Goose bumps rose on her arms as he sat down on a split-log bench less than a foot behind her. She had always been able to tell when he was watching her; the scrutiny of those drooping, deceptively lazy green eyes was a searing force. She felt it now.

"You dress like a Mex peasant," he commented.

"I am a peasant. And glad for it. There's a great deal of freedom in having nothing and wanting nothing except to live and be left alone."

Without looking around, she tossed her shawl onto the pile of grass and blankets. She refused to give in to the urge to straighten her stained, much-mended white blouse. She tucked her bare ankles and crude leather sandals under the coarse brown material of her skirt.

He swore softly. "You were too damned proud to take the finery I bought for you in New York?"

"Too proud to take what Blue Song gold had purchased? Hardly. I took what I liked best and left the rest behind. I also took twenty thousand dollars from our bank account. Don't worry—there's many times that left."

He leaned forward. She felt his blunt fingers on the back of her neck. The contact made her blood race even more swiftly. She twisted halfway around and grabbed his wrist as he pulled the gold nugget from inside her blouse. "Don't touch me again," she warned.

His eyes glittered with emotions she couldn't read. He knotted his hand around the sturdy leather necklace and pulled slowly. She cried out in dismay but had no choice except to face him. She looked up with a mixture of defi-

ance and despair. "It is mine. You gave it to me. Just as"
—she winced inside—"you gave me your name."

Abruptly she snatched at the necklace, trying to lift it
over her head. "Here. Neither was mine to keep. Take it.
Give it to your real wife."

"No, dammit. Proud hellion." He wound the leather
thong around his fist so that it was too snug for her to
remove. "Forget about Amarintha. She's not my real
wife. You are. You and me still got a lot to share—a fortune to build. I came clear to the end of nowhere to bring
you back."

Disbelief turned quickly to fury. "One wife for profit
and one for respectability! You were forced into your first
marriage by the threat of jail, but the second one you
chose of your own free will! Now go back to the wife you
picked voluntarily! And your child! Your other child, the
respectable white one. Was it yet to be born when you
left on this vengeful quest to find me? Didn't Amarintha
protest your leaving her before the birth—or did you de-
sert *her* without warning too?"

He grasped her shoulders roughly. "The babe wasn't
mine! I never touched Amarintha!"

Shaking with anger and grief, she sprang at him and
slapped his face. "Don't insult me with more lies! Tell me
the truth! Even though you didn't love me, how could
you dishonor me? How could you break your word?"

"Katie! Listen to me!" He grabbed her in a confining
hug and pinned her between his knees. "There were reasons—"

"I trusted you!" she yelled. Popping sounds echoed
from somewhere in the valley. Justis's head jerked up as
he listened to them. "I believed in you!" she continued,
trying to break free of his embrace. "Oh, God, God." She
groaned in defeat. "I loved—"

"Quiet!" He pressed a hand over her mouth. His eyes
alert, he tilted his head toward the noise in the distance.

Breathing heavily, Katherine frowned in bewilderment as it registered in her mind. *Gunfire.*

In a smooth movement he lifted her out of his way and vaulted to his feet. With two long steps he was at his gear, pulling pistols and rifles from it. The popping sounds continued, growing louder. She heard shouts and screams and ran toward the heavy log door.

"No," he said, blocking her way. "Here." He pressed a pistol into her hand, then laid a rifle on the table. "I reckon you remember how to use 'em?"

"Of course, but—"

"I'm goin' outside." He tucked a pistol in his belt and cradled a rifle in his arm. "Slam the door behind me." With no more warning than that, he flung the door open and disappeared into the black, overcast night.

Katherine could no more hide in the cabin than he. She ignored the long rifle, knowing that she was likely to trip over it. With the pistol clutched calmly in one hand she stepped outside and pulled the door shut behind her.

At the other end of the valley she saw the bright flare of torches carried by men on horseback. The torches threw hellish yellow light over more than two dozen vaqueros, several of whom were shooting into the livestock corraled in a large communal pen beyond the missionaries' cabins.

The others were setting fire to the cabins. The missionaries and their families, including children barely old enough to walk, had been herded into a tight knot at the center of a group of vaqueros, who were brandishing pistols and yelling orders in heavily accented English.

Katherine's heart stopped when she saw a particularly tall rider on a stallion whose coat gleamed like new gold under the torchlight. *Vittorio.* He had come to drive the Americans out and take her back. Even Justis couldn't win against the mob of men he'd brought with him. Terror surged through her. Vittorio would love an excuse to make certain her "dead" husband remained dead.

"Justis!" she called in a low, desperate voice.

A moment later he was beside her, gripping her arm angrily. "Woman, if you ever do what I tell you to do, I'll probably faint from shock."

"We have to run before they come this way!"

"Who are they?"

"Some of the rancheros didn't want Americans settling here. I'm sure that's why they're destroying the settlement." She turned to him frantically. "We can't fight them—surely you see that! There are too many! We can hide—"

"Is it Salazar?"

She trembled inwardly. "What difference does it make?"

"Have you got anything to fear from him?"

"I—I don't, but he'll kill *you*!"

"Thought he was a damned gentleman. A dandy. An educated—"

"I haven't got time to argue with you! Follow me!" She shoved past him, grabbed his arm, and tugged him toward the wooded hills a hundred paces away. "Please, Justis, please!"

"All right, but move careful in the dark. Gimme your pistol." He tucked both his and hers into his belt. Carrying the rifle, he grabbed her hand and they ran toward the woods. Already Katherine could hear the sound of horses galloping up the trail to her cabin.

She and Justis made the edge of the forest and stopped. When they looked back they saw five or six vaqueros, led by Vittorio, stop near the cabin door. Vittorio dismounted from his palomino and strode to it, then knocked gently.

Justis cursed softly and viciously. "Thinks he's comin' to Sunday tea, looks like to me."

Vittorio opened the door and glanced inside. Obviously agitated by her absence, he turned and yelled something in Spanish to his men. Katherine jumped. "He's telling them to spread out and look for us. *Us?*"

"He must've found out I was at his ranch yesterday." She moaned. "I told him you were dead."

"Pretty damned thorough about puttin' me out of your life, weren't you?"

"You *were* dead to me."

The horsemen scattered, but two started toward the woods. Justis took her arm. "Move slow and quiet." They eased up a low rise. The two vaqueros guided their horses among the trees, their torches held high.

"Señora Gallatin!" they called. *"Por favor! Vamonos, Señora!"*

To Katherine's right, some kind of large night bird flew out of a tree with great commotion, rattling the branches. The vaqueros urged their horses into a trot and turned straight toward the sound. Katherine ducked, but the far edge of torchlight flickered on her face.

*"Señora!"*

One vaquero spurred his horse forward. Justis shoved Katherine behind a tree and gave her a pistol again. "Don't shoot me by accident—or on purpose," he muttered. The other vaquero pointed his rifle upward and fired to alert the rest. Then he, too, sent his mount loping forward.

Justis blocked the path. He swung the barrel end of his rifle into the first rider's midsection, tumbling him off his horse in a groaning heap. The torch fell from the rider's hand and sputtered on the wet earth. Justis turned toward Katherine. "Run!"

"No!"

The second vaquero quickly swung a well-oiled reata. It caught Justis around the neck as he lifted his rifle and fired. The shot went wild and the vaquero's horse reared. Justis made a strangling sound as the rawhide lariat jerked him flat onto his stomach. The woods began to fill with men and horses.

Katherine leveled her pistol at the vaquero as Justis scrambled to his feet. He grabbed the lariat and heaved backward on it before the vaquero could anchor it to his saddle. The man yelped in surprise as the incredible power at the end of his rope snapped him off his horse. He crashed, facedown, on the forest floor.

But there were other vaqueros now, lots of them, their reatas cutting the air with vicious whipping sounds. Katherine fired the pistol, and one man fell, clutching a wounded arm. Another lasso settled around Justis's neck, choking him. Two more pinned his arms to his sides. Still he managed to dig his heels into the ground and stay upright, struggling to reach the pistol tucked in his belt. Katherine ran to him and pulled it free.

"*Alto!*" she screamed, and pointed the gun at the rider nearest her. From behind her a vaquero brought the hard wooden shaft of his torch down on her wrist. The gun flew from her grip and she staggered against Justis, gasping in pain.

The attack on her wrung a deep primal bellow of rage from him. It startled the vaqueros for a second, and he jerked one arm free. He slid a knife from a sheath on his belt and sliced the taut lariat lines apart with a swift stroke.

The vaqueros yelled in dismay and closed in on him as a group. Katherine was hauled, kicking and punching, across a rider's saddle. With the help of another he held her facedown while she struggled and screamed every oath she knew.

She heard the heavy thuds of the vaqueros' fists and torches falling on Justis; she heard their agonized curses before they bludgeoned the knife out of his hand. Then there was only the scrambling and grunts of a dozen men intent on beating one man unconscious—and having a difficult time doing it.

"*Alto! Por favor!*" she begged. "Give him mercy!"

But they didn't, not until he was limp on the ground,

his hands and feet tied. The vaqueros holding Katherine finally let her go. She tumbled from the horse and crawled to Justis. His face had several bad gashes and was covered in blood. Red spittle showed on his lips when he coughed. She cradled his head in her hands and ran her fingers over the knots already swelling beneath his scalp.

"Catalina, you brought this on him and yourself. It is your fault. If you had stayed at my rancho, all would have been well."

She looked up to find Vittorio watching calmly from the back of his huge golden horse. "What are you going to do with us?"

"I am simply going to take you and your husband back to my rancho, along with all the troublesome Protestants."

Justis stirred weakly. She wet her fingers and cleared blood away from his eyes. He looked at her, dazed at first, then with recognition. "Help me sit up," he said in a tortured whisper.

She eased him upright and sat behind him, bracing him with her body. His hands were tied behind him and she bit her lip to keep from crying out when she saw their bleeding knuckles. Judging by the number of vaqueros who lay on the ground clutching various parts of their anatomies, he had put up even more of a fight than she realized.

"Greetings, Señor Gallatin," Vittorio said pleasantly. "Welcome to California. I heard that you visited my rancho yesterday and coaxed some of my servants to sing for your gold. They have been punished for that. I thought you were dead. Catalina said you were killed in a mining accident."

"Not . . . dead . . . yet," Justis muttered, coughing. "Came to get Katherine away from you."

"Away from me? She might have run temporarily, but she never intended to stay away for long. Hasn't she told you what she and I have shared? She was my mistress before she left."

"Don't believe it," Justis answered.

Katherine bit her tongue to stop her own denial. Vittorio's mind wasn't normal. If she were going to save Justis's life, she had to plan unusual negotiations. "My husband doesn't understand our relationship, Vittorio. But I'm sure that once I explain it to him, he'll leave us in peace."

"Explain," Justis ordered in a pained, rasping voice.

Vittorio smiled. "After we return to my rancho I will tell you what she and I did together, Señor. Perhaps I will even demonstrate."

"God damn you to hell," Justis said weakly, and spat blood at him. He tried to twist his head enough to look at her. "Explain."

"Be patient," she said. "Be quiet." She cast a calm, inquisitive gaze at Vittorio. "What will you do with him? And the missionaries?"

Vittorio flicked a long quirt back and forth over his horse's neck, making the stallion dance nervously. The Californio's dark eyes gleamed at her, full of victory and anticipation. "The overzealous missionaries have to leave my country, I fear. They are troublemakers. I have already spoken to the governor about them. He agrees. As for your husband—he has bribed my servants, hurt several of my men, and insulted me to my face. I think he will have to be punished. Here we rancheros hold our own trials. I will have one for him. It will be fair."

"Thank you," she said. "I knew you would be reasonable."

He nodded, mollified by her polite attitude. As always, he set great store by pleasant manners and gentility. "Now come with me, Catalina." He gestured to his men. "Find a wagon and put this Mr. Gallatin in it."

She almost sagged with relief. For the moment, at least, Justis was safe. Her worst fear had been that Vittorio would shoot him on the spot. "Try not to cause any more trouble," she told Justis sternly, and got to her feet.

*"Katie."* He said her name like a warning. His ravaged face made her fight for control with every shred of her willpower. He was so badly hurt, he could barely sit up now that she no longer braced him. Listing to one side, his breath wheezing, he stared up at her groggily. "I don't believe it."

"I never asked you to come look for me. Do you expect wifely concern from the woman you humiliated and deserted?"

"Katie. Don't." He sank to one side, helpless.

Katherine walked to Vittorio and held up her arms. He lifted her in front of him on the saddle and reined his horse around. She forced herself not to look back. It was the most difficult thing she'd ever done.

## CHAPTER 19

His entire head throbbed with pain, and at times Justis was so dizzy, he would have toppled forward had not his wrists been tightly manacled to the post behind him. He could barely breathe through his broken nose, and one eye was swollen shut. The itching of the caked blood on his face was enough to drive him half crazy, and he couldn't bend forward enough to scratch it on his knees. Whenever he moved he felt as if someone were kicking him in the ribs.

He leaned his head back against the post and shifted gingerly on the matted straw under him. He was in some sort of empty wooden shed that was too clean to have been used—recently at least—by any kind of livestock. Posts were sunk in the ground at odd places, with iron eyelets embedded deeply in them. He decided finally that the place had been designed for shearing sheep.

The vaqueros had dumped him there around midday, after traveling all night to return to the rancho. They'd brought in a bucket of water and doused him with some of it, then thoughtfully set the bucket across the shed where he could stare at it all day without any hope of getting a drink. His pain-racked senses had only managed to note that Katie had walked voluntarily into Vittorio's fancy hacienda.

What was her game? Why had she acted afraid of Vittorio, then gone to him gladly? What had he done to her that made him claim her as his mistress? She wouldn't enjoy being beaten like some pitiful whore. Justis groaned. Or would she?

He wasn't sure how much time passed, but when he heard a lock rattling on the shed door, the sunlight had faded from the cracks in the shed's walls. The door creaked open and Salazar stepped in, looking immaculate and very much the Spanish nobleman in a pleated white shirt, short black jacket, and the black trousers that flared from the knees down. Heavy silver spurs jingled on his black boots.

He stood to one side, bowed, and waved for someone to enter. Katie came in wearing an ornate white dress with matching slippers. Her gleaming onyx hair was pulled up artfully, so that it was easy to imagine it still hung to her heels when undone. A blue lace mantilla cascaded from a tall comb worked into the hair at her crown.

She was so lovely, Justis wanted to hate her. She gazed down at him with a stoic, unfathomable blankness in her dark eyes and clasped her hands in front of her.

"I want you to see how happy your wife is with me," Salazar said cheerfully as he shut the shed's door. "And I want you to see why she and I are so perfect together."

In a few short, utterly obscene words, Justis gave him an opinion. The whole time he stared up into Katie's eyes, trying desperately to decide if what he saw there was acceptance, apathy, or disgust. It was as if she had frozen every thought and feeling behind black ice.

"Do what we discussed, Catalina," Salazar told her. "The trunk is over there, in the corner."

She nodded and walked gracefully to a plain wooden box. She knelt down, opened the lid, and retrieved something from inside. As she carried the items to Salazar, Justis stared at them in sick horror. *Manacles and a short thick rawhide whip.*

"As we discussed, Catalina," Salazar murmured.

She nodded, knelt down on the straw, then stretched out on her stomach and put her hands near one of the posts. Salazar hummed a merry fandango as he squatted beside her and chained her wrists to an eyelet at the post's bottom. Almost gently he pushed the trailing mantilla to one side.

"Do you like this?" Justis asked her, his voice so strained, it was barely audible.

"Yes," she murmured, her face turned away from him. "Don't say anything. Just watch."

"It is very entertaining," Salazar said, smiling. He snatched at the line of pearl buttons all the way down the back of the dress and impatiently wrenched the material apart, his hands quivering with excitement. She wore nothing underneath, and the gaping dress bared smooth cinnamon skin from her neck to the rise of her hips.

Justis shut his eyes and struggled for breath. He would never believe this, that the woman he had known for more than two years, the proud, dignified woman with whom he had shared so much grief and passion, could be such a stranger to him.

When he looked again Salazar was watching him with a pleased expression. He dangled the end of the whip on her back, as if he wanted to tickle her. "You hate your wife for her infidelity, Señor?"

If it were true, he could hate her. But a deep part of his soul could not comprehend it, and something in Salazar's careful scrutiny struck a warning chord. "No, I don't hate her," he said casually. "I'd have to love her to care what she does. I don't love her. Never have."

From the corner of his eye he saw the slow tightening of her hands on the chain of the manacles. Then they relaxed, but as if with great effort. When Justis glanced at Salazar, the ranchero seemed disgruntled by his lack of response.

Salazar sighed. "I understand. You cannot love a lady who has given herself to another in such unique ways." He continued in a low, conversational tone, stroking the whip up and down her spine as he explained the things he had done to her before she left with the missionaries.

Justis shrugged, while his hatred for Salazar evolved into something so black and vicious, pinpoints of light danced in front of his eyes. "I hope she enjoyed herself," he told Salazar finally.

The ranchero cursed sarcastically and jerked her dress open even farther. "Let me see what you think of this, then."

Justis couldn't help his swift, agonized groan as Salazar cocked his arm and brought the whip down on her back. She never moved or made a sound. Salazar looked at Justis quickly. "You are not as strong as she is." He swung the whip again. Again she was completely still; not even her fingers twitched.

"What you're doin' doesn't bother me," Justis assured him. He pulled against his own manacles so hard that his hands went numb. "I think I even see why you enjoy it. She's a challenge, I reckon. That's what makes her so special?"

"Indeed." Salazar nodded. "She doesn't feel pain the way a Mexican or white woman does." He sneered. "You lie—you do not enjoy watching. You are a crude, insensitive man who cannot comprehend the beauty of her devotion to me. I will prove it to you. Tonight I will beat her until she bleeds."

He pulled the whip back farther, his face contorted

with the strain of concentration, but paused at the sound of hurried footsteps outside the shed door. "Don Salazar!" someone called politely. Justis didn't understand anything else the servant said except the word *visitador*, for visitor.

Salazar answered tersely, tossed the whip down, and reluctantly unlocked the manacles on Katie's wrists. "Later, *querida*. You stay here."

He left, and the servant fastened the shed door again. An emotion-laden silence settled on them. His throat raw, Justis stared at Katie. She slowly pushed herself upright, sitting straight and proper in the straw even though her dress hung open and two red welts crossed her back.

She tugged her mantilla off and reached behind her to fumble with her buttons. They were hopelessly out of reach. Her hands moved slowly to her lap, and she simply sat.

"Katie?" he finally managed to whisper. "Tell me the truth about what just happened."

She got up and went to the water bucket. He glimpsed her face in profile and found the expression completely shuttered, her mouth a tight line. She carried the bucket over to him and sat down, then tore a strip from the soft cotton underlining of her skirt.

"I will clean your face for you," she said crisply.

He nearly exploded with frustration. He struggled against the manacles for a few seconds before he slumped wearily, panting. "You cold bitch! Tell me the truth! Do you love him? Do you love bein' beaten?"

She dropped the cloth into the bucket and turned away from him. "I don't like it. No."

"Then you love him so much that you put up with it?"

"N-no."

"Then why? Why?" His voice was harsh. "He must be right. That tough hide of yours doesn't feel a damned thing!"

In the space of a breath her strength crumpled. Burying her face in her knees, she sobbed like a broken-hearted child, making desperate little noises and trembling all over. "It hurt. It hurt so much."

Justis groaned loudly. "Oh, God, Katie, *Katie*. I can't come to you, gal. You come to me. Please come here. *Please.*"

She turned just enough to hide her face against his shoulder and slip one arm around his waist. He kissed her hair frantically as she muffled racking sobs on his bloodstained shirt. "It w-would have been worse if I had acted the way he wanted," she whispered. "He g-gets tired sooner this way."

"I'll kill him. I swear."

"He wanted you to b-be horrified. He would have hit me more, not less, if you had been."

"I got that idea, but I wasn't sure. It nearly choked me to watch and pretend I didn't care." He rubbed his cheek against her hair, caressing her the only way he could. "What power has he got over you? Why didn't you go to Adela for help after he hurt you the first time?"

"I didn't know if Adela would believe me. If she didn't, I would have had no one else to turn to." Her shoulders shook. "And I couldn't risk fighting him as long as I had Mary to think of. When the missionaries came through I escaped with them."

"But why let him hurt you today? What can he threaten you with now?"

Her arm tightened around his waist. "Did you think I wouldn't try to help you? If Vittorio is satisfied that you are no rival, he may let you go. So I'll do whatever it takes to make him forget his jealousy."

"You'll let him beat you, and act like you like it, for my sake?"

"You—you have rescued me more than once. Now I can try to return the kindness." She raised her head from his shoulder. Her eyes were steeped in sorrow. "When he

comes back you must act as you did before. No matter
what he does to me, you must act unconcerned."

Justis shook his head. "He's not goin' to let me go. He'd
be a fool to do it, and he knows that. All I hope is that
you can get free of him somehow."

She laid a hand along his face. Her gaze held so much
tenderness, it made him feel better. Remembering the
look in her eyes would help him endure whatever
Salazar had planned.

"Don't worry," she urged him. "You and I have sur-
vived too much together to let a petty tyrant rule us
now." She cleared her throat brusquely and studied his
bloody, battered face. "Look at you. I've never seen such
a messy *a-Yu-ne-ga.*"

Her hands very gentle, she cleaned him up using the
torn strip from her dress as a washcloth. She cupped water to his swollen mouth so that he could drink and made
a cushion of straw between his lower back and the post.
He watched her in silent adoration while she rubbed his
shoulders and arms, trying to ease the muscles cramped
from the manacles' confinement.

"Last night at the church," he asked at last, "did you
think it was Salazar comin' to get you? Was it him that
you wanted to kill so bad?"

She nodded wearily. "After Mary died my whole aim
in life was to have revenge on Vittorio. Now my whole
aim is to get you away from here safely. I think I can
convince him to put you on a ship bound for the Sand-
wich Islands or the Orient—someplace he won't expect
you to return from. Then I'll—"

"No. You and I go together, or not at all." He lifted his
head and eyed her as sternly as he could. "You still have
to learn me what I want to know about manners and shit
like that."

She laughed, a gentle, tragic sound, and kissed his
bruised mouth with great care. *"Teach* you," she whispered, as he had known she would.

He rested his forehead against hers. "We may not have much time," he told her gruffly. "Sit closer to me and put your head on my shoulder."

With a soft whimper of emotion she nestled to his side and held him.

"KATIE, GAL. It's time."

Katherine woke to Justis's hoarsely whispered warning in her ear. The shed was very dark and she strained her eyes to see the moonlight that edged around the door. Her nerves on fire, she heard the soft rattle of the iron lock.

She brushed one last kiss across Justis's mouth. "I may never have another chance to say this. I want you to know that I—"

"Señora!" a male voice murmured outside the door. "I am here to help you." The door eased open and a short, stocky man crept inside the shed. "Doña Mendez sent me a few days ago to find out how you were doing. She grows worried because Don Salazar said you were too busy to visit her. My name is Diego."

He knelt beside them and felt the manacles that bound Justis's wrists. *"Por Dios!* These will take some work to remove without the key."

"Don Salazar may come back at any moment," Katherine said.

"No, he has visitors. They are drinking and talking politics."

Katherine heard the grating rasp of metal filing metal. Justis shifted to give the man as much room as he could. "Can you get us a pair of horses?"

"No, Señor, only one for you and the Señora to share. I will ride ahead and bring help back to meet you on the trail."

"How long a ride is it to the Mendez rancho?"

"You could make it by dawn if you ride hard. By noon

if you let the horse walk." He panted a little and filed faster. "I saw you when they carried you here, Señor. You will need all your strength to ride a *very* slow horse all the way to the rancho."

"I know," he said grimly. "That's why I want you to take my wife with you. I'll follow alone."

"We go together or we don't go at all," Katherine reminded him. "No arguments. Save your breath. You're too weak to boss me around."

"Katlanicha—"

"Don't try to work Cherokee medicine with my name. *We go together.*"

"I think you will need her help," Diego commented.

Justis cursed softly. "Can you loan us a gun in case Salazar catches us?"

"*Sí.*"

"How about a knife?" Katherine asked eagerly.

The man's hands paused in their work. She could see him well enough to know he was staring at her in amazement. "*Sí*—if that is what the Señora wishes."

"The doc needs her scalpel," Justis said, his voice droll despite pain and exhaustion. "The cat needs her claw."

Katherine nodded to herself with bitter satisfaction. She had lost too many battles. This time she would save herself and Justis, or die.

THE TRAIL WAS lit only by a white sliver of moon in the sky. Katherine guided the big bay mare up the side of a ridge until she reached a meadow at the summit. Suddenly it seemed that they were at the top of the world, surrounded by starry sky. Justis's arm tightened around her waist. "Too risky," he murmured, his mustache brushing her ear. "Too easy to be seen up here."

"If Vittorio is following us, he must be hours behind."

"Depends on when he found out we were gone. And

how fast he's pushin' to catch up with us. Cut across the
other side and angle back later."

"It will cost us time, but all right."

She held the bay to a slow walk as she descended from
the ridge. Justis leaned against her back, his big body
almost shoving her out of the saddle at times. When he
gripped her tightly she winced in discomfort. "Dizzy
again?" she asked.

"Yeah. Am I squashin' you?"

"Not at all," she lied. "Just don't fall off. I can't imagine how I'd ever get you back on."

"You'd have to leave me. If it comes to that, promise
that you will."

"I promise."

"Liar."

"It isn't polite to call a lady a liar."

"Still lookin' for the perfect gentleman, are you?"

"I've given up on gentlemen."

"What are you lookin' for, then?"

"Nothing."

"Still don't need a man around?"

"I need one."

"What kind?"

"One who doesn't mind cavorting with a divorced
woman."

"You're not divorced."

"I was married, but my husband married someone
else. I think 'divorced' is the closest to a description for
me."

"Are you tryin' to make me mad so I won't think
about the pain in my head?"

"No, I'm telling you the truth."

"I think you're tryin' to make me mad."

"Pshaw. Accomplishing that is easy. I don't have to
try. I'm merely talking to you so that you won't fall
asleep and slide *arse* first onto the ground."

"After all this mess is settled we're goin' back to New York, you hear?"

"No. I like California. It's wild and free, the way home was when I was little, and it's one of the few places where I might be accepted on my own terms." Her voice quavered. "And it's where my only child is buried."

After a second he said, "My only child too."

She shook her head. "You have a child in Gold Ridge. With Amarintha."

"You *are* tryin' to make me mad!"

The bay leapt sideways as a cougar screamed from the woods to their left. Katherine brought her to a halt but she stood shivering, ready to bolt without warning. Justis groaned softly. "One more bounce like that and I'm done for."

Katherine was riding astride, the skirt of her dress tucked under her thighs. She swung one leg up and over the horse's neck, as she had seen the vaqueros do, and dropped lightly to the ground. Holding the bay's bridle in a tight grip, she led her back to the open meadow at the top of the ridge.

Justis slid forward and wrapped his hands around the saddle horn. "Can you manage better that way?" she asked him.

"Yeah. But you can't walk the whole night—"

"I walked all the way from Tennessee to Illinois. I can walk to the Mendez rancho. Don't worry about me."

He laughed dully. "I always forget—you can do anything you set your mind to. Be a doctor, raise a babe without a husband to help you, travel halfway around the world, and make a decent life for yourself among foreigners. You don't want my help, and there's not a damned thing I can do for you, is there?"

"You could tell me the truth about why you married Amarintha Parnell."

"If I make it to the Mendez's place, I'll tell you. *That*

promise ought to inspire you to tug this hoss along faster."

"I'll get you there," she vowed. "And I'll get the truth." And then what? she asked herself sadly.

ONLY THE BAY'S uncanny ability to pick out the trail in sheer darkness kept them from bumping into towering redwoods on either side. The forest was a majestic cathedral with a night breeze for a choir. Exhausted, Katherine stumbled over her own feet and braced a hand on the bay's neck to steady herself.

"Stop," Justis said. She pulled the horse to a halt. Holding tightly to the saddle horn, he leaned forward, swaying with the effort, and laid a hand on her shoulder. "Climb up behind me. It'll be fine."

She was too tired to disagree. When she was settled against his broad back she slipped her arms under his and latched her hands over his stomach. The November night was very cool, and he was deliciously warm. Katherine rested her face against his shoulder and sighed with happiness, remembering all the nights in their hotel room in New York.

She had loved his sneaky way of whispering good night to her as he placed a sweet, sentimental kiss on the tip of her nose. He had always waited until he thought she was asleep. Reliving those moments, she nestled her cheek against his sweaty, bloodstained shirt.

"You missed me," he said.

"Missed your fur and your heat."

"Hah. Can't miss those without missin' me a little too."

"I missed you more than you missed me, I'm sure. You had Amarintha to distract you."

"And you had our baby." There was only sorrow in his voice, not rebuke. "Tell me about her, Katie. Everything. From the day you realized you were carryin' a babe until the day she died."

She hugged him gently. "All right. It's a good thing you have the rest of the night to listen."

"You sound like it might be the only night you'll give me."

"You'll be leaving California soon."

"Not alone, I won't."

"I'm not your wife any—"

"But you're the mother of my babe. Now tell me about her."

Katherine nodded slowly. Mary was the one bond he would always want to share with her. She began.


JUST AFTER DAWN, as the light revealed steep hillsides covered in brown autumn grass, the mare grew excited and began to flick her ears backward, as if listening. "Dammit," Justis said softly. "I bet she hears her own kind. They must be close."

Katherine's heart thudded as she glanced at the land around them. Except for a few clumps of trees the hills offered little in the way of cover. Justis reined in the mare halfway up a hill and stopped. He looked over his shoulder at Katherine. "Walk to the top, but keep down so nobody can see you."

She dismounted and crept up the hill, then flattened herself to the ground near the summit and crawled on her stomach the last few feet. When she peeked over, she saw what she'd feared most—a group of vaqueros in the distance, led by a tall man riding a palomino. She ran back to Justis.

"Vittorio. Maybe ten minutes away."

"Let's go." Sagging with the effort, he helped her climb up behind him. "Hold on."

"Can *you* hold on?"

"I'd rather try than be caught."

As the bay scooted down the hill, Katherine snaked one hand around Justis's waist and gripped the saddle horn with the other. "You're anchored to me," she assured him.

"You may be sorry for that."

"No, never," she said softly, but the wind whipped the words away.

Katherine prayed for luck. If Vittorio continued leading his men in a path that was parallel to theirs, staying in the narrow valleys between the hills, he might never discover them. Their mare loped along at an easy speed she could probably maintain for miles.

But only minutes later the landscape became their enemy. The hills began to recede, and ahead Katherine saw a large, shallow valley with a stream winding through it, banked by skeletal winter sycamores.

Justis slid the mare to a halt. "We'll hide. Let Salazar pass through first." He backed the mare into the shadow of a hill and they waited in tense silence.

"Rest," she whispered.

He leaned back into the harbor of her arms, shut his eyes, and let his head lie on her shoulder. She winced at the mass of cuts and bruises on his face. In the few spots without injury the skin was sickly pale.

"You need a lot of doctoring, sir. I hope you don't mind an old Cherokee method. It will help." She licked as much of his face as she could reach, using her tongue gently to wash and soothe.

"Hmmm. Remember that time in New York when we saw those African lions at the sideshow?" he asked.

"Yes. Penned up. It was sad."

"The he-lion had a torn ear, and the she-lion was lickin' it so sweet you could tell she liked him. I feel like the he-lion."

"If your hair gets any thicker, you'll *look* like the he-lion."

The mare swung about suddenly, and they both nearly fell off. Katherine looked toward the hills behind them and cried out in dismay. One of Vittorio's men had crested a rise. He spotted them immediately and wheeled his horse, shouting and waving as he did.

"We'll make a stand at the stream," Justis said grimly, and urged the bay toward it at a gallop. When they neared the bank he guided her into a dense grove of sycamores.

"At least it will be difficult for them to drag us out of here," Katherine said. Her pulse roared in her ears. She touched icy fingers to the knife Diego had loaned her. It was tucked in a belt she'd made from her lace mantilla. Justis pulled the borrowed pistol from a sling on the saddle.

They watched the approaching horsemen. Katherine's heart sank at the sight of Vittorio and a dozen of his vaqueros bearing down on the stream. There were too many to win against. She nuzzled her cheek to Justis's shoulder, knowing he must be thinking the same thing.

"Well, let's get to it," he said gruffly. "Climb down, gal."

Salazar and his men thundered into the stream and drew their horses to a stop. Their guns drawn, they formed a line facing the trees. "Bring Catalina and come out, Señor Gallatin!" Vittorio yelled. "It is finished!"

Katherine slid off the horse and held up her arms to Justis. "Easy, now. I'll brace you. Don't fall." She tried to smile. "I don't want you to tumble on your arse in front of anyone besides me."

"Wouldn't look too impressive," he agreed. For a second the world grew still and quiet. Her gaze held Justis's and everything faded except the sharing of strength and devotion.

A strange sensation shivered down her spine. Katherine curled her fingers in a beckoning gesture. "Come down." She heard a pleading note in her voice and realized she was holding her breath. "Stand beside me and let's give them hell together."

His eyes never left hers. Slowly he shook his head,

then reached down and brushed one scraped, swollen finger across her lips. "Adela's men ought to get here soon," he murmured. "I'll buy you some time."

"Señor Gallatin! Catalina!" Vittorio called. "You have no choice! Come out!"

Katherine's heart pumped cold horror. She spoke to Justis through gritted teeth. "Get off that horse, sir, or I'll never forgive you."

He cupped her cheek with his hand. His gaze roamed over her face as if he were memorizing every feature for a long journey. "The day we met I said you were the kind of lady who made a man want to fight dragons for her. Remember?"

She cried out desperately. "I won't let you—"

"Believe whatever else you want to believe about me, Katie Blue Song Gallatin, but don't ever doubt that I fell in love with you that day and have loved you more every day since."

*"Justis!"*

He slapped the mare's neck and sent her plunging out of the sycamores. Justis slid her to a stop in the stream, defiantly blocking Salazar and his men. Katherine ran to the edge of the bank and stood watching, her heart frozen with fear.

"Let's talk about gold, Señor Salazar," Justis said pleasantly. "I could make you the richest man in the Californias."

"Diplomatic negotiation, Señor Gallatin? That has never been your way."

"I'm older and wiser."

"And desperate. I do not care about your gold."

"But it's my wife's gold, too, and she's anxious to have the rest of it. If you want her to stay with you and be happy, you need the gold."

"She will be happy without it."

"Hellfire, Mex, you don't know her the way I do.

She'll make your life pure living misery if you don't give her what she wants."

Salazar laughed coldly. "You do not know how to tame a woman the way I do."

"You won't ever tame her. Not without the gold."

From the distance came gunshots. Salazar's men spurred their horses into alertness. Katherine saw a group of riders coming up the valley from the south. *Help from Adela.*

"Your sister-in-law knows what you're up to," Justis told Salazar. "One of her men went to tell her. Back away, you sick sonuvabitch! You've lost your chance!"

Salazar's face contorted with surprise, then rage. "I will not be humiliated by lies!"

"It's too late to act innocent. Adela knows the truth. This is the end of your scheme."

"No. This is the end of *you*, Señor."

Katherine screamed as Vittorio pointed a pistol and fired. Justis fell sideways from the mare, which bolted away. Katherine leapt into the stream and stumbled as her feet hit slick rocks. Falling to her knees, she struggled to get up. The rumble and splash of Adela's horsemen racing to the scene was a bitter sound. *Too late.*

Justis crouched in the knee-deep water, one hand clutched to his stomach, the other bracing himself weakly. Vittorio jumped down from his horse, another pistol in his hand, the hand already lifting toward Justis's head.

Katherine vaulted to her feet and jerked her knife free. "Vittorio!" she screamed. He kept advancing on Justis, his murderous concentration locked on one goal, his thumb pulling the pistol's hammer back. Katherine threw the knife with all her strength. It sank to the hilt in Vittorio's stomach.

Chaos surrounded them—Adela's men closing in, Vittorio's men milling their horses in confusion. Vittorio swung toward her, his mouth open in agony, his free hand quivering near the knife handle. He staggered forward. "You . . . are . . . cruel. No lady . . . is cruel." Lifting the pistol, he pointed it at her chest and fired as he fell.

Katherine reeled from the force of his body striking hers. They went down in the stream with him on top. Pinned beneath him, she choked as water filled her mouth and nose. Was his weight squeezing the life from her chest, or was she dying from her wound? What did it matter if Justis had been fatally shot also? As blackness stole over her, she prayed that she would find him on the other side of it.

"Katie!"

Hands dragged her upright and shoved Salazar's body away. She slumped into strong, familiar arms. Gasping for breath, she threw her head back to gaze up in wonder. She cried out happily as Justis pulled her close to his chest. "Are you alive?" she asked, clutching his shoulders.

"I hope so," he said.

She pushed him back a few inches and looked at him. The stream rushed around his waist, lapping at the blood-stain on the side of his shirt. "Oh, God, you *were* shot."

He shushed her and grasped her hands when she tried to examine him. "Just snipped. Enough to give me another scar for my collection." He ran his own hands over the front of her bloody dress.

"Am I shot?" she asked fervently, beginning to care now that she knew he was safe.

"No, but you'll have to fix your sleeve."

She yelped in giddy amazement when she saw the ragged hole Salazar's pistol had put there. "What happened?"

"I shot him about a gnat's breath before he fired at you."

She put her arms around his neck. Holding each other,

they looked around warily. Two vaqueros were hauling Salazar's lifeless body from the stream.

"I shot him in the back," Justis murmured. "Wasn't time for anything more gentlemanly. I didn't care. Still don't. It saved your life."

Crying, she kissed his battered face. "He didn't deserve better."

"Katherine!" a woman called. Adela climbed down from the sidesaddle of a prancing white horse and waded toward them with her arms outstretched. "I did not know, my friend! Forgive me, I did not know what he was doing!" She knelt in the stream, hugged Katherine tearfully, and looked at Justis wide-eyed. "Not dead in a mining accident?"

"No." He smiled gingerly, his face a terrible, beautiful sight, Katherine thought.

Adela crossed herself. "Did Vittorio let his men do that to you?"

" 'Fraid so, Señora."

The three of them looked toward the far bank. Vittorio's men were standing around his body, talking quietly but gesturing in a way that suggested disagreement. Katherine stared at the bloody corpse but could barely believe he was dead.

Very dead—knifed and shot. By Americans. She touched Adela's shoulder. "What now? Will we be tried for murder?"

Adela nodded, her mouth a firm line. "Yes. In accepted California style. Vittorio would approve, I am sure." She stood up, regal despite her short and wiry stature, and the fact that she was immersed to her knees in the stream. She called Salazar's men over and asked them terse questions in Spanish. Then she called her men over, including Diego, and asked him questions while everyone listened. At last she raised her hands and announced the verdict. Looking relieved, Salazar's men nodded and walked away.

"Innocent, guilty, or what?" Justis asked Katherine, swaying a little.

She touched his face and found the skin cold with sweat. Suddenly she realized he had been strong only by necessity and was now on the verge of collapse. He needed doctoring, rest, food, and all the restraint her stunned willpower could muster. His words came back to her.

*Don't ever doubt that I fell in love with you.*

"We are innocent, dear man," she whispered. "And free."

He thought for a moment, then smiled crookedly. "And married," he insisted, and passed out in her arms.

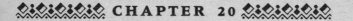 

## CHAPTER 20

THEIR room at the Mendez rancho was a pleasant, simple place of whitewashed adobe walls and a gently creaking plank floor covered with colorful rugs. A crucifix hung over the bed where Justis lay sleeping. Katherine's gaze moved from him to it. *Thank you for watching over him.*

She rose from her chair by a shuttered window and straightened the blanket he had bunched around his waist. Yesterday and last night he had slept soundly, but this morning he shifted often, frowning and wincing as his painfully abused body began to wake up.

She scooped a dollop of salve from a pottery jar on the table beside the bed, then brushed it over the stitches she had placed in a particularly bad cut along his jaw. She eased the blanket down and smoothed more salve on the deep furrow Vittorio's pistol shot had left in the skin on his right side.

Tenderness welled in her throat. She bent over and kissed his mustache, which was possibly the only unin-

jured spot on his face. It wouldn't do to disturb his rest.
There would be time enough for that after he felt better.
What she had to say to him would certainly be a shock.

Pensively she walked back to the window, opened one
side of the shutters, and propped her elbows on the adobe
sill. Gazing out into a sunshine-filled courtyard, she remembered what he had told her. *I've loved you more every
day.*

Even now those words sent a shiver down her spine.
Had they merely been the gallant offering of a man who
thought he was about to die? Thinking back on all their
months together, she knew that the differences in their
backgrounds and her determined independence would
never have made it easy for him to admit loving her any
more than her doubts and rigid pride had made it possible for her to admit that she loved him.

But if he were telling the truth, why had he married
Amarintha, taken her to bed, and fathered her child?
Was his definition of love so practical that he could put it
aside to promote his standing with his own people?

Katherine folded her arms and rested her chin on
them. Regardless of all her questions, certain facts were
clear—he wanted her back, he had risked his life to protect her, and if they conceived other children together,
he would cherish them. She shut her eyes. There was one
other fact, the most important. She loved him more than
her own life and would give up everything—even pride
—to be with him.

"Hey. Com'ere."

She pivoted at the deep, rumbling sound of his sleepy
voice. He surveyed her through half-shut eyes and curled
a brawny hand, beckoning her. Despite the swelling and
bruises, his face held a distinctly jaunty expression.

"You arrogant, lazy oaf," she said softly, smiling as she
crossed the small room to him. She took his hand and sat
down on the bed. "How do you feel?"

"Like all my bones were put together with rusty nails, My face feels like it's been twisted inside out."

"Looks that way, too, I'm afraid." She feathered a fingertip across one bruised cheek and added, "But all the pretty blues and purples complement the green of your eyes." She kissed the tip of his nose and stroked his hair. "What would you like first? Something to eat? To drink?"

"I'd like to talk. I promised you the truth about Amarintha."

Katherine inhaled sharply. "Maybe you'd like me to bring you the chamber pot. Or give you a back rub. Or—"

"Don't you want to hear why I married her?"

Her shoulders slumped. "Yes. I might as well get it over with."

He cupped her face between his swollen hands. "I never deserted you. I married Amarintha for show, nothing else. Not one damned thing passed between us except hate and blackmail. She sent you that god-awful newspaper clipping out of spite because she wanted me to stay in Gold Ridge another few months—make the marriage look good n' solid—but I was determined to head back to New York."

"Blackmail?" Katherine murmured.

She listened in growing distress as he explained how he'd secured the Blue Song land for her. She was crying by the time he finished. "You tied yourself to Amarintha so you could protect my land? That's the only reason?"

Justis nodded. He stroked her face with quick, loving caresses. "I could have given up my businesses without a backward look—plus saved Sam and Rebecca's share of the profits somehow—but I couldn't win a court fight over your land. So I married Amarintha and built her a big house and set up a grand bank account for her. That was all she wanted from me."

"But . . . Amarintha's babe. If it's not yours, whose is it?"

"The judge's."

Katherine gaped at him. "That's impossible. He's Amarintha's own father."

"Impossible?" He gave her a gently rebuking look. "Doc, I thought you were a little more worldly."

"But why would a father take his own daughter—" She nearly gagged. "Oh, God, but then, why would Vittorio take pleasure from pain? I ought not to be surprised by anything anymore." She frowned, trying to picture Amarintha and the judge together. "That would explain so much about Amarintha, why she acted so oddly at times. She must have been carrying an awful torture in her heart."

"He'd branded her," Justis said in a low, soft voice.

Horrified, she stared at him. "Do you mean actually—"

"Yeah. On one shoulder blade. I came back to the house early one evening and surprised her washin' herself over a bucket in the kitchen. She had her clothes down around her waist. She screamed at me and damn near clubbed me with a fryin' pan. Said she wouldn't have any man starin' at her again. I cornered her and told her I wasn't leavin' the room till I got a close look at the mark on her shoulder."

Justis shook his head and his eyes darkened with regret. "It nearly broke her spirit. She crumpled up in a ball like a scared kid and made terrible little noises. For a minute or two she thought she *was* a kid again, and I was the judge."

He exhaled, looking a little sick. "She made me promise not to hurt her ever again. I asked her how I'd hurt her already. The things she told me would make a devil cry, gal. I've never heard anything so awful. And the worst of it for me was the brand. The judge has a big ol' fancy ring with some sort of Parnell family crest on it. As best I can figure from what she told me, when she was real little he heated that ring on the stove and burned her with it. Put his mark on her forever, he said, so she couldn't ever show herself to a man without shame."

Katherine leaned forward and rested her head on his shoulder. "I can't hate her," she told him simply.

He stroked her hair. "Can you forgive me for marryin' her? I know I did a god-awful thing to you—to us—but she'll never be anything but a wife in name only, and we'll never cross paths with her. And if it makes you feel any better, I told Sam and Rebecca the truth about everything. They know that you and me are married and why I had to marry Amarintha too. They know that I left Gold Ridge to go back to you, and they don't expect to see me again."

"Amarintha. Poor Amarintha. She deserves to find a little happiness. Do you think she has?"

"Yeah. Now that she's got her escape from the judge she'll be all right. Not like other folks, but happy in her own way. She wanted the babe, and I suspect she'll dote on it."

Katherine gently slipped her arms under him. She hugged him and turned to lay her head against his shoulder. So this was the worst of it—she would have to live with the fact that she would always share Justis with Amarintha, though only in name.

"Do you believe everything I just told you?" he asked.

"Yes."

"I love you," he murmured. "I know you don't want to hear that a second time, but you might as well. I figure that it's gotten pretty obvious to you, anyway."

Her throat closed with tears. She swallowed hard, trying to put together the perfect words to tell him that it was exactly what she wanted to hear, had always wanted to hear. Someone knocked on the door.

Rubbing her forehead in frustration, Katherine went to open it. Adela peered around her at Justis. "He is better?"

"He is awake and more or less aware of the world, I think."

"Can I speak with you both for a moment?"

"Certainly."

"Thank you, Señora, for all your hospitality," Justis told her as she pulled a chair up to the bedside. "You're a true friend."

She scrutinized him, intrigued, as Katherine sat down by his legs. "You have changed," she said finally, nodding. "There is something, perhaps a kind of satisfaction, in your eyes."

"My wife's safe from Salazar. That's a load off my mind." He hesitated, thinking. "And I feel like a part of my life has come to an end."

"Oh? You are happy to see your life change?"

His eyes met Katherine's for a moment. "I don't know yet. I've got to ask some questions first."

"Ah." Adela cleared her throat. "I will say what I came to say and leave quickly so that you can talk with Katherine. You will have even more to discuss." She looked at Katherine. "Your missionary companions? They are moving north. They say California has too many Catholics and not enough heathens." She smiled wryly. "Although I think they are not sure which they want to convert most. But they are going. Good."

"Good," Katherine murmured. "They saw this beautiful land only as something to tame."

"Do you love that wild valley they left behind? The Valley of the Sun?"

Katherine nodded and avoided looking at Justis.

"It is yours if you want it," Adela said softly. She glanced at Justis. "For both of you."

"How can that be?" Justis asked in amazement.

"A land grant from the governor will be easy to arrange for a nominal price." She laughed merrily. "His pen will sign the deed pronto for five hundred of those Yankee gold pieces Katherine brought with her. My husband has already sent men to retrieve all her money from Vittorio's safe."

Katherine's pulse was thready with both exhilaration

and despair. She could have a home, a home of her own choosing, in a place where she would be respected! But it was not Justis's plan to stay in this remote part of the world, and she had already made up her mind to go wherever he asked.

She hid her troubled thoughts by idly studying a loose thread on the blue skirt she wore. "How much land?"

"How much do you want? My husband can ride the width of our land in three days. Would a rancho that size be enough for you?"

"Three *days*?" Justis repeated slowly.

"Well, yes, but that is riding from dawn to dusk," Adela explained in a sheepish tone. "I did not mean to make ours sound like the grandest rancho in California." She stood up, placed a hand on Katherine's shoulder, and squeezed affectionately. "My husband and I would love to have the Gallatins for neighbors. You will let me know your decision soon, yes?"

"Yes," Katherine answered, trying to sound neutral. "Thank you, dear friend."

"*Gracias,*" Justis added, his southern drawl lending a honeyed slur to the words. "*Mucho gracias, Señora.*"

Adela applauded. "We will make you a Californio, I bet!"

Katherine followed her to the door and hugged her tightly. After Adela left she pretended to fiddle with the latch, thinking about what she was about to say.

"You want to stay here," Justis said wearily. "I can see that. It's the home you've been craving. It's almost like an omen. You came from the Sun Land, so it seems right that you'd find the Valley of the Sun. You don't need anything or anybody else. God, I wish you could love me the way I love you."

Her restraint shattered. With a soft, garbled cry, she ran to the bed and knelt on the floor near his side.

"What the—" he began, startled.

She grasped his hand and kissed his battered knuckles,

then rested her cheek against them. She looked up at him with all the devotion in her soul. "I'll make a home wherever you want. I'll go wherever you ask me to go. I'll be the best wife you could dream of, and I'll raise your children proudly. I've always wanted to have them —half-breeds though they will be. If we teach them to be strong, they'll do well in the world regardless."

He shoved himself upright, his pain momentarily forgotten, a stunned look on his face. He grasped her shoulders and made her sit on the bed beside him. "What are you tellin' me, Katie?"

"That I love you. That I always have. I knew it that day in Gold Ridge when you gave me a scalpel to cut you with. You told me to take out my grief and hatred on you. I cried because I knew I'd never find another man as special as you, but I thought we had no future together."

"You love me?" he repeated, shaking her a little. "Do you know what you're sayin'?"

She nodded. "I've had more than two years to decide for certain, haven't I? But the hard part was that I knew for certain right away, and nothing could change it. Even when you were ashamed of me—remember back in Gold Ridge when you decided you couldn't be seen with me in public?—even when I was mad and humiliated I couldn't stop loving you. Don't you see? For all my pride, I was a hopeless wreck."

He gripped her shoulders fiercely. "I was never ashamed of you. I had a deal with Amarintha. She used her influence with Captain Taylor to get you into the stockade to doctor folks. In return I had to agree to act 'respectable' accordin' to her rules. All those weeks of not seein' you nearly killed me."

Katherine made a sound of sorrow. "So many things came between us."

"But . . . *you love me*?" He still looked incredulous.

"I don't just love you. I love you desperately, completely, and, at times during the past months when I thought you'd deserted me for good, to such a miserable degree that I wished I could cut my heart out and feel nothing."

He gazed deeply into her eyes. "Say it again."

"I love you." Half crying, half laughing, she ran a hand over his chestnut hair. "You shaggy, badly mauled hellion, I love you dearly and want to spend the rest of my life with you."

He brought her to him and kissed her as best he could. She licked his mouth and made mewling sounds of pleasure. "We'll go back to New York and start anew—"

"No. I'll never belong there, Katie. I'll never be civilized or respectable. I'm sorry, gal, I really am. It's time I admitted the truth. I'm a wild Irishman, and I'm proud of it."

She smiled at him. "I don't mind your change of heart a bit. I've long suspected that you'd always be a wild Irishman. But where do you want to go if not New York?"

"Could you teach a wild Irishman to speak Spanish?"

The breath stopped in her throat. "You mean—and stay here?"

"Yeah. I thought . . . How would it be with you if we built a house near Mary?"

"You should know her real name." Katherine leaned forward and whispered in his ear, "Dahlonega. It's the Cherokee word for gold. I wanted to honor her past—and her father's past."

He slid his arms around her. A quiver ran through his body. "Thank you."

She placed loving kisses on the side of his neck. "Her real name is a secret between you and me. We are the only ones who know it. Yes, yes, let's build a house near her."

"Do you really want more younguns?"

"Yes. Do you?" she asked anxiously.

He chuckled. "As many wild little Gallatins as you can bear and I can manage."

She raised her head and burned him with a look of sheer desire. "More children should be easy to accomplish, sweetheart."

"Sweetheart." He smiled, savoring the endearment, the first one they'd ever shared. "I'm lonely under this blanket, *honey.*"

She eased him onto his back. "I'll be very, very gentle with your poor, battered self."

Katherine stripped off her clothes and stretched out beside him, one leg draped over his thighs, her head on his shoulder. They held each other in silent wonder, both still stunned by the love that could be shared so openly now.

"We have a lot to talk about," Justis whispered, his lips against her hair. "God, so many things to explain, so much I want you to understand about things I said and did."

"No need to hurry." She looked up at him with pure adoration. "I will always stand in your soul. We have forever to share."

"Glory," he said as her hands began to replace his pain with pleasure. "Glory."

GLEN MARY. They both spoke the rancho's name aloud as they stood atop a hill looking over the valley. "We'll be happy here," she told him.

He nodded contentedly, then reached into his trousers pocket and retrieved something. "I've got a present for you."

She watched as he opened a small leather pouch. "Hold out your hand," he said. When she did, he filled it with gold nuggets. "All straight out of the Blue Song property," he told her gruffly. "I got 'em when I was in Georgia the last time."

She curled her fingers over the magnificent gift. "They

have such power," she murmured. "I can feel the Sun Land in them. Thank you, my love. Thank you."

He hugged her and she cried a little, a bittersweet sound that made him kiss her hair in sympathy. "You'll always miss the old homeland," he whispered. "I know. But at least you've got some of its treasure—and something that ain't so much a treasure—me. I'll always love you."

"My best treasure," she said, smiling.

They kissed, then she drew her head back and looked up at him. "I've dreamed that we'll go back there someday. It's a very unusual dream, filled with people I don't know, and yet I *do* know them. We'll go back—or our children will, or perhaps their children. I'm not certain. It's puzzling, my dream, but very reassuring." She removed his gold nugget from around her neck and slipped the leather thong over his head.

He frowned. "Why did you give it back?"

"Because I want to share the spirit of home with you," she said, touching the nugget as it lay gleaming against his shirt. "Because I never want to be apart from you again, and the gold is a talisman that will always lead us to each other if we're lost."

He kissed her tenderly. "Build us a future, gal. Weave it with your dreams. I'll always be there."

A breeze swept over the hillsides, whispering promises. The legacy of their love would reach far beyond the sunset.

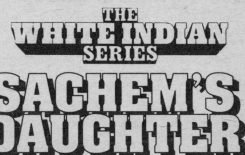

# NORA ROBERTS

☐ 28578  **PUBLIC SECRETS**  $4.95

☐ 27283  **BRAZEN VIRTUE**  $4.50

☐ 26461  **HOT ICE**  $3.95

☐ 26574  **SACRED SINS**  $4.50

☐ 27859  **SWEET REVENGE**  $3.95

Buy them at your local bookstore or use this page to order:

# THE LATEST IN BOOKS
# AND AUDIO CASSETTES

## Paperbacks

| | | | |
|---|---|---|---|
| ☐ | 28671 | **NOBODY'S FAULT** Nancy Holmes | $5.95 |
| ☐ | 28412 | **A SEASON OF SWANS** Celeste De Blasis | $5.95 |
| ☐ | 28354 | **SEDUCTION** Amanda Quick | $4.50 |
| ☐ | 28594 | **SURRENDER** Amanda Quick | $4.50 |
| ☐ | 28435 | **WORLD OF DIFFERENCE** Leonia Blair | $5.95 |
| ☐ | 28416 | **RIGHTFULLY MINE** Doris Mortman | $5.95 |
| ☐ | 27032 | **FIRST BORN** Doris Mortman | $4.95 |
| ☐ | 27283 | **BRAZEN VIRTUE** Nora Roberts | $4.50 |
| ☐ | 27891 | **PEOPLE LIKE US** Dominick Dunne | $4.95 |
| ☐ | 27260 | **WILD SWAN** Celeste De Blasis | $5.95 |
| ☐ | 25692 | **SWAN'S CHANCE** Celeste De Blasis | $5.95 |
| ☐ | 27790 | **A WOMAN OF SUBSTANCE** Barbara Taylor Bradford | $5.95 |

## Audio

| | | |
|---|---|---|
| ☐ **SEPTEMBER** by Rosamunde Pilcher<br>Performance by Lynn Redgrave<br>180 Mins. Double Cassette | 45241-X | $15.95 |
| ☐ **THE SHELL SEEKERS** by Rosamunde Pilcher<br>Performance by Lynn Redgrave<br>180 Mins. Double Cassette | 48183-9 | $14.95 |
| ☐ **COLD SASSY TREE** by Olive Ann Burns<br>Performance by Richard Thomas<br>180 Mins. Double Cassette | 45166-9 | $14.95 |
| ☐ **NOBODY'S FAULT** by Nancy Holmes<br>Performance by Geraldine James<br>180 Mins. Double Cassette | 45250-9 | $14.95 |

Bantam Books, Dept. FBS, 414 East Golf Road, Des Plaines, IL 60016

Please send me the items I have checked above. I am enclosing $_____
(please add $2.50 to cover postage and handling). Send check or money order,
no cash or C.O.D.s please. (Tape offer good in USA only.)

Mr/Ms _____

Address _____

City/State _____ Zip _____

FBS–1/91

Please allow four to six weeks for delivery.
Prices and availability subject to change without notice.